Praise for the

'Great fun!' –

'Chapman delivers on every level in this intriguing murder mystery' – *Lancashire Evening Post*

'A delightful Dales tale to warm the cockles!' – *Peterborough Telegraph*

'A rollicking read' – *Craven Herald*

'For above all else, there is warmth and heart to her novels' – *Yorkshire Times*

'Bags of Yorkshire charm and wit' – *Northern Echo*

'A delightful read' – *Dalesman*

'A classic whodunit set in the spectacular landscape of the Yorkshire Dales, written with affection for the area and its people' – Cath Staincliffe

'Charming . . . full of dry wit and clever plotting . . . will delight and entertain the reader' – *Countryside*

'Nicely told and rather charming, so it should give traditionalists hours of innocent delight' – *Literary Review*

'An engaging twist on the lonely-hearts-killer motif . . . should leave readers eager for the sequel' – *Publishers Weekly*

'An engaging cast of characters and a cleverly clued puzzle move Chapman's debut to the top of the English village murder list' – *Kirkus*

Date with Deceit

Julia Chapman is the pseudonym of Julia Stagg, who has had five novels, the Fogas Chronicles set in the French Pyrenees, published by Hodder. *Date with Deceit* is the sixth in the Dales Detective series, following on from *Date with Danger*.

Also by Julia Chapman

Date with Death
Date with Malice
Date with Mystery
Date with Poison
Date with Danger

Julia Chapman

DATE WITH DECEIT

PAN BOOKS

First published 2021 by Pan Books
an imprint of Pan Macmillan
The Smithson, 6 Briset Street, London EC1M 5NR
EU representative: Macmillan Publishers Ireland Ltd, 1st Floor,
The Liffey Trust Centre, 117–126 Sheriff Street Upper,
Dublin 1, DO1 YC43
Associated companies throughout the world
www.panmacmillan.com

ISBN 978-1-5290-4957-2

Copyright © Julia Chapman 2021

The right of Julia Chapman to be identified as the
author of this work has been asserted by her in accordance
with the Copyright, Designs and Patents Act 1988.

All rights reserved. No part of this publication may be reproduced,
stored in a retrieval system, or transmitted, in any form, or by any means
(electronic, mechanical, photocopying, recording or otherwise)
without the prior written permission of the publisher.

Pan Macmillan does not have any control over, or any responsibility for,
any author or third-party websites referred to in or on this book.

5 7 9 8 6 4

A CIP catalogue record for this book is available from the British Library.

Typeset by Palimpsest Book Production Limited, Falkirk, Stirlingshire
Printed and bound by CPI Group (UK) Ltd, Croydon, CR0 4YY

This book is sold subject to the condition that it shall not, by way of
trade or otherwise, be lent, hired out, or otherwise circulated without
the publisher's prior consent in any form of binding or cover other than
that in which it is published and without a similar condition including
this condition being imposed on the subsequent purchaser.

Visit **www.panmacmillan.com** to read more about all our books
and to buy them. You will also find features, author interviews and
news of any author events, and you can sign up for e-newsletters
so that you're always first to hear about our new releases.

For everyone on the frontline of coronavirus . . .

Thank you

1

Stuart Lister was trying to show initiative. But he was also placing his career in jeopardy.

He checked his watch. Another three quarters of an hour at least before there was any danger of being interrupted. The silence of the place felt heavy, disturbed only by the throaty whirr of the ancient fridge in the kitchen area. Beyond the large double-glazed windows people were crossing the cobbled marketplace, going about their business, just a regular Wednesday in Bruncliffe.

The normality of it all only served to heighten his awareness of the risk he was taking.

With a deep breath, he stepped into the office, palm damp against the door handle, and swallowed, the sharp edge of his Adam's apple raking down his throat. He shouldn't be here. This was so out of character. Effectively breaking and entering when the most criminal thing he'd done up until now was lie about his age in the pub. He should be out in reception getting on with his work.

But this *was* work. It was a burst of resourcefulness, motivated by two things: a desire to impress and a broken boiler.

Having been malfunctioning for a week, the ancient water heater in his flat had finally given up entirely that morning, choosing to die a noisy death during his shower.

With an alarming bang originating from the cupboard that housed the contraption, the tepid water he was washing in had suddenly turned into an icy waterfall that had made him yelp.

Wrapped in a towel and shivering, Stuart had called the landlord again and been met with promises of action, none of which he had any faith in. So he'd dressed in a hurry, pulling on yesterday's shirt which he'd hung in the bedroom doorway to air, ensuring that it now smelled less of him and more of the sickly sweet-and-sour aroma of Chinese cooking that seeped through the floor from the takeaway below. To compound his misery, he'd arrived at work to a scrawled note from Julie, the receptionist, informing him that she was away on a training course for the day and he would have to man the office.

His heart had plummeted. Not so much at having to take on her role. More at the fact that she was going to be absent. With her open manner and infectious laugh, Julie was what got him through the hours toiling away for Taylor's Estate Agents. It certainly wasn't the pay, his salary still barely above minimum wage despite his increased responsibilities. *Lettings Manager* – it sounded impressive; in reality it meant nothing. He was the head of a department that consisted solely of himself, responsible for everything to do with the rental properties the agency had on its books. Well, almost everything. Much to his frustration, Mr Taylor still didn't trust him with the high-end properties, handling the lettings and inspections for those himself.

Standing at his desk reading Julie's note in a rumpled suit reeking of prawn crackers, Stuart Lister had had a moment of insight, wondering if the lack of trust his boss placed in him came from image. After all, it was hardly impressive that the lettings manager's own living quarters were so shoddy. A tiny flat above the Happy House take-away – flat being a generous description for the bedroom that just about accommodated a double bed, the narrow lounge with kitchenette and the cramped, mouldy bath-room – didn't really suggest success. But without a substantial increase in pay, Stuart had no other option. With holiday rentals yielding good income in the pictur-esque Dales, there was a shortage of standard lets and those that did come on the market were often larger properties which were actually up for sale, rented out while waiting for a buyer.

Of course, there was the possibility of moving back to Skipton. But that would mean moving back in with his mother and, while he loved her dearly, she fussed over him too much. When he'd told her he was relocating to Brun-cliffe, all of fifteen miles to the north, she'd gone into a panic, warning him how folk 'over there' were different. He couldn't go running back with his tail between his legs. Which meant if he was to improve his lot, he needed money so he could afford a better flat. Which meant he needed a promotion. Hence the initiative he was currently showing.

He took a step into his boss's office, grip still tight on the door handle, anchoring him on the right side of the law. For now. Vertical blinds on the small window opposite sliced the bright light of the day across the empty desk, Mr Taylor in tuxedo and his wife in long dress smiling out from behind bars of sunshine in the sole photograph adorning its surface. A couple of certificates and awards decorated the wall behind. And to one side, the large metal filing cabinet that was the motive for Stuart's trespass.

Another glance at his watch. Another minute had passed while he dithered.

One more deep breath and Stuart Lister crossed the floor in quick steps, long legs covering the distance to the filing cabinet in seconds. The key. That's what he needed first. Picking up the pot that contained the flourishing peace lily which resided on top of the cabinet, he took the small silver key from the plastic saucer beneath it.

The worst kept secret in the estate agency's history. Having once lost the key and having had to fork out a fair amount to the local locksmith to get access to his private papers, Bernard Taylor had decided to keep a second one in the office. His employees weren't supposed to know about it. But Julie had discovered it when watering the plant one day and had mentioned it to Stuart in passing as an example of how tight their boss was, risking security for the sake of calling out a locksmith again.

And now here he was, Stuart Lister, about to break the law with it.

Before he could change his mind, he unlocked the filing cabinet and pulled open the top drawer.

Financial accounts, payroll info, VAT records . . . Stuart flicked through the tabs on the dark green suspension files, nothing of interest catching his eye. He eased the drawer closed, wincing as it screeched on its runners. A panicked glance over his shoulder to the reception area, checking there was no one to witness his wrongdoing. He turned back to the cabinet, opened the second drawer.

Personnel files. Along with information packs on

employment law, health and safety regulations, insurance and a raft of other documents. Half of the contents, Stuart suspected, were probably already obsolete, revised versions easily available online. He moved onto the third drawer. More out of date material, this time old brochures and flyers for the business, along with printed specs from an age when digital house-selling hadn't been an option.

Impatience overriding his nerves, he bent down to the fourth drawer and knew straight away from the weight of it that this one was different.

Bingo.

A drawer full of fat files. The first section held what he was after. Eight folders, neatly arranged, documenting the more expensive rentals handled by Taylor's. The ones Stuart wasn't trusted to manage. Before his conscience could interfere, he scooped them up, closed the drawer and turned towards the reception. And through the large windows either side of the front door, he saw the stout figure of Bernard Taylor crossing the cobbles of the market square.

He was early. There was no time to get the files back where they belonged without being caught.

Frozen in the doorway of his boss's office, forbidden folders clutched to his chest, Stuart Lister felt his heart start to thunder.

Funerals were generally good for business. It was a fact that Troy Murgatroyd, landlord of the Fleece, never admitted to anyone, but had long observed in a lifetime spent behind a bar. Folk came in from the cold needing a bit of cheer – because the graveyard could be a bitter place even in late spring if a northerly was blowing down the dale – and the pub was the perfect place to find it. A fire in the grate, the company of good friends and a fine spread laid out by his wife in the back room, all conspired to keep them chatting and drinking. And spending. And hey presto, a quiet week-day morning could suddenly become lucrative.

Looking at the muted group of locals who'd attended the funeral of Pete Ferris, Troy sensed today would buck that trend. There was no food on offer for a start, the few family members who'd bothered to show up having left town the minute the formalities were over. All in all, it hadn't been much of a send-off.

For someone from one of the cities to the south, Leeds perhaps, or even Lancaster across the border to the west, maybe it wouldn't seem so strange that a man's passing could be marked by so few and in such a lacklustre way. After all, cities were places of anonymity where you could live – and die – alone. But this was Bruncliffe. A tight-knit community nestled in the Yorkshire Dales. Surrounded on three sides by the embrace of the fells, it was a place where people knew each other and knew how to show respect. Strange then, that the good folk of the town hadn't turned out in their best suits, collars tight on unaccustomed necks, shoes polished.

Some would say the dead man deserved no more.

He'd been a poacher. Not the most popular of professions in an area devoted to farming and country pursuits. He'd lived his life on the outskirts of civilised society, rarely seen in the marketplace and rarely sober when he was. Little surprise then that, by all accounts, the church had been close to empty. And of those people who'd bothered to pay their respects and made it as far as the Fleece, there was a dark cloud hanging over them, no doubt arising from the manner in which the man had gone to meet his maker.

'Suicide.' Will Metcalfe shook his head and stared into the bottom of his empty pint glass. 'What a way to go.'

'Drugs too,' muttered Troy, hand hovering above the Black Sheep tap, waiting for Will to offer over his glass. 'Not the route I'd choose.'

No one asked the sullen landlord to expand on his preferred choice of exit from this life. Nor was anyone making any move to order more drinks.

Will Metcalfe sighed. Put the empty glass on the bar and glanced at Samson O'Brien, who was standing next to him. And drinking a coffee. It was enough to curdle the landlord's already sour temperament. Folk frequenting a public house and not ordering ale.

'I just wish I could have thanked him in person,' Will said. 'You know, for what he did for Nathan.'

Surprised to hear Will mention his nephew in the same context as the poacher, Troy moved away from the beer pump and leaned in towards the oldest Metcalfe sibling. 'What did Pete Ferris do for young Nathan?'

'He saved his life,' said Will, attention back on the landlord. 'When Nathan went missing up on the fells back in March, Pete found him and brought him down safe.'

It wasn't often that the man behind the bar was surprised by his clientele, having lived in the Fleece all his life. He was proud to know his customers. To be able to predict their behaviour. And while Pete Ferris hadn't been as regular as some, no doubt owing to a lack of spare cash to pay for his beer, the ferret-faced man had been in often enough to give Troy a sense of his nature. Furtive. Feral. The poacher certainly hadn't been known for his philanthropic nature.

Yet here was a revelation about him Troy hadn't been expecting. The dramatic return of Nathan Metcalfe to Bruncliffe after several days on the hills in bad weather – a return that had seen the anxious townsfolk expressing a universal sigh of relief at the teenager's safe delivery from what could easily have been an untimely death – was thanks to Pete Ferris.

'I had no idea,' he said.

Will shrugged. 'I only found out myself after Pete died. He didn't want folk knowing.'

'He wouldn't even accept a reward,' added Samson O'Brien, draining the last of his coffee and placing the cup on the bar, next to Will's empty glass. 'Lucy wanted to pay him for saving her son's life, but Pete wouldn't hear of it.'

If Troy had been astounded at the first disclosure, this second one was enough to make his jaw drop. 'He refused payment?'

Samson nodded. 'Wouldn't take a penny.'

'And like I said,' muttered Will, 'I didn't even get the chance to thank him.'

James 'Herriot' Ellison, the town vet, had been standing quietly next to Samson, not one for getting involved much in conversation. He was a man who went about his business with a level of care and a discretion that endeared him to the farmers he worked with. But now he spoke up.

'Nathan taking in the lurchers is thanks enough,' he

said. 'They'd have struggled to find a home and being confined to a kennels would have killed them.'

Troy grunted in agreement. The two dogs that had been the permanent companions of the poacher were legendary for their ferocious protection of the man and his ramshackle caravan, people approaching the premises unannounced at their peril. There were few who would have been happy to take on a couple of dogs with that kind of temperament. But by all accounts, young Nathan seemed to have a rapport with them akin to that they'd shared with Pete Ferris. Until Pete had decided to kill them along with himself . . .

It had been all over town – that Samson O'Brien and Delilah Metcalfe had discovered the dead poacher in his caravan, and his two lurchers left for dead outside.

'What kind of man rescues a kid he doesn't really know and then a matter of a few weeks later, decides to kill his own dogs in a joint suicide?' mused the landlord.

Herriot shook his head. 'We can't be certain what Pete's intentions were.'

There was something in the way the vet said it that made the three other men turn to him.

'You saying they weren't poisoned?' asked Samson.

'Oh, they were poisoned all right. I'm just saying that the quantities used aren't conclusive. We can't say for sure that he meant to kill them.'

'What was it?'

'Ketamine,' said the vet.

'Ketamine?' Will Metcalfe's voice was sharp. 'What the hell is it with that stuff?'

He had a point. Other than in connection with horses, Troy had never heard of it until six months ago, and now the area seemed to be awash with it. 'There's definitely a lot of it about,' the landlord muttered, shaking his head in disgust.

'Sure is.' Herriot lowered his glass and looked at Samson O'Brien. And Troy Murgatroyd, with all his years of experience gleaned from a life working in a pub, noticed the stillness that had settled on Bruncliffe's private detective.

If he'd been inclined to bet, the landlord would have put good money on the man sensing a case.

He made it to his desk just as Bernard Taylor stormed in, metal and glass crashing behind him as he let the door slam shut.

'Morning, Mr Taylor.' It came out in a squeak of tension. Stuart Lister shoved the folders he'd stolen from his boss's office under a pile of papers and wiped his palms on his trousers, wondering if the violent thumping in his chest was the portent of a heart attack.

'Where's Julie?' Mr Taylor snapped, looking at the unoccupied seat behind the desk nearest to him.

'She's at a training course. She said you'd authorised—'

'Christ! Like we can afford to be understaffed. Here. Get this into the system!' A rental contract dropped in front of Stuart, Mr Taylor mopping a podgy hand across the sweat sheening on his forehead. The man was perspiring like a wrestler three bouts in and it wasn't even hot outside. 'And call someone about that bloody fridge. That rattling is driving me crazy.'

'Yes, Mr Taylor.' Stuart shifted in his chair, acutely aware of the hidden folders.

But Bernard Taylor was turning away, still mopping his

face as he headed for his private office. The danger was far from over, however.

Concentrate on work. Just act normally. Stuart pulled the contract that had been deposited on his desk towards him. A letting agreement for a large house on the fells above Keasden, it was standard fare. Apart from the blank space at the top.

'Mr Taylor,' he said, standing up on legs that were quivering. 'Erm . . . what name should I put on this?'

His boss wheeled round. 'Name?'

Stuart gestured at the empty space on the page in his hand. 'For the tenant?'

Plump fingers flicked at the air as though they were conjuring an answer and Mr Taylor's face contorted. 'Erm . . . name . . . yes . . . erm . . . Fred Lambert. Forgot to write it down. Too busy . . .'

'I could help with that.' The words slipped from the young man, as though something in him recognised that this was his chance to impress without resorting to underhand means.

'Help?' Mr Taylor was staring, walking back towards him.

'With the rentals. I could help you out with them. Do more of the inspections—'

A heavy hand thumped down on Stuart's desk, halting the nervous stream of language gushing from the lad and sending a pile of papers cascading over the edge. 'Just do what I bloody asked!' barked Mr Taylor.

'Sorry . . .' spluttered Stuart, aware out of the corner of his eye that some of the paperwork now littering the laminate flooring included pages that should be under lock and key. If his boss so much as looked down, Stuart's career with Taylor's would be over. 'I just thought . . .'

'I don't pay you to think! So how about you get on with the work I do pay you for.'

To Stuart's relief, Mr Taylor swung back towards his office, oblivious to the origin of the rental contracts scattered on the ground. He slammed the door behind him and Stuart dived to the floor, shaking hands gathering up the incriminating evidence, heart thundering in his ears.

Pages and folders in a jumbled heap in his gangly arms, he slumped into his chair.

That had been close. Too close. Even now, if Mr Taylor decided to work on one of the contracts he kept to himself . . .

The thought was enough to make Stuart squirm. Which is when he felt something dig into his leg. Metal, with sharp edges.

Already feeling a cold cloak of dread stealing over him, Stuart put a hand in his pocket and pulled out a key. The key to the filing cabinet in his boss's office, which he'd stolen from and then forgotten to relock.

With a quiet groan, he sank down even further in his chair and waited for the axe to fall.

2

'Hmph!' The sound was part approval, part disbelief, Norman Woolerton running a hand over his bald head and squinting at the computer screen before him. 'You seem to be getting there at last.'

On the other side of his desk was the sombre figure of Delilah Metcalfe, the young woman clad in black, having come straight from a funeral to a meeting with her bank manager. Who also happened to be a family friend, married to Delilah's father's cousin and known more commonly, outside the confines of his office, as Uncle Woolly.

There was nothing woolly about the man when it came to banking, as Delilah could testify. Six months ago he'd hauled her in for a frank talk about her escalating debts – her small cottage and her business premises mortgaged and her two enterprises, a website-development company and a dating agency, failing to yield sufficient turnover to cover her costs. Insolvency had been looming and Norman Woolerton had been determined to make it as painless as possible by refusing to extend Delilah's loans, there being no point in throwing more good money after bad. But Delilah had put forward a passionate defence, begging him for one further extension, just enough to tide her over the rough patch that had followed her divorce. She'd backed up her faith in herself with detailed spreadsheets of projected income, talking about the growing dating agency membership, the fact that she'd taken on a tenant in her office building.

It had been enough to sway the bank manager. But not enough to turn him into a fool. So he'd put a time limit on her attempts to pull herself back from the brink. Six months.

With those six months having passed, Norman Woolerton was pleasantly surprised to see from the information in front of him that the lass was almost there. There'd been a small but steady upturn in subscribers to the Dales Dating Agency; the IT side of the business had pulled in a couple of decent accounts; and then there was the work Delilah had been doing with Samson O'Brien's detective agency. Not to mention a substantial payment more recently from local farmer Clive Knowles, described as a consultation fee.

'I didn't realise there was scope for setting up websites amongst farming folk,' said Norman, indicating the substantial figure that had been handed over by Mr Knowles.

Delilah blushed, shaking her head. 'That's not what it was for,' she murmured.

'So what kind of consultation was it?'

'Marital.'

Norman blinked, picturing the unkempt man who lived out past Horton on a farm that was as badly kept as its owner. The fact he was a confirmed bachelor was a matter of course, for what woman in her right mind would take him and his ramshackle premises on? Hence there was more than a touch of astonishment in the bank manager's next words.

'Clive Knowles asked you for advice on getting wed?'

A brief nod from across the desk was the only answer.

Norman looked at the computer screen, at the sizeable deposit and then back across to his client.

'I take it from this you were successful!'

'Kind of,' muttered Delilah.

Norman Woolerton stared at her. Reappraising her in light of what she'd achieved. For Delilah Metcalfe – a woman with such a chequered history when it came to love, not to mention already being divorced and not yet thirty – had been ridiculed when she set up the Dales Dating Agency. But here was evidence that she knew what she was doing.

'Any sign of more lonely farmers asking for similar advice?' he queried, ever the businessman. 'Because another couple of payments like that and you'll really be out of the woods.'

'Not that I know of. Besides, it was a fluke.' Delilah's head dropped and her shoulders slumped, causing Noman to regard her with narrowed eyes, like a spreadsheet refusing to yield its secrets.

It was strange. The lass should have been jumping up and down, celebrating the fact that she was well on the way to turning her businesses into profit. Yet she was the most subdued he'd seen her since . . . He cast his mind back to the dreadful days three years ago when Delilah's world had been rocked: first by the death of her brother Ryan while on duty out in Afghanistan; then by the repeated philandering of her husband, Neil Taylor, and the break-up of their marriage.

Young Delilah hadn't been one to mope. Instead she'd thrown herself into rescuing the enterprises she'd set up with that rascal Taylor. But she hadn't been herself, her warm smile not often seen. All that had changed of late, though. To be precise, since last October when Samson O'Brien had returned to Bruncliffe and opened his detective agency in the downstairs office of Delilah's building. Since then, the two of them had become quite a team, solving cases together. And getting into all sorts of danger, from all accounts. Delilah had seemed to be thriving on it.

Yet here she was, looking like the weight of the world was upon her.

The bank manager didn't know what to make of it. Nor did he know how to address it, being far more at ease discussing profit and loss than anything personal, even when it pained him to see one of his favourite people looking so glum.

'Anyway,' he said, clearing his throat, 'whatever you're doing, keep it up. Another couple of months of this kind of growth and you'll really be on solid ground. This love lark clearly pays!'

There was a strangled noise from Delilah, who then coughed, stood, and came around to the other side of the oak desk that served as a barricade to every other client except her.

'Thanks, Uncle Woolly,' she said, kissing his cheek. She managed a small smile and as the door closed after her, the puzzled bank manager couldn't help thinking that something was ailing Delilah Metcalfe. Something that was beyond his professional help.

'Who's a good boy, then?'

The large grey dog sitting upright by the radiator in the reception area of the bank turned his head at the sound, an

eyebrow raised in what could be classed as query. Or haut-
eur. From behind the safety of the glass partition that
separated her cashier's position from the rest of the foyer,
Mrs Pettiford couldn't interpret the look. Suffice to say, it
wasn't one of affection.

'A good doggy,' she persisted, nodding her head at the
regal Weimaraner, his pale eyes fixed on her now.

It was a quiet morning in Bruncliffe's bank. A morning
she'd wished she'd not had to work as it had prevented her
from attending the funeral that had taken place within the
stone walls of St Oswald's down on Church Street. Not
that she'd known Pete Ferris. Well, not personally. She
didn't associate with that kind of person. But one had to
admit that his life – and subsequently his death – was fas-
cinating. A poacher. Slinking around the hills with his gun
and his lurchers, living beyond the line of legality. And
then killing himself.

It was most annoying to have missed the sending off of
such a character. Especially as such occasions often proved
fertile ground for the harvesting of gossip. So, as she stood
behind her counter with no customers to entertain her, Mrs
Pettiford was feeling more than a little left out. Hence she
was trying to make conversation with Delilah Metcalfe's
dog.

'Not long now,' she cooed. 'Mummy will be out any
minute.'

Although that might not be true. For Mrs Pettiford
knew a bit about the state of Delilah Metcalfe's finances
and the concerns Mr Woolerton had about them. Rightly
so, too. The bank couldn't afford to be propping up frivo-
lous concerns like a dating agency, especially if it wasn't

paying its way. If asked her opinion, which regrettably Mr Woolerton never sought to do, she would have added that it was high time the youngest of the Metcalfe brood settled down to a proper career. Something with prospects. Like working in a bank.

Even if that bank was quieter than Mrs Pettiford ever remembered it, no longer filled to bursting point on market days with a queue of farmers out the door, the floor left as mucky as a shippon at the end of winter. Those days were gone. Now entire mornings went by without a single person coming through the double doors, despite the fact that this was the last bank standing in Bruncliffe, the two others having pulled down their shutters for the final time over a year ago, one now a fancy cafe, the other an Indian restaurant. It was a sorry state of affairs. And when she allowed herself to think about it, her own position no longer seemed the safe haven it had always been—

The rattle of the front door and the low woof of greeting from the dog pulled Mrs Pettiford away from such morbid thoughts as her first customer of the day entered.

'Good morning,' she said, smile in place.

She was rewarded with a wan-faced nod of acknowledgement from a middle-aged woman, dressed immaculately in a cashmere jacket, moleskin trousers and smart ankle boots, none of which had come out of Betty's Boutique on Back Street. Which was hardly surprising, as Mrs Pettiford's customer was none other than Bruncliffe royalty – Nancy Taylor, wife of the successful estate agent Bernard Taylor, who was also the town's current mayor. She was a woman more at home in the boutiques of Harrogate and one who wore her wealth well.

'How can I help you?' asked Mrs Pettiford, as her eyes took in the fine cut of the woman's clothes, the subtle accents of jewellery and the exquisite leather of her handbag, trying not to let her jealousy show. Or her surprise at seeing the ugly black holdall the woman was placing on the floor, the one jarring note in what was otherwise style perfection.

'I need a statement for our account. The bank's website is down,' said Mrs Taylor.

'Oh. Right.' Mrs Pettiford's heart lifted. The website was down again – another cyberattack no doubt. Last time it had seen a huge influx of customers coming through the doors and, even though most of them had been irate at the inconvenience, for the woman behind the counter it had briefly felt like the old days when her position had been one of value. 'I can give you up to six weeks' worth of transactions but anything beyond that will need to be posted to you, I'm afraid. Is that sufficient?'

'It'll have to do.'

'Business or personal?'

'Personal . . . actually, make it both, please.' Nancy Taylor shifted on the other side of the glass and stared down at the holdall. There was something about her not as self-composed as her tailored clothing would suggest, fingers tapping on the counter briefly before she thrust her hands into her pockets.

That movement – the suddenness of it; the stealth of it. It caught the bank clerk's attention, but only for a second as the printer chose that moment to start its usual trick of chewing up paper.

'I think it's not awake yet,' Mrs Pettiford simpered,

pulling out the ruined pages and resisting the urge to slap the damn machine like she normally would. 'There you go.' She passed the reprinted pages under the partition. 'Is that everything?'

'Yes. Thanks.' With her left hand firmly in her pocket, Nancy Taylor pushed the statements into her handbag, picked up the holdall and walked out of the door.

'Well,' murmured Mrs Pettiford as the bank settled back into silence. 'Not exactly talkative, was she?'

The Weimaraner didn't even look up from where he was now lying on the ground. But the bank clerk was unaware she'd been snubbed. Her mind was too busy trying to work out what it was she'd just seen. Something about Nancy Taylor. Something about those slender fingers tip-tapping away—

A door in the back of the building closed and the sound of footsteps roused the Weimaraner in a way Mrs Pettiford's attempts at conversation couldn't, a low whine emitting from his long throat as he looked hopefully towards the far corner of the room. And sure enough, Delilah Metcalfe emerged from the corridor, a smile fleeting across her pale face at the enthusiastic tail-wagging of her dog.

'Sorry, Tolpuddle,' she murmured, untying his lead. 'Didn't mean to be so long.' She began heading for the door, the dog pulling her on in his desperation to be outside. 'Thanks for keeping an eye on him, Mrs Pettiford. Bye.'

Unusually for a woman known for her garrulous nature, Mrs Pettiford didn't reply. She was staring at the counter. At the precise spot where Mrs Taylor's hands had been only moments before. It was only as the door to the bank closed behind Delilah that a sudden spark of comprehension lit up the clerk's face.

Those slender fingers. That's what it was! They'd been bare!

With no band of gold decorating the left hand, it could only mean one thing. And then there was the ugly hold-all . . .

'She's leaving him!' Mrs Pettiford exclaimed to the empty room. 'The mayor's wife is leaving him!'

This dazzling insight, perhaps the richest vein of gossip Mrs Pettiford had ever unearthed in a lifetime of digging, was only marred by one thing – that it hadn't happened slightly earlier when there had been someone in the bank to appreciate the brilliance of her deductions. And who better to have been the first person to share this shock revelation with than Delilah Metcalfe, former daughter-in-law of the for-now Mrs Taylor?

But Mrs Pettiford didn't spend long ruing her missed chances. After all, Delilah wasn't the most receptive of audiences when it came to scandals, having starred in a few herself. And besides, this was sensitive material. The kind of thing that, if got wrong, could really backfire, the mayor having plenty of powerful friends in the town. So instead, the bank clerk stored the nugget away. She would do a bit more surreptitious digging around the subject and bide her time before unleashing this earth-shattering news on the unsuspecting folk of Bruncliffe.

It felt like an age. Sitting there waiting for his boss to come storming out and sack him. Knowing that when it happened, his fledgling career as an estate agent would be over, for such was the power of Taylor's in the area that few would hire someone rejected by that agency.

Despite the perilous situation, somehow Stuart Lister managed to work, fingers busy on the keyboard creating a digital file for the latest tenant. But all the while, his nerves were stretched taut, sweat gathering on his top lip, his breath that of a cornered animal, fast and shallow.

There was no way out of this. As soon as Mr Taylor tried to open his filing cabinet, he would know something was up. The missing key, for starters. And when he opened the unlocked drawers and found all of the high-end rental properties missing from the files, he would come looking for Stuart. For the young man, it was tempting to simply get up and leave before he was fired.

The muffled sound of a ringing mobile made him turn towards the closed office door and he heard the rumble of Mr Taylor's voice.

A distraction. Thank God. Although Stuart knew it was only prolonging the inevitable. At some point his boss was going to discover the extent of Stuart's betrayal. He'd mucked it all up, trying too hard to impress. He was an idiot.

It had seemed like the perfect plan – if a bit risky. While on the computer the day before, Stuart had noticed a backlog in the inspections on some of the rentals Mr Taylor oversaw. Three of the houses were supposed to have had their six-monthly visits at the end of April but there was no record of those reports having been completed. As the entire IT system was in the process of being overhauled by Delilah Metcalfe, Stuart hadn't liked to jump to conclusions, thinking that maybe it was simply a glitch and that the paper files would show that the inspections had in fact been carried out.

His first instinct had been to ignore the omission. Bernard Taylor had never been the most considerate of employers, but the last couple of weeks he'd been even worse, taking out his moods on the office furniture and his staff. And while this unpredictable behaviour held the silver lining of giving Stuart the excuse to strike up conversations with the lovely Julie – there being nothing like a shared sense of being treated unfairly for breeding camaraderie – it was mostly Stuart who bore the full brunt of Mr Taylor's temperament. So, for someone who shunned confrontation, asking his more-irascible-than-ever boss if he was doing his job properly wasn't a move Stuart favoured. Best just to let it lie.

But that morning, arriving at work to an empty office and no prospect of anyone being around for at least an hour – his boss out with rental clients, Julie on her training course and the cleaner, Ida Capstick, long finished and gone – Stuart had seen a way to show his resourcefulness. He'd have a look at the paper files himself. If there had been an oversight, he'd find a way to raise it with Mr Taylor without revealing that he'd been checking up on him. Because, Stuart had reasoned as he made the decision to be proactive, with the way his boss had been acting lately, he needed a hand or the business was going to suffer.

Taking the files without permission had seemed like a sensible option.

How then, had it come to this? Mr Taylor about to discover the extent of his employee's errant behaviour, an abrupt dismissal looming.

A loud curse from the office and Stuart felt his stomach curl tightly in on itself, long fingers clenching into tense fists. Footsteps and then the office door being flung open.

'Stuart!'

The shout made the young man jump. He turned slowly towards his fate, his boss advancing on him, hands on hips, face puce.

'Yes, Mr Taylor?' Even to his own ears, Stuart sounded scared.

'If anyone calls, I'll be out for an hour,' snapped Bernard Taylor. 'Get that fridge sorted before I get back.'

Stuart Lister watched in bemused relief as his boss stalked past his desk, across reception and out of the front door. It was only then that the young estate agent felt the air rush back into his lungs, hands shaking as his fists unfurled.

Somehow he'd dodged a bullet.

He reached for the pile of folders that he'd retrieved from the floor, papers sticking out all over the place from their fall. He'd sort them out and then put them straight back in Mr Taylor's filing cabinet without delay. No more trying to impress. No more initiative. It wasn't worth it.

But the first piece of paper he picked up changed all that. His hands went still and he found himself staring at a rental contract.

It was odd. Odd enough to make him rethink. And this time his actions weren't driven by anything other than curiosity.

3

Samson O'Brien didn't have far to go to get to work. Stepping out of the gloomy interior of the Fleece into the bright sunshine of a late morning in May, blinking at the sudden change in light and still finding himself surprised at the warmth in the air despite the good weather having held for the last week, he crossed the narrow tarmac of Back Street to the three-storey building opposite.

Automatically, he glanced up at the first-floor window where the shared kitchen looked out over the road. No shadow behind the glass. Delilah Metcalfe, his landlady, his supposed partner and the woman he was trying to pretend was only a friend, wasn't back. After a meeting with the bank manager, she would be needing to refuel and would have already been in the kitchen putting the kettle on, brewing up a pot of tea in true Yorkshire fashion. Samson's stomach shrank at the thought of it, the strength of his hometown's cuppa something he'd lost a taste for during his years down in London.

It wasn't the only thing he'd lost a taste for while he was away. The cold of a North Yorkshire winter was another. After six months back in Bruncliffe, most of them spent freezing and wet, it was little wonder that he was inclined to mistrust this change to soft breezes and balmy temperatures, not a single rain cloud in the sky. He was still having to fight the instinct to put on his parka every time he left home.

Home.

His gaze drifted to the top floor of the building. Thanks to Delilah's generosity, that was where he was living. Because home was something else he'd lost while he was down south. The farm out in Thorpdale, which he'd left in a blaze of anger, had no longer been in the family when he'd returned fourteen years later. But on the plus side, his father was no longer drinking. Just as he couldn't quite get himself to trust the sudden change in season, so Samson still couldn't get used to seeing his father at the bar in the Fleece, nothing stronger than an orange juice in his hand. But that's where he'd just left him, talking away to Arty Robinson and his friends from Fellside Court retirement apartments, the pensioners having turned out for the funeral of Pete Ferris, partly through sentiment but also out of respect for what the man had done for Nathan Metcalfe.

Samson let his eyes drop back down to the window spanning the ground floor, the bright letters 'D D A' picked out in a gold arch across the glass. Freshly applied, the letters glinted in the sunshine, mirroring the more faded characters on the window above. Two lots of D D A. Two businesses that shared the same initials, shared the same office building, and of recent times, the same personnel. The Dales Detective Agency and the Dales Dating Agency – they couldn't be more diverse and, some would say, they couldn't be more niche, in an area not known for crime or for lovelorn folk. And yet both businesses had started to thrive in the last couple of months. Delilah had achieved success with her Speedy Date nights and her online matchmaking, and Samson, having solved a number of cases – several of them with Delilah's help – was beginning to believe his fledgling venture might prosper.

So they'd gone into business together. A combining of forces, Delilah's technical knowledge lending an element to the detective services that Samson couldn't have offered, and it seemed to be working. On a superficial level at least. Beneath the surface . . .

Samson sighed and let himself into the office building. Human relationships weren't his forte. Not after years working undercover for the National Crime Agency, where he was used to lying and manipulating and never opening himself up to trust. And here he was—

A noise. From the back of the building. A small clatter of metal.

Samson froze in the hallway, soundlessly easing the door closed behind him, feeling his heart rate increase, every fibre of him alert to the danger. He had no weapon to hand. Which wasn't an ideal state of affairs, because danger was on the horizon. The very past that had driven him out of the police force and back up north to Bruncliffe was closing in on him, and he'd been warned to expect the worst. An attempt on his life.

Was this it?

His hand slipped into his pocket, feeling the cold screen of his emergency mobile. The one his old boss, DI Warren, had given him, the one that was supposed to serve as an alarm, alerting him when the threat came calling.

There'd been no message. No forewarning. Samson clutched the phone in his fist. At the very least he could throw it.

Another noise from the back. Footsteps. Wary. Not the confident steps of someone who had nothing to hide.

Samson tried to remember whether he'd locked the back door when he'd left for the funeral that morning. It was something he wouldn't have had to think about in London, the idea of leaving a door unlocked not one that he would ever have entertained. Yet six months back in his home town and he'd fallen into old ways, nipping down the shop without bothering to secure the premises.

He was going to have to change his habits, given what was hanging over him. If it wasn't already too late.

Moving quietly, he edged down the hallway, his back to the wall until he got to his office. A quick glimpse inside the open door revealed just the old desk, a couple of chairs and the filing cabinet. And the dog bed to the far side. Nothing out of place. Nothing he could use in a fight either, his laptop upstairs in Delilah's office where she'd been updating his software.

But at least the room was empty. Whatever this threat was, it had come alone, then. Because if there were two of them, they'd have split up, one in the front, one in the back.

Feeling like the odds might be a bit more in his favour, Samson moved further along the hallway towards the downstairs kitchen, which was now used as a utility. He could see the basket of dirty laundry that he'd forgotten to put on that morning on top of the washing machine and, in the reflection from the window, a figure hidden around the corner of the L-shaped room.

There was definitely someone in there. And it wasn't Delilah. Because Delilah came in a package that included an excitable Weimaraner who adored Samson. There was no way he could be this near to the hound without being met with some serious canine affection. Then he saw the reflected image shift and his blood ran cold.

Whoever was waiting around the corner for him was holding a gun, arm outstretched, pointing it towards the doorway. And Delilah was due back any minute. She was about to walk in on a situation that was deadly. About to fall into a situation that he had been worrying about since he'd heard that danger was heading his way.

He needed to act. And now.

In one swift movement he lunged into the kitchen, grabbed the plastic basket of clothing and, as he dived to the floor, flung it around the corner at his assailant.

There was a stunned yelp, the clatter of metal on tile and Samson was already springing back up onto his feet, turning to face whoever had been sent to do him harm as they flailed blindly around the small kitchen space, the basket over their head, dirty laundry draped all over them. He caught an out-swinging arm, devoid of gun, and grasped it hard, preparing to twist it up behind the attacker's back. But he felt his fingers dig into soft flesh beneath the jacket. A smart jacket, made from wool of some sort. Not normal assassin attire. Then he heard the moan from under several layers of clothing.

A woman.

'What the hell—?' No longer confident he'd read the situation correctly, he dropped her arm, stepped back and lifted the basket off her. With a shake of her head, a dark bob appeared, not as immaculate as usual, a stray sock still caught in it. 'Sorry . . .' Samson stuttered, realising the magnitude of his mistake as he stared at the familiar figure. 'I thought . . . I didn't know . . .'

'No, I'm sorry.' The woman brushed the remaining articles of clothing to the floor and retrieved her mobile – a mobile, not a gun – from next to the washing machine before turning to face him. And Samson got a sense that her pale features were only partly a result of the assault she'd just endured. 'I didn't want anyone to see me. So I came in the back. The door was unlocked . . .'

Samson swallowed. Nodded. And wondered if Nancy Taylor had any idea how close she'd just come to being seriously hurt.

'Come on in,' he said, embarrassed now, a week of his dirty washing strewn across the kitchen. 'Delilah will be back soon. I'll make you a drink while you wait.'

But Nancy Taylor was shaking her head. 'I'm not here for Delilah,' she said, tension tightening her face into a grimace. 'It's you I came to see.'

'Me?' Samson felt his eyebrows shoot into his hairline. What on earth would the mayor's wife want with him?

'Yes, you. Thing is . . .' The woman faltered, a hand going out to the worktop to steady herself. 'Thing is, I need someone to spy on my husband. Would that be something you'd do?'

The sunshine was having no effect on Delilah Metcalfe. As she walked across the cobbled marketplace, Tolpuddle pulling at the lead in his eagerness to be back at the office, she felt none of the joys normally associated with the month of May. While she may have thrown off her coat and braved the day in just a jumper and jeans, she didn't feel buoyed by the arrival of this lovely weather. The bright colours of the bouquets outside the florists didn't catch her eye. Even the delicious scent of baking wafting over the square from Peaks Patisserie failed to turn her head in anticipation. Instead she trudged on, her spirits as heavy as a Swaledale's fleece on a wet winter's day.

What was the point? All that excitement and adventure. A near-death experience that had brought them so close. Close enough to almost kiss. And when she'd slipped into a frozen sleep, he'd kept her warm, wrapped in his embrace. He'd saved her life.

And now? He might as well have been a brother. A surplus sibling for a woman who already had enough older brothers and had no need of another.

Just over three weeks since they'd been locked in a freezer together facing certain death, and Delilah was despairing over the state of her relationship with Samson O'Brien. While the staff at Airedale hospital had been amazing, bringing thawing limbs back to life, things between the Dales Detective Agency staff seemed to have remained frozen.

It wasn't like he was giving her the cold shoulder. In fact, for an outsider, it would be hard to fault Samson's behaviour towards her. He was friendly. He was considerate. And unfailingly polite. So actually, he was nothing like a brother at all. More like a colleague. An affable colleague.

Nothing more.

It was her own fault, this depression that had settled upon her, causing her to lose her appetite, draining her enthusiasm for daily life. Because after their escapade, after the intimacy they'd shared in the dark tomb of the freezer when Samson had told her everything about the events that had forced him to leave London, she'd been convinced things would be different. That just as they'd survived, so too would this new-found warmth that had blossomed in the icy temperatures.

But it hadn't. When they were released from hospital and normal life returned, things between the two of them had become . . .

What? Not strained. Not on Samson's part anyway. He seemed to be genuinely happy to be her friend, and no more. Which was the problem. Delilah wanted so much more. She knew that now. But how to broach the topic? This was a man who'd been suspended from his role as an undercover detective with the NCA on corruption charges; a man who was facing the possibility of a court case if he couldn't clear his name; and a man with a very real threat against his life. Her aching heart seemed so trivial a subject to burden him with.

And on a more pragmatic level, they'd hardly seen each other in recent weeks.

Work was partly to blame. Delilah had been caught up trying to complete two website-development projects that she'd had to abandon when events at the auction mart had taken over their lives. And Samson had been hit with a flurry of enquiries from folk who only a month before would have shunned him on the street. Word was getting round about what he'd done to help save Bruncliffe's livestock auction and gratitude was bringing him cases. What kind of cases, Delilah had no idea, as he'd not asked for her help on any of them.

In fact, she'd seen more of Frank Thistlethwaite, the Leeds-based policeman, in the last couple of weeks. A night out in the pub. A meal at a restaurant over in Skipton.

Delilah knew that with just a bit more encouragement on her part Frank would happily develop their friendship into the kind of relationship she'd been hoping for with Samson.

'God, you're never happy,' she muttered at herself as she turned down Back Street, trying to take cheer from the day around her.

For it was a wonderful day. The sun was shining on the narrow road, high enough to clear the slate roofs and brighten the normally sullen stones of the Fleece. It bounced off the rainbow-coloured array of merchandise outside Plastic Fantastic. And it had turned the letters spanning the glass of her building into a golden arc.

A golden arc behind which she could see two figures as she approached the front door. Samson had a client in with him. She knew better than to go barging in like she would have done a month ago. There was no point. Samson would politely tell her he had no need of her services. Something that she wouldn't have accepted before, but now she was reluctant to add to his worries by forcing the issue of their relationship out into the open. Plus, with her heart so bruised, she was wary of exposing it to any more harm.

Fixing a smile on her face, she slipped the key into the lock and took a deep breath. She'd do her best to keep a firm lid on her temperamental nature, curb her tendency for rash behaviour, and respect Samson's need for distance. Even though it was driving her mad. Full of good intentions, Delilah opened the door.

A crying woman sitting opposite him was never a great way to start work. Samson O'Brien loosened the black tie that had been threatening to choke him for the last hour, sensing that this day which had begun with a funeral and continued with him attacking an innocent person – who just happened to be part of Bruncliffe's elite – wasn't about to improve any.

'Tissue?' he asked, passing across the box he kept in a drawer and wishing that Delilah Metcalfe was there with him. The same Delilah Metcalfe he'd been keeping at arm's length for the best part of three weeks, despite it almost killing him.

He pushed back such futile thoughts and concentrated on his unexpected visitor.

Nancy Taylor was sobbing gently, a tissue now pressed to her eyes. Like everything the woman did, it was elegant. But no less heartbreaking for that. And Samson didn't have a clue how to deal with it.

Make tea, maybe? That's what Delilah would do. And then she'd sit with Mrs Taylor, an arm around her, offering the comfort and warmth that came so naturally to her. Whereas he . . . he was offering this classy woman some tissues from the Spar.

Samson shoved the box back in the drawer and cleared his throat.

'Perhaps we could start at the beginning?' he suggested softly.

'I'm sorry . . .' Mrs Taylor's voice broke and her shoulders shook. And Samson felt completely out of his depth.

The dog let her down, as he always did. While she was making every effort to respect the distance Samson had put between them, despite her confusion about it, Tolpuddle was doing no such thing. And so the second he managed to squeeze his nose between the front door and the door-frame, he started pushing hard, forcing his large grey body against the wood.

'Tolpuddle!' Delilah snapped. But it was too late. The door sprang out of her grasp and smacked against the wall, the dog already racing into the hallway and towards . . .

'Tolpuddle!' she tried again.

He wasn't listening. He was heading straight into Samson's office, an affection-seeking missile that she had no power to avert.

'Bugger.' She hurried after him as his wagging tail disappeared out of sight through the doorway. 'Sorry,' she was already saying, 'he's been cooped up in the bank and—'

She halted abruptly on the threshold, eyes taking in the identity of the woman sitting opposite Samson, sideways on to Delilah, head bent down, black holdall on the floor beside her.

'Nancy?' Delilah didn't hide her surprise. Her former mother-in-law was the last person she'd expected to see visiting the Dales Detective Agency. 'What are you—?'

She paused again, noticing the ball of tissue in the woman's hand, the slight smudge of mascara on the high cheekbone. Nancy Taylor, the most composed person Delilah had ever known, had been crying. In front of someone.

Delilah went to move, automatically wanting to console and comfort this woman who'd offered her daughter-in-law unexpected support when young love had turned sour. But then she remembered where she was. In Samson's office. It was no longer a place she felt at liberty to enter without invitation. She glanced at him and found his eyes fixed on her, something akin to panic in their depths. Then his lips moved, silently communicating.

Help! He tipped his head at the woman opposite him, who was crying openly now.

Delilah was in the door in a flash, pulling up a chair next to Nancy Taylor and placing an arm around her shaking shoulders.

'I'll make tea,' said Samson, getting to his feet. The relief in his voice was audible.

4

'Bernard's having an affair.' Nancy Taylor placed her cup on its saucer and her shoulders sagged, as though the admission had drained her.

So shocking was the bare statement, Delilah found herself unable to take it in, distracted instead by the crockery in the hands of the mayor's wife, wondering how far back in the kitchen cupboards Samson had had to dig in order to find something that was more appropriate for his prospective client than the chipped mugs the Dales Detective Agency normally offered its customers.

The rattle of china drew her attention back to the astonishing announcement that had come from the woman sitting next to her, who was now leaning forward to place her cup on the desk.

'Sorry,' said Nancy. 'I can't seem to stop my hands shaking. So stupid of me. I'm behaving like a teenager.'

'No need to apologise.' Delilah placed her own hand over Nancy's, surprised at how cold they felt despite the warmth in the office.

Samson cleared his throat. 'An affair?' he asked. 'What makes you say that?'

A twisted smile prefaced Nancy's response. 'It was a gut feeling at first. Late nights that were always blamed on work. Phone calls cut short when I walked in on them.' She turned to her ex-daughter-in-law with a contrite look. 'You know what I mean.'

Delilah nodded. Only she didn't know. Not really. Because when her husband – Nancy's *son* – had cheated on her, she'd been the last person to find out. She'd placed her blind trust in the man and had never suspected that the loving persona he showed to her and the rest of Bruncliffe was masking a serial adulterer.

'And have you asked Bernard about any of this?' Samson's pragmatic response brought another small smile to Nancy's face.

'No. That would be the sensible option, I agree. But I'm feeling far from sensible about all of this. In fact, if I had to be honest, I'm afraid to ask him.'

'You think he could be violent?' The surprise in Samson's voice was understandable, the idea of Bruncliffe's rotund mayor being capable of physical aggression not one many in the town would sign up to.

Nancy's smile turned into a dry laugh. 'No, not at all. I'm afraid to ask him because I can't bear the thought that it's all been a sham – the lifestyle we've built up together; all the hard work getting him to where he is . . .' She shook her head. 'I'm a coward.'

'You're here asking for help,' countered Delilah. 'I'd hardly call that the action of a coward.'

'About that,' said Samson. 'I don't mean to sound callous, but if you already know Bernard is having an affair, what do you need a detective for? Surely you'd be better off seeing a solicitor?'

'I thought about it. Until I found this when I was going through Bernard's wardrobe this morning.' Nancy picked up the holdall from the floor, unzipped it and then stood, turning the bag upside down as she did so. Bundles of rolled-up banknotes thumped down onto Samson's desk.

'Jesus!' Samson stared at the money piled in front of him and then at Nancy. 'That's a lot of cash!'

'You're not kidding,' murmured Delilah, stunned.

'It's one hundred and twenty-five thousand pounds, to be precise,' said Nancy. 'And it's why I'm here. I not only want to know if my husband is having an affair, but also if he intends to rob me blind in the process.'

'I want out!' Bernard Taylor was on his feet, leaning across the desk, face ashen, jaw tense, looking like a man one pulse away from a coronary.

Sitting in his office in the Low Mill development his company owned, Rick Procter eased back in his chair, mind racing. His instinct was to cut the man loose, let the people they both worked for step in and take charge – a euphemism if ever there was one. The concept didn't cause the property developer any qualms. He held no allegiance to Taylor, despite the fact they were deep in this together; that he had actually been the one to bring the estate agent on board with his ingenious idea to incorporate remote rental properties into the business.

But it was too risky. If the organisation they answered to got wind of the fact that part of Rick's operation was getting cold feet, their response would be to close down his whole set-up. Another euphemism, and one Rick didn't want to be on the other end of.

So he was going to have to calm the man down and get him back in line, because there was too much at stake.

Taylor knew everything about Procter Properties – well, almost everything. Enough to sabotage the image Rick had carefully cultivated over the years and to expose the murky dealings behind the facade. Enough to secure both of them a lengthy prison sentence, or an early death. He couldn't have him simply sauntering off into the sunset. Or losing his nerve and developing a conscience. In fact, the timing of Taylor's meltdown couldn't have been worse.

'I understand your concerns, Bernard,' he began. 'I really do. But now isn't the right moment—'

'I don't care. I can't take any more of this.' Taylor started trembling, legs going weak and depositing him into his chair with a thud. He ran a hand over his face and for one awful minute, Rick thought he was going to cry. Instead, the estate agent shook his head mournfully. 'I'm not sleeping. Ever since Pete Ferris . . .' The words trailed off into an edgy silence.

Bloody Pete Ferris. Taylor had been getting more and more twitchy since the poacher launched his blackmail attempt. A couple of photographs, taken from a hiding place at a remote property on Henside Road, and Ferris had had them over a barrel – the golden boy of the Bruncliffe business world and the town's mayor caught in the act of running a cannabis farm. Never one to miss an opportunity, the poacher had contacted Bernard Taylor and outlined his demands: £250,000 in cash.

There had never been a question of paying the man. It simply couldn't happen. But Taylor had allowed himself to believe that the money would be handed over and Pete Ferris would be satisfied, never to darken their doors again. So, nearly four weeks ago, when the poacher was found to have committed suicide the very night the ransom was supposed to have been paid, Rick had presumed Taylor would accept it with relief, a lucky break that allowed him to keep his half of the potential ransom. As early as the next day, however, the estate agent had started getting anxious, querying the cause of Ferris's demise. And undeterred by Rick's repeated warnings that this was a course of inquiry best left alone, he kept coming back to it.

The fact his doubts were justified didn't change anything: Bernard Taylor had become a liability. One look at him was enough to see he was right on the edge. But there was no get-out clause in the unwritten contract they had with the people they were doing business with.

'Look,' Rick said softly, 'let's just get this networking event at the weekend out of the way and then we can discuss this.'

But Taylor was shaking his head again, more vigorously this time. 'I'm revoking all of the rental contracts. The farms need to be gone within the week.'

'And the rest of the business?' Rick's tone was deceivingly genial, concealing his rising temper at the naivety of the man opposite.

Taylor shrugged. 'We can sort something out.'

Sort something out. An enterprise that was pulling in millions for the criminal organisation behind it all, and the estate agent was talking about ending it like he was negotiating a divorce settlement.

'Okay,' Rick said, hands flat on the desk in front of him – the safest way to stop them from reaching across and fastening themselves around Taylor's chubby neck, which would at least solve this current problem. 'I promise I'll raise it with the bosses, but you have to swear you'll leave it with me. These aren't men who take rejection lightly.'

The mayor nodded eagerly, happy yet again to consign the dirty work to his partner. 'Thanks,' he muttered, getting to his feet.

'So, can I still count on you for Saturday?' Rick kept the question light, despite the weight it carried. Because his partner had no idea of the magnitude of the coming few days, Rick having made the decision to keep him in the dark as long as possible in the hope it would contain the man's jitters. Judging by the man's demeanour, it had been the right call.

'What time?'

'Eight thirty at Mearbeck Hall Hotel. Don't be late.'

Bernard Taylor nodded and, looking no more composed than when he'd entered the room, took his leave. Half an hour later Rick Procter was still staring into the distance, trying to come up with a solution. One that didn't involve shutting down the operation as his companion in crime was insisting. Because if there was one thing he was sure of, telling this particular bunch of men that you no longer wanted to be part of their organisation wasn't an option. Especially when the next time Rick met them, they would be carrying fully loaded shotguns.

Fred Lambert.

Stuart stared at the name on the piece of paper in his hand. It was a rental contract that had fallen out of one of the folders he'd taken from the filing cabinet, drawn up for an old manor house with four bedrooms and lots of out-buildings on a secluded plot out past Horton. The property had come on the market last June for a hefty eighteen hundred a month before being snapped up by a Mr Lambert.

Needless to say, being at the pricier end of the lettings market, it was a property Mr Taylor hadn't let Stuart near, so while it had been entered on the computer system, this was the first time the lettings manager had paid attention to the details. Or the name of the tenant. It wasn't an unusual name, not around these parts, there being plenty of Lamberts in the Dales. But it was striking a chord.

Fred Lambert was the same name Mr Taylor had given him just now for the newly leased house up above Keasden – a five-bedroomed barn conversion set back from the road on a couple of acres, out of sight of what little passing traffic ventured up onto those fells.

A coincidence, maybe? If not, then the man had deep pockets. And a seemingly insatiable need for large houses in isolated areas.

Curious to see if there were any more instances of Mr Lambert's appetite for high-end rental properties, Stuart pulled the rest of the folders towards him. Separating the contracts from other paperwork, he spread them out on his desk.

No more Fred Lamberts. But bizarrely, there were a couple of other oddities. For a start, it appeared that Mr Lambert shared an address with a Mr Dugdale, who'd rented the former farm on Henside Road, because both contracts had the same details listed as the tenant's contact information.

Stuart automatically turned to his computer and googled

the address, zooming in on the map to see a large house on a leafy road in Roundhay in Leeds. A house easily as big as those the two men had rented here in the Dales.

But that wasn't all. A couple of the phone numbers listed were the same. For different tenants. Two people with different names renting separate properties months apart yet they had identical phone numbers? Now that was bizarre. And then there was the small matter of references. For eight separate properties, one source was cited as a referee for all of them. A Kingston Holdings.

The rattle of the fridge startled Stuart and he glanced at the clock on the far wall. He'd already spent half an hour looking at the documents. If Mr Taylor came back early and found him going through them, there'd be no explanation for what he was doing.

Gathering up the contracts, he set about placing them into their respective folders, deciding that whatever was going on, it was none of his business. Perhaps it was a network of businessmen who, for some reason, were renting large houses in the middle of nowhere—

He paused, struck by the fact that there was very little paperwork in the folder in his hand. One of Mr Lambert's properties. There was the contract, which Stuart was just replacing, room-by-room specifications including a floor-plan, and an inventory.

No evidence of credit checks on the tenant.

No copies of references.

No copy of ID either.

Despite having only a smattering of experience behind him, Stuart took his career seriously and had read enough articles online to know that, while the regulations for rental properties were not as strict as for sales, agents were still expected to carry out basic checks to comply with the 'know your customer' remit established by the government. Yet this file contained nothing to show that Mr Taylor had followed procedure when it came to establishing the background of his clients. Or their money.

Stuart picked up the next folder. Likewise, there were no references and no proof that a credit check had been carried out. Nor was there a photocopy of a passport or driver's licence. Not even a single utility bill. He hurriedly checked the other six.

They were all missing essential documentation.

Concerned now, he logged on to his account and pulled up the digital files for all eight properties, quickly clicking through them. According to the information on the screen, all of the tenants had been vetted and paper records stored on file, as was company policy. Yet there was no evidence of that process in the folders.

Not only that, but five of the eight properties were listed as being up to date with their six-monthly inspections. However, there were no copies of any of Mr Taylor's inspection reports in the folders.

Stuart didn't know what to make of it.

Before he knew what he was doing, he was reopening the folders one by one, laying the scant paperwork on his desk. Heart racing and with one eye on the marketplace beyond the windows, he pulled out his phone and started taking photographs.

If he'd been asked the reason for his actions, he couldn't have answered precisely. It was a feeling. A hunch that something wasn't right, even though the rational part of him was trying to believe it was all nothing more than an administrative hiccup. Five minutes later, however, having taken photos of every one of the rental properties that Mr Taylor guarded so tightly, Stuart returned to his boss's office and opened the bottom drawer of the filing cabinet and knew instantly that his hunch had been justified. Because the tab on the suspension file directly behind the rental one said 'Kingston Holdings'.

Stuart Lister reached in and took out the contents.

High above the town, on the slopes of a fellside that looked down upon the collection of slate roofs and the two tall mill chimneys that made up Bruncliffe, Gareth Towler was having a bad day. Despite the wonderful weather.

Shaking his head at the latest development, he shoved his mobile back in the pocket of his waxed jacket and took a deep breath, making himself appreciate the gentle spring morning, the touch of warmth in the air, the sound of lapwings in the distance. For a few minutes he felt his worries recede and was reminded why he loved being a gamekeeper. Then he focused back on the problem in hand.

Bloody shooting parties. They were often the worst part of his job. Back when he'd been a nipper helping out beating, things had been different. More respect for a start. More of an understanding about the effort that went into rearing the birds and the parts everyone played in bringing a successful shoot together. Nowadays, he often found himself overseeing events for people who didn't know one end of a shotgun from another. Rich folk pretending to be gentry for a day without a jot of the manners the likes of old Mr Lupton, the owner of Bruncliffe Manor back in Gareth's childhood, had displayed as a matter of course.

Those had been the days. Mr Lupton had run a good estate – well stocked, well managed and well loved. An invitation to shoot at Bruncliffe Manor had been considered an honour, Gareth recalling a dazzling array of finery and impeccable behaviour amongst the guns, while an army of knowledgeable beaters, loaders and pickers-up worked the drive, all aided by immaculately behaved Labradors and spaniels. For a child like Gareth, it had been one long carnival. And while his love of gamekeeping had sprung from early mornings and late evenings tending pheasants out on his own on the fells, the magic of those smoothly run shoots had made an impression.

But when Mr Lupton had passed away, that affection for Bruncliffe Manor had passed with him, his son seeing the huge manor house and the acres of fellside that came with it purely as an asset. One that would pay off death duties if managed correctly. Fast forward a few decades and the current generation of the Lupton family rarely ventured this far north from their London home to avail themselves of the sport the manor had to offer, leaving the running of the estate to Gareth, as head gamekeeper, and a grey-faced accountant who appeared once a quarter to place even further restrictions on the funds available to Gareth and his team. In the absence of that personal connection, the manor was now run as a profit-making enterprise, offering commercial shoots to anyone who could pay the daily rate; no discernment as to the quality of the guests so long as they had the money.

It was a far cry from the estate Gareth remembered

---

from his youth. But there was something about the place that kept him there, even when he'd received offers of employment from some of the grandest manors in the country. Something that made him desperate to keep his job, even on days like this.

'Bloody Bruncliffe,' he muttered, looking down at the town of his birth with a wry grin.

A soft nose nuzzled his hand, as if in sympathy.

'Aye, Bounty,' Gareth said, addressing the springer spaniel by his side, his hand running over the brown head. 'Can't help but love the place, eh?'

Even when it threw up problems like the one he had now. A shoot all set for the weekend, eight guns expecting a thrilling day of clays and fine food. But while Gareth could guarantee one of those essential elements, he'd just found out he couldn't provide the other.

'Bugger it!' he muttered, scratching the thatch of russet hair beneath his cap. The group had already shown themselves to be awkward, putting pressure on him to provide a drive of pheasants even though it was out of season, something he'd resolutely refused to do. Then the standard vehicles he normally provided for the day – reliable Range Rovers he hired in – had been deemed unsuitable and a demand placed for Jeep Grand Cherokees. Unfortunately, 250 miles north of London, the Jeeps had proved impossible to get hold of and only after a day of searching had Gareth been able to find an alternative.

Three Jaguar F-Pace SVRs. A breed rarely seen in these parts. He hoped they would be grand enough to impress the clients. Especially as he was now left scrabbling to find a caterer with only a couple of days to go before the event.

Perhaps the swanky cars would detract so much from the food that he could get away with using some sandwiches from the Spar.

A booming laugh burst out of him at the thought. And was promptly silenced by a sigh.

He was worried. A deep-seated concern about this shoot, which under normal circumstances would see him cancelling it. He had few rules when it came to running such events, but the most important was that if he wasn't sure about people, he didn't let them book. Working with shotguns and live ammunition didn't lend itself to second chances when it came to judging folk.

But this was different. This was being organised by Rick Procter and Bernard Taylor, men of huge influence in the area, with the town council in their pockets. They weren't men to be crossed when it came to business. Cancelling the shoot this late in the day would definitely come under the heading of crossing them and, with everything that was in the pipeline, that could have fatal consequences for Gareth's prospects as gamekeeper of Bruncliffe Manor.

In fact, it was fair to say that Procter and Taylor held Gareth's future in their hands.

So the booking had to be honoured. But perhaps with a few reinforcements for the minimal staff that normally accompanied him on simulated shoots? A few bodies that knew how to handle themselves and would be able to help should the visitors turn out to be obnoxious City types, as Gareth suspected they might. He'd seen it before. Only last August he'd had to terminate an event early when two of the guns – part of a group of blokes from the financial sector trying to bag grouse for the first time – had started openly taking cocaine while at the peg, ready to fire.

There'd been no arguing as he'd escorted them all off the moor, Gareth imposing enough when calm, let alone when he was trying to keep a grip on his temper. So it wasn't as though he'd never experienced a difficult shooting party before. But this one was niggling at him. So much so that he felt the need to beef up his ranks.

Two names sprang to mind. And as he scrolled through his contacts on his phone to get their details, he was struck with even more inspiration. The answer to all his prayers, delivered neatly under the one family name.

Metcalfe.

With a grin, Gareth turned towards the Land Rover waiting on the track, Bounty following at a trot.

'Let's go girl,' he said, getting into the 4x4, the spaniel hopping straight over from the back to sit next to him on the passenger seat. 'This favour needs to be asked in person.'

5

'So what do you think? Is Bernard capable of having an affair?'

Samson's question was addressed to Delilah's back. She was standing over at the office window, her attention on the departing figure of her former mother-in-law walking away down the street. With her focus elsewhere, he allowed himself a moment to appreciate the woman who had stolen his heart. And he felt a pang of concern. She was losing weight, her jumper failing to conceal the sharp point of her shoulder blades, her profile as she began to turn towards him offering a prominent cheekbone below pallid skin. In three short weeks she'd lost the healthy bloom that characterised her, and he'd only just noticed.

He cursed silently. She was still in shock – still reacting to the trauma they'd endured. And he'd failed to pick up on it. He was so used to the consequences of a dangerous existence that he hadn't given a thought to how Delilah was coping after their confinement in the freezer. He could have kicked himself. Despite her tough exterior, Delilah had never faced anything like the ordeal she'd been subjected to, and post-traumatic shock was no respecter of persons.

She was fully facing him now, a wry smile below weary

eyes. 'You think I'm some kind of expert or something, just because I've had experience of a philandering Taylor?'

The words had bite to them and had Samson scrabbling to apologise. 'Sorry . . . I didn't mean . . .'

She waved a hand at him, dismissing his attempts to backtrack. 'To be honest, I haven't a clue. If I learned anything at all from my brief attempt at marriage, it was that I'm not a very good judge of people.'

Samson shifted uncomfortably in his seat, knowing her acquaintance with him had done nothing to advance her understanding of human behaviour.

'So I can't help you there, I'm afraid,' she continued. 'But what I will say is that Nancy Taylor doesn't air her laundry in public. When Neil and I divorced, she kept very quiet about it, despite the clamour in Bruncliffe for the inside story. So it would have taken a lot for her to walk in here today and confess her concerns about Bernard to you. I wouldn't take that lightly.'

'Agreed. She's a classy lady.'

There was an awkward pause, about the point at which Delilah would have normally drawn up a chair, sat at his desk and asked him how they were going to proceed with the latest case. But instead, she turned back to the window, shrugged and then walked towards the door.

'I'm thinking it'll be straightforward,' he blurted out.

Delilah paused. 'What will?'

'This case. A simple tail on Bernard for a couple of days and we'll . . . I'll know whether or not he's seeing anyone.' He could feel his cheeks beginning to burn under her calm gaze.

She nodded.

'What I mean is, I'll be fine on my own with this one,' he said, even though he wondered if he would be.

Finding out whether the town's mayor was seeing someone on the sly was one thing; working out the origins of the holdall stuffed full of cash that Nancy Taylor had stumbled on in her husband's wardrobe was another. The bank statements she'd had with her only confirmed that it hadn't come out of either of the Taylor accounts in the last six weeks, so it was still possibly a legitimate withdrawal from an earlier date. But then again, why would Bernard be squirrelling money away like that? And in his wardrobe? For a wife already suspecting him of infidelity, presuming he was hiding assets ahead of a divorce seemed a reasonable conclusion to leap to. Proving that was the sort of puzzle that would benefit from a bit of Delilah's IT expertise, but Samson simply couldn't allow it.

'Okay,' she said.

A buzzing sound drew her eyes to the edge of the desk and, too late, Samson saw his emergency mobile, out in full view. In his attempts to placate the crying Nancy Taylor, he'd left it down and forgotten all about it.

'New phone?' she asked.

He opted for the truth. 'DI Warren gave it me when we met up last month. Said I should keep it on me at all times . . . You know, so he can contact me if he hears anything.' He shrugged. Tried to make light of it, even though she knew the reality of the danger he was in.

She stared at it for a second. 'Good idea. You should do what he says.' Then she gestured towards the dozing Tolpuddle in the dog bed in the corner. 'Can I leave him with you for a while?'

'Sure.' Samson waited for an explanation as to where she was going but none was forthcoming. Instead, Delilah Metcalfe left his office, crossed the hallway and went out, quietly closing the front door behind her.

It was more disconcerting than if she'd blown up into the full Metcalfe rage he'd grown to expect.

Already unsettled, Samson reached for the emergency mobile and read the screen. The succinct text from his former boss unsettled him even further:

Danger imminent. Don't trust police!

Coming from a detective within the force, the warning was a stark reminder that Samson was on his own. And it confirmed that he'd made the right decision to try and keep a bit of distance between himself and Delilah – as much as possible given their situation. No more working together. No more socialising in the Fleece. For the last few weeks he'd been putting their relationship back on a professional footing so that anyone intending him harm would think she meant nothing to him. If being a bit more aloof meant keeping her safe, then that's what he had to do. Even if his heart thought otherwise.

'Is now a good time?'

The voice from the doorway cut through Samson's thoughts and sent him shooting up in his chair.

'Sorry! I didn't mean to startle you.' Edith Hird, one of his father's friends from Fellside Court, was standing in the doorway leaning on her stick, looking pale in her funeral attire, the black making her seem even thinner than usual.

'Edith,' he said, taking in the concerned look on the retired headmistress's face. 'Is everything okay?'

She came into the room with a nervous glance across the road to the pub. 'I need your help,' she said. 'But I don't want anyone to know I'm here.'

'Discretion,' said Samson, pulling out a chair for her, 'is my middle name.'

When the door slammed shut over at Peaks Patisserie some minutes later, Lucy Metcalfe didn't even look up. She was too busy sliding lemon-and-ginger scones out of the oven – her second batch that day and it was only just gone lunchtime – and trying not to trip over the broom which was lying in the middle of the floor next to a pile of broken crockery.

'Need a hand?' The new arrival was Delilah, already coming around the counter into the kitchen and pulling on an apron, tying the cords with ferocity, her face set in a scowl as she started loading the dishwasher. Signs her sister-in-law knew all too well from a lifetime spent around Metcalfes.

'Not if you're in a bad mood,' said Lucy with a smile. 'We're mad busy and I've already got Elaine forgetting orders and dropping plates. I don't need anything else getting damaged.'

'I didn't drop the plate,' protested Elaine Bullock, appearing in the kitchen carrying more dirty dishes, her glasses askew and plaits coming undone. 'It leapt from my hands. A suicide bid to escape the mayhem out there!' She glared back over her shoulder at the busy cafe, tables crowded with tourists lured to the Dales by the sunshine and mild temperatures. 'Don't they have somewhere better to be?'

Lucy laughed. 'As long as they're spending money, they can stay here all day if they want.'

'But it's so nice out there!' Elaine tipped her chin in the direction of the blue sky stretching across the gothic turrets of the town hall beyond the windows of the cafe, her gesture accompanied by a rattle of china from the precariously stacked dishes in her hands. 'They could be up on the fells, or down by the river—'

'Or collecting rock samples in some outlandish place.' Delilah's reply earned a grin from her friend.

'Touché! I should be outside, too,' Elaine admitted ruefully, a part-time waitress who was really a geologist, waiting on tables to help pay for field trips abroad that her meagre hours lecturing didn't quite cover. 'But at least I have an excuse – my Monument Valley excursion is only four months away and still not paid for. You, however – what are you doing in here on a beautiful day like this?'

'Escaping,' muttered Delilah. Her reply was accompanied by a clatter of cutlery being thrust into the dishwasher that suggested her temper hadn't improved.

Lucy and Elaine shared a look.

'Want to talk about it?' asked Elaine, placing her dishes on the counter while Lucy regarded her sister-in-law with concern.

'No.' With a yank, Delilah pulled down the lid of the industrial dishwasher, momentarily drowning out conversation as the machine thrummed into life.

'Fair enough.' Not one for cajoling, Elaine took the abrupt answer at face value and flipped open her notepad to consult the orders she'd just taken. 'So, I need four more cream teas and we're running short on cupcakes. Oh, and a large group are waiting to be seated so don't expect a breather any time soon.'

'Crikey.' Lucy wiped her brow. 'We've not had a day quite this crazy in a long time. But I can't complain—'

'Lucy!' A large voice interrupted them from the entrance to the cafe, where a ruddy face bookended by a thick thatch of hair and a full beard – both dark auburn – topped a body of immense proportions. Taller even than any of the Metcalfe lads and with shoulders straining beneath his waxed jacket, the man strode across the room towards the kitchen. 'My saviour!'

'Gareth! How lovely—' Lucy's greeting was cut off as two huge hands grabbed her by the waist and lifted her into a bear hug, enveloping her in the smell of the hills, with an underlying aroma of pheasant and grouse.

'How's my favourite chef?' asked the gamekeeper, planting a kiss on her cheek before dropping her back to her feet. 'And her minions?'

A tea towel whipped across the back of his legs, doing nothing more than making him laugh, and a fist landed on his arm with the same impact as a gnat on a hippo.

'*Minions?*' Elaine and Delilah were both glowering at him, Elaine twirling her tea towel for another go and Delilah rubbing her fist.

Gareth Towler raised both hands in surrender. 'Steady on, ladies. I come with an offer of work.' He turned to Lucy. 'Quite a bit of work, actually. I need catering for a shoot.'

'When?'

'This weekend . . .' said Gareth with a hopeful wince, but Lucy was already shaking her head.

'Sorry, no can do. Even if I could get the food ready in time, I don't have the staff to cover it. What happened to your regular caterer?'

'They've had to close down for a while. Turns out the coronation chicken scones they served at a wedding on Saturday came with added salmonella.'

Lucy looked horrified. As did her sister-in-law. 'The poor clients,' said Delilah. 'They must be distraught.'

'You can say that again.' Elaine pulled a face. 'I mean, coronation chicken? At a wedding? The caterers should have been sacked for the menu, let alone the food poisoning.'

A boom of laughter broke from Gareth's wide chest and he slapped Elaine on the back. 'I agree. But they've always done well for us. Until now.' He turned back to Lucy, voice coaxing, a pleading look on his face. 'Which is why I need your help. And it'll be a good chance for you to impress. If this goes well, it could be a regular thing.'

'I'm sorry but I can't just drop—'

'How much does it pay?' Elaine cut across her boss to address Gareth directly.

'A lot,' he said. 'Rick Procter's organised it and money's no object.'

'*Quelle surprise*,' muttered Elaine dryly at the reference to Bruncliffe's successful property developer.

'Seems him and Bernard Taylor have got some investors coming to town they want to impress. Bound to be good tips too,' he added with a wink at the waitress.

'Final question,' she said, a fierce look on her face. 'Are you shooting live game?'

'No. It's out of season so it'll be a simulated shoot.'

'Then we'll do it,' announced Elaine, holding out her hand to shake on the deal.

Lucy's mouth dropped open. 'Elaine! I can't just take on all that work. Besides, we need at least two more members of staff—'

'One,' said Delilah.

'One what?' asked Lucy, confused.

'You only need one more member of staff. I'll help.'

Gareth grinned. 'I take it that's a yes, then? Chef and minions all on board?'

'I'm sorry, no—' Lucy began, only to break off at the sight of the gamekeeper's suddenly strained expression, the flippancy of moments ago gone as he caught hold of her by the shoulders.

'I'm begging you, Lucy. Please. There's so much resting on this.'

She stared at him for a second, then threw up her hands in resignation. 'Okay, okay, I'll do it. But you two,' she said, turning to her friends, 'had better know what you've let yourselves in for! I'm going to work you so hard, you'll earn every penny. Understand?'

Elaine snapped to attention. But Delilah's attention was elsewhere. Because her offer of help hadn't been motivated by financial reward or even a desire to do her sister-in-law a good turn. Instead she was already planning the best way to use the event to keep tabs on Bernard Taylor, the good intentions she'd had of not interfering in the case fading as quickly as mist over the Ribble on a summer's morning. Whether he wanted Delilah's assistance or not, Samson O'Brien was about to get it.

*

Lucy Metcalfe was as good as her word. By late evening, when the shops that surrounded the market square were shuttered, workers and customers either at home or in one of the town's three pubs, lights still shone out into the spring twilight from Peaks Patisserie. Most people passing by gave a curious look towards the windows to ascertain the reason for this unusual turn of events and some were rewarded by catching a glimpse of one of the three figures working away in the kitchen at the back of the cafe. But as he made his way home from Taylor's, having been kept late waiting for the repair man to finish fixing the fridge, Stuart Lister didn't so much as glance towards the cafe's glowing facade. Nor did he see the furtive shape scuttle down the ginnel next to the butcher's.

He had far too much on his mind.

Forehead furrowed with concern, he hurried across the marketplace and turned down Church Street, crossing the road towards the police station.

It was tempting to go straight in. To lay out his worries in front of Sergeant Clayton and PC Danny Bradley. But what if he was wrong? What if he'd misread things?

It would be the end of his career with Taylor's and he could forget about walking into any similar positions any-where in the Dales. He would have to start again. And that was too big a gamble for a lad with little to his name and a personality that had made it hard making the move from Skipton to Bruncliffe. He'd never survive if he had to re-locate somewhere as metropolitan as Leeds.

So he reluctantly walked past the sturdy building with the police cars parked outside and on towards the bright neon sign of the Happy House takeaway, where Mr Lee was already busy behind the counter, a queue of people waiting for food. Nodding through the window to his neighbour, Stuart unlocked the door that led to the hallway he shared with the restaurant.

'Good evening!' Mrs Lee was standing in the foyer, a grizzling baby on her hip and a plastic bag in her hand. 'Are you hungry?'

The question was clearly rhetorical, as before Stuart could even formulate a response in the negative – food being the last thing on his mind – Mrs Lee was pressing the bag into his hand.

'House special chow mein and spring rolls,' she declared with a warm smile and a shake of her head, reaching out to pinch his cheek gently. 'You're getting too thin.'

Stuart blushed. Took the bag and mumbled his thanks, before nodding at the baby, whose wailing had kept him awake most of the night before, the walls between the two upstairs flats seemingly as thin as the prawn crackers his neighbours made in vast quantities. 'How is he? Still teething?'

Mrs Lee grimaced and then laughed. 'I think he's going to have big teeth, judging by the crying. Sorry.'

'It's fine. I can't hear him,' Stuart lied.

His neighbour laughed again, knowing the realities of the property they were both renting. Then she shooed him away with her free hand. 'Go,' she said. 'Eat it while it's hot.'

With a final word of thanks, Stuart headed up the stairs to his flat and let himself in. He set the bag of food on the top of the gas cooker, there being no other worktop space in his cramped kitchenette, and sat on the sagging sofa, a fug of stale cooking smells engulfing him as he sank into it. He pulled out his mobile and began scrolling through the photos he'd taken at the office and felt his chest start to tighten.

Pages and pages of documents. The first lot from the high-end rental folders, detailing the absence of evidence that due diligence had been carried out in any of those transactions. Stuart had thought that bad enough. But what he'd subsequently discovered when he went to replace those files . . .

He stared at the photos and could barely breathe.

Rental contracts for properties that had never crossed Stuart's desk, despite his title of Lettings Manager. And all of them rented to the same tenant: Kingston Holdings.

As soon as he'd seen them, Stuart had known that there was something up. Then he'd noticed the rental amounts. Astronomical figures, even for the Yorkshire Dales. Kingston Holdings was renting more than thirty properties across the region and paying over the odds for every single one of them. But that wasn't the most disturbing thing. What worried Stuart the most was that he recognised several of the houses.

They had been sold by Taylor's in the past six months and were now lived in by very contented purchasers. In other words, they weren't on the rental market.

And yet . . .

Time had been against him in the office. He'd spread a few of the documents out on the floor and quickly taken photos before placing them all back, heart thudding the whole time. Because this couldn't be explained away as an admin error. This was something much bigger than that. And something Stuart sensed he couldn't afford to be caught prying into.

With the filing cabinet locked and the key replaced on the saucer under the plant, Stuart had barely had time to sit down before Bernard Taylor came back into the office, his mood no better than when he'd left. A sudden clatter from the fridge had sent him into a prolonged rant about ineffectual staff and sent Stuart scrabbling for the phone to find someone to repair it. Thus distracted, the afternoon passed in a blur and it was only now, in the solitude of his flat, that Stuart could try to fathom out what exactly he'd stumbled on. A quick google of Kingston Holdings seemed like a good place to start.

Two hours later, the trainee estate agent was still sitting on the couch, crouched over his mobile, its light casting a blue-white glow onto his face in the darkened room. He let out a sigh and tossed the phone aside. He was out of his depth, not even sure what he should be looking for. What he needed was professional help. But who could he trust?

He'd only lived in Bruncliffe a short while but it was long enough to know that allegiances in the town were often based on ancestry. And relationships interwoven over the centuries meant that an offhand comment in the wrong ear could result in disparaging someone unwittingly to their next of kin. This was a sensitive issue and Stuart couldn't afford for his enquiries to get back to Bernard Taylor. So he needed someone who wasn't in the back pocket of the town's mayor. Or related to him.

It came to him in a flash of inspiration. Picking his

mobile back up he started scrolling through a list of Bruncliffe businesses. On top of the cooker, the bag of chow mein and spring rolls continued to go ignored, and it would be morning before Stuart realised that his boiler had finally been fixed.

6

It was raining. Of course it was. Over a week of May sunshine and gorgeous spring days but the minute he was outside tailing someone, the heavens opened and the temperature plummeted from the high teens back down to barely double figures.

Such was life in the Yorkshire Dales.

Samson pulled up the hood of his parka, the coat back in use thanks to the sudden change in the weather, and huddled closer to the stone wall on his left, trying to get some shelter from the chill wind that was gusting down the ginnel he was hiding in – a ginnel that reeked of damp dog. At the end of the alleyway, a slice of the marketplace was visible, wet cobbles glistening in front of the three shops framed by the walls of Samson's hideout. He had his focus on only one of them: the double-fronted expanse of glass that was Taylor's Estate Agents.

Two days into the case and Samson had seen nothing to justify Nancy Taylor's misgivings about her husband. So far, Bernard had behaved exactly as you'd expect of a successful businessman who happened to also be the current town mayor. He'd spent most of his working hours at his offices in the marketplace, leaving only a handful of times: once to attend a meeting at the town hall and twice for a long lunch at the brasserie in Rick Procter's development in Low Mill. Samson had followed him effortlessly on all three occasions, confident his target knew nothing about being shadowed, but he'd witnessed nothing sinister. Unless you counted the fact that on both days Bernard's lunch partner had been Rick Procter himself.

For Samson – not being a fan of the head of Procter Properties – that was grounds enough for divorce. Frustratingly, though, there were few in town who shared his view of the man, most of Bruncliffe's citizens hailing Procter as a role model and saintly benefactor – but then they hadn't had their family farm stolen from them for a song. An alcoholic father abandoned by his son and an unscrupulous developer with an eye for a killing were a heady mix; Twistleton Farm no longer being in the O'Brien family was testimony to that.

Associating with Rick Procter aside, Bernard Taylor had done nothing over the last couple of days to suggest he was having an affair. Samson had tailed him the short distance from his home at the top end of the square to his work and back home again. But this wasn't London with its swarm of humanity and warren of streets, where a man could hide in plain sight, shrouded by the anonymity of a huge city. This was Bruncliffe, and so there was a limit to how long Samson could conceal himself in this ginnel off the marketplace and not arouse suspicion. So far he'd only been disturbed a couple of times, the path not much used and the rain reducing the number of folk walking around. On both occasions he'd avoided scrutiny by shrinking back within the hood of his parka and concentrating on his mobile, keeping his face turned away from the passers-by. But it wouldn't be long before someone either recognised him or raised the alarm about a strange man loitering in a dark alley. Which meant that if Samson was going to keep tabs on the estate agent, he was going to have to be a bit more creative than simply standing opposite Taylor's offices for hours on end.

Technology. That's what he needed.

Delilah immediately sprang to mind – it didn't take much for his thoughts to wander in that direction these days. She'd have just the gadgets he needed to track Bernard Taylor without having to get soaked out in the elements. A GPS device of some sort. She'd probably even be able to get access to his mobile or his computer. In fact, wasn't she working on Taylor's IT system, upgrading it or something? With that as a cover, she'd be able to get inside the offices and deploy some of her spy tools, the easiest way to ascertain whether the stash of money Nancy uncovered was the prelude to the end of a marriage and a difficult divorce.

Perhaps he should give Delilah a call? Apologise for being so rash as to cut her out of the case?

Rain pattering on his hood, Samson pulled out his mobile, stared at the screen for a couple of seconds and then shoved it back in his pocket.

He couldn't do it. It would be putting her at risk, providing an easy target for whatever shape the menace was going to take that was coming from his past. It would be putting his heart at risk, too. Because ever since those cold hours in the freezer when the thought of losing his maverick partner had forced him to acknowledge how much she meant to him, he'd been struggling not to let his feelings for Delilah show. It was pure torture – even the briefest of time with her and he was biting his lip to stop himself from telling her. From pulling her into his arms and—

'Is that you, Samson?'

Samson whipped round to see his father's friend and neighbour, Arty Robinson, standing behind him in the alleyway, umbrella over his bald head, and a puzzled look on his face.

Stuart Lister wasn't cut out for cloak and dagger nonsense. He'd already stretched his meagre skills by lying to his boss, asking for the morning off for a fictitious dental appointment. The prospect of having a root canal seemed preferable right now compared to what he was actually doing – leaving the safety of his flat for a meeting that could land him in hot water. Or worse.

Closing the door behind him, Stuart scanned the wet street for anyone he knew before pulling up the hood of his waterproof. He was probably the only person in town who was grateful for the inclement weather. At least it offered him an excuse for keeping his head covered. He'd debated going full beanie hat and scarf, but while the wind was cold and the temperature had plummeted, it was still May and wearing that many layers in what was deemed to be spring in the Yorkshire Dales would draw attention rather than deflect it. Besides, he'd reasoned, he belonged here now. Folk knew him to see him and, given his profession, no one would question him being out on the streets during the day. They were far more likely to register surprise if he tried skulking around in disguise.

Thus encouraged, he turned into the cold wind that was blowing along Church Street and began walking briskly towards the viaduct. He'd devoted as much thought to the best route to take to his rendezvous as he had to the issue of camouflage. He couldn't make a direct journey. This was Bruncliffe – the chances of him getting there unseen were practically zero. So he'd hatched a plan to approach his destination from an unexpected direction which, should he be seen and recognised, would seem innocuous. Sticking to his original deception, he was heading for the dental surgery, next door to the vet's on a side street not far from the primary school.

Cutting left down Station Road, he walked parallel to the train tracks for a while before taking a succession of turns through quiet streets to arrive at the far end of a narrow road of houses, grey stones sombre in the rain, slate roofs glistening. Halfway down were the only two non-residential properties: the vet's and the dentist's.

This was where it would get tricky. Up until now, Stuart had held a legitimate excuse for his journey. Once he walked past the opaque glass window of the dental surgery, he would find it harder to justify his presence.

Pulling his hood a little lower to cover his face as much as he could, he picked up his pace and strode down the damp pavement. Past the vet's. Past the dentist's. And with his heart thundering, he turned left out onto High Street.

No one he knew was coming towards him, the rain keeping a lot of folk at home. A few long, nervous strides and he was able to duck into the ginnel that would bring him onto Back Street. Almost there. Hustling along the gloomy alley, he emerged next to the wool shop, where he paused. Back Street was never the busiest of places, being somewhat overlooked when it came to Bruncliffe's commercial concerns, but even so, he looked left and right.

Not a soul to be seen. Even the glorious rainbow of plastic items that normally brightened the pavement outside Plastic Fantastic had been pulled inside, leaving the road to wallow in the gloom of a grey, wet day.

Stuart checked his watch. He had five minutes to make his appointment. He'd timed it perfectly. But he still had a bit of distance to cover.

Stepping out from the cover of the ginnel, he hurried up the road. As he approached the windows of the Fleece, he twisted his head to offer only the back of his hood to any curious gaze that might be looking out, forcing his own focus onto the golden letters spanning the glass across the road.

The Dales Detective Agency. Maybe that was where he should have gone? But it was too early for that. He wanted to make sure his suspicions were valid before he sounded the alarm.

So instead he kept walking, huddled inside his waterproof, shoulders hunched over, the back of his neck prickling as though a thousand eyes were watching him from the windows he was passing. Hugging as close to the buildings as he could, he followed the natural curve of the road round onto the marketplace. A couple more long strides and he'd reached the doorway that had been his objective, his heart truly rattling, his breathing coming in short gasps.

With one final desperate glance around the exposed square that extended across the cobbles to the multitude of shops and business that surrounded it, Stuart stretched out his hand and pushed open the heavy wooden door. Slinking around it into safety, he was satisfied that he had made it undetected.

He was wrong. Because just as he turned his head, his face visible in profile, the young estate agent was noticed. Not by Ida Capstick, the cleaner, who was wheeling her bike down the opposite side of the square. Not even by Mrs Pettiford, who had nipped out from behind her counter at the bank to go to the post office, too distracted by a snippet of gossip she'd just overheard to pay attention to a lanky figure disappearing into a doorway up by the town hall.

Instead, in a complete freak of fate, Stuart Lister, trainee estate agent with problems on his mind, was seen by the worst person possible.

As his anxious face turned up towards the town hall, a man just happened to emerge from the car park around the back. It wasn't the man's custom to park right at the top of the square. Being a busy entrepreneur, normally he left his Range Rover as close to his appointments as possible. But the rain had ensured that anyone visiting the town today was coming in by car and so his usual parking spot had been taken. Hence he'd been forced to use the facilities at the town hall. Blond hair already wet, he was walking down towards the marketplace, thoughts troubled by his own worries, when he just happened to see the thin features of a lad he recognised.

It took a while to place him. In fact, it was only as Rick Procter entered Taylor's and saw the empty desk to the left of the reception area that he realised who it was he'd just seen.

Taylor's pet letting agent. Hired for his incompetence

and lack of backbone – someone who wouldn't get in the way of what they were doing. Rick couldn't even remember his name.

'Has he left you in the lurch, then?' he asked the attractive lass on reception, gesturing towards the unoccupied chair across the room. He only asked as a way of flirting with her. If she'd been older or less bonny, he'd have walked straight past to where Bernard Taylor was waiting for him in the doorway. Instead he lingered at her desk, waiting for her answer as she laughed and graced him with a warm smile.

'Seeing as poor Stuart's having root canal work done as we speak, I think I have to forgive him,' she said.

Rick laughed back. Nodded and walked towards the office at the rear of the room. All the time his brain was whirring.

Because Stuart, the lad who was supposed to be innocuous, hadn't been going into the dentist's when Rick had seen him.

Rick filed the incident in the back of his mind. It could be nothing. Or it could be something. Either way, it was yet one more example of how Bernard Taylor was becoming a liability.

'I thought that was you! What are you doing out here, lad? Spying on someone?' Standing in the ginnel, grinning despite the weather, Arty Robinson regarded Samson with a look of mischief.

'No . . . just waiting for Delilah.'

'In the rain?' Arty was peering round Samson towards the mouth of the alleyway, trying to get an idea of where the detective might have had his focus. His gaze settled on one of the few businesses visible across the cobbles. 'Something going on at Rice N Spice, is there?'

'I told you, I'm just waiting—'

'Or has our mayor been fiddling the town expenses?' Arty laughed. Then stopped and stared at Samson, eyes widening. 'Is that it? You're watching Bernard Taylor?'

'No. I'm not.'

But Arty wasn't having any of it. 'It *is* Taylor you're after! I can tell from your face!'

Samson groaned and slumped back against the stone wall. He'd been right. Bruncliffe was way too small for old fashioned surveillance techniques. Especially as it appeared he was so rusty when it came to undercover work that he'd been quickly rumbled by a retired bookie.

A retired bookie who was now glancing across at the estate agent's and then back at Samson, excitement making him hop from one foot to the other. 'What's going on, lad?' he demanded. 'And how can we help?'

We. Samson noted the use of the plural pronoun with a sinking heart – Arty was offering the well-meaning interference of his gang of friends in Fellside Court retirement complex, one of whom just happened to be Samson's own father. It was the last thing that was needed on a case already so close to home. And so sensitive in terms of local politics.

'Seriously,' Arty continued, undaunted by Samson's obvious lack of enthusiasm for his proposition, 'you can't do this on your own. Taylor knows you. He knows what you are. Whatever you're watching him for, one sniff of you on his tail and he'll slip through your hands. You need help. And me, Joseph, Eric and the girls can offer just that. We could sit in Peaks Patisserie all day, sipping coffees and keeping an eye on that place and no one would question it. Might give Clarissa something else to talk about other than this new beau of hers—'

'No,' said Samson, firmly. 'It's not going to happen. Just forget you saw me and don't tell a soul about this.'

'But—'

Samson held up a hand. 'Arty, I'm sorry but I don't need your help, okay? I've got this covered.'

It was like popping a balloon. Arty's shoulders drooped, his round face fell and he nodded glumly. 'I understand. Sorry. Didn't mean to bother you. Just thought it might be a break from sitting around doing nothing, especially for Edith. She's been a bit down of late.' He sighed. 'You'd be surprised how long an afternoon can be when you've nothing to fill it.'

The guilt hit Samson in the gut like a headbutt from a boisterous calf. Forty-eight hours since Edith Hird – sister of Clarissa Ralph and the other of Arty's 'girls' – had asked for his assistance and he'd done nothing about it. And here was Arty worried about her . . . As the pensioner moved past him, heading for the marketplace, he put out a hand to halt him.

'Hang on,' he found himself saying. 'Maybe we can work something out. But you have to promise me complete discretion.'

'Totally sealed, boss.' Arty zipped a finger across his grinning lips. 'So when do we start? I mean, you'll need cover for when he's at the shoot. The two of you won't be able to do it all.'

'The shoot?'

Arty blinked and took a step back. 'You don't know about the shoot? It's all anyone is talking about round town the last couple of days. I'm surprised Delilah didn't mention it seeing as she's been helping Lucy out with the prep – that's why your dad's been looking after Tolpuddle the last couple of days. Did Delilah not say?'

Samson shook his head, not wanting to reveal that he hadn't seen Delilah in two days and even then, it had been in passing. Not for the first time, he realised how much he was missing by keeping her at arm's length – not just her company but her in-depth knowledge of everything that was going on in Bruncliffe. She really was his ear on the ground when it came to local affairs.

'Rick Procter's organised it,' Arty continued. 'A huge affair to impress some investors that him and Bernard Taylor are trying to woo. It's tomorrow, up at Bruncliffe Manor.'

'Damn,' muttered Samson. A shoot on the large estate to the east of Bruncliffe, with no access for the uninvited. There was no way he'd be able to keep Taylor under surveillance in a place like that, despite all the natural cover. He'd worked as a beater on a few occasions in his youth before he left town and knew that crawling around in the undergrowth trying to spy on someone was most likely to end up with a backside peppered with shotgun pellets.

If he was going to uncover any illicit assignations in Bernard Taylor's life, it was looking like he was going to need Delilah's help after all. A tracker or something—

'Anyway,' continued Arty, 'not to worry. Luckily for

you, the organisers got caught short on the catering front and had to ask Lucy to step in.'

'And that's lucky how?' asked Samson, puzzled as to the sudden turn of direction the conversation had taken.

The pensioner's head tipped to one side and his eyes narrowed. 'Well, it gave you the perfect excuse, didn't it?'

'Sorry?'

Arty gestured towards the estate agent's. 'Whatever it is you're following Taylor for, Lucy doing the catering offers you the perfect excuse to get someone on the inside. I mean, isn't that why Delilah volunteered to work at the shoot in the first place?'

For the second time in what was turning out to be a long morning, Samson groaned.

7

'How can I help?'

From the comfort of one of the two armchairs in the corner of his office, Matty Thistlethwaite regarded the lanky young man sitting opposite and knew he'd made the right decision not to sit at the desk. The fidgeting hands, the tapping foot – whatever had brought Stuart Lister to Turpin's, it was making him nervous, a situation the formal setting of the desk would only have exacerbated. And as the lad was unmarried and with youth on his side, Matty presumed it probably wasn't divorce or death that he had on his mind, the normal preoccupations for many who visited the solicitor. Matty doubted it was a house purchase either, as someone who worked in real estate wouldn't be looking this uneasy about getting onto the property ladder.

'Thanks for seeing me,' Stuart said, gaze flicking from Matty to the window and back again. He coughed, cleared his throat and glanced down at his hands.

Matty waited. Patience was something he found worked well with anxious clients and he'd cultivated an aura of calm that made him seem a lot older than his thirty-odd years. Which was no harm when he was dealing with customers who expected their solicitor to be grey, both at the temples and in personality.

The silence stretched and then suddenly Stuart stood,

77

long limbs snapping him upright. 'I should go,' he muttered. 'I'm wasting your time.'

'Not at all,' said Matty, remaining in his seat as the young man hovered by his chair. 'You're a welcome break from conveyancing.' He leaned forward and poured coffee from the cafetière on the small table between them. 'So,' he continued in his relaxed manner, holding out a cup towards Stuart with a smile, 'tell me what's new in the property world. Anything I should know about?'

The lad's face went white and he sank back into his seat. 'That's exactly what I wanted to talk to you about.'

Samson knew the moment he stepped into the cafe and saw Delilah's guilty glance in his direction that Arty had hit the unsuspecting nail on the head. Her offer to work at the shoot was motivated by the investigation into Bernard Taylor.

'Any chance of a couple of coffees?' he asked Lucy, as Delilah scuttled into the kitchen, blushing. 'And a chat with Delilah if she's got a couple of minutes?'

'A couple of minutes is about all I can spare her for,' grumbled Lucy, rubbing the small of her back. 'I think this shoot will be the death of me.'

'How many are you catering for?'

'Eight guns, plus entourage, whatever that means.'

'Local?'

Lucy shook her head. 'Out of town. And from what Gareth said, they're already proving a nuisance.'

'Gareth Towler?' Samson recalled a large, tousle-haired lad a couple of years below him at school who'd been besotted with raising game birds, always skipping classes to help out with feeding pheasants at Bruncliffe Manor. He seemed to remember him being one of a gang of many children who hung out at the Metcalfe farm, Samson amongst them. 'Ash's mate?' he asked, referring to the youngest of Delilah's brothers.

'The same. He's head gamekeeper on the estate now, and organises all the shoots. Good at it too. He runs a tight ship and takes no nonsense. Ryan used to do the odd session beating for him when he was home on leave and Nathan's been a couple of times. In fact, it was Gareth who helped coax Nathan out of the dark place he was in after Ryan died.' A shadow crossed Lucy's face at the memory of her son's pain. And her own. Then she smiled. 'He took Nathan fishing whenever he could and just got him back into enjoying life. So I shouldn't be complaining about doing this for him, really.'

A sharp cry from the kitchen was followed by a crash of china. Lucy rolled her eyes.

'Is Elaine helping out by any chance?' asked Samson, the reputation of the waitress known around the town.

'Helping is one way to describe it! But beggars can't be choosers. Gareth didn't give me much notice so I'm short-staffed and I've already had to pay over the odds to get someone in from a temping agency for the actual shoot. I can't afford to hire someone else at those rates. Besides,' she said with a grin, 'Elaine's handy to have around at events like this if any of the customers decide to get fresh with the waitresses.'

Samson could well believe it. The geologist had a sharp way with words and took no nonsense. She also habitually wore Dr Martens and he imagined she wouldn't be averse to using them for purposes other than walking, should the need arise.

'Anyway,' concluded Lucy, 'I'll get you those coffees. And a couple of scones too.'

While the busy chef headed back into the kitchen, Samson made his way towards Arty Robinson, who'd already secured a table next to the window and was studiously watching the front of Taylor's. The retired bookie had been right about the cafe being the perfect milieu for him, thought Samson as he surveyed the room, the average age of the clientele this Friday afternoon north of fifty. Arty's shining bald head blended in completely, more so than the dark locks gracing Samson's wet parka.

'Anything?' he asked, as he took off his coat and hung it over the back of the chair before sitting down opposite his new-found partner.

Arty consulted the napkin on the table in front of him, an indecipherable scribble inked across its surface. 'Just Rick Procter exiting the premises at ten thirty-eight hours,' he read, voice clipped in a military manner. 'Alone.'

Nothing unusual there, especially given that Procter was organising an event with Taylor for the weekend.

'No one else?'

'Not a soul.' Looking up from his notes, Arty glanced over towards the counter, eyes resting hopefully on the mouth-watering display of cakes. 'Hungry work, this surveillance,' he said. 'We might need to have an expenses account. You know, to cover sundries.'

'An expenses account?' Delilah had approached the table from behind Samson and kept her concentration on the older man as she deposited three mugs of coffee and three scones in front of them. 'Who you working for, Arty?'

Grinning at the sight of the scones, Arty leaned over to Delilah as she took a seat next to him and whispered to her in a loud voice, 'The Dales Detective Agency!'

Delilah frowned and looked at Samson, eyebrows raised. 'In what guise?'

'Relief cover,' said Samson, enjoying the confusion on her face. 'You know, for when you're at the shoot.'

'I guessed you two were staking out Taylor's offices,' continued Arty, oblivious to Delilah's discomfort as she took a swig of her coffee. 'And suggested that me and the Fellside Court gang could keep watch here over the weekend while you're busy at Bruncliffe Manor.'

'Oh, right . . .' Behind the rim of her mug, Delilah's cheeks were on fire.

'Right,' echoed Samson dryly. 'Arty reckons it'll take their minds off Clarissa's love life.'

Arty grinned at him and then let out a curse. 'Pretend you didn't hear that,' he said to Delilah. 'It's supposed to be a secret.'

'Don't worry, Delilah excels at keeping secrets,' said Samson, tone still arid.

Delilah shot him a glance before turning back to Arty. 'Clarissa has a boyfriend? Since when?'

'Since two weeks ago. Not sure he can be called a boyfriend as such at our age, though.'

'How did she meet him?'

It was Arty's turn to look awkward. 'That's the bit I'm not supposed to say.'

'Why ever not?'

He scratched his scalp and then shrugged. 'She met him online. Although technically, she hasn't actually met him yet. They're still just exchanging messages.'

Delilah smiled. 'What's wrong with having met online?'

'Well, she didn't use your agency so, you know, she's afraid you'd be annoyed.'

'Not at all,' said Delilah. 'It's good that she's happy.'

'Aye. She's in better form than her sister, that's for sure.'

'What's up with Edith?'

'Hard to put a finger on it. She just seems out of sorts.' Arty sighed, reached forward for his coffee and then stood, face contrite. 'Blast! That's one of the drawbacks of old age. I've got to spend a penny. Can you keep watch?'

He hurried off towards the toilets, leaving a strained silence at the table behind him. It was Delilah who finally broke it.

'That's great news about Clarissa,' she said, with what she hoped was a distracting smile.

'Forget about Clarissa,' growled Samson. 'Do you want to tell me what the hell you're doing?'

Delilah knew exactly what he was talking about. She shrugged. 'It seemed like a good opportunity to keep tabs on Bernard.'

'I'm perfectly capable of doing that on my own. I told you – I don't need help on this case.'

'And Arty?'

'He came across me in the ginnel and guessed what I was doing.'

Delilah laughed. 'So much for being an undercover expert.'

Her reaction drew a smile from Samson. 'I must be losing my touch. But then he offered to help and when I refused, he looked so crestfallen, I didn't have the heart to say no again. So I'm setting him up in here to watch Taylor's place during the day.'

'Is your father going to be involved?'

The answer came on a sigh. 'Apparently so. Eric, Edith and Clarissa too.'

Delilah crossed her arms over her chest, chin lifting. 'So you'll take the help of a group of pensioners but you won't take mine?'

'It's different,' Samson protested. 'I only suggested this as a way of giving them something to do. They won't be actively involved. Whereas you're going waitressing at an event where we know Taylor will be. What if he gets suspicious about you being there? You could blow the whole case wide open.'

'He won't get suspicious.'

'How can you be so sure? If he is having an affair or up to anything shady with his finances, he's going to be on high alert. You won't be able to let him see you, which is going to be nigh on impossible out on the moor. So what use will you be?'

A small smile crossed Delilah's lips. 'He won't see me. I promise. And besides, what other option do you have? I can't see you getting access. Unless you're planning on dressing up in a deer suit so you can blend in with the countryside—?'

Samson's mobile interrupted them, Nancy Taylor's name showing on the display. Turning his back to the room, he answered it.

'Nancy? Everything all right?'

A torrent of words tumbled through the phone and Samson realised his options for running the case had just changed. He could no longer do it all by himself. Which meant he was going to have to eat an awful lot of humble pie.

'Can I trust you?'

Matty spread his hands wide at the young man's question. 'I'm a lawyer. I'm used to being discreet.'

'Sorry. Yes. I didn't mean to suggest . . .' Stuart reached for his coffee, took a gulp and placed the cup back on its saucer with a rattle. 'It's just . . . shell companies. How do you spot them?'

'Shell companies?' Matty hid his surprise. This hadn't been what he'd expected the lad to say. 'In what context?'

Stuart shook his head. 'Just in general. Nothing specific.'

It didn't take much to see he was lying. Wary of spooking him again, Matty took the question at face value.

'First of all, it helps if you have the company name. If it's registered in the UK then a good place to start is Companies House—'

'UK? Don't they have to be registered overseas?'

Matty gave a dry laugh. 'No. While the weather might be better in some of the more traditional jurisdictions that shelter shell companies, it's actually cheaper to set one up here. Apply online with an address in some offbeat office block and hey presto, you're in business.'

'How easy is it to find out if a company is a shell or not, then?'

The intensity accompanying the question told Matty all he needed to know. The estate agent was worried about someone, probably someone connected to a property deal, and was trying to do his due diligence.

'That's a question with two answers,' said the lawyer. 'Often they're easy to spot if you know what you're looking for. But if you want to find out anything more, that's the tricky bit.'

Stuart sat back in his chair, face twisted in thought and long fingers rubbing against each other anxiously. He looked like a man trapped between the devil and the deep blue sea.

'Whatever it is,' said Matty, 'I can help. Just tell me the name of the company and I'll do the legwork. Absolute discretion guaranteed.'

'I don't have a name—'

Matty cut him off with a raised eyebrow and a smile. 'You do. Otherwise you wouldn't be here. And given your profession, I suspect you're trying to do the right thing – a thing required by law – which isn't easy in a small town where the walls have ears. So let me have the name of the company that's bothering you and I'll do what I can to uncover who's behind it.'

There was a pause, Stuart looking both hopeful and yet still reluctant. Then Matty took in the lad's jacket, frayed at the cuffs, his shirt creased and crumpled, and the faint odour of Chinese spices that permeated from him.

'Pro bono, of course,' the lawyer added with a smile. 'For a fellow professional.'

The estate agent's shoulders sagged and he gave a single nod of relief. 'Thanks. That'd be a great help. But I have to stress, this is just curiosity. It might lead to nothing—'

'The name?'

Stuart Lister gulped. And then threw caution to the wind. 'Kingston Holdings,' he said.

'Well?' asked Delilah, leaning across the table as Samson placed his mobile back in his pocket. 'What did Nancy want?'

'She seems to have reason to believe that Bernard is meeting the woman he's having an affair with tomorrow.'

'At the shoot?' Delilah's eyebrows shot up. 'Seriously? How on earth has she found that out?'

'I'm not sure she has,' said Samson, frowning. 'She said Bernard's just called her to say he'll be out all day Saturday with work and she could tell from the tone of his voice that he was lying. How reliable that is as a source, I'm not sure.'

Delilah gave a dry laugh. 'You're asking the wrong person. Bernard's son lied to me for the duration of our marriage and I never sensed a thing. But would the town's mayor be so foolish as to flaunt his new woman at an event like that? Even if it's invited guests only, it's still a bit risky.'

'Maybe that's the entourage that Lucy is having to cater for,' mused Samson. 'Entertainment for the boys. And Bernard is joining in. Either way, Nancy is insistent that we tail her husband and find out.'

'Well, there's only one way to do that,' said Delilah, a smug tone entering her voice. 'If only you had an insider already booked to work the event . . .'

Samson sat back, glaring at her. She was insufferable. And she was also right. He needed her help. But that didn't stop him worrying about her, particularly as he was supposed to be keeping her at a distance.

'If you do this,' he said, 'you have to wear a wire.'

'What on earth for?'

'That's the condition. If you don't agree, I'll tell Lucy that you're putting yourself in danger and she'll sack you in an instant.'

Delilah's chin tipped even higher. Then she simply nodded. 'Okay, I'll wear comms equipment but I'll supply it. And it won't be a wire,' she added with a mocking laugh. 'They went out with the ark.'

'A wire?' Arty Robinson was back at the table, rubbing his hands in excitement. 'Are we getting rigged up with wires? Wait till I tell the gang. This day just gets better and better!'

He reached for his scone and took a big bite, eyes glued back on the estate agent's across the square.

Fighting back a smile, Samson glanced over at Delilah to see her grinning at him and he felt his heart swell with love. Arty was right yet again. This day just kept getting better. Basking in being back in her company once more, Samson allowed himself to ignore the kernel of concern at the thought of Delilah spying on someone in an environment where guns would be in use.

Many hours later, in one of the apartments at Fellside Court retirement complex, Phyllis Walker was trying to remember when she'd last had such fun.

Hands twisted with arthritis, she was doing her best to wield the tools of her former trade. And without being arrogant, she thought, as she stood back to admire her work, she was doing a pretty good job. Especially considering how little notice she'd been given.

She'd been finishing off the last of her solitary evening

meal when there'd been a frantic knocking at the front door and she'd opened it to see a group of excited fellow residents in the hallway. Arty Robinson had been the first to speak, but it had all been so garbled and delivered in a stage whisper so loud the others had to keep telling him to keep his voice down, thus effectively drowning him out. In the end it had been easier to invite them all in.

Arty and his companions – including Tolpuddle, the gorgeous Weimaraner – had all filed in, leaving Phyllis's lounge somewhat overcrowded. It had taken them a few minutes to outline what they wanted – something to do with an undercover operation which they weren't at liberty to talk about, which at first made the conservative Phyllis reluctant to be involved. But when she realised it was all connected to the Dales Detective Agency and Joseph O'Brien's son, Samson, a young man she'd found to be most charming in her previous dealings with him back in February, she'd relented. And consequently was having an evening unlike any she'd had recently.

Entertaining for a start. Exciting too. And so rewarding, to know that she hadn't lost her touch, even if her hands were no longer as agile as they had once been.

'It's all about light and shade,' she explained to her audience. 'A strip of pale here and the shape changes. A bit of dark there and everything becomes more hollow.'

'Christ,' muttered Arty Robinson, watching on from the safety of the couch alongside Joseph O'Brien and Eric Bradley. 'Who knew it was all so complicated?'

'And what the hell is all that stuff?' wheezed Eric, a frail hand resting on his oxygen tank in reassurance, the excitement of the day having taken a toll on his breathing.

He nodded towards the table, which was littered with brushes, puffs, powders, tubes and vials of God knows what, and an instrument that looked like a pair of scissors designed by the Devil.

'Best off not knowing,' murmured Joseph with a bemused smile. 'Let them keep their secrets.'

Sitting in a dining chair to one side, Edith Hird let out a sharp laugh. 'Don't include me in that,' she said, shaking her stick in the direction of the three men on the sofa. 'I'm as perplexed by all this as the rest of you.'

'I think it's magical,' breathed her sister, Clarissa Ralph, who was busy pouring tea for everyone. 'The things you can do, Phyllis! You're a real artist.'

Phyllis gave a little bow. She'd been raised in a household that didn't hold with self-aggrandisement, but she felt a thrill at having her talents recognised. Especially after all these years of being defined as simply a pensioner.

'Happy to help,' she said truthfully.

'I'll have to get you to work on me before Robert comes over,' continued Clarissa with an infectious smile. 'He's taking me to Bettys tea rooms at Harlow Carr for our first date.'

'Is he now?' said Edith sharply. 'When was that decided?'

'This morning. We haven't fixed on a day yet because he's got a lot on. But I can't wait to meet him.'

'Aye, well just make sure he has his wallet with him,' muttered her sister.

From his seat on the couch, Arty saw the change in Edith's mood. That frown of concern, which had disappeared since his return from his meeting with Samson, had crept back onto her forehead.

'Maybe we should get Phyllis to do us next,' he threw out, hoping to distract his friend once more. 'You know, go for deep cover?'

'Duvet cover, more like,' quipped Eric. 'That's about the only thing that would work on that face of yours.'

Edith laughed and Arty did his best to look hurt. When in truth, hearing the sound of her laughter, he was anything but.

So far his plan to raise her spirits had been working. When he'd arrived back at the retirement complex with news of an assignment for the Dales Detective Agency, the gloom had been lifted off what had been an uneventful afternoon. More like her old self, Edith had joined her sister in making lists of what they would need to take and drawing up a rota of shifts – and comfort breaks – amongst the group of friends, while Joseph, Arty and Eric had discussed the best way for them to operate 'comms', as Arty kept referring to it. Having been denied access to any of Delilah's gadgetry, they were going to have to rely on their mobiles, and so Joseph had spent the best part of an hour getting his head around creating a WhatsApp group. Arty had subsequently spent the next half an hour driving them all mad by repeatedly posting in it.

With little prospect of getting any sleep, such was the excitement amongst the group, they were sitting in the residents' lounge discussing last-minute arrangements, when their day had taken yet another unexpected turn. One that had necessitated a trip to see Phyllis – a former beauty-salon owner and, more importantly, former make-up artist for Bruncliffe Operatic Society – in her first floor apartment.

And now Phyllis was standing back, letting them see the fruits of her labour.

'Well,' she said, 'what do you think? Have I still got it?'

There wasn't a sound. Just a line of open mouths as the pensioners took in the transformation Phyllis had brought about.

'Bloody hell!' Arty finally said, Edith not even turning at the blasphemy as they all stared at the person standing in front of them. 'Your own mother wouldn't know you.'

'That,' said Delilah, 'is exactly what I wanted to hear.'

From his place on the floor lying at Joseph's feet, Tolpuddle lifted his head at her voice and tipped it sideways in puzzlement, letting out an apprehensive whine.

'It's okay, boy,' Delilah said, rubbing his head. Then she caught sight of herself in the antique mirror above Phyllis's sideboard and she understood his confusion.

Arty was right. Even her mother wouldn't know her. More importantly, neither would Bernard Taylor.

Nor, Delilah thought with a laugh, would Samson. Going undercover was going to be fun.

8

Delilah Metcalfe was running late. As always. Seven o'clock Saturday morning, the sky streaked with light from a sun yet to lift above the limestone crag that dominated the town to the east, and Samson was already at work. But Delilah was nowhere to be seen.

Under the guise of helping to pack the Peaks Patisserie van ready for the shoot, Samson had agreed to meet her at the cafe so they could get whatever communication system she had in mind up and running, all without Lucy being any the wiser as to the real reason Delilah had volunteered to be on the catering staff. So far, though, the youngest of the Metcalfe clan had failed to materialise.

Stifling his irritation, Samson went back inside the cafe to get yet another load, Lucy seemingly taking everything but the kitchen sink to the event. As he walked through the door, he saw a middle-aged woman coming towards him, struggling with three boxes piled up in her arms, her grey hair barely visible above the top.

'Here, let me,' he said, taking the boxes from her with ease.

Blue eyes sparkling, a plump face beamed up at him, the woman rubbing at her lower back. 'Thanks,' she said. 'I think I'm getting too old for this.'

'Nothing of the sort,' said Samson gallantly. 'I'm Samson, by the way.'

A laugh met his introduction. 'I know,' said the woman, with an arch look. 'I've heard all about you. I'm Denise, the hired help.'

'I see you two have met.' Lucy had emerged from the kitchen looking harried, a list in her hand. 'Denise, if you've got a minute, could you go out and check with Elaine that we've got the cutlery. Oh, and the tablecloths.'

Denise nodded and headed outside to where Elaine Bullock's trouser-clad backside and Dr Marten boots were sticking out of the van she was busy packing, leaving Lucy with Samson.

'Looks like you've got a good worker there,' he commented.

'Who? Denise?' Lucy nodded. 'The agency really came through with her. But I should have known the minute I met her she'd be good. She's related to Ida Capstick somehow, second cousin or something.'

Samson looked at the older woman again, short grey hair above a round face, a plump body beneath it. He couldn't see any similarity to the rake-thin cleaner. Except perhaps a sharpness around the eyes.

'Right, we're almost done,' said Lucy, pointing at the boxes in Samson's arms. 'Just those to get in and that's it.'

Taking the hint, Samson turned and went back out to the van, Lucy following him. Elaine was standing to one side talking to Denise and simply pointed at the one patch of remaining space in the rear of the van as Samson approached.

'You sure you've got enough food here?' he asked dryly, as he placed his boxes where she'd indicated, the vehicle looking close to bursting.

It was the wrong thing to say to a chef before an event. Lucy's face contorted with panic.

'Do you think I need more? I mean, I've done enough for twenty people. But what if we run out. It won't look good. I might not get another contract—'

'Lucy!' The sharpness of Elaine Bullock's tone was counteracted by the gentle hand she placed on her friend's arm. 'Ignore him. He's joking. There's enough here to feed three rugby teams, so stop worrying.'

'Sorry,' muttered Samson, as Denise directed a glare in his direction.

'It's okay. I'm just nervous,' said Lucy with a small smile. 'I always get like this. Once we're up at the manor and start feeding people, I'll be able to relax.'

'Is that everything, then?' asked Denise, taking the list from Lucy's hands and running a finger down it.

'Think so.'

'In that case, let's get going,' said Elaine, closing the rear doors of the van with a slam. With her trademark plaits in place, her smudge-free glasses slipping down her nose, her white shirt clean if already creased and her usual purple Dr Martens exchanged for a pair of black ones, it was as professional as Samson had ever seen the geologist look. But even so, she was a far cry from the practical Denise, with her sensible shoes, crisply ironed shirt and loose black trousers. Suddenly, Samson was glad of the presence of the older woman. If there was any trouble at the shoot – whether as a result of Delilah's attempts to keep an eye on Bernard Taylor or simply through customers getting too friendly with the staff – given Denise's shared DNA with the formidable Ida Capstick, she would be good to have around.

Not that Delilah would be an issue, seeing as she hadn't turned up yet. He snuck a look at his watch. Where the hell was she?

'Right, we're off,' said Elaine, throwing Samson a wave as Denise and Lucy moved with her towards the front of the van.

Samson watched them with bemusement. 'Aren't you forgetting something?' he asked.

They turned, one blonde, one brunette, one grey, all three looking puzzled.

'Or someone?' he elaborated. 'Delilah said she'd meet me here.'

Lucy looked at him with wide eyes. 'Didn't she tell you? She texted me this morning to say she'd decided to spend the night up at Ellershaw. We're picking her up on the way.'

Ellershaw Farm – the Metcalfe home where Delilah's parents lived along with her brother Will and his family. It was off Hillside Lane, the road that led up to Bruncliffe Manor, and so it made sense for Delilah to be picked up rather than coming all the way into town and back out again. But why hadn't she told him about the change of plan?

'Oh, right. Thing is, I need to . . .' Samson paused. Lucy didn't know that Delilah was going to the shoot to keep an eye on Bernard Taylor and he wasn't sure she'd be best pleased if she found out.

'You need to what?' asked Elaine with a glint in her eye. 'Declare undying love for her?'

Denise made a strangled sound and got in the van while Samson felt his cheeks burn.

'No. Just wanted to have a word with her, that's all.'

'Right. Well, send her a text. We've got work to get to. Come on, Lucy.'

As Elaine sat in next to Denise, Lucy leaned over to Samson and kissed him on the cheek. 'Thanks for the help.'

Samson just nodded. He was still standing outside the cafe as the van turned right off the marketplace and disappeared down Back Street, heading for the hills behind the town. With a sense of concern, he started walking back to the office building.

No wire – or whatever the up-to-date equivalent was. That was what was making him so unsettled. He didn't like the thought of Delilah working a case when he had no way of knowing what was going on. It was only when he reached the front door of the office that it hit him.

Ellershaw Farm. Lucy lived in a converted barn on the hill up above it. Her route to work this morning would have taken her past the end of the farm's drive. So why hadn't she picked Delilah up then?

Puzzling over this incongruity, he let himself into the hallway and was promptly greeted by an enthusiastic Weimaraner.

'Tolpuddle!' he exclaimed in surprise as the dog leaped up at him. 'What are you doing here?'

'Does tha really expect him to reply?' came a sharp retort from the top of the stairs, making Samson jump. He looked up to see Ida Capstick standing there, arms folded across her thin frame, face in its customary sour expression, and on a day she didn't usually clean at the office building.

*

'Do you think he knew?'

'Not a clue.' Elaine looked sideways at the woman called Denise and let out a loud peal of laughter. 'Some bloody detective.'

'You can hardly blame him,' protested Lucy, as she turned the van onto Hillside Lane. 'I'm not sure I'd have twigged if I hadn't been forewarned. I mean, you look so . . .'

'Old?' From behind her disguise, Delilah grinned.

'Plump,' suggested Elaine, pinching her fellow waitress's waist and feeling a soft resistance. 'That get-up has really done the trick.'

Get-up wasn't the word Delilah would have used. Her transformation had taken over an hour, sitting impatiently in Phyllis Walker's lounge while the former salon owner worked her magic in front of an unruly audience. A wig, lots of make-up and some foam padding in the right places, and Denise had been born.

'Poor Samson. I don't know how you kept a straight face,' continued Lucy.

'Me? What about you?' Delilah looked at her sister-in-law, normally a woman incapable of telling untruths. 'You were lying through your teeth without even blinking!'

Lucy grinned. 'It was fun. I even embellished your backstory a bit and said you were Ida's cousin. Samson swallowed it whole!'

Delilah's mouth dropped open while Elaine let out a raucous laugh and slapped her thigh.

'I wish I could see his face when he works it out,' said the waitress.

'If he does,' said Lucy. 'Are you going to tell him, Dee?'

'Once we're at the manor. I figured if he finds out after I've successfully managed to fool him, he's less likely to worry. Or feel the need to come haring up here!' Delilah was busy putting on a pair of glasses, the thick frames changing the shape of her face even more. She tapped the left arm by her ear, fiddled with her phone and then smiled, holding it up for Elaine to see as the same vista of stone walls and steep fields visible out of the windscreen rolled across the screen. 'Hidden camera and microphone in my specs. I'll send him a link to this for now, just to whet his appetite.'

Lucy shook her head. When her sister-in-law had approached her the day before and revealed her genuine reasons for helping out at the shoot, Lucy had been reluctant to get involved at first. She had vivid memories of a series of Dales Detective Agency cases that had ended with Delilah placed in jeopardy, the last one being the worst. Delilah, however, had protested that this wasn't the same, but refused to elaborate on what it was about. Eventually, sensing Lucy was going to refuse to sanction her presence at the event in disguise, Delilah had confessed.

The Dales Detective Agency was investigating Bernard Taylor at the behest of his wife.

Lucy had been shocked – both at the thought of the town's mayor having an affair and at the fact that the serene Nancy Taylor had resorted to setting detectives on his tail. But she could also see why Delilah was insistent that this case was straightforward and removed from danger, especially now there was no chance of deadly coronation chicken scones, given that Lucy was in charge of the catering.

It had been enough to make Lucy yield. And with

Elaine Bullock in on the secret, neither woman the type to find keeping confidences a burden, Denise had been allowed to take Delilah's place on the catering roster.

'Just as long as you stay out of trouble, that's all I ask,' said Lucy.

'I'll do my best,' grinned Delilah.

Up ahead, the drive to Ellershaw Farm came into view on the left and, opposite it, the turn-off for Bruncliffe Manor. Time to let Samson have contact. Fingers flying, Delilah wrote down a few brief instructions and sent him a link to the spy cam app. She waited a couple of seconds and then pressed the arm of her glasses again to turn the camera off: battery conservation. If her gadget was to last the day, she'd have to use it sparingly. Feeling like a real undercover operative, a thrill of excitement shot through her. She was completely incognito, and completely solo.

'Morning, Ida!' Samson aimed a grin at the familiar fierce features staring down the stairs at him. Having grown up at Twistleton Farm with Ida and her brother George as his nearest neighbours, he'd long ago learned that there was a generous heart beneath the cleaner's granite exterior. 'You do know it's a Saturday?'

She scowled at him. 'I'm making up for not being here yesterday morning – not that tha noticed!' She tipped her chin towards Tolpuddle, who was still writhing around on the floor as Samson rubbed his belly. 'Check his collar.'

Samson did as he was told, pulling out a note from under the band circling the dog's neck. It contained a scrawled message from Delilah, asking him to look after Tolpuddle for the day. Nothing more.

'Seems as tha's been left in charge of that gorgeous hound,' Ida commented, revealing that she'd had no qualms about reading the note, too.

'It would appear so,' muttered Samson. He stared at the piece of paper, wondering what was going on. Clearly Delilah had been down to the office at some point that morning in order to drop Tolpuddle off. Yet she hadn't come to the cafe to share whatever monitoring system she was intending to use.

Maybe that was the point. Maybe she didn't want him having access to whatever she was up to; Delilah Metcalfe was going it alone. The thought chilled him.

From upstairs in Delilah's office came the sound of a phone ringing and Ida let out a snort of annoyance.

'Blasted thing's not stopped all the time I've been here,' she muttered, casting a glare along the landing towards the open office door. 'Can't see as how a dating agency could be so busy at this time on a Saturday!'

The phone gave one last ring and fell silent, Ida nodding her head in satisfaction, as if her ferocious scowl had cowed the device into submission.

'There's a brew on,' she called down in Samson's direction, before turning away towards the upstairs kitchen. 'Happen as there's bacon in the fridge too.'

Not having had his breakfast yet, Samson didn't need asking twice and he made his way upstairs, Tolpuddle following.

'Has tha been left in the lurch, then?' the cleaner asked, standing at the stove as she placed several rashers in a frying pan, the dog watching her every movement with anticipation.

Date with Deceit

'You could say that.' Samson sat at the small table, a mug of strong tea already set out for him with enough milk in it to turn it an unappetising shade of beige. He took a swig anyway, having finally accepted after more than six months back home that his southern-influenced concept of tea would never hold sway with people in Bruncliffe. With the mug in his hands and the comforting sound of bacon sizzling in the pan, he let his thoughts settle on the enigma that was Delilah Metcalfe.

He couldn't get his head around her. She was acting in such an irresponsible way, going undercover at the shoot with no backup. It wasn't professional. And he was worried.

Would he be worried if she was a man? Probably not as much. Besides, he consoled himself, Delilah was able to take care of herself. Goodness knows she'd proved that over the last couple of months with the scrapes they'd got themselves into. Plus, Lucy and Elaine were with her. And Denise, a sensible woman if ever he'd met one.

A thump on the table brought Samson back to the kitchen, a bacon sandwich now in front of him.

'Eat,' instructed Ida. 'Tha looks half starved.'

'Thanks,' he said. He took a bite, groaned in appreciation and nodded towards Ida. 'You're a star. Just what I needed.'

The cleaner made a noise somewhere between a grunt and a cough, as much acknowledgement as she ever gave for praise. 'Lucy's off to the shoot, then?' she asked, placing a saucer on the floor for Tolpuddle, two rashers on it. One of them had already been eaten by the grateful hound before she'd turned back to the stove.

'Lucy, Elaine and your cousin, Denise, too,' said Samson. 'She seems like a nice woman.'

Ida looked at him, spatula in mid-air, a frown creasing her forehead. 'Tha's talking daft. There's no Denise in our family.'

Sandwich halfway to his mouth, Samson stared at her. 'You sure?'

Even as he asked it, he knew what the response to his question would be. This was Ida Capstick; she never spoke unless she was sure.

Ida snorted in derision. 'Happen I'd know my own family. Tha's got the wrong end of the stick. What did the lass look like?'

'Middle-aged, grey hair, plump. A bit nondescript really.'

'And called Denise?' The cleaner shook her head. 'No one I can think of.'

'That's odd. Lucy was adamant she was your cousin.'

'Someone's playing tricks, lad,' Ida muttered, turning her attention back to the pan and her own bacon, which was starting to stick. 'And given the line of work tha persists in pursuing, I'd be worried. Because whoever this Denise lass is, she's no Capstick, that's for sure.'

'But why would Lucy . . . ?'

'Aye, that's a surprise all right. Thought as young Lucy would know who's who in Bruncliffe given her pedigree. Not like she's of offcumden stock or owt. She should know better than to be passing someone off as Capstick kin when they're not.'

With an indignant toss of her head, Ida flipped the bacon onto the waiting white teacake and turned towards the table. It was a moment of terrible timing. For just as the cleaner was twisting towards him, Samson – who'd been deep in thought, staring at his phone – shot to his feet with an oath, eyes wide, sending his chair flying backwards and sending the crockery on the table clattering. His reaction startled both the cleaner and Tolpuddle, who'd been watching hopefully as the last of the bacon was served, his own breakfast long finished.

Ida came off worst.

Leaping backwards in alarm, her right hand jerked, the plate in it flew upwards, and the bacon sandwich flew even higher – up into the air, twisting and turning like an edible frisbee. She moved to catch it. But she was too late.

The plate fell to the floor and smashed into pieces. The sandwich fell into the waiting mouth of the hungry Weimaraner.

'Sorry Ida, got to dash,' Samson was saying, moving towards the door at a run. 'Come on, Tolpuddle!'

With a couple of frantic gulps, the dog swallowed his unexpected treat and bolted out after him, the sound of six lots of footsteps racing down the stairs preceding the slamming of the back door. And then silence.

Ida stared at the floor. The broken plate. The smear of ketchup. And at the puddle of undrunk tea on the table.

Life had been a lot less chaotic before Samson O'Brien had returned home. But, she admitted to herself with a rare smile, it was a lot more interesting with him about. The smile disappeared as the phone in Delilah's office started up again. Muttering to herself, Ida strode across the landing towards it.

*

The Peaks Patisserie van had turned onto a curving tree-lined drive that spoke of wealth and history. To the right, beyond the trees, were sloping fields filled with contented looking sheep. To the left, rolling parkland could be glimpsed through the trunks of the limes marching up the road, whetting the appetite until the stunning facade of Bruncliffe Manor materialised around the next bend.

'Wow,' said Elaine, staring at the stone-built Georgian manor, ivy clambering up its sides, double-storey central bow windows looking serenely out over a south-facing terrace with steps leading down to pristine grass. 'Imagine living in that!'

'Hell of a lot of cleaning,' said Delilah.

'I doubt they do it themselves,' remarked Lucy with a laugh as she pulled the van up on the gravel forecourt beside the huge house.

Ahead of them, standing to one side of the imposing entrance, was Gareth Towler. Resplendent in his formal shooting attire, the big man looked every bit the gamekeeper. A brown tweed jacket stretched across broad shoulders, covering a matching waistcoat and a checked shirt and tie, while plus fours and long boots completed the look. By his side was a liver-brown English springer spaniel, alert and eager for a day's work, and a young man, dressed more casually in combat trousers, T-shirt and fleece, a walkie-talkie in his hand.

But while Gareth's attire conveyed dignity and poise, the expression on his face as he shoved his mobile into a pocket conveyed a man holding onto his temper. With a dark scowl, he left the young man and strode over to the van, the dog trotting alongside him.

'Morning all,' he muttered, leaning on Lucy's open window.

'Everything okay?' asked Lucy.

Gareth shook his head. 'Got a bad feeling about today, is all. That was the manager of Mearbeck Hall on the phone,' he said, referring to the five-star spa hotel to the south of Bruncliffe. 'He's a mate of mine and thought I ought to know that our clients are already proving to be a handful. Seems they decided it would be a laugh to go for a midnight swim last night so they broke into the spa and jumped in the pool. And then got aggressive when the staff tried to get them to leave. The manager had to step in and sort it out.'

'Were they drunk?'

'Aye. More than. Caused a bit of damage too.' He grimaced. 'It's not the sort of behaviour I want to hear about before I hand over loaded shotguns. If it weren't for Rick Procter organising it, I'd be tempted to call the shoot off.'

'You think that's necessary?'

The gamekeeper removed his cap and scratched his head, his thatch of russet hair left sticking up in tufts. 'I don't know. There's something about this group that makes me wary.' He sighed and slapped his cap back on before straightening up. 'Anyway, we'll see how it goes. But just a heads up for you girls, I'm going to run this one as a dry shoot. No alcohol allowed. So if they start pressurising you to break out the hooch, send them to me, okay?'

The three women nodded. And it was only then that Gareth frowned, bending back down to stare at the older woman sitting between Elaine and Lucy.

'No Delilah?' he asked.

'Oh, sorry,' said Lucy. 'This is Denise. Delilah couldn't make it.'

Gareth leaned across and held out a huge hand towards this new person. 'Good to have you on board, Denise,' he said, shaking hands. Then he turned back to Lucy. 'Shame about Delilah. She knows how to handle herself and that might prove useful with this lot.'

Denise grinned. And got a sharp elbow from Elaine in her ribs in return.

'I think we'll be okay,' said Lucy. 'Any problems and you'll be the first to know.'

'Aye, well, just remember – don't take any nonsense from them. I don't care how much money or influence they have, they don't get to behave badly. Not on my shoot.'

'How about you?' asked Elaine. 'Will you be able to manage them?'

Gareth grinned. 'I've ordered in reinforcements,' he said enigmatically. Then he tipped his head at the lad waiting by the front door. 'Right, I'd best get Tommy set up. He's operating the traps today so I need to make sure he's clear on what drive's when and where. So, I'll let you get on. The fourth member of your team is already round the back waiting for you. Good luck!'

With a slap on the roof of the van, he stood back and let Lucy pull away across the gravel. When she turned around the far side of the house onto a small track that led to the rear, a sigh of relief came from the seat next to her.

'Well, that's the first test passed,' said Delilah, with a nervous laugh. 'Gareth didn't even blink when he shook my hand.'

'He's too worried to think straight,' said Elaine. 'Poor

bugger. These clients sound a complete delight. Kind of glad I'm going to be stuck in the kitchen.'

Given her propensity for clumsiness, it had been agreed that Elaine would stay with Lucy preparing the food, leaving Delilah and the agency temp to serve the customers. It was a thought that now troubled the owner of Peaks Patisserie.

'Will you be okay working front of house?' Lucy asked, regarding Delilah with concern.

Delilah laughed. 'I grew up with five older brothers, remember. A few raucous blokes won't faze me. It's whoever was sent by the agency you need to worry about.'

'Who is the fourth member of the team? Anyone we know?' asked Elaine.

Lucy pulled a face. 'Er . . . kind of.'

'Someone we *know*?' Delilah shot her sister-in-law a look. 'What about my disguise? We can't let on who I really am.'

'We might not have a choice,' muttered Lucy, pointing towards a figure standing by the back door of the manor. 'There she is.'

Delilah took in the blonde hair pulled back in a ponytail, the pale face, the sharp cheekbones and the unmistakable beauty of a woman she hadn't seen since Christmas Eve. Ana Stoyanovic, former manager of Fellside Court, was back in Bruncliffe.

9

'You were supposed to be incognito!' Elaine Bullock was still laughing a short while later as they brought the catering supplies into the kitchen. 'Talk about blowing it!'

As an undercover operative, Delilah had had a steep learning curve, her first lesson being that you can't go running up to someone and throw your arms around them without giving the game away. Which is precisely what she'd done when she'd seen Ana Stoyanovic waiting on the back step of Bruncliffe Manor. The minute the Peaks Patisserie van pulled up, Delilah had leapt out over Elaine and gone sprinting across to the Serbian, who'd suffered the enthusiastic embrace with a puzzled look, clearly trying to place this middle-aged woman greeting her so enthusiastically. Which meant yet another person had to be let in on the Dales Detective Agency's latest case, Ana needing some explanation as to why Delilah was in such a convincing disguise.

'A grand total of three minutes of successful deception,' said Lucy, tapping her watch. 'All joking aside, Delilah, how the hell do you think you're going to fool Bernard Taylor and Rick Procter for an entire day?'

Delilah shrugged. 'I'll be fine. I just wasn't expecting Ana to be here, that's all.'

'Rick Procter is going to be here today?' Ana asked,

freezing in the doorway, her arms full of tea towels and serviettes.

Lucy nodded. 'He's organised it. He's trying to woo some investors – something to do with a new development project. Why, is that a problem?'

'I'm sorry, I didn't realise. If I'd known . . .' Ana set down her load and ran a hand over her face, which had turned even paler than usual. 'I'd rather he didn't find out I'm in Bruncliffe.'

'Are you afraid he'll put pressure on you to return to Fellside Court?' asked Delilah, knowing that, as the owner of the retirement complex, Rick had been left scrabbling to find a replacement at short notice when Ana suddenly left town. And also knowing that, having been caught up in the murderous events at Christmas that had targeted the pensioners she'd been working with, Ana might not be so keen to resume her old job. 'Because if it's any consolation, he's already filled the position.'

'It's not that,' said Ana. 'I'd go back there in a heartbeat if it wasn't for running the risk of Mr Procter finding out the real reason I left in the first place.'

'He doesn't know?'

'No.' Ana shrugged and gave a twisted smile. 'I didn't think it was wise to tell my boss that I'd been working here illegally on my cousin's Bulgarian passport. Especially not a man as powerful as Mr Procter.' She shuddered. 'He would be a bad enemy to have.'

Delilah glanced at Lucy and gave a slight nod of her head. Ana was right. When she'd made the decision to return to Serbia, tired of living a lie and living apart from her young son, she'd left Rick in the lurch – yet here she was kitted out in the same white-shirt-black-trousers uniform that the rest of the Peaks Patisserie team were wearing, about to set to work as a waitress. At the very least Rick Procter would be curious as to her reappearance.

'But you're here legally now,' protested Elaine. 'Aren't you?'

'Yes. On a Hungarian passport, thanks to my great-grandfather.'

'So what's the problem? Rick would understand.'

Ana dipped her head to one side, as though she doubted the property developer's magnanimity, and Delilah found herself sharing those reservations. Having always been an admirer of Bruncliffe's self-made man, in the last few months she'd seen a side of Rick she didn't like. Beneath the bonhomie he presented to the world, he had a ruthless streak, his open hostility to Samson just one facet of it. And if that wasn't enough, Tolpuddle had developed a deep aversion to the man, the dog's opinion finally tipping the scales; unlike the majority of Bruncliffe, Delilah was no longer a fan of Rick Procter.

'Even if he did understand,' Ana replied, her words more clipped than her Eastern European accent normally rendered them, 'he would want to know why I am working here as a waitress and not using my nursing qualifications.'

'It's a good question,' said Lucy gently. 'Why are you temping? You could earn a lot more doing what you're trained to do.'

'Yes, but I don't have any references I can use for a full-time post.' Ana's expression turned sheepish. 'All of my previous positions in the UK were under my fake persona. I've got a couple of hours at a care home in Skipton, but until

I can build up enough to get a proper reference, I'm supplementing the income by helping out at catering events. It's all a bit unsettled . . . and I'm planning to bring my son over, so . . .' She spread her hands in a helpless gesture.

'So you don't want Rick or anyone rocking the boat by stirring it all up again,' concluded Delilah. 'Fair enough.'

'I'm so sorry,' said Ana, looking at Lucy. 'Maybe the temping agency can send someone else?'

Lucy let out a groan at the thought of losing a third of her workforce before she'd even started, knowing the chance of getting a replacement at this short notice was next to zero. 'You're leaving . . . ? Isn't there a way . . . ?' she stuttered.

'Of course there is,' said Elaine, untying her apron and tossing it at Ana. 'Here, get that on. You can have my role in the kitchen and I'll go front of house with Delilah.'

'Brilliant idea,' said Delilah with a grin, as Ana started putting on the apron, a smile of relief on her face. 'But I think you mean Denise.'

Elaine laughed, flicked her plaits over her shoulder, pushed her glasses up her nose and snapped out a sharp salute in Lucy's direction. 'Denise and Elaine reporting for duty, ma'am!'

Lucy Metcalfe looked at her troops and wondered which unnerved her more. Having Elaine and Delilah – both blessed with sharp tongues and no-nonsense attitudes – serving her customers. Or knowing that those customers, who already had a reputation for poor behaviour, would have free access to firearms.

More than ever, she was regretting becoming involved with Rick Procter's shoot.

*

Standing in the car park of Mearbeck Hall Hotel next to a fleet of top-of-the-range, black Jaguar F-Pace SVRs, Rick Procter was beginning to think the whole thing was a bad idea.

Correction. He'd thought it was a bad idea from the outset. Now he was beginning to think it was a *really* bad idea.

Already there'd been trouble. A call in the early hours from the manager of the hotel – a man he'd had plenty of dealings with in the past and had a good business relationship with – had informed him in frosty tones that his guests had caused damage during robust night-time partying, and that Mr Procter should be aware that there would be a substantial indemnity added to the bill as a result. And while the manager had gone on to say that he would honour the original booking and provide hospitality for the men that evening, Mr Procter's guests would not be welcome to stay at the hotel in future.

Only thing was, the group of men causing havoc at the hotel weren't Rick's guests. Nor were they investors looking to sink capital into a building project in Bruncliffe, as was the pretext for their visit. No, the men Rick would be hosting for the next twenty-four hours were his bosses, which was precisely why he'd had no choice but to go along with what they wanted, despite his qualms. And what they wanted was a weekend away in the countryside, playing at being English gentlemen, while also inspecting their ventures in this remote part of the country. Ventures that included cannabis farms currently being overseen by Rick and Bernard.

The plan had so many potential pitfalls – not least of

which was that Rick's 'guests' might cause themselves to get arrested. But what worried Rick even more was that the entire trip had been motivated by more pragmatic – and potentially deadly – objectives.

Over the course of the last few months there'd been several incidents which would have given those in charge cause for concern. The trouble at the property in Leeds for a start, Samson O'Brien's innocent trespassing at the big house in Roundhay having been enough to trigger moving that business to the more remote Dales. Enough to leave one of the guards responsible for that incident floating face down in a canal, too.

With Rick and Bernard already on thin ice, Rick had dealt with the latest foul-up himself, not foolish enough to try the patience of the people he worked with by revealing yet another hiccup in the Bruncliffe operation. But what if they'd got wind of it? What if word had got out that Pete Ferris had managed to take photos of the newly installed business on Henside Road and instigate a blackmail plot?

It begged the question as to the real purpose of this visit: a business trip or a weekend to tie up loose ends?

Rick tugged at the collar of his checked shirt, feeling a breathlessness that had nothing to do with the tie pushed tight against his neck. The choking sensation only intensified as he spotted Bernard Taylor approaching from the far end of the car park.

Dressed for the occasion, like Rick, but possessing none of the property developer's natural style, the stout figure of the mayor looked vaguely ridiculous in plus fours and a matching jacket, the material of both items straining over the generous contours of his frame. More Toad of Toad Hall than a member of the English nobility. Even from a distance, Rick could tell the man was sweating, and that was before he found out the true identity of the people they were about to be hosting.

'Morning,' Rick said.

Taylor nodded, his face waxen, a haunted expression in his eyes, like he was the prey for the day's shooting. 'They're late,' he muttered, pulling out a handkerchief and mopping his brow. He stuffed the handkerchief back in his pocket with a trembling hand.

Christ. Things were going from bad to worse.

'There's something I need to tell you,' Rick said, as a burst of raucous laughter came from somewhere inside the hotel. 'These investors we're taking up to the manor, they're a bit more than that.'

Taylor turned to him, beads of perspiration forming once more on his forehead despite his recent ministrations. 'What do you mean?'

'It's the Karamanski brothers. They're over here on business and asked if they could catch up with us.'

The name was enough to paralyse the mayor, mouth part open, a tick above his left eye the only movement on his stunned face.

Rick gave a shrug as though this was just another piece of mundane networking, the kind that kept the world of commerce turning. Pretending that his heart wasn't thundering at the prospect of negotiating the tightrope of this day with the deadweight of Taylor on his back, threatening to tip the pair of them off into the abyss.

But he'd had no alternative. Taylor was there at the

insistence of the men they were about to meet, the heads of the organisation they worked for. It was a command that concerned Rick more than he liked to think about, the two brothers never having shown any interest in meeting Bernard before. Why now?

Taylor's shock finally broke into a babble of panic. 'What's this about? Did they say? Why the hell didn't you tell me—?'

'Take it easy!' The grip Rick placed on his partner's arm was forceful enough to secure silence. 'We don't have time for this. Let's just get through the bloody day and by the end of it, I'll have sorted everything. I promise.'

In the background, the laughter got louder, the hotel doors swinging open, and Rick sensed Taylor weighing up his options. Deciding whether or not to flee – which was precisely why Rick hadn't forewarned him of what was at stake. A no-show by Taylor today would have placed them both in danger.

He gave the mayor a shake. 'Bernard, I need to know you're with me on this.'

Taylor pulled his arm from Rick's hold. 'Jesus . . . yes! Yes!' he snapped, words taut with tension.

Another burst of voices and a group of men appeared on the steps in the spring sunshine. Four large bodyguards walked ahead, black leather jackets pulled tight across physiques that owed their origin to chemicals as much as hard workouts in a gym. But their muscles counted for nothing compared to the real power contained in the six men walking behind them.

Or more specifically, two of the six, the smallest of the group: Niko and Andrey Karamanski, brothers in life and partners in crime. Despite their lack of stature compared to their friends, there was a compact energy about them, an alertness that crackled with intelligence. And danger.

Rick had met them once before and had come away both impressed and terrified by their ruthlessness when it came to business. And here they were, on his turf, taking everything in while they laughed at their rowdy comrades. They made the property developer nervous, even when they were smiling.

Especially when they were smiling.

Decked out in brown camouflage, sunglasses and rugged boots, the six men followed the bodyguards across the car park like a band of mercenaries, a swagger to their walk, an arrogance to their posture and a genuine menace exuding from them. The mayor was staring at the approaching group with the enthusiasm of a vole that had fallen into a nest of vipers.

'For Christ's sake, Bernard, smile!' hissed Rick.

As Taylor pulled his nervous features into a rictus grin, Rick Procter had a premonition that the day was not going to end well.

Samson could have kicked himself. As he coaxed his borrowed transport up the hill out of town, he had to laugh at how he'd been hoodwinked. The grey hair, the blue eyes, and the body that looked nothing like Delilah's athletic frame . . .

'Best not think too much about that, eh, boy?' he murmured to his companion.

Sprawled out on the back seat, Tolpuddle barked in return.

It had taken a while for the penny to drop, Samson having to admit that if it hadn't been for Delilah's message arriving just as Ida was denying the existence of anyone called Denise amongst the current crop of Capsticks, he might not have made the connection. But when he'd opened the link Delilah had sent and saw the view from her spy cam, things had fallen into place. It had only been a snippet of video, the sound no more than a fierce crackle, and then the screen had gone blank. But it had been enough.

Because the video had been of the very road he was travelling up now, Hillside Lane. The road that led to Bruncliffe Manor and, of course, Ellershaw Farm, where Lucy was purportedly picking up Delilah. It was a road Samson knew well. In fact he had a particularly fond memory of travelling up it on a day in December, the stone walls grey against the white canvas of the snow-covered fields, his scarlet Royal Enfield motorbike a streak of colour on a two-tone palette. And behind him on the pillion, Delilah, her arms wrapped tight around him as she laughed at the beauty of the day.

So he'd recognised the rolling vista taken through the windscreen of the Peaks Patisserie van straight away. He'd also spotted that the turn off for Ellershaw Farm was still some way ahead. Which begged the question – how come Delilah was already sending him live feed from inside the van if it hadn't yet reached her pick-up point?

As he'd been mulling over this point, he'd had one ear on Ida, who was continuing her rant about misappropriated relations. So when the cleaner had expressed her surprise that someone of Lucy Metcalfe's pedigree had managed to get local connections so mixed up, Samson had found himself taking the thought even further.

Why would Lucy, a Bruncliffe local, born genetically coded with an in-built register of who was who in the town, be claiming Denise was a relation of Ida's when she clearly wasn't? Unless she was trying to establish a credible identity for someone who wasn't what they seemed, and, like many rookies, had made the fatal mistake of over-embellishing the legend, adding too many layers in an effort to gain authenticity. Which meant Denise wasn't Denise. Which meant . . .

Bloody Delilah!

The unmasking of Denise's true identity had had Samson up on his feet and running out the door, Tolpuddle on his heels, concern for Delilah in her first attempt at going undercover driving the detective to be nearer the scene. Given that his current partner wasn't as pillion-able as the woman who'd been with him for the same journey back in December, Samson had gone for Plan B. Out through the back yard, past his redundant motorbike, and into the ginnel, and then a sprint up the steps that rose sharply to the foot of the Crag. With the bulk of limestone towering over him, he'd panted after Tolpuddle, who instinctively knew where they were headed. But as they approached Delilah's cottage on Crag Lane, Samson hadn't entered the small front yard as the confused hound had anticipated. Instead, he'd continued on to the bright-red Nissan Micra that was parked on the other side of the house.

Praying that his landlady had continued to ignore his advice about making her car more secure, Samson had reached up into the front-right wheel arch and felt his fingers curl around metal. The key. Relieved, he'd opened the door and let Tolpuddle in the back. Not waiting to get approval of his unauthorised loan of Delilah's car – an action he justified by her deception of him that morning – he'd shoved the driver's seat back to a distance more suited to the average human, and took off through the town. Ten minutes later, man and dog were almost at their destination. If the car coped with the last bit of hill.

'Come on,' Samson muttered as the Micra's engine groaned in protest at the incline. He glanced in the rear-view mirror and saw three black Jaguar 4x4s speeding into view, racing up the hillside like a presidential motorcade at speeds his little car could barely manage on the flat.

Too fast, in fact, because up ahead the road curved blindly around the fellside and the Jaguars weren't going to have room to overtake before the bend.

Samson pressed his foot even further to the floor, willing the Micra to go faster, the black vehicles almost upon him. And the bend even closer. But still they showed no sign of slowing, the one in the lead so close now he could see the occupants. Two large men in the front seat, a couple of shadowy figures in the back.

'Ease up,' he shouted into the mirror, the bonnet of the first Jaguar filling his view.

It didn't stay there long. With a growl of acceleration and a screech of tyres, it pulled out, going past in a blur of glass and black metal. Close on its tail, the second 4x4 sped by and cut across the Micra, the bend right in front of them now.

A quick look in the mirror. The third car was still

behind, no time for it to overtake as, around the curving road, the large shape of a milk tanker was coming into view.

But the 4x4 driver had other ideas. Engine roaring under the strain, the Jaguar started pulling out.

'Jesus! What the hell—?'

With the tanker bearing down on them, Samson had no option but to brake hard, trying to create more space on the road in front as the last 4x4 drew recklessly alongside. Bracing himself for the inevitable collision, he risked a sideways glance and caught the malevolent glare of a man staring out from the rear of the Jaguar, a thick scar visible on his shaven scalp. In front of the man, Bernard Taylor, eyes fixed ahead, an expression of pure terror on his face, hands flat against the dashboard. And over it all, the bellow of the milk tanker's horn, lights flashing, brakes screeching, the driver having nowhere to go on this narrow country lane, hemmed in by stone walls, a sheer drop down the fellside the only option.

Everything seemed to slow as, seconds from impact, the Jaguar swerved sharply in front of the Micra with no more than a couple of feet to spare, and whipped around the bend, leaving the milk tanker to rumble past, the driver shaking his head in shock and disapproval.

'Jesus!' Samson muttered again, heart thumping, hands slick on the steering wheel. In the rear, Tolpuddle was looking equally stressed at the commotion.

'It's all right, boy,' murmured Samson, giving the hound a reassuring pat.

But in reality, he didn't think it was all right at all. Because the convoy of Jaguars being driven by maniacs had been the men heading for the shoot. The same men who would be spending the day toting loaded shotguns.

Having made the decision to drive up Hillside Lane so he could be on hand should Delilah's disguise be rumbled, Samson's concern for his partner was no longer about her being recognised. It was now more about her and her co-workers surviving the day unscathed.

10

'Stop scratching your head! People will think you've got nits,' hissed Elaine, as she followed Delilah out of the kitchen, through the breakfast room and into the long corridor that led to the grand entrance hall of Bruncliffe Manor.

'I can't help it,' came Delilah's muttered reply, one hand balancing a tray of non-alcoholic hot toddies and the other fingers-deep in her fake grey hair as she tried to alleviate the burning itch that was plaguing her scalp. 'This bloody wig is driving me crazy.'

It wasn't only the wig that was tormenting her. It was also the layers of make-up that made her unaccustomed face feel plastic and rendered a smile an act of contortion. Add to that the generous amount of padding, which was making her hot, and Delilah was feeling far from comfortable. At this rate, the text she'd just sent Samson confessing to her undercover identity might be redundant, because she was in danger of ripping the whole outfit off. And the day hadn't even started.

She gave her scalp one last decent scratch, setting the glasses rattling precariously on the tray in her other hand and knocking a squeak of alarm out of her fellow waitress before she managed to steady them.

'And people think *I'm* the clumsy one,' said Elaine with

a relieved grin, her own grip tight on the tray of breakfast rolls she'd been entrusted with, knowing that certain death awaited her from a stressed Lucy if she dropped them. Each one an exquisite swirl of pastry, sausage and egg, the waitress was also doing her best not to drool.

'Perfect timing, ladies!' Gareth Towler greeted them from where he was standing on the front steps looking out over the drive, the double doors wide open, letting in the warm spring air. As they joined him beneath the curved portico, his spaniel turned towards them eagerly, nose in the air, sniffing. 'Something smells good, doesn't it, Bounty?'

'Lucy's worked her usual magic,' said Elaine. She held out her tray for the gamekeeper to inspect the delicious-smelling rolls. 'Not sure I'll be able to resist eating them much longer.'

Gareth groaned in sympathy. 'Good job our guests will be here any minute.'

At his words, the sound of an approaching vehicle came from the tree-screened drive. Standing slightly behind Elaine, still not convinced her disguise would hold up to close scrutiny, Delilah discreetly tapped the arm of her glasses to activate the camera as a battered Land Rover came into view.

'Ah! My reinforcements have just arrived,' said Gareth.

'Batman and Robin?' quipped Elaine.

Gareth let out a boom of laughter. 'Bruncliffe's equivalent!'

While Elaine was grinning, the humour wasn't shared by Delilah. Instead her knees had gone weak, her legs wobbling. Because getting out of the Land Rover were two men, one tall and lithe, the other stocky and dark. Both were dressed in khaki trousers, shirt and gilet, ready for shooting. Both were carrying shotguns broken over their arms. And both were Delilah's brothers.

'Will and Ash Metcalfe!' said Elaine in genuine surprise, a sharp glance going to her co-worker to her left as the men started walking towards them.

'Aye,' said Gareth. 'Couldn't think of anyone better to have around if trouble breaks out. Morning lads!'

'So is this the trouble you were expecting, Gareth?' asked Ash, a broad smile creasing his face at the sight of Elaine Bullock, his glance barely registering the woman next to her. 'They look like a handful all right.' Then he spotted the tray of breakfast rolls and he whistled. 'Lucy's outdone herself. They look amazing!'

But while Ash only had eyes for Elaine and food, Will Metcalfe was a different beast. He was staring at the other woman on the steps.

'I don't think we've been introduced,' he said.

Fixed in her oldest brother's gaze, Delilah managed a squeak in reply. 'Denise,' she said. Her words were accompanied by the gentle tinkle of glass as the tray in her hands began to shake.

Samson was just in time to witness the drama.

Knowing he couldn't enter the grounds of Bruncliffe Manor without creating suspicion and possibly spooking Bernard Taylor, he parked in the turn-off for Ellershaw Farm. Opposite the driveway to the manor, it was close enough to act should any problems arise, but still out of sight. Besides, it wasn't just Bernard he didn't want to spook – he didn't want to undermine Delilah by showing up. His presence would be as good as telling her he had no faith in her abilities to carry off the deception she'd put so much effort into. So he settled for the layby, switched off the car, gave Tolpuddle a few strokes to calm him after the tension of the drive up, and checked his mobile.

He had a text from Delilah confessing to her alter ego and telling him not to worry. Or come up. He grinned. How well she knew him. And then the video feed went live. What he saw was enough to make him swear.

Will and Ash Metcalfe approaching Delilah.

This could blow the entire case.

Convinced it was going to be the end of a short-lived undercover operation, Samson could barely watch as the two men came closer. While she'd duped him that morning, now Delilah was facing her brothers, and that was a different prospect entirely. Plus, she was notoriously bad at lying.

'Come on, Delilah,' he muttered.

Ash was talking, his eyes doing no more than flicking in the direction of the camera before his attention was back on Elaine Bullock. So far so good. Then Will was staring straight down the lens with that intense focus of his, the kind of look that would put anyone on edge.

'*I don't think we've been introduced*,' he was saying.

Samson could hear the quiver of nerves in Delilah's voice as she replied. And she had every right to be nervous, because Will Metcalfe was one of the shrewdest people Samson had ever met.

'*Denise? You're not from Bruncliffe?*' It was both a statement and a question, Will's solid gaze, unwavering, skewering Delilah.

'*No . . . I mean . . . I'm not . . .*' Panic trembled through the words.

'*She's from the agency,*' said Elaine, cutting across Delilah's stuttered reply. '*What's with the third degree, Will?*'

Will's focus switched to Elaine and Samson heard the soft rush of a held breath being released. It was overlaid by the sound of engines, faint at first but getting louder.

'*They're here,*' muttered Gareth, glancing around his group of workers. '*Remember, everyone, the slightest sign of any nonsense and you let me know. All right?*'

No one got a chance to reply. Because at that moment, three Jaguars tore around the corner, coming to a halt in front of the house in a screech of brakes and a clatter of sprayed gravel. The doors flung open, and some of the biggest men Samson had ever seen got out of the cars. What was more worrying, given that he'd lived a life amongst the underworld, they were also some of the most menacing.

He found himself feeling strangely grateful that Will and Ash Metcalfe were at Bruncliffe Manor.

'Christ!' muttered Ash, watching the men unfold from the 4x4s. 'Rambo's got nothing on these guys.'

There were ten of them, eight of them easily big enough to make a living as heavyweight boxers; judging by a couple of the misshapen noses, it wasn't just their size that made them suitable candidates for the ring. And while the other two were smaller in stature, they carried a self-possession that only came from power. None of the group were the kind of men the Metcalfe brothers would want to meet in a dark alley in Leeds on a Friday night. Nor were they what any of the welcoming committee had been expecting – with four wearing leather jackets and the rest dressed in camouflage, they looked like they knew how to handle guns, and were a far cry from the usual chinless rich-boy investors, up from the capital for a day's sport in the country.

A suave Rick Procter and an ashen-faced Bernard Taylor completed the party.

'Welcome to Bruncliffe Manor,' Gareth said, going down the steps to greet them, Delilah and Elaine on his heels bearing the trays of hot toddies and breakfast rolls.

The two smaller men came forward, hands outstretched as Rick Procter made the introductions.

'Nikolay and Andrey, this is Gareth, who will be running the shoot today.'

'Call me Niko, please,' said the older of the men, shaking hands with the gamekeeper, his English carrying the accent of a non-native speaker.

There was something captivating about the man, his smile warm with an aura of authority that the gamekeeper imagined was seldom questioned.

'Welcome to the Yorkshire Dales,' said Gareth. 'Have you come far?'

'From Bulgaria,' said Niko. Then he grinned. 'Via the Mearbeck Hall Hotel.'

Gareth's laugh was echoed by Rick Procter, a trifle late and a trifle forced, warning the gamekeeper not to be lulled by the Bulgarian's affable manner. He'd had enough dealings with Rick over the years to know the man was a fearless businessman who never lost his cool. Yet here he was on edge. And as for Bernard Taylor . . .

The mayor was standing slightly apart from the group,

a smile fixed on his waxen face, like a badly formed resident of Madame Tussauds.

'Right,' said Gareth, as Niko made no move to introduce the rest of his party. 'Well, let's have a bite to eat and I'll run you through some ground rules.'

He gestured at Delilah and Elaine, who stepped forward, holding out their trays. The tallest of the men, a white scar scything across the left side of his scalp, stared at the two women and made some wisecrack in Bulgarian, prompting raucous laughter from the others.

'Get the feeling that wasn't complimentary?' Elaine murmured to Delilah, as the men began to help themselves to the drinks and breakfast rolls, still laughing.

'Just a bit,' Delilah whispered. She was suddenly grateful for the suffocating padding and the itchy wig – for providing a barrier to the unpleasant attention.

The man was bad news. Samson watched the images with growing disquiet, his eyes fixed on the tall Bulgarian, the same man he'd seen in the last Jaguar as it sped past him. While Gareth outlined the rules, reminding the guns of basic safety measures, the guy was constantly making asides, fooling around like the class joker. And when the gamekeeper announced that the shoot was to be dry, no alcohol allowed, the man rolled his eyes and then patted his pocket with a grin.

Gareth didn't seem to notice. But judging by the focus of the spy cam, Delilah's attention was fully on the man with the scar. At least it suggested she'd spotted him as potential trouble, which was some consolation for Samson, who was feeling more and more frustrated at not being by her side. As for Bernard Taylor, the true subject of the Dales Detective Agency's investigation, there was nothing in his behaviour to suggest that this outing was anything other than what it was purported to be: a chance to curry favour with would-be investors. If anything, the mayor looked like a man out of his depth, his face strained, his smile slipping when no one was looking. Whatever Nancy Taylor suspected in terms of extramarital relationships, there was no evidence of it so far.

Perhaps it would be wise to call Delilah and tell her to leave?

Although there was still the matter of that bag full of banknotes . . . Maybe today would shed some light on the origins of that? Besides, Samson knew that if he suggested his partner call it a day this early in proceedings, the answer would be blunt and to the point. He'd just have to hope that once the men headed off to the first drive, Elaine and Delilah would be able to return to the kitchen. The game-keeper's next words indicated that moment was imminent.

'*Right, let's go and get kitted out*,' Gareth was saying, pointing towards the back of the house.

Over the rattle of glasses being put down and the crunch of boots on gravel as the group moved away, Delilah's murmur was just about audible. '*Here, take this*,' she said, passing her tray to Elaine.

Much to Samson's consternation, she set off after the men.

The first sign of dissent came in the gun room in the con-verted stone stables at the rear of the manor. With a guttural laugh of disdain, the man with the scar picked up a shotgun and grunted at Niko.

'Is there a problem?' asked Gareth.

Niko gave a small smile. 'My cousin Milan is more used to Kalashnikovs.'

'Right. Well, we don't tend to shoot with them in these parts,' came the dry response. 'Besides, it takes more skill to hit clays with a shotgun.'

'Clays?' Niko looked from the gamekeeper to Rick Procter, frowning. 'We're shooting clays?'

Rick swallowed. Nodded. Spread his hands in apology. 'I was meaning to tell you. It's out of season here for game birds.'

'I see.' The clipped words were belied by a soft smile, Rick shifting uneasily under the man's steady gaze. The Bulgarian turned to Gareth. 'It's really not possible? There's no way we can persuade you to change your mind? A few birds. Who's going to know?'

Gareth shook his head, wide arms folding across his broad chest. 'Not happening. No live game,' he said. 'Rules are rules and while I don't make them, I sure as hell don't break them either. So, what's it to be? Are we shooting clays or not?'

'We will shoot clays. It's a long way to come for no sport, eh boys?' Niko smiled at his friends but there was a hardness to the look that rested on Rick.

Not as easily placated, a snort of disgust came from the man called Milan. He followed it with an outburst in English. 'We should stay home and shoot. Boar, stag, birds – no stupid rules!'

Niko barked something abrupt in Bulgarian and Milan turned away, snapping the shotgun shut, slinging it over his shoulder and striding towards the door, where Will Metcalfe was standing.

'Break your gun, please,' Will said, a hand out to stop the man, another gesturing at the shotgun. 'We don't walk around with them closed. Safety reasons.'

Milan halted, stared down at Will, who barely came up to his chin, and there was a long silence, Will meeting the man's look unflinchingly. Then the Bulgarian slowly, provocatively, lifted the gun off his shoulder so it was aimed at Will before proceeding to break it open. He pointedly laid it over the crook of his arm and, with a mock salute, carried on out of the door.

'Everyone else ready to go?' asked Gareth, trying to muster an enthusiasm he didn't feel.

Like a group of sullen teenagers, the men filed out of the room, Will keeping guard as they trooped past him, until only Bernard Taylor was left.

'Here,' said Gareth, smiling as he handed the mayor the last shotgun. 'I take it you don't want a Kalashnikov?'

But the mayor didn't share the joke. Instead he took the weapon with a glower. 'It wouldn't have hurt just to have said yes,' he snapped. 'Like the man said. A few birds. No one would miss them. We're supposed to be showing these people a good time.'

Gareth shrugged. 'Sorry, Bernard, I'm not willing to lose my job just to keep some of your investors happy.'

'Keep going like this and you might lose it anyway! Those plans haven't got approval yet!' retorted the mayor, before striding out of the door.

The gamekeeper stared after him, a dark flush creeping up from his beard.

'Jesus!' said Will. 'Did he just threaten you?'

Gareth tried to brush it off. 'Local politics,' he said with

Julia Chapman

a dry laugh. 'Not sure which is worse – that or this bunch of Bulgarians. They're going to be a handful.'

'Aye. That Milan lad especially. Glad you called us in.'

'Me too.' The comment came from behind the game-keeper and he spun around to see the waitress called Denise standing in the corner of the room, blue eyes wide behind her glasses.

'Shouldn't you be in the kitchen?' he asked, surprised – not only by her presence but that he hadn't noticed her at all.

'Oh . . . yes . . . I mean . . . Lucy asked me to see if you want coffee and tea taking over to the pegs.'

Gareth nodded. 'Good idea. Wouldn't harm to have a bit of extra refreshments for this lot. Try and keep them sweet. Can you bring it over in the van?'

'I'll drive her over,' said Will. 'Ash can go with you.'

'Great. Thanks. I'll see you over there.' With Bounty at his heels, the troubled gamekeeper headed out towards the 4x4s, the Bulgarians already getting into their Jaguars, engines racing, waiting for him to lead the way.

He didn't see the look of concern flicker across the face of the waitress behind him at the thought of a journey in close proximity with Will Metcalfe.

Things were going smoothly in the kitchen of Bruncliffe Manor. The nerves that had plagued Lucy in the early morning when they were packing the van had completely disappeared now that she was in a familiar environment. Not that it was like any environment she'd ever cooked in before.

Two fridges, a large La Cornue range in matt black with

132

a highly polished stainless-steel splashback as well as two Miele built-in ovens, enough work surface for three or four chefs to work at one time without problem, and a huge central island offering more prep area – it was the kitchen of her dreams. Add in an orangery-style glass-and-metalwork ceiling letting in the May sunshine, a mosaic tiled floor and two windows looking out over the back courtyard and the L-shaped stone stables, and it was perfect. After an hour and a half of hard work, with delicious smells coming from the range and an array of cakes and pastries laid out on the island, Lucy was feeling in charge.

She was even beginning to hum while she worked. Much to the amusement of Ana Stoyanovic, who was standing at the sink, rinsing salad and enjoying the warmth of the sun that was streaming through the high arching window in front of her. Lucy's good mood was infectious, Ana too already looking lighter of heart. But when the door to the kitchen flung open and Elaine walked in, promptly catching one of the two trays she was carrying on a worktop and sending it crashing to the ground, the loud clatter of metal on tile cut short the tuneful humming of Lucy and made Ana jump.

'Sorry!' the waitress exclaimed, depositing the second tray, loaded with glasses, on the counter before bending over to retrieve the one she'd dropped. She stood back up with a grin. 'At least it wasn't the one with the glasses on!'

Ana laughed and Lucy just shook her head with a rueful smile. And then frowned. 'Where's Delilah?'

'Snooping around the gunroom with the Bulgarians.'

'What Bulgarians?' asked Ana.

'The property investors Rick's brought to the shoot. They're from Bulgaria, and I tell you what, they look a bit menacing.' Elaine shuddered.

But Lucy wasn't bothered about the origin of the guests. She was purely concerned about the whereabouts of her staff. 'What on earth is Delilah doing in the gunroom? I need her in here helping to prep!'

Ana turned back to the sink, still smiling, just in time to see a large man dressed in camouflage come storming out of the stables across the yard, a shotgun in his hands and a fierce scowl on his face. Along the side of his head was a jagged scar. She couldn't help but stare. So when he glanced over and saw her there, spotlit by the morning sun inside the window, she was trapped by his gaze. The scowl slipped from his face, transformed into a leer as his colleagues emerged from the building behind him, some of them in camouflage, others in leather jackets bulging over huge physiques. He half turned, still staring at her, and made a comment, eliciting loud laughter from the group.

Ana dropped her gaze. Dropped the salad leaves she was holding into the sink. And span away from the window, further into the sanctuary of the kitchen where she couldn't be seen.

'You okay?' Elaine asked, as Ana stood against the island, a streak of pink on her pale cheeks and a flustered look about her.

'Those men,' she said. 'They're investors?'

'That's what Gareth called them. Why?'

'Because I recognise them. Not the men, as such, but the type. Those leather jackets, the way they walk . . .' Ana shivered. 'They're mafia.'

'Mafia?' Lucy turned from the stove, eyebrows raised. 'Seriously?'

Ana nodded.

'Bloody hell,' muttered Elaine. 'We'd best tell Delilah.'

Concerned, Lucy Metcalfe stared out into the courtyard at the group of men moving away towards the front of the house. If Ana was right, these were not the sort of people who would react well to finding out someone was spying on them while wearing a disguise. Whatever she had planned, Delilah would need to be extra careful or she was going to find herself in the kind of situation that not even Samson O'Brien would be able to get her out of.

11

Down in Bruncliffe, the three Metcalfes who'd been left in charge of Peaks Patisserie were doing a brilliant job. Will's wife Alison was waiting on tables, Lucy's lad Nathan was manning the dishwasher and the matriarch of the Metcalfe clan, Peggy, was baking up a storm, a batch of Yorkshire curd tarts and two tea loaves already cooling on a wire rack. With a tray of spinach-and-feta mini quiches in the oven and some lamb-and-mint pasties currently underway, things were running smoothly. Despite the hectic start.

The makeshift team had had to hit the ground running, having arrived at the cafe at eight to see a huddle of people already waiting at the door. Peggy hadn't had the heart to leave them out there for half an hour until the official open-ing time, especially when they were all residents of Fellside Court.

'What on earth are you doing here so early?' she'd asked as she ushered the group into the cafe. 'Did you get kicked out for misbehaving?'

The last question was aimed at Arty Robinson, who'd grinned back at her. 'Not this time,' he'd said.

He'd offered nothing more by way of explanation and they'd settled themselves at a table next to the window. And promptly ordered coffees and breakfast rolls. That had been the catalyst for a manic morning. People passing by had seen the pensioners sitting in the cafe, and had been drawn in despite the early hour. Before the cafe was even supposed to be open, every table had been occupied and the temporary staff rushed off their feet.

Two hours on, and things had quietened down a bit. Apart from the table by the window.

'What do you think they're up to?' Peggy asked Nathan, as they stood behind the counter grabbing a breather and watching the pensioners chattering away. 'They've been here ages and show no sign of moving.'

'A stake-out, I'd say.'

'Seriously?' Peggy glanced at her grandson to see if he was joking but the lad was slouched on the counter, long body draped over it as he contentedly bit into a blueberry muffin. There was no sign of laughter on the face that was almost a mirror-image of his father's at that age. 'What on earth makes you say that?'

Nathan shrugged. 'They keep taking it in turns to sit looking out of the window. And they're drinking a lot of coffee. Classic signs of a stake-out.' He sounded so authoritative and a lot older than his fourteen – soon to be fifteen – years. 'They must be on a job for Samson while he's up at the shoot.'

Peggy turned back to reassess the group across the cafe. Ludicrous as it might sound, Nathan's observation held a ring of truth, particularly when the group included Joseph O'Brien, Samson's father. She shook her head, amazed both at her grandson's prescience and her own easy acceptance of what he'd suggested.

A stake-out in Bruncliffe. Only last year that would have been considered ridiculous. Like Bruncliffe had any crime! But since the return of Samson O'Brien in the autumn and the opening of the Dales Detective Agency, such events had become commonplace, at least for the Metcalfe family. It was only a few weeks ago that Delilah had nearly lost her life—

Peggy's breath caught in her throat, her hand involuntarily going to her heart as though to ease a pain at the thought. She'd already lost one child; she wasn't sure she could cope with losing another. Which is why, much as she cared for the O'Brien lad, Samson having been a fixture in the Metcalfe family since his mother died, she sometimes wished he hadn't returned home and got Delilah embroiled in his escapades. It was only going to end in someone getting hurt and Peggy had a sneaking suspicion that person would be Delilah. Even if she survived the physical danger that seemed to come with the job, surviving with her heart unscathed was another matter. For Peggy had seen the way her only daughter looked at the returned detective and suspected the attraction Delilah felt for the Dales Detective Agency wasn't simply based on an interest in sleuthing.

'You okay, Gran?' Standing up straight now and towering over her, Nathan was watching her with concern, the last bit of the muffin halfway to his mouth.

'Yes, yes, sorry.' Peggy forced a smile. 'I was miles away.'

'Dad?' he asked, not fooled for a minute.

The pain in her heart flipped to love as she looked at her grandson, offering her comfort for a loss that had affected no one more than him. She smiled again, genuine this time.

'Your father would be so proud of you,' she said, reaching up to stroke a stray lock of hair off his forehead.

Nathan grinned down at her. 'Proud enough to let me have one of those quiches? I think they're done.'

Peggy laughed, remembering a son who'd had a similar appetite and a similar cheeky manner. 'Okay – but don't burn yourself!'

The lad headed into the kitchen and Peggy was about to follow him when a scrape of chairs from the table over at the window caught her attention. Arty Robinson was swapping places with Clarissa Ralph and Joseph O'Brien was giving up his seat to Clarissa's sister, Edith.

Nathan was right. Whatever they were up to, the residents of Fellside Court weren't simply having a prolonged coffee morning, that was for sure.

Intrigued, Peggy Metcalfe went into the kitchen to rescue her quiches before they all disappeared. That would be one mystery which wouldn't require solving by Bruncliffe's detective agency.

Up on the fells above the town, Peggy's only daughter would rather have been investigating a missing quiche than sitting in a jolting Land Rover feeling like she was going to be sick, all the while being interrogated like a stranger by her oldest brother. As he guided the vehicle over the rough track that led to the shooting pegs, Will fired questions at the woman he knew as Denise.

Where was she from? Were her family local? When did she start temping for the catering agency? Had she known Lucy long . . . ?

Getting a taste of what it was like to be an offcumden in her own community, Delilah was doing her best to provide plausible answers, but the physical effort of being in disguise was starting to take its toll. With her face red and a sheen of sweat on her forehead – the foam padding around her midriff making her feel like an over-lagged pipe – she was beginning to think she might have bitten off more than she could chew.

And that was before she factored in what she'd learned when she'd called into the kitchen to sweet-talk Lucy into dropping everything to provide unscheduled coffee and cake for the guns.

Mafia! What the hell?

Ana had been convinced about it, that the men she'd seen in the courtyard bore the hallmarks of organised crime. While it was a substantial allegation to be based on appearance alone, if she was right it changed the nature of what lay ahead entirely.

Delilah was about to go undercover amongst men who wouldn't take kindly to being spied on.

She'd been tempted to call it a day on hearing Ana's bombshell, a move the Peaks Patisserie team had strongly advocated. And one Delilah knew Samson would be already pushing for if the spy cam had been on during the conversation in the kitchen. After all, there was no sign of any femme fatale with her sights on Bernard Taylor, unless one of the Bulgarians had an even more convincing disguise than Delilah. So the need for stealth was redundant. She could abandon her suffocating outfit, send her alter ego home 'sick', and serve out the rest of the shoot as herself, a waitress and nothing more.

But Delilah had a stubborn streak as wide as Malham Cove. This was her first covert operation and she wanted to prove she could do it. Even if just for a little while.

Besides, there was still the matter of the financial aspect of the investigation. Given Ana's suspicions, the day could well yield something that might cast light on Bernard's hoard of cash: a careless conversation, for example, which was unlikely to be held in front of the Dales Detective Agency's Delilah Metcalfe.

And then there was Samson . . . Or rather, a desire to impress him. To get a reaction out of him and get their relationship back to something other than the intolerable politeness that had shrouded it recently.

With this reasoning in mind, Delilah had sworn her friends to silence – knowing that if Samson got wind of Ana's theories about the men, he'd insist on Denise making a swift exit – loaded up the old Land Rover with a couple of crates of provisions and a folding table, and clambered up into the passenger seat next to Will, determined to carry out her mission.

Fast forward ten minutes and as the 4x4 lurched and bumped along the grass track, it was taking all of her will-power to stick to that resolution.

'Here we are,' said Will, finally turning off the track to pull up where the Jaguars were parked on a patch of grass next to a small copse.

Almost falling out of the car with relief, Delilah discreetly tapped the side of her glasses to reactivate the camera, dabbed the worst of the sweat off her face with a tissue and, with Will helping her carry the supplies, walked down the sloping grass to join the shooting party.

'Gareth's starting them off on the tough stuff,' murmured Will with a small smile as he took in the terrain of the first drive, the copse giving way to bare fellside rising sharply to the left, bursts of yellow gorse along its ridge, breaking up the green. Facing into the hillside were eight pegs spaced out along the rough grass. 'High pheasants.'

Delilah just nodded politely. While she was totally at home in this environment, she wasn't sure how much a woman like Denise would know about the world of clay shooting. Best to say nothing.

'They're harder to hit,' Will carried on, taking the woman's silence for ignorance. 'Reckon he's trying to put our delightful Bulgarians in their place.'

'They need it,' she said with passion, and was rewarded with a sharp look from her brother.

'It's funny,' he said, still staring at her as they set down the crates a safe distance from the pegs, 'you really remind me of someone. Are you sure we haven't met before?'

'Quite sure,' Delilah muttered, bending down to pick up the folding table, using the action to hide her burning face.

'Right. Well make sure you stay well back out of the way. These buggers don't look like they'll be the most respectful guns ever and if anyone is going to get hurt, I'd rather it wasn't one of us. Okay?'

Thinking he didn't know the half of it, Delilah let a brisk nod suffice and busied herself with erecting the table and laying out the coffee flasks, cups and cakes while Will headed over to the group gathered around the gamekeeper.

'So if everyone is clear,' Gareth was concluding, his spaniel Bounty at his heels, 'we'll commence and finish the drive on my whistle. Okay?'

The responses were mostly nods, the men already turning away and pulling on their ear defenders, eager to get shooting as they headed for the pegs they'd been allocated in the draw. Moments later, at the shrill blast of Gareth's whistle, a flurry of clays flew over the top of the fellside and a barrage of gunshot began cracking around the dale.

From her position behind her table, Delilah tried to tell herself that this wasn't the stupidest thing she'd ever got herself into.

Huddled over his phone in the cramped confines of the Micra, Samson was also kicking himself for an act of stupidity, but of an entirely different nature. He'd left the office in such a hurry, he hadn't thought to grab any sustenance, so now he was stuck on a remote road up on the fells with no chance of getting any supplies. And he was being tortured.

'Stop focusing on the food,' he groaned, as Delilah's spy cam treated him to the array of cakes provided for the shooting party, dipping close to a divine looking tea loaf as she began to cut it, the pop of gunshot audible in the background. The images were breaking up slightly, as though the distance out to the fells was having an impact, but they were clear enough to make him salivate.

God he was hungry. And less than half a mile down the drive opposite, Lucy Metcalfe was baking up a storm in the kitchen of Bruncliffe Manor. The thought of it was agony.

A whimper came from the back seat, followed by a gurgle of canine intestines. Tolpuddle, dreaming, a paw across his nose. Perhaps his stomach was empty too, leading to fantasies of tasty sausages. Or juicy steaks. Although the greedy bugger had managed to get himself two of Ida's bacon butties, so maybe that gurgle was simply one of satisfied digestion.

More in hope than expectation, Samson leaned across to open the glovebox. Insurance documents, a dog-eared manual, a packet of tissues, a ballpoint pen and the tail end of a roll of Polo Mints that looked like they'd got damp at some point.

Faced with Hobson's choice, he seized on them eagerly, fingers working the twist of wrapping to discover three mints. He glanced at his watch, dismayed to see it was still only mid-morning. With the shooting party being treated to five drives spaced out over elevenses, a leisurely lunch and afternoon tea, there was every chance he could be sitting in the Micra for another six hours. So, half a mint an hour.

Samson sighed. Broke a mint in two and placed it in his mouth, throwing the rest on the seat next to him before reverting his attention back to the live feed playing out on his mobile. Delilah had finished setting out the food and was watching the shoot. And he could tell from the way the camera was moving from side to side that she was shaking her head, unimpressed by the abilities of the Bulgarians.

He didn't blame her. The men were haphazard, peppering the sky with erratic blasts, most of the clays flying over their heads unscathed. But at least they were trying. The camera swung to the far peg to show Rick Procter, who didn't even seem to be taking aim properly, firing before the barrel of his shotgun was fully lifted. Either he was a dreadful shot or he was deliberately missing in an effort not to embarrass his guests.

The image froze for a second then restarted, Bernard Taylor now in the frame. There was no play-acting in the mayor's lack of skill with a firearm. Flinching every time the large Bulgarian next to him fired, he had a grip on his gun that even death couldn't have released. And unless Samson was mistaken—

'*He's not shooting!*' Delilah's whisper came over the speaker in a rustle of static, anticipating Samson's own observation. '*Bernard isn't firing his gun.*'

She was right. She was also the only one who'd noticed – Gareth was further down the line with Will and Ash, and the four bodyguards were standing behind the Karamanski brothers. No one was paying any attention to the rotund man at the end who was going through the motions, tracking the clays with his barrel, yet never pulling the trigger.

'*What's wrong with him?*' Delilah muttered into the microphone.

A bark in reply came from the seat behind Samson, Tolpuddle waking up at the sound of her voice.

'It's okay boy,' said Samson, reaching a hand back to pat the dog, focus still on the screen. 'She's not here.'

He felt the wet touch of a nose, the lick of a tongue and then a low whine.

'What's up?' he asked, looking at the Weimaraner now.

Tolpuddle gave another bark and licked Samson's hand again, nose twitching. Hauling himself up from his sleeping position, he stretched forward between the seats. Towards the remainder of the Polos.

'Oh no you don't!' yelled Samson, lunging for the precious rations at the same time.

But the dog was faster. In a blur of grey, he grabbed the twisted end of the wrapper and dived back into the rear of the car.

'That's our only food,' Samson pleaded, trying to reach back to snatch the mints. Tolpuddle wasn't having it. He shuffled to the far side of the seat. Samson resorted to threats. 'Okay, go ahead and eat them. But I'm warning you, that'll be you and me finished. No more stake-outs. No more sleepovers in my office. You'll be dead to me.'

With his head tipped to one side, the dog regarded him solemnly, the mints dangling from his jaws. Then Delilah spoke again.

'*I think there's going to be trouble,*' she murmured, in a voice filled with concern. '*Samson, are you watching?*'

Samson turned back to his mobile as Tolpuddle barked again, the mints falling onto the back seat. But they went ignored. Because Delilah was right. Trouble was about to break out.

If she'd had to put money on where the trouble would come from, Delilah Metcalfe would have placed her entire life savings – which didn't amount to much – on Milan, the tall Bulgarian. Since he'd got out of the Jaguar back at the manor, there'd been an air of malcontent about him, a dark cloud of looming aggression. That cloud had only got more and more ominous as the first drive had progressed and the clays remained untouched by the majority of his shots.

While his compatriots had settled into the sport, getting better with each round they fired, Milan had continued to miss the mark, his reckless style more suited to a shoot-out in a Wild West saloon. Aware he was lagging behind the others, he'd begun grunting his discontent. Then he'd started shouting in Bulgarian at every missed target. Now he was gesticulating at his shotgun, seemingly blaming the weapon for his lack of success. Until he spotted a target that offered more entertainment.

A brown hare, emerging out of the copse onto the fell-side to the left of the guns. Startled by the noise, it stopped, sat upright and turned, ears lifted as it gazed around with wary elegance.

'I think there's going to be trouble,' Delilah murmured, watching a sly smile cross the Bulgarian's face. He reloaded his gun, attention on the hare rather than the blue sky through which the clays were flying, and Delilah went cold. 'Samson, are you watching?' she asked, unable to keep the concern from her voice.

There was no opportunity for a reply, the comms one-way only. All Delilah could do was keep her glasses fixed in the direction of the Bulgarian, and hope that Samson was seeing this too. Fingers clenched on the knife she'd been using to cut the cake, she heard Milan give a roar of delight as he swung his gun across the land towards the creature.

Finally realising the danger, the hare began racing back the way it had come, but Milan was cunning. He fired both barrels ahead of it, between the animal and the cover of the trees. Wheeling around, the hare broke up the hill, across the exposed fellside, legs pushing it on to the safety of the gorse on the ridge as Milan raced to reload. His compatriots were turning now, seeing the live target for the first time. And they were changing their aim too, only Rick and Bernard holding back, a look of distaste on the property developer's face; one of terror on the mayor's.

Six shotguns. One hare.

It wasn't a fair fight.

A hail of shots rang out, Delilah, breath caught in her chest, willing the animal on. Urging it upwards, away from the guns which were firing wildly, her own legs tensed at the effort she knew this uphill dash was taking. The men were shouting and hollering against a volley of gunfire. And over it all, the shrill sound of Gareth's whistle going ignored.

The hare was so close to safety. Only a few leaps away from the yellow flowers of the thick gorse that would allow it to disappear. But the men were determined, adrenalin pumping as they fired and reloaded, Delilah holding her fists clenched, eyes fixed on the fleeing creature—

She didn't see who shot it. All she saw was the brown body flip up into the air and then down, still, the gorse a whisker away. And then the men were cheering and hooting, Milan holding his shotgun above his head in triumph, while an annoyed Gareth tried to bring order back to the group.

'The drive is over!' he was shouting. 'Put your guns down!'

The men were ignoring him, until Niko barked something in Bulgarian and a resentful silence settled on the gathering, shotguns broken and laid over arms as they stared at the gamekeeper.

'What the hell was that all about?' Gareth seethed at Milan. 'No live targets, I said. Was I not specific enough?'

Milan shrugged, not looking apologetic in the least.

'Sorry,' said Niko, smiling. 'It's the red blood, you know?'

Gareth took a deep breath, clearly wrestling with his

temper. Then, with a calm command, he cast his arm out towards the hillside. 'Fetch, Bounty.'

In a streak of muscle, the springer spaniel scarpered up the steep rise straight towards the fallen hare and then gently, almost respectfully, gathered it into her mouth and came back to lie it at the gamekeeper's feet.

'Good girl,' murmured Gareth, patting the dog. He stared down at the limp creature she'd retrieved, and slowly turned back to the men. 'No more bloody live targets. Understand?'

Milan just glared at him. But Niko nodded.

'Right, let's all have a break and try to cool off a bit,' said Gareth. 'I suggest coffee and cake.' He turned his back on the group, heading for Delilah and the table of refreshments, and as his broad back presented itself to the Bulgarians, Milan, like a surly teenager, lifted his right hand into a mime of a gun and mock-fired several rounds into it.

'You okay, Denise?' Ash had moved up next to Delilah, face concerned, almost undoing the tight hold she had on herself and her disguise. She bit her cheek and forced back the anger that was threatening to undo all her hard work.

'Yes,' she murmured. 'Kind of.'

'That was all a bit barbaric,' he muttered with a shake of his head.

She knew what he meant. They'd grown up around guns and had witnessed plenty of shoots. But nothing Delilah had ever seen had been as savage as this. Judging by the disdain on Rick Procter's face as he followed the men to the table, he wasn't enamoured with what had just happened either. But it was Bernard Taylor's reaction that caught Delilah's attention. As the Bulgarians crowded around her, laughing and joking at their prowess, she caught a glimpse of her former father-in-law standing alone at the pegs, staring down at the dead hare with horror, his lips working silently as though he was murmuring a prayer.

For some reason, Delilah didn't think it was for the slaughtered creature.

12

'What the hell are Rick and Bernard playing at, inviting this lot to a shoot?'

Watching the Bulgarians carrying on rowdily as they stood around the table of refreshments, Will Metcalfe was seriously bemused. In all the years he'd known Rick Procter and Bernard Taylor, the men had never put a foot wrong when it came to business. But this was a disaster waiting to happen. One that had already happened, judging by the animated discussion the mayor was having with the property developer to one side.

Face puce, Bernard Taylor was leaning into his business partner in a manner that wouldn't go down well at a council meeting, while Rick seemed to be trying to placate him.

Ash shook his head, equally puzzled. As a carpenter, he'd worked for the Procter Properties group on and off for a couple of years, supplying and fitting bespoke kitchens for their high-end developments. Like his brother, he'd never seen Rick make a mistake when it came to investments or to partnerships. But he was looking at one now. 'I just don't get it,' he muttered. 'That lot don't look like business investors to me.'

'Me neither. Especially not that Milan. That scar wasn't the product of a boardroom dispute.' Will turned his attention to Denise, who was pouring coffee and cutting cake, all the time keeping her eye on the men. 'She's got her head screwed on,' he said grimly. 'Thank God she's here instead of Delilah.'

Ash grunted, and raised his mug to his lips.

'Do you know her?' continued Will, still watching the waitress, unable to shift that feeling of recognition.

Another grunt from his brother, this time with a shake of the head.

'She doesn't remind you of anyone?'

'Nope.' Ash took a long drink, mug lifted high.

Will shrugged. 'Must be just me,' he muttered.

Across the grass, Gareth was approaching Rick Procter, the gamekeeper frowning and tapping his watch.

'Looks like we're about to restart,' said Will. 'I'd best get some of that cake before we're back at it.'

As he walked off, Ash Metcalfe lowered his mug and let the smile he'd been hiding stretch across his face.

Recognise her? He'd known Denise the minute he'd clapped eyes on her outside Bruncliffe Manor – the way she stood, that little tick she had of tipping up her chin when she was trying to be defiant. He'd also recognised the sheer effort she'd had to make in keeping her temper after Milan's callous attack on the hare. But if his brother was fooled, far be it from Ash to set him straight. Their little sister clearly had her reasons for being here in disguise and Ash wasn't about to ruin it by alerting their hot-headed older sibling and creating a fuss. Which is exactly what Will would do if he twigged. And in the current company, creating a fuss and unmasking Delilah could create a situation of the sort none of them wanted.

*

'This isn't something we can rush, Bernard,' Rick was saying, one eye on the man in front of him and the other on the rest of the group, aware of the Metcalfe brothers watching them. He forced a smile. 'As soon as I get the right moment, I'll speak to Niko. But until then, please, leave it with me as we agreed.'

'We agreed that when I didn't know what today entailed,' hissed the mayor, the white patches of strain around his eyes vivid against a florid face. 'So either you tell them soon or I will. I can't keep this up any more. These men . . .' He cast a look towards the group over by the table and swallowed, no need to verbalise the fear that held him as taut as a bow.

'And that is exactly why I need to do this carefully,' murmured Rick, keeping his voice steady. They were at the edge of the abyss he'd foreseen and the weight of his business partner had never felt heavier on his back. One wrong move and they would both be damned. 'I'll do it, I promise. I'll speak to Niko when I get a chance and organise your withdrawal from the business. But this whole shoot was his idea, don't forget. If I'm to have any chance of getting what you want, we need it to go smoothly in order to keep him sweet. So for God's sake, play along for the rest of the day. That's all I ask.'

Taylor made a guttural sound, part terror, part acceptance. Then his shoulders slumped and he nodded. 'I just want out,' he said.

It was the statement of a child. Someone who had no idea of consequences, or of how deadly they could be. Someone who wasn't going to have to clean up the resulting mess.

Conscious of his temper building, Rick was almost relieved to see the large figure of Gareth Towler approaching, a suggestive tap of his watch in the property developer's direction. Despite having no appetite for the resumption of what already felt like the longest day of his life, Rick nodded in response and the gamekeeper's voice boomed out.

'Second drive is about to start. Take your positions please, gentlemen.'

Praying this one would go smoothly, Rick Procter followed the reluctant steps of the mayor across the grass towards the pegs.

'I wonder how Delilah's undercover operation is going,' mused Arty Robinson. 'Do you think she's seeing more action than we are?'

Head propped on a hand, his third cup of coffee in front of him, his second scone already eaten, he was staring out of the window of Peaks Patisserie, the front door of Taylor's not having moved since the receptionist opened up the premises first thing. If it was a slow day for Bruncliffe's property market, it was an even slower one for an amateur detective.

'You'd have to hope so,' said Joseph.

Arty yawned and rubbed his eyes. 'Honestly, I don't know how Samson did this day after day. I mean, it's not exactly high-octane.'

Edith tutted and gave him her 'look', refined over years as headmistress of Bruncliffe Primary School. 'If you'd adhered to the schedule, you wouldn't be here. Clarissa and I were down to do the first shift. You boys weren't meant to relieve us for another hour.'

The boys in question, Arty, Joseph O'Brien and Eric Bradley, totalling over two hundred years on the planet between them, looked bashful. Caught up in the excitement of a stake-out, they'd been unable to resist the lure of joining the sisters at the cafe, throwing Edith's schedule into disarray.

'Besides,' said Edith, with a softer tone, 'where would you rather be – here or at armchair aerobics in the residents' lounge?'

'If he keeps eating cake at this rate, he's never going to fit in an armchair again,' wheezed Eric Bradley.

Arty laughed. 'Good point,' he said, slapping his protruding stomach.

'My Robert doesn't have to worry about his weight,' said Clarissa. 'Which is just as well, seeing as we're going to Bettys for our first date. I'm thinking I'll just have a plate of macaroons . . . or maybe push the boat out and order afternoon tea . . .' Her face had taken on a dreamy smile. 'What would you have, Edith?'

'Neither. I've no time for idle pipe dreaming.' The words came out brittle, casting a pall across the table, Joseph toying with his teaspoon and Eric leaning over to fiddle with his oxygen tank.

Clarissa's cheeks reddened. Her smile dimmed slightly, then grew even brighter as she stood up and excused herself, heading towards the ladies. Arty waited until she was out of earshot before speaking.

'That was a bit harsh, Edith.'

Edith turned to face the three men, no sign of contrition. 'Was it? You don't think she needs telling?'

The men looked at each other, nonplussed. 'Telling what?' asked Joseph.

'That this is all a bit suspect. I mean, the man keeps making all these promises—'

'It's a trip to Harlow Carr and a bite to eat at Bettys,' said Arty. 'Where's the harm in that?'

'The harm is that he might not be who he says he is. And Clarissa is already throwing her heart into this. You know how soft she is. I just don't want her to get hurt.'

'You mean you think he's out to trick her?' Arty had read about such people in the paper. Scamming folk online by pretending to be what they weren't. Conning old dears out of their life savings by offering the promise of romance. Or even love. 'You think this Robert is a cuttlefish?'

Eric let out a snort of laughter. 'Catfish,' he said. 'They're known as catfish.'

Arty shrugged. 'Catfish, cuttlefish, they're both ugly buggers.'

'That's exactly what I think,' said Edith, nodding.

But Arty was shaking his head. 'I think you're over-reacting. A meal in Bettys isn't exactly going to yield much if he is a scam artist.'

'I don't know,' muttered Eric. 'Have you seen the price of the macaroons?'

Joseph laughed but Edith didn't join in, her lips remaining pursed. And Arty realised this was it. This was what had been bothering her. She was fretting about her sister.

'Look,' he said, reaching out to put a hand on her arm, 'if you're that worried, perhaps you ought to do something about it.

'I already have,' said Edith, a hint of red on her cheeks. 'I've asked Samson to look into it.'

The three men stared at her, Arty finally finding his voice. 'You've got Samson spying on your own sister?'

Edith nodded, chin tipping up in defiance.

'So,' asked a breezy voice – Clarissa was sitting back down, 'have I missed anything exciting?'

'Not a thing,' said Arty, turning back to stare out of the window, more concerned about Edith than ever.

By the time Delilah had packed away the crockery and what remained of the cakes, ready to transport everything back to the Land Rover, the second drive was well underway.

It had begun with a truce of sorts. Having reiterated his warnings about shooting live game, Gareth had rejigged the order on the pegs to give each man a turn at the better positions and, so far, everything seemed to be progressing calmly. As calmly as it could when clays were whizzing overhead and a line of men were trying to shoot them.

Stacking the last crate of repacked supplies on the grass, Delilah straightened up and stretched her aching back. The sun was high in the sky now, a fine May day shining down on the narrow dale where the drive was taking place. Sheltered from the light breeze that was wafting soft clouds across the blue above, it was getting warm. In fact, thought Delilah, as she fanned her face, it was getting downright hot.

Blasted padding.

She felt like she was slowly cooking, the huge doughnut around her middle making her combust. Wiping a tissue across her forehead, she was startled to see it come away with a streak of tan across it. Her make-up. The sweat was making it run.

If she had to stand out here much longer, Denise would melt into Delilah.

'Want a hand with that?'

Delilah quickly stuffed the tissue in her pocket before turning to see Will behind her, pointing at the bare table. Not even waiting for an answer, he flipped it onto its side, smoothly folded down the legs and stacked it next to the crates.

Already hot and tired, a familiar flare of annoyance surged through Delilah at his presumptuous manner and she was about to make a sharp comment, but caught herself just in time. She was Denise, a woman working as a waitress for a caterer; not Will's little sister who'd spent a lifetime trying to prove she was his equal. Maybe Denise, flushed with heat and beginning to feel weary, wouldn't mind a little help. In fact . . .

'Thanks,' she said with a wide smile before making a show of rubbing her back. 'I don't suppose you could carry this lot over to the cars for me while you're at it?'

Will smiled back at her. 'Not at all. Glad to be of help. Here,' he said, passing over his shotgun, which he'd been holding broken over his arm, 'look after that for me. And don't worry, it's not loaded.'

Delilah gave what she hoped was a cautious smile and took the shotgun with tentative fingers like she'd never handled a gun before, all the time fighting the urge to grab a few cartridges, snap them in the barrels and show the Bulgarians how to shoot clays.

Another four hours of being Denise. Sweltering in this

plump body, make-up running, eyes irritated by the contact lenses and her head itching like a family of ants had taken up residence beneath the wig, let alone constantly curbing her behaviour. Delilah didn't know if she'd be able to stick it.

Or, to be frank, if it was worth it. She'd seen nothing of note in terms of the Dales Detective Agency investigation and had overheard even less, the one conversation that might possibly have been of interest – the heated discussion between Rick and Bernard – having taken place out of hearing distance when she was busy serving tea and coffee to the others.

Perhaps she should call it quits. Plead a headache at the end of this drive and get Will to drop her back at the manor. Lucy would be glad of the extra help in the kitchen in the run-up to lunch.

Buoyed by the thought that she could soon be shedding her fake persona, padding and all, Delilah turned her attention to the shoot with renewed enthusiasm.

The coffee break hadn't done anything to improve skill levels. She watched with a critical eye as the line of guns fired up at the clays whipping over the fellside, Niko and Andrey by far the best shots, their bodyguards standing alert behind them, no ear defenders, impervious to the loud blasts. Rick Procter was next to Niko, appearing competent as he reloaded and fired in a smooth movement, but still looking like he was holding something back. The rest of the Bulgarians, however, were no better than they'd been in the earlier drive. In fact, if anything, they were slightly more haphazard, snatching at targets and missing wildly, a crazed recklessness to them.

And Bernard Taylor? He wasn't even trying to pretend any more, his gun held down towards the ground, the man twitching at each shot from the men either side of him despite the ear defenders he was wearing.

It would have been better if he'd at least made an effort. Particularly as his neighbour was Milan, who'd once more grown frustrated at his lack of success with the clays and looked to be itching for trouble. As the Bulgarian lowered his gun from a spectacular miss, shouting what were no doubt obscenities in his own language and clearly blaming his weapon yet again, his gaze fell on the immobile mayor and he let out a laugh devoid of humour. He snapped open his shotgun, the cartridges flying out, and quickly reloaded, focus on the mayor the entire time.

Delilah recognised his expression. It was the same look he'd had before he started shooting at the hare; a predator lining up its prey. Sensing trouble, she took a step forward, aware of the useless gun draped over her elbow. Aware that Milan now had a loaded shotgun, which he was swinging to his left. Not up into the air where the clays were. At shoulder height now, pointing towards the rotund figure in plus fours on the next peg—

'No!' she shouted, moving forward in horror.

Her voice was lost in the boom of the gun as Milan let loose both barrels, right across the front of Bernard Taylor's peg.

Down the road in the layby, Delilah's panicked shout had an impact on both occupants of the Micra, Samson snapping upright in his seat, causing his left calf to cramp, and Tolpuddle waking abruptly from his dreams with a confused bark.

'It's all right, boy,' murmured Samson, reaching back to pat the dog gently while simultaneously rubbing his own aching leg muscle.

But it wasn't all right at all. Samson was staring in disbelief at his mobile, the image breaking up but good enough to show Bernard Taylor staggering back from a hail of pellets, a shrill yelp of terror escaping from him as he fell to the ground, seemingly uninjured. In the background, Milan was laughing wildly, impervious to the furious remonstrations of the gamekeeper, who'd brought the drive to an abrupt halt with his whistle.

Jesus! The big Bulgarian was lethal. First the hare and now he'd almost shot someone, and he thought it was just a joke.

The situation was far from ideal. Especially when the camera that was Samson's only link to Delilah seemed to be going on the blink. What if the battery was running out? How long should it last? Or was it internet reception that was the problem?

Having used cheap burner phones for the majority of his life, as befitted his clandestine profession, Samson hadn't acquired much technical knowhow and the person who could tell him the answers to those questions was on the other end of the staccato images.

One last flicker of video and his screen froze.

'Damn it!' he muttered.

He sat there for a few minutes, considering his options. It was so tempting to interfere. A simple text and he could tell Delilah to call the whole thing off. It wasn't like she was getting anywhere in terms of the Taylor case and from what he'd just seen, she was putting herself in jeopardy for nothing. There was no telling what the crazed Milan might decide to do next. And God forbid her disguise should be rumbled . . .

But on the other hand, she was doing so well, handling herself like an undercover professional in an environment that was proving more and more complex. She'd be furious if he suggested she stop now, taking it as a sign he had no faith in her.

It was a risk he'd just have to take, Samson decided. Being on the brunt of Delilah's temper was a small price to pay to ensure she was safe. Keeping his message short and to the point, he sent the text. Of course, whether or not Miss Metcalfe would heed his advice was another matter.

A whimper came from the back seat and Samson glanced over his shoulder at Tolpuddle, the dog looking anxious as though he could sense Delilah was in trouble. And alone.

'It doesn't feel right, does it?' said Samson, scratching the grey head. 'Not being with her.'

Even when they'd been locked in that blasted freezer a month ago, facing an uncertain outcome, at least they'd been together. He'd been able to tell himself he'd done all he could for her. This time he was sitting idle in a Micra over a mile away and she didn't even have her faithful hound with her.

Soothed by the affection, the hound in question began to relax. He stretched. Yawned. And then pushed his nose towards the discarded Polo Mints wrapper, sniffing optimistically. He looked up, eyes forlorn, and a small whine escaped his throat. Another. Then a third, the gap between them getting smaller as the Weimaraner geared up to his infamous howl, which he could sustain indefinitely and which could drive a person to distraction.

'Oh no you don't!' said Samson, recognising the signs of hunger, his own stomach growling in response. 'Come on, let's get out and stretch our legs. Take our mind off food.'

And off the perilous situation that Delilah seemed to have got herself into.

Slipping one of his wireless earphones in his right ear and his mobile in his back pocket so he could at least hear if the camera started working again, Samson got out of the car, the dog scampering after him. A walk. That would do them both the world of good. Without really thinking, he put a lead on Tolpuddle and began crossing the road. It was only as he stepped through the open double gates that he realised where he was going.

Bruncliffe Manor.

He paused, the Weimaraner pulling on the lead and looking back at him, as if Tolpuddle too felt the same urge. Whether the dog's urge was motivated purely by hunger pangs, Samson couldn't say. But either way, his own gut instinct was to head up to the manor. It wasn't an instinct he felt inclined to ignore, even if it ran the risk of wrecking everything, including his relationship with Delilah if he blew her cover.

He glanced at his watch. According to what Gareth had said at the introduction, the shooting party were staying on the fells for elevenses. Which meant the coast was clear. Samson could go up to the manor, beg some sustenance for him and his canine partner from Lucy, and be that bit nearer to Delilah. Maybe get access to the WiFi for better coverage from the camera too. It was the sensible thing to do and not motivated at all by concerns over Delilah's ability to look after herself.

Samson was still telling himself this as he resumed following Tolpuddle up the tree-lined drive.

13

'Give me one good reason why I shouldn't end the bloody shoot!' Gareth demanded, every inch of his huge body radiating anger.

'I can give you a thousand reasons why you shouldn't. In cash. No tax payable.' Rick Procter was trying to soothe ruffled feathers in the only way he knew how. But the gamekeeper wasn't one to be bought off.

'Fat lot of good your money will do me if someone dies out here. I'll be out of a job and stand a good chance of going to court, if not worse. They're a bloody liability, this lot. Not fit to be let out with loaded firearms.'

Rick nodded. The gamekeeper was right. While Rick hadn't grown up around shotguns the way many in Bruncliffe had, and wasn't the best when it came to marksmanship, he knew enough to show respect around them. Niko, Andrey and their friends didn't seem to share that caution. They were behaving like a bunch of hoodlums. Or men who were accustomed to holding all the power.

'I understand. Believe me I do,' he said. 'But I've got a lot at stake here, too. As does Bruncliffe. If I can persuade these guys to invest in the projects I've got lined up, there'll be jobs and financial benefits coming to the town, including here at Bruncliffe Manor . . .' Rick spread his hands in a gesture of altruism, letting the gentle hint sink in, all the while his smooth patter hiding the frantic panic beneath the surface. He glanced to his left, where the rest of the shooting party were gathered around the Jaguars, laughing and joking. Apart from Niko, who was leaning back against one of the cars, watching Rick with that steady gaze, like a cobra planning its next meal.

While Gareth had been confronting Milan over his actions, berating the man for being an idiot and threatening to bring the day's events to a premature conclusion, Niko had walked up to Rick and stood by his side, silent but yet still managing to be menacing. Then he'd spoken, calmly and quietly; the words had been enough to freeze Rick's blood.

'Stopping the shoot would not be good,' was all he'd said.

Rick hadn't needed it spelling out, understanding perfectly who would be the unlucky fall guy in such a scenario. So when Gareth had sent everyone to the cars, Milan throwing his gun to the ground and stalking off without it in a final act of petulance, Rick had lingered behind and tried to negotiate a truce with the gamekeeper. All under the watchful eye of Niko.

The scrutiny was adding extra passion to Rick's plea. 'I'm begging you, Gareth, please. There's more than just a day's fun riding on this. For both of us.'

Gareth took a deep breath, glanced over at the group and shook his head in resignation. 'Okay. But I'm warning you, one more stunt from your trigger-happy friend and the day is over. Understand?'

'Totally. Thanks.' Rick held out his hand to the gamekeeper and noticed a moment of hesitation. As though the man was unwilling to shake hands. It wasn't something that afflicted Rick Procter in Bruncliffe normally, people falling over themselves to acknowledge the property developer, who was one of the town's greatest benefactors. But here was a man who was showing reluctance to press the flesh with him and it was a direct result of the company Rick was keeping.

'I owe you one,' he added, smiling gratefully as Gareth finally grasped his hand.

'Aye, well you can start by picking up that idiot's gun. I'm buggered if I'm doing it,' growled Gareth, before walking off towards the Metcalfe brothers at their Land Rover.

Feeling his grip on the day slipping, Rick turned to retrieve Milan's abandoned shotgun and was met with the steady gaze of the plump waitress, her eyes fixed on him from behind her glasses.

There was something about the way she was holding her head, disapproval in every line of her being. She reminded him of someone.

He stared back until she looked away but even so, he couldn't shrug off the sense that this day was going to be ruinous in so many ways. Even the bloody hired staff had lost respect for him. Associating with Niko and his brother was putting an end to Rick's good reputation in his hometown. But failing to associate with them could put an end to his life.

Back in Peaks Patisserie, things had picked up a bit on the stake-out front. There'd been a steady run of customers coming and going at Taylor's through the mid-morning, the pensioners watching from the cafe now having a good idea of which folk were thinking of buying or selling property in the town. But so far, there'd been nothing that seemed out of the ordinary. It had been enough, however, to distract the group and, apart from the earlier hiccup, Edith's mood was back on form.

Until her sister's phone went.

'Oh, sorry,' Clarissa said, standing, a wide smile lighting up her face. 'That's Robert. I'd better take it.'

She moved away from the table, mobile to her ear as she left the cafe to stand outside, and the clouds descended over Edith. But she didn't say anything. Which meant Arty just had to.

'So what's Samson going to do?' he asked.

Edith shrugged. 'I asked him to run a background check on this Robert Webster. See what turns up. But there isn't much to go on.'

Joseph whistled softly. 'What if Clarissa finds out?'

'She won't.' Edith looked at the three of them. 'I wouldn't be doing this if I wasn't really worried. So I trust I can rely on you to keep it quiet.'

They all nodded. But Arty felt a twinge of apprehension. It was a bit underhand. And Clarissa was such a trusting soul . . .

'Wonderful news!' Clarissa was back, the joy in her voice returning the sunshine to the table that had descended into gloom. 'Robert's taking me on a cruise!'

Edith's head snapped round so fast, Arty was afraid she'd tear a ligament. 'A cruise? Seriously? You've not even been on a date yet.'

Clarissa's smile didn't waver. 'I know! He's so romantic.

Date with Deceit

A trip around the Greek islands. All inclusive. I can't wait. You should see the ship.' She clasped her hands together and sighed happily as she sat down.

Her sister, however, had turned back to look out of the window, a frown darkening her brow.

'This Robert, chap,' asked Arty, for the first time feeling some of Edith's apprehension, 'is he paying for it?'

'Arty Robinson,' said Clarissa with a laugh, 'this isn't the Dark Ages! I'll pay my own way, thank you! Which means I'd best start saving.' She gave another delighted laugh.

Edith's lips compressed even tighter, as though she was biting back a retort. And Arty made a decision. He remembered the last time he'd not taken the concerns of a friend seriously. It had led to a series of dreadful events and nearly cost the lives of two others he held dear. This time, he wouldn't make that mistake.

'He sounds like a great bloke,' he said with a smile he hoped would hide his treacherous intentions. 'What else do you know about him?'

Glad to have a receptive audience, Clarissa began to chat away and Arty felt his heart grow heavy with deceit.

If the weight of Arty's deception was metaphorical, Delilah's was all too real. Out on the fells, a stern-faced Gareth had announced that the shooting party was heading back to the manor for elevenses and, as she clambered into the Land Rover next to Will, she couldn't help but feel relieved.

That last incident had been no joke, no matter how much Milan had found it funny, Bernard Taylor lucky not to have been injured. And for one awful moment, as Gareth

169

confronted the big Bulgarian over his behaviour, Delilah had thought it was going to escalate into something even worse, her brothers moving up behind the gamekeeper in a show of support.

But somehow Rick Procter had smoothed things over and instead of the shoot coming to an early finish as had seemed likely, they were driving back across the fellside in a line of 4x4s, the journey giving everyone the opportunity to cool off.

Cooling off was exactly what Delilah needed. Apart from the day having been wrought with tension, the over-bearing heat being generated by her disguise was wearing her down, beads of sweat slipping between her shoulder blades, the wig making her scalp crawl. She was grateful to be sitting in the Land Rover at the rear of the convoy, window wound down, her face turned to catch the breeze.

And grateful to have come to a decision.

It was Samson's text that had done it. A concise message, urging her to call off the undercover operation on safety grounds, especially when it seemed to be a waste of time. She'd already been considering it, not wanting to be around should Milan decide to go for a hat-trick of idiotic behaviour. But now—

'My sister has a daft dog that does that!' Will's comment, coming out of a tense silence, made her jump. He was looking at her, a small smile breaking up the frown he'd been wearing since he got behind the wheel. 'Sticks his head out the window like that. Only, his ears flop around a lot more than yours.'

Delilah laughed and Will's smile stretched some more. Then he sighed and his features lapsed back into a grimace.

'What a bloody business this is. I can't believe Gareth's still going ahead with it. What the hell is he thinking?'

'That Rick Procter has a lot of power in the town and shouldn't be crossed lightly?' As soon as the words left her mouth, Delilah knew she'd slipped up.

'You know Rick?' Will glanced at her.

She gave a casual shrug, hoping the heavy foundation on her face would hide the heat she could feel stealing up her cheeks. 'I read the *Craven Herald*. He seems to be Mr Bruncliffe. I wouldn't imagine Gareth would want to annoy a person with that much influence.'

Will snorted. 'Bloody high cost to pay if one of them Bulgarians hits something bigger than a damn hare!' He shook his head in disbelief but as he looked at the woman next to him, his tone became gentle. 'Don't take this the wrong way, Denise,' he said, 'but try and stay in the kitchen for the next drive if you can. Be a lot safer than being out on the pegs with this lot.'

Delilah gave a soft laugh. 'You sound like someone I know.'

'Is he wise and knowledgeable, too?' Will was grinning at her now.

'Something like that.' Too choked up to say any more, Delilah turned back to face the open window, marvelling at the irony that it was only when she was in disguise that she could see her brother for who he really was – a compassionate man with a genuine concern for others.

And for once, she had every intention of taking his advice.

In the lead Jaguar, a fraught silence had filled the first half of the journey as the convoy made its way back to the manor. One Rick had been reluctant to break. Sitting in the back with Niko, two bodyguards in the front seats, he felt himself being assessed. He doubted it was positively. It wasn't until they were almost at the end of the rough track that the man next to him spoke.

'Your partner . . .' Niko twisted his right hand and tipped his head. A gesture filled with misgivings. 'He doesn't seem very stable.'

'He's stressed,' blurted Rick, knowing that it wasn't just Bernard Taylor being judged. 'He's got a lot on his plate, that's all.'

Niko nodded. Reached across the central armrest and patted Rick on the hand. 'He needs to be dealt with – and soon. We can't afford loose ends. Or loose mouths.'

Then he flipped up the lid of the armrest and pulled a small bottle of clear liquid from the chiller within. He unscrewed the lid and offered it to Rick.

'*Nazdrave!*' he said as Rick tipped the bottle up and drank. 'Cheers!'

It was like drinking fire. The burn of pure alcohol scorching his gullet, Rick managed a smile, nodded and handed the bottle back.

'Homebrewed rakia,' said Niko, taking a swig. 'The best way to seal a deal.'

With a look of satisfaction, whether at the business or at the drink it was hard to say, Niko placed the rakia back in the chiller and flipped the lid closed, leaving Rick to wonder what exactly was the nature of the deal that had just been sealed. Or if he had the courage to keep his end of the bargain.

*

'You should have pulled the plug,' said Ash, noticing the white of Gareth's knuckles as he gripped the steering wheel of his 4x4.

Almost back at the manor and the man was still seething. Which, even for Ash Metcalfe, one of the most affable men around, was understandable.

'Bloody Rick,' muttered the gamekeeper. 'If it wasn't for him, I would have done.'

'Why does it make any difference that Rick's involved?'

Gareth gave his passenger a sideways look, a russet eyebrow raised in disbelief. 'Come off it, Ash. You know what it's like around here. Rick and Bernard wield a lot of influence when it comes to business in Bruncliffe.'

'And?'

A sigh met the question. 'The Luptons have submitted plans to develop some of the manor's estate on the other side of the road. For lodges and the like, holiday accommodation. They've been doing everything they can to keep the council on side. So if word gets back to them that I cancelled a shoot for the current mayor and his pet developer, they won't look too kindly on it. And I can't afford to lose this job.'

'Is it worth getting shot over?'

'Nothing's worth that,' agreed Gareth. 'But I've told Rick, one more foot wrong and they're all out of here.'

Ash nodded. Then looked at his friend. 'Aye, sounds good in theory. Just wonder how easy it'll be for us to get rid of them if it comes to that.'

A grim look settled on the gamekeeper. 'We'll cross that bridge when we come to it,' he muttered.

'Let's hope we don't have to,' murmured Ash.

With a jolt of wheels, the Land Rover bounced off the track and back onto the main drive, turning towards the large property, its grey stone walls just visible through the trees. Ash twisted in his seat and glanced over his right shoulder at the convoy behind, his brother's battered Land Rover bringing up the rear, and wondered how he could ensure that Delilah stayed as far away as possible from the next drive.

If he'd twisted the other way, he'd have seen a flash of movement in the trees to his left, two shapes diving for cover.

They'd walked up through the trees, staying parallel to the winding drive but keeping as much as possible to the scant concealment offered by the broad limes, Samson presuming that any cars would come from behind, from the direction of the main road. So when the sound of engines burst upon them from a small track that led off the drive, there was barely time to react.

'Down!' hissed Samson, flinging himself to the ground as a Land Rover bumped up onto the tarmac from their right.

Tolpuddle hesitated for a second and then flopped beside him with a soft sigh. While Samson was fortuitously dressed in a forest green jumper and khaki trousers, standing some chance of blending in with the long grass beneath the trees, the same couldn't be said for the grey mass of dog next to him. He placed a hand on the Weimaraner's back, pressing gently until Tolpuddle relaxed onto his side.

Praying that if anyone glanced their way they'd mistake the hound for a lump of limestone, from his prone position,

Samson watched the Land Rover speed past. He caught a glimpse of fair hair, Ash Metcalfe twisted away from them, looking back at the other cars which were following the 4x4.

What the hell? The shooting party. What were they doing back? Had Gareth cancelled it after the last incident?

Cursing his bad luck, Samson kept a hand on the dog as the first of the Jaguars bounced up onto the drive. A low whine came from the Weimaraner.

'Stay,' murmured Samson, patting him softly, focus on the convoy. A familiar face was staring straight ahead from the nearest rear seat: Rick Procter, his profile oozing tension. Then the next Jaguar, the occupants laughing, a familiar scar cutting through the short hair of the man in the passenger seat. No heads turned their way.

The last Jaguar turned off the track. Four people in it, three of them looking up towards the manor. Sitting in the back, however, forehead leaning against his window, Bernard Taylor was staring vacantly out. As the car turned, his gaze skimmed across the grass, over the shape of the man lying on the ground, the dog next to him . . .

'Shit!' murmured Samson, wondering how he was going to talk himself out of what was a questionable situation.

But Bernard's expression didn't change, no shock of surprise registering on the blank features. Instead his focus simply drifted on by, as though Samson and Tolpuddle were invisible and he was seeing right through them.

The Jaguar moved away and the final car came into view – Will Metcalfe's beat-up Land Rover, Will at the wheel, Delilah next to him. Or Denise, because she didn't look anything like Delilah. Samson pressed his body even deeper into the grass, watching the profile of the woman in the passenger seat as the 4x4 swung right, onto the drive. She was looking down at her lap, Will saying something to her. She nodded demurely. Nothing at all like Delilah, thought Samson, suddenly overcome with the urge to laugh. The 4x4 pulled away, towards the manor, and Samson rolled over onto his back, grinning.

He'd missed this. The adrenalin rush of an operation going wrong. The sudden improvisation, the thrill of danger that made your skin go cold and your heart race, the taste of fear at the back of your throat. And then the relief, a dopamine high that made you feel invincible.

A whine came from the grey shape next to him, Tolpuddle nosing Samson's pocket, hopeful of finding a treat. Samson laughed softly and rubbed the dog's head, thinking that he'd never had an undercover partner do that before.

Another whine. Either he got his partner some food or no amount of crawling through undergrowth would keep them concealed once the siren Tolpuddle was capable of let rip.

Getting to his feet, Samson gathered up the dog lead, and set off once more for the manor. Food and information, in that order. Lucy would know whether or not Gareth had called time on the shoot and, as long as Samson was cautious, Delilah need never know he was there until the operation was all over.

Panic had taken hold inside the luxurious kitchen of Bruncliffe Manor. No matter how many expensive appliances or acres of worktop, nothing could help a head chef whose well devised plans had been thrown to the wind. Nothing, apart from more time. And with the Land Rover pulling into sight beyond the tall windows overlooking the court-yard, that time had just run out.

'Gareth's here,' said Ana, glancing up from the mini pork pies she was topping with apple sauce.

'Damn, damn, damn, damn, damn!' Lucy growled. When the call had come through to say that not only were the guests returning to the manor for elevenses, but they were also coming early, the gentle harmony that had reigned in the large room all morning had dissolved into frantic work. And lots of cursing. Most of it coming from the mild-mannered Lucy, much to Elaine's surprise. 'Ana, I need those pies finished and plated up. Elaine, are those aperitifs ready to go? If so, get out into the foyer with them. And where the hell is bloody Delilah when I need her?'

'I'm on my way,' said Elaine, picking up the tray of drinks she'd been preparing and making for the door, relieved to be heading out of the stress-filled kitchen.

'Make sure you come straight back when you've handed them out, too!' Lucy shouted after her. 'I need you in here!'

Moving as fast as she could considering her load – and her tendency to drop things – Elaine made her way through the breakfast room and along the back corridor, coming out into the large space of the foyer. Through the open front doors, she could see the Jaguars pulled up on the gravel beyond the curved portico, Will's Land Rover tucked in next to them, car doors opening and closing as the shooting party got out.

Just in time. She took up her position by the doorway

and at the sound of heavy footsteps crunching across the gravel, held up the tray of drinks and tried not to gag.

Bullshot, Lucy had called the odorous cocktail. Non-alcoholic. It smelt like a cow's backside as far as the geologist was concerned, the waft of beef consommé making her feel vaguely sick. Or perhaps it was the frantic preparations for the returning guests, Elaine having spent most of the last twenty minutes scurrying between the kitchen and the drawing room, laying out the refreshments for the premature break.

'Aperitif?' she asked with a smile as the Bulgarians entered the hallway, the tall one with the scarred head at the front of the group, a scowl on his naturally sullen face. Then she saw he was still carrying his shotgun. 'I'm sorry, sir, no guns allowed in the house.'

There was a sharp comment from the man called Niko, prompting Scar Head to growl something at Elaine in Bulgarian before striding across the hall to stick the gun in the umbrella stand. With a final black look in her direction, he stormed past her into the drawing room. Much to the amusement of the group.

'Sir, sir,' she called out, as the other men crowded around her, laughing and taking drinks, 'you can't leave it there, sir.'

Her words fell on deaf ears, the men following their compatriot into the room, the gun left sticking up out of the ceramic pot, surrounded by a variety of colourful umbrellas.

'Bloody idiot!' muttered Elaine.

'That doesn't narrow it down much with this lot,' came a low rumble from the far side of the hall. Gareth was approaching her from the rear of the house, looking like the world was on his shoulders, his gorgeous spaniel noticeably absent from his side.

'Where's Bounty?' asked Elaine in surprise.

'In the back of the Land Rover, for her own safety.'

'I take it it's not been a good morning?'

The gamekeeper gave her a grim smile. 'That's putting it mildly.'

'Sorry to add to it,' she said, tipping her head towards the umbrella stand, 'but one of the Bulgarians has left his gun over there.'

Gareth groaned. 'Stupid sod. I'd best take it out to the gunroom—' A loud crash came from the drawing room, the unmistakable sound of breaking glass. 'Jesus! What now?'

'Don't worry about the gun,' said Elaine, her heart going out to the beleaguered gamekeeper. 'I'll take it back through with me when I've got rid of these drinks.'

There was a pause, Gareth's brow furrowed as he weighed up her offer against a backdrop of rowdy laughter from his unruly clients. 'Have you handled one before?'

'Yes, although I've happily avoided them for years.'

The gamekeeper's frown eased slightly. 'Thanks, Elaine. You're a star.' He was already turning away to deal with whatever the latest trouble was, leaving her to serve the last few arrivals.

'Aperitif?' she asked hopefully, as Rick Procter and Bernard Taylor crossed the hallway towards her, side by side but not speaking.

The property developer shook his head, stony faced, and as for the mayor . . .

Elaine tried to think of the right expression to describe

the man she was accustomed to seeing full of vigour. Deathlike was the word that sprang to mind, his skin grey, his eyes glazed. It would take more than Lucy's Bullshot to revive him.

Close on their heels was Will Metcalfe, looking thunderous, like the time he'd caught Elaine and Delilah sneaking back into Ellershaw Farm at one in the morning on a school night. Elaine didn't even bother holding out her tray. But behind him was finally a friendly face, Ash Metcalfe, who took a drink, pulled one of her plaits and gave her a wink before disappearing into the drawing room.

Last up the stairs and into the hallway was Delilah, panting slightly and sweating, as though she'd just run up Pen-y-ghent and back.

'What the hell happened out there?' whispered Elaine. 'They've all returned like they've been in front of a firing squad, not out enjoying themselves.'

'You wouldn't believe it,' said Delilah, dabbing her forehead with a tissue. 'It's been chaos—'

'Denise! Elaine!' Gareth's voice called out from inside the room. 'Can one of you come and clean this up, please?'

With a look of resignation, Delilah headed into the room, leaving Elaine to hurry back to the kitchen.

Across the hall, the shotgun remained forgotten in its temporary home.

14

They'd run out of cover. Having reached the last of the majestic lime trees, Samson and Tolpuddle were looking out from behind its broad trunk at the gravel forecourt before them, the cars parked up, the front doors of the manor wide open, revealing the expansive foyer beyond. No one around. But they couldn't stay here. They were too exposed. If anyone came out into the hall or even onto the terrace that swept down the south side of the building in front of the bow-shaped window, they'd be spotted.

The kitchen. That's what they were looking for. It would probably be around the back. Scanning the terrain, Samson's eyes settled on the thick copse that climbed the hillside to the north of the manor. It ran down the full length of the house and would offer the perfect solution, allowing them to get to the back of the building unobserved. But reaching it would be problematic. The expanse of gravel offered no shelter, apart from a hedge which separated it from the sloping pasture to Samson's left and ran all the way round the parking area, almost to the copse. Between the lime tree and the start of the hedge, however, there was nothing but bare grass.

They'd have to make a dash for it, across the grass to the hedge and then crawl along behind it before making a second dash to reach the more substantial protection of the far trees.

A whimper from beside him brought his attention back to Tolpuddle, the dog's nose in the air, catching the delicious aroma of cooking. Eager to sample the origin of the tantalising smell, he was pulling on his lead, glancing up at Samson in confusion when he didn't budge.

'Ready?' whispered Samson, crouching down to the dog's level, lead gathered in his hand.

It was only then he heard it. A tinny sound, like the buzz of a bee in a trapped room. He glanced down and saw his earphone snagged on his jumper. It must have fallen out earlier when he hit the ground. He slipped it back in place and a blast of loud laughter erupted in his ear.

Either he was back within range or Delilah had reactivated the camera – whichever it was, it sounded like the Bulgarians were enjoying the food and drink that had been laid on for them. Then, over the hubbub, a sound that made him freeze. The scrape of a door being opened. And suddenly he could hear voices in both ears.

The men were coming out onto the terrace. He twisted to his right and saw broad shoulders emerging through French windows. One of the bodyguards, his head already turning, surveying the landscape for possible threats—

'Run!' Samson hissed at Tolpuddle, and set off sprinting for the hedge.

Across the grass, totally exposed, the dog racing along beside him, Samson didn't even dare look towards the house. Another couple of yards and they'd be there. Three long strides, expecting to hear a shout at any moment. Then a headlong dive to the ground, a roll and Samson was sitting on the grass behind the hedge, panting, Tolpuddle pulling up sharp next to him, barely out of breath.

'Good boy,' he whispered, and was rewarded with a lick on the ear.

Twisting to face the house, he peered through the thick laurel, the bodyguard now joined by most of the shooting party out on the terrace. Jesus – that had been close.

With a grin, Samson gathered up Tolpuddle's lead and began crawling on his hands and knees along the back of the hedge towards the far side of the gravel forecourt.

'What took you so long?' demanded Lucy as Elaine entered the kitchen, the chef already pointing to several trays of food waiting to be taken into the guests, Ana busy at work preparing more. 'And where the hell is Delilah?'

'She got held up,' said Elaine. 'The Bulgarians have been causing mayhem—' She broke off, an image of the shotgun left amongst the umbrellas coming to mind. 'Damn. Sorry, I've got to go and get something—'

She was already turning, empty-handed, towards the door, but Lucy's tone of voice stopped her in her tracks.

'Don't you dare!' The chef thundered, pointing at the refreshments. 'This has to be taken. Now! And by you, because of my other two supposed waitresses, one hasn't been here all morning and the other can't go in that room because Rick Procter might see her. So whatever it is you have to do can wait—'

'But it's a gun—'

'I don't care if it's a bomb about to go off! I've spent all morning and the best part of three days working to get this ready – an event I wouldn't have taken on but for your insistence – so the least you can do now is get the food in to the guests on time.'

Elaine wouldn't normally have argued. Not with a chef this close to meltdown. But the thought of that gun and her promise to Gareth made her try one more time. 'But Lucy, it's a matter of health and safety—'

Lucy growled.

'I can get it,' Ana interjected. 'I've finished here and I need the toilet. Where is it?'

'Thanks, Ana. It's in the umbrella stand in the hall. Can you leave it out in the gunroom in the stables?' With a cheeky grin and a wink at the irate chef, Elaine picked up two trays and hurried out of the kitchen.

They were stuck behind the hedge. Squatting down on his haunches, Samson was peering through the laurel barrier at the cause of their confinement.

Two of the bodyguards, feeling sufficiently relaxed about their charges in this environment, had wandered down from the raised terrace outside the room hosting the elevenses and sauntered across the gravel towards the cars. At which point they'd promptly lit cigarettes and proceeded to chat.

With the men too close for comfort, Samson had pulled the Weimaraner down beside him out of sight, calling a halt to their journey towards food – much to Tolpuddle's consternation. But the bodyguards were taking their time over their cigarette break.

'Not long now boy, I promise,' Samson murmured, stroking the dog's head.

Tolpuddle replied by issuing a low whine, leaning into

Samson and almost knocking him over. With the beginnings of cramp in his left leg and an impatient Weimaraner next to him, Samson wasn't sure how much longer they could stay hidden.

While Samson was concealed behind a hedge, Ana Stoyanovic was hiding in the ladies' toilets.

She'd tried to time her visit as best as she could, having waited a while after Elaine left the kitchen so that the guests in the drawing room would be preoccupied with the snacks the waitress had delivered, and thus less likely to notice someone walking past. As it turned out, the outward journey had been easy. But getting back to the kitchen was going to prove tricky.

The problem was, the corridor that led out from her current hiding place joined the hall exactly opposite the opening to the drawing room, which would leave Ana completely exposed as she made her way back to the foyer to retrieve the shotgun. Anyone coming out of the gathering would see her. Face on. So she had to get this right.

Peering around the toilet door, she could see the path was clear. So she crossed her fingers and slipped out into the corridor, hurrying towards the grand entrance space, her steps sounding loud on the tiles. Reaching the hallway, she looked to her right. There. The umbrella stand, tucked around the corner. A shotgun sticking out of it.

A burst of laughter came from the open door opposite, beyond which she could see Elaine and Delilah silhouetted against the light streaming in the large bow window, hard at work carrying trays of food around the guests. And there, in the background, Rick Procter, blond hair unmissable as he spoke to two short, thickset men.

It was enough to galvanise Ana into motion. Grabbing the gun, she scuttled across the vast space and back towards the sanctuary of the kitchen, a smile lifting her lips, thinking that she had the makings of an undercover operative herself.

Only she didn't. Because she hadn't looked behind her. If she had done so, she would have noticed the door to the other downstairs toilet easing open. A figure emerging just as Ana turned to take the gun. A figure that saw her profile before she hurried away in a manner that could only be described as furtive.

'Ana Stoyanovic!' muttered Bernard Taylor. For a man already under a lot of stress, the unexpected appearance of a woman who used to work for Rick Procter could only be interpreted in a negative light.

'I've been to funerals that were more joyous,' muttered Elaine as she joined Delilah at the back of the grandiose room that was hosting the shooting party.

She had a point. In the midst of the antique furniture and opulent furnishings of the stately space that looked out through a huge curved bay window over meticulously maintained lawns, the atmosphere was strained. While some of the men had moved through the bay's French windows onto the terrace and were laughing and carrying on loudly, there was an underlying tension between the main protagonists.

Rick Procter was talking quietly with the two brothers, Niko and Andrey, but from the facial expressions, Delilah doubted they were discussing their earlier performances with the clays. From all appearances, it looked like Rick was getting a telling off. And while Gareth was deep in discussion with Will and Ash, it was clear the gamekeeper had a wary eye on his troublesome guests, waiting for yet another ruckus to claim his attention.

'You're not going back out there with these idiots for the next drive, are you?' Elaine asked. She'd been appalled when, in a lull between serving the men, Delilah had given her an edited version of the morning's activity, and that was without even hearing about the incident with the hare. Delilah had deliberately failed to mention it – not out of sensitivity for Elaine so much as for the sake of the Bulgarians. Because Delilah knew Elaine was capable of walking up to Milan and cracking him over the head with her tray if she knew the full story.

'No, thank God,' confessed Delilah, fighting the urge to scratch, her scalp on fire under the wig. 'This is Denise's last outing. I'm officially retiring her once this lot head out on the fells. Although part of me feels I ought to go, just to keep an eye on him.'

She gestured towards the lone figure of Bernard Taylor, who'd just re-entered the room, the rigid set of his face suggesting that he wasn't finding the morning enjoyable.

'What's up with our esteemed mayor?' asked Elaine with a dry tone.

'I don't know. I've never seen him like this. He tore into Gareth before we'd even set off for the shoot and then had a barney with Rick while we were up there. He just seems totally on edge. And being almost shot hasn't helped things. I'm worried about him.'

Elaine snorted. 'I didn't see him showing the same concern for you when you were going through a very public divorce from his cheating son.'

The response drew a shrug from Delilah. 'I know. But he was my father-in-law for a while, for what that's worth.'

'Well, I'm just glad you've seen sense. This lot are dangerous and you'd be putting yourself in harm's way if you went back out there—'

'More food!' came a rough demand from the terrace.

With a smothered sigh, Delilah reached out to pick up a tray of Lucy's fabulous apple-sauce-topped mini pork pies from the table, but Elaine put a hand out to stop her.

'Let me,' she murmured, with a wink. 'You've had to put up with them all morning.'

Delilah wasn't about to argue. She'd had a gutful of the Bulgarian investors and, despite her concern for Bernard Taylor, was glad to know that soon she'd be able to divest herself of the infernal wig and the rest of Denise's outfit. Even in the cool of the room, she was beginning to wilt underneath all the padding.

'Thanks,' she said, leaning over to kiss her friend. 'You're a star.'

'And don't forget it,' retorted Elaine, walking away with a wide grin.

Delilah watched her go, still smiling. Then turned and caught the frowning regard of Rick Procter. He'd moved away from the Bulgarian brothers and was staring at her. Like she was a puzzle that needed working out.

She dropped her gaze and busied herself with loading the empty Bullshot glasses onto a tray, intending to make a hasty exit. But as she turned to leave the room, he was there, in front of her, a hand out to stop her.

'I feel like I know you,' he said, really staring at her now.

'I'm sorry . . .' she spluttered, heat rising through her. 'I don't see how . . .'

'We haven't met before?'

She shook her head, mute with panic, feeling like the disguise had been stripped from her, the tray in her hands beginning to tremble.

'You're sure? Because I'm really good with faces,' Rick persisted.

'I'm sure.' It came out as a squeak, the man still fixing her with that intense scrutiny.

'Funny, because I could have sworn—'

'*Idiot!*'

The loud exclamation came from Milan out on the terrace and was followed by an almighty clatter of metal on concrete as the tray that had been in Elaine's hands fell to the floor, a cascade of pork pies following it, most of them bouncing off the tall Bulgarian's chest in the process.

'Look what you did!' He gestured furiously at his T-shirt, the brown camouflage pattern now smeared with apple sauce.

'I'm so sorry! Let me wipe it!' Elaine offered, glasses askew as she dabbed frantically at the man's clothing with a napkin, knocking something out of his T-shirt pocket in the process and only serving to make things worse.

Cursing fluently in English, Milan swatted her hands away, and looked on the verge of reacting even more violently but for an interjection from Niko. It was quiet and in Bulgarian but whatever he said, it had the effect of making Milan pause.

Which was when Elaine noticed the small plastic bag on the floor.

'I think this is yours,' she said, picking it up, holding it aloft and only then realising what it was.

White powder. In a ziplock bag.

Milan went to snatch it from her, but for a big man Gareth Towler moved fast, crossing the room in long strides to take the bag from Elaine.

'Is this what I think it is?' he growled, the room completely silent now. 'Well? Is it?'

The Bulgarian just stared at him, lips curled in a sneer.

'Bloody cocaine? You've been taking cocaine while we were out on the shoot?'

'It's nothing—' Milan started to say with a dismissive shrug. But the gamekeeper cut him off.

'Nothing? You call nearly shooting someone nothing? You were off your head out there!' He swung round to Rick Procter, who was watching on with a look of disquiet. 'I warned you. One last straw. Well here it is!' He shook the bag of drugs. 'The shoot's off.'

'You can't cancel it!' The shout of protest came from an unexpected source, Bernard Taylor the only person to speak up in the tense silence that followed the gamekeeper's pronouncement.

'Yes I bloody can. And I just have done. So finish off your drinks, get in your cars and bugger off, the lot of you.'

Gareth made to move out of the room but the mayor was persistent, stepping into the bigger man's path.

'I strongly suggest you reconsider!' he snapped, jabbing

a finger in the direction of the gamekeeper. 'Or the Luptons will be holding you to account when their planning permission goes awry.'

Delilah couldn't believe her ears. It was a blatant threat, one that had made Rick Procter blanch. Yet Bernard Taylor, normally a master of small town politics, seemed unrepentant at his crass manoeuvrings, his face contorted in an inexplicable rage. For a man who'd looked like he was under duress for the entirety of the morning, his sudden fury at the thought of the shoot being terminated early made no sense.

'Leave the Luptons out of this, Bernard,' said Gareth, with a quiet calm that belied the tension radiating from him. Placing a firm hand on the mayor's chest, he pushed him aside and strode out of the room.

'I'm warning you, Towler!' Bernard Taylor shouted after him. 'You'll lose your job over this.'

The hush that had held while the gamekeeper was in the room broke in his wake, voices rising, drowning out the mayor who was now being spoken to by an ashen-faced Rick Procter. Delilah felt the breath she'd been holding escape her lungs.

'Bloody hell!' The muttered curse came from Elaine, who'd moved next to her. 'All I did was spill a few pork pies to distract Rick Procter's attention from you and look what happened!'

Delilah's jaw dropped. 'You did it deliberately?'

Elaine nodded, pushing her glasses defiantly up her nose. 'Didn't know this would be the result, did I?'

'You two, okay?' Ash had joined them, one eye on the large Bulgarian who was having a heated conversation with his cousins, dark looks being cast in Elaine's direction. 'Might be a good moment for you both to head for the kitchen. What do you think, Dee?'

Delilah was about to reply when Ash's use of her family nickname registered. 'You know?' she said in a stunned whisper.

'About who you really are? Yes. About why you're in disguise? Not a clue. But I strongly suggest you and Elaine make a quick exit. This isn't the time for someone else to figure out your true identity.'

She could see he was expecting an argument. And under normal circumstances, Delilah would have given him one. But the close call with Rick Procter and the overwhelming desire to shed her false layers swayed her.

'Okay,' she said. 'But if these guys kick off, don't do anything stupid, Ash.'

Ash nodded. 'Don't worry. Will and I won't be taking any chances.'

She gave his hand a discreet squeeze and then hurried out of the room after Elaine, wondering how they were going to break this news to a chef who'd spent hours pre-paring food that was no longer needed.

Ana Stoyanovic was oblivious to the drama unfolding in the drawing room. She was too busy trying to avoid a drama of her own.

The damn shotgun!

She'd carried it through the house and out into the courtyard, only to find that the gunroom, which was located in the old stables, was locked.

What to do? She couldn't leave the gun just lying on the

floor. It would be no safer than it had been in the umbrella stand. But she also couldn't take much longer getting rid of it because a harried Lucy had already banged on the kitchen window, wanting her back at her workstation.

There was only one option.

The gamekeeper's Land Rover was parked on the cobbles. Shotgun held gingerly out to one side, Ana crossed over towards it.

In the rear, a brown spaniel lay tucked up asleep in its cage, head on its paws. Careful not to wake it, she eased open the passenger door and laid the shotgun down on the seat, before gently closing the door again.

That would have to do for now. She'd get Elaine to tell Gareth where it was and the gamekeeper could take it from there.

Another frantic knock on the window from the chef had Ana running back to the kitchen.

Samson and Tolpuddle were still stuck behind the hedge, the dog lying on the grass, head on his paws looking desolate, while Samson was glued to the images on his mobile.

The video had proved compulsive viewing. The cascade of pork pies, the cocaine, the announcement from Gareth and the outburst from Bernard Taylor . . .

Drawing on all of his years of experience undercover, Samson had a horrible feeling that the whole thing was brewing into a potential catastrophe, something far more deadly than events so far. And Delilah and her friends were right in the middle of it.

As were the two bodyguards standing chatting by the Jaguars, muscles bulging under their leather jackets. Jackets which had remained resolutely on, despite the warmth of the day, making Samson wonder if there wasn't a reason for that. A concealed weapon or two, maybe?

What a mess. A bunch of trigger-happy hoodlums strung out on cocaine, who'd just been told to bugger off . . .

The more he thought about it, the more Samson grew concerned. It wasn't going to be easy if the Bulgarians dug their heels in and refused to leave the premises. Not only could Gareth be putting himself in danger, but the Metcalfe brothers and the Peaks Patisserie team, too.

Perhaps now was the time to put in a request for some official reinforcements, just as a precaution? It was amazing how folk calmed down a bit at the sight of a uniform or two.

He was still debating whether or not to make the call when footsteps descending the front stairs made him lift his head to peer through the thick laurel.

Gareth Towler had appeared, a hand to his temple as though his head was throbbing, face like granite. He was speaking into a walkie-talkie. Giving the bodyguards a wide berth, he walked along the front of the house. Towards the hedge.

'Yes, I said cancelled, Tommy. So don't bother setting the next traps. Just get yourself back down here.' With a grunt, the gamekeeper shoved the radio in his pocket and stood for a moment, staring at the ground.

Tolpuddle let out a low whimper of hunger, Samson quickly laying a hand on his head to silence him as loud voices floated out from inside the foyer. The rest of the Bulgarians. Heading outside.

With a weary glance over his shoulder, Gareth resumed walking, picking up the pace before turning down the track on the north side of the building away from his troublesome guests, the curve of the hedge taking him out of Samson's sight.

Make the call to Bruncliffe Police Station or not? Samson decided to give it a few minutes. Give the Bulgarians a chance to go quietly. Which he sincerely hoped they would, because the alternative was too concerning to contemplate.

15

'Cancelled?' Lucy was staring at the two messengers looking like she would happily shoot both of them. Given the news they'd brought with them from the drawing room, it was hardly surprising. 'You're joking!'

'Nope,' said Elaine. 'Gareth shut the whole thing down. Never seen him so angry.'

The chef looked at the range, the pots bubbling away on top, a huge side of beef roasting in the stove. Then she looked at her staff, all three of them finally in the room at the moment they were no longer needed.

'All that work for nothing,' she murmured, slumping against the worktop. 'I need a drink.'

'I'll put the kettle on,' said Delilah, casting a worried glance at Elaine.

'A proper drink,' muttered Lucy, as Ana placed a stool next to her and eased her onto it. 'Something stronger than tea!'

'There's a drinks cabinet in the drawing room,' said Elaine. 'I'll go see what I can find. Back in a sec.'

The door closed behind her and Lucy lowered her head into her hands, letting out a groan. 'I can't believe he's cancelled it.'

Witnessing her sister-in-law's dejection, Delilah felt a pang of guilt. She'd been nothing but relieved since the gamekeeper's decision and, now that she was back in the kitchen, couldn't wait to begin peeling off the layers of her disguise.

'I'm sure Ash and Will would be happy to have lunch before they go,' she said helpfully. 'They'll appreciate all your efforts.'

But Lucy wasn't yet in a mood to be consoled. 'There's enough food for twenty people. Even Ash at his hungriest can't eat all that! God, I knew this bloody event was a bad idea.'

'Couldn't you use the beef cold?' Ana asked. 'In the cafe maybe?'

'Great idea,' agreed Delilah. 'Sandwiches. Or pies of some sort?'

A flash of movement reflected in the stainless-steel splashback caught Lucy's attention and she turned to see Gareth crossing the courtyard, the stress on her friend's face cutting through her own frustrations. The fact that he'd pulled the plug on an event his clients would have paid up to a grand a person for gave some idea of the gravity of the situation.

'Poor bugger,' she muttered. 'It must have been difficult for him to make this call.'

'Bernard Taylor threatened him with his job,' murmured Delilah. 'But Gareth did the right thing. Those men aren't safe around guns.'

The word was like a trigger, Ana suddenly slapping her head. 'The shotgun! Got to go!'

In a whirl of movement, she was gone out of the door.

Lucy shook her head as yet another member of her staff disappeared. 'Next time,' she said, with a smile, as Delilah pulled off her wig with a groan of relief before taking her glasses off and starting to remove her contact lenses, 'remind me to hire proper bloody waitresses!'

With eyes of different colours, Delilah grinned back at her.

He needed to persuade Gareth Towler. Threaten him some more if necessary. Whatever it took to make sure the shoot wasn't cancelled, Bernard was prepared to do it.

Rick Procter had tried to stop him. But the noise of anxiety in the mayor's head was so loud, he didn't hear what was said. Just words. More words. When what was needed was action. If the shoot went ahead, he could be freed from the chains that bound him to the rottenness emanating from his association with Procter Properties. With these men.

That Niko . . . Bernard had never met someone so terrifying. The pressure of his terror was pushing against his chest, making him feel his heart would explode. That something was about to snap.

With only one objective in mind, Bernard Taylor hurried down the long corridor that led off the foyer, the direction the gamekeeper had come from when they'd arrived back for elevenses. He emerged into a room with a dining table, a set of double doors directly ahead, women's voices audible behind them.

Presuming they must lead to a rear exit, Bernard rushed across the room towards the doors. He pushed them open, and froze.

Samson was watching the Bulgarians and growing more uneasy by the minute.

They'd been standing on the forecourt for a while but

were showing no signs of getting in the Jaguars and leaving. And while he didn't know what they were saying, the body language was easy to read, several of the men gesticulating wildly, throwing loud comments back at Ash and Will who were on the front steps, arms folded, heavily outnumbered. Outsized too, even without the big lad, Milan, being in the group, wherever the hell he'd got to.

As for the Karamanski brothers, they were doing nothing to calm their compatriots down. Standing to one side, they were watching on passively, impossible to read.

Samson had seen their likes before. Men who held real power. They were the most dangerous type to deal with. It was that experience – combined with the knowledge that there were several shotguns in the back of each Jaguar, and no doubt cartridges, too – that finally made him reach for his mobile.

Bruncliffe Police Station wasn't exactly buzzing. A couple of calls – a stolen bike that had turned up half an hour later, seemingly taken as a prank, and a missing cat – were all that had disturbed the morning's peace as PC Danny Bradley tried to catch up with paperwork that had been mounting on his desk. Opposite him, Sergeant Gavin Clayton was propped back in his chair, hands resting on his ample stomach, his eyes half closed. Either the boss was almost asleep or he was meditating.

Meditating on all the food he couldn't eat now that he was dieting, thought Danny with a grin.

'What you grinning at, lad?'

Danny looked up to see the sergeant regarding him with a raised eyebrow.

'Nothing . . . that is . . .' Stuttering, a blush stealing up over his uniform collar, the constable was saved by the sharp trill of the station phone.

'I'll get it,' muttered the sergeant, thumping his chair to the ground and letting out a grunt as he stood up. 'Happen it'll be nowt.'

As Sergeant Clayton answered the phone, Danny stifled a sigh and got back to his filing. In the last few weeks, things had been quiet. Too quiet. After the excitement of the previous month with the drama at the auction mart – not to mention the fact that he'd lost his heart to a bewitching beauty – the young constable was finding the days on duty tedious. How he yearned for some action, something that would—

'Speak up, O'Brien! I can barely hear you.'

O'Brien. The name was enough to make Danny look up in hope and stare at his sergeant, who was shaking his head wearily, a hand on his brow as though a headache was already starting at the mere mention of the man who'd turned policing in Bruncliffe upside down since he returned home.

'You're behind a hedge? What the hell are you doing—?' The sergeant frowned. Listening intently.

Danny reached for the car keys.

Delilah was bent over the worktop removing the second contact lens when the kitchen doors flung open.

'Did you find any whisky?' she demanded with a laugh, looking up and expecting to see Elaine in the doorway.

Instead it was Bernard Taylor, his mouth open as he stared at her, the wig on the counter, the discarded glasses next to it, the lens on her fingertip, the padding still around her waist . . .

'You!' he exclaimed.

There was a second of silence, Delilah staring back at him, Lucy casting worried glances between the pair of them. Then Bernard seemed to collapse upon himself, deflating before their eyes, a hand clutched to his chest.

'I can't take any more of this,' he muttered, backing away into the breakfast room. 'First the Stoyanovic woman and now you . . .'

The doors slapped shut behind him.

'Shit!' exclaimed Delilah, still rooted to the spot. Then she popped the lens back in and grabbed the wig, pulling it onto her head, using the splashback behind the range as a mirror.

'What are you doing?' asked Lucy.

'Going after him. I need to explain.'

'Explain what? That you were spying on him? There's no way to explain this, Delilah. Just stay out of it. The damage is already done.'

But Delilah was adamant. She'd seen the look on Bernard Taylor's face. Sensed that he was a man on the brink. She put the second lens back in, shoved her glasses back on, automatically tapped the arm to activate them, and headed for the door.

Delilah Metcalfe! The dumpy waitress who'd been following them around all morning had been none other than Delilah Metcalfe in disguise. Which could only mean one thing.

The Dales Detective Agency was investigating them.

As he staggered through the breakfast room, Bernard Taylor felt a tidal wave of panic crash over him.

He was finished. They knew. About the properties. The drugs. The connection to the Bulgarians. Why else would Delilah be snooping around?

And the Stoyanovic woman too. Creeping around the hallways, keeping herself hidden. Was she in on it? Did she have information from her time working for Procter at that bloody retirement complex?

Collar tight around his neck, he veered across the room and into the dining room next to it, a set of French windows already open onto the rear of the property. Air. He needed air.

He stumbled into the empty courtyard, legs trembling. There was no coming back from this. He was ruined. And suddenly he had a moment of calm acceptance. His fractured mind knew what he had to do. He still had time.

Pulling his mobile out of his pocket, he called her. Two rings and it answered. Voicemail.

'Nancy,' he spluttered, moving towards the game-keeper's Land Rover, opening the driver's door, the caged dog in the back setting up barking but Bernard collapsing onto the seat anyway, before his legs gave way. 'Nancy, I'm so sorry . . . I love you so much . . . I never meant to hurt you.'

Lucy was alone in the kitchen. Again.

With a wry shake of her head at the impulsive nature of her staff, she stood up and returned to work. The meal might have been cancelled, but that didn't mean all the cleaning up would miraculously be done for her. Plus Ana had made a good point. The meat could be used in the cafe. And the desserts, too. In fact—

Her thoughts were interrupted by a flash of brown across the splashback, making her turn to the window, aware of a dog barking frantically out in the yard. She was still turning when there was a loud explosion. It rattled the glass in the long windows and burst violently into the kitchen, making her drop the pan she'd been holding and leap backwards as boiling water and peas cascaded all over the kitchen floor.

Moments later, a woman's scream tore through the air.

A shotgun. Both barrels by the sound of it. Samson was already rising up from behind the hedge, the dog getting to his feet beside him.

He didn't care that he was about to blow his cover. He didn't care that he was still on the phone, Sergeant Clayton's startled squeaks coming out of the receiver.

All he cared about was Delilah.

Then he heard the scream. A woman.

He started running, down along the hedge, Tolpuddle sprinting beside him. Aware that the Bulgarians and the Metcalfe brothers were all running too. Everyone heading the same way, towards the back of the building.

Cutting out through a gap in the laurels, Samson hit the track some distance ahead of the others, Tolpuddle barking now. Another dog somewhere barking too. Then they were round the corner and into the courtyard, Gareth's Land Rover there, a dog in the back going crazy in its cage. Ana Stoyanovic beside the open passenger door, screaming, a shotgun at her feet. Rick Procter. Gareth. Lucy bursting out of a back door. All of them looking at—

What?

On the driver's side. On the floor. A woman slumped over, her shirt covered in blood.

'Delilah!' he shouted, racing towards her. He reached her. Collapsed beside her. 'Delilah?' he said again, this time in a whisper of dread. For if he'd ever doubted the strength of his feelings for this woman, with the prospect of losing her suddenly so real, Samson O'Brien felt his heart lurch inside him.

She lifted her head. Dark shadows under the eyes, cheeks smeared with blood and tears.

'He's been shot,' she said, twisting slightly so he could see the man, head in her lap, her hand pressed uselessly against a large wound in his chest.

Bernard Taylor. An alarming amount of blood under him.

Samson was already raising his mobile to get help, even though he knew it was too late.

16

Down in Bruncliffe's marketplace, blissfully unaware of the events playing out on the hills above them, the pensioners finally had some excitement of their own.

'Oh!' exclaimed Clarissa, reaching for her pen and the notebook in front of her. 'Action stations!'

Three grey heads and one bald one swivelled to look out of the window as a gangly figure approached the door of Taylor's.

'Is that the lad that was nearly killed back in the autumn?' asked Arty, peering at the young man who was now entering the estate agent's. 'In that near miss with a tractor?'

'The very same,' said Joseph. 'Stuart Lister – he's the lettings manager over there. Poor soul got caught up in that whole mess when Samson first arrived home.'

Mess was putting it lightly. Several people murdered, Stuart almost one of them, and a dramatic opening case for the Dales Detective Agency. It had been a homecoming for Joseph's son like no other.

'Subject duly logged.' Clarissa checked her watch and bent over the notebook, the page split into three columns. Carefully writing down the time in the left hand column, she then added Stuart's name in the centre, along with his professional position, and in the final column she wrote 'subdued'.

'Subdued?' queried Arty, glancing at the neat copperplate handwriting. 'What's that about?'

Clarissa shrugged. 'That's how he looked. Subdued.'

Edith nodded. 'Yes, he definitely didn't seem eager to get to work, slouching along like he's got a lot on his mind.'

Clarissa was busy adding Edith's comments to her notes while Arty watched on, incredulous.

'What the hell has any of that got to do with our stakeout?' he asked. 'This is supposed to be an exercise in observation. Not speculation!'

'It's not speculation,' argued Edith. 'Observation is all about noticing significant details. The more meat we can put on the bones of our notes, the better.'

'But you can't just guess at a man's mood by the way he walks,' protested Arty. 'You might as well claim that you can tell a person's character by the way they take their tea. It's illogical!'

Edith pointed to the mug of milky tea in front of her friend. 'I could tell you straight away that you're from Yorkshire just by looking at that. And seeing as you're being stubborn and have yet to buy a round of drinks, I'd say you're living up to that stereotype.'

A laugh from Eric turned into a gasping cough while Joseph smiled, patting an indignant Arty on the back.

'I think the girls have a point,' he said, apologetically.

'Huh!' grumped Arty to his friend. 'So much for male solidarity. You'll be telling me you believe in women's intuition next.'

Joseph grinned and turned back to the window, just in time to see a police car go screeching across the square, lights flashing, its siren starting as it reached the other side.

'Bloody hell!' exclaimed Arty.

Edith Hird didn't say a word about the profanity. She was too stunned. As was the entire cafe. It had to be something very serious indeed to make Bruncliffe's Sergeant Clayton resort to blues and twos.

'What on earth can that be about?' asked Clarissa, face troubled as the siren faded into the distance.

Arty glanced at his friend, both men having the same thought. While Joseph O'Brien didn't know much about women's intuition, something was telling him his own son and the lovely Delilah Metcalfe might be in trouble.

Resurrecting a habit long since idle, he found himself muttering the rosary beneath his breath.

Staring at the Land Rover in the courtyard of Bruncliffe Manor, Sergeant Clayton had never felt more out of his depth.

On the other end of the phone back at the police station, he'd heard everything. The shotgun going off. The scream. The panic in Samson O'Brien's voice before the line went dead. The sergeant had been running for the door, Danny on his heels, not even knowing who'd been shot. That news had come through as they were racing up the steep hill out of town, Danny taking the call.

Bernard Taylor.

Not just shot. Dead. The mayor of Bruncliffe already beyond help by the time the paramedics arrived, the air ambulance not even having to land.

With backup on its way in the form of two detectives and a forensics team from Harrogate, the local sergeant should have been reassured. But, with all due respect to his urban-based colleagues, they wouldn't understand the magnitude of what they were dealing with here.

Not only was the deceased the mayor of the town, but one of the key witnesses – or suspects, depending on what forensics revealed – was none other than Rick Procter, another of Bruncliffe's leading lights. The whole thing was a powder keg, with a lit match being held way too close for comfort.

And at the heart of it, Samson O'Brien and his sidekick, Delilah Metcalfe.

'What do you think, Sarge?' Danny Bradley was by his side, the normal flush of youth that graced his cheeks blanched by the sight before them.

'I think we'd best call Frank Thistlethwaite.'

At the mention of the Leeds-based detective, Danny glanced at his boss. 'You think that's wise? I mean, it's not even his jurisdiction.'

'I'll tell you what's wise – not going on a bloody diet while Samson O'Brien is still in town! Even the mention of his name makes my stomach burn in anticipation of trouble,' snapped the sergeant. 'DCI Thistlethwaite has requested we keep him in the loop about O'Brien and I'd say this is a big bloody loop. So just do as I say!'

Feeling a sense of betrayal, Danny reluctantly did as he was told.

Detective Chief Inspector Frank Thistlethwaite was already out of his jurisdiction when his mobile rang. In fact, he was sitting in the sunshine outside a camping pod a mere seven miles north-west of Bruncliffe. Which meant he was firmly in Sergeant Clayton's patch.

As to what he was doing there? Officially, he was on two weeks' leave, starting the day before. Unofficially? He was keeping an eye on the magnet for trouble that was Samson O'Brien.

The man had got under his skin. A suspended police officer facing accusations of corruption who'd somehow become involved in an unsolved murder in Frank's own city of Leeds – not to mention the drama that had unfolded the last time Frank was in Bruncliffe, O'Brien at the centre of things yet again. There were too many questions left unanswered when it came to him, and Frank wanted to get to the bottom of it all.

That's what he told himself. That his determination to bring down O'Brien might have more to do with the attractions of a certain Delilah Metcalfe, or even residual jealousy from a son whose chief superintendent father had paid far more attention to O'Brien's career over the years than he ever had to his own child's, was something Frank was forced to admit in his more candid moments.

Whatever the real motive, the desire to nail Bruncliffe's reprobate had brought him here. But now that he was in touching distance of the town and the disgraced officer, Frank had been wondering how to proceed with his private investigation.

And then his mobile rang.

Constable Danny Bradley kept it concise. A shooting up at Bruncliffe Manor with both Samson O'Brien and Delilah Metcalfe as witnesses.

Frank hung up, thinking that he should have known not to worry about finding a way to get O'Brien. Because O'Brien had a very good habit of putting himself right in the frame. And with what Frank happened to know was coming down the line in the corruption case, the net was about to close even tighter on the former undercover officer.

They'd commandeered the breakfast room and the dining room for holding interviews, Sergeant Clayton claiming that the proximity of both to the crime scene made this a logical choice. Constable Danny Bradley couldn't help but think that it was also the proximity to the kitchen, and the array of wonderful smells coming out of it, that had swung the decision for his sergeant.

Not that they'd had much time for eating.

By the time they'd cordoned off the Land Rover and calmed down the irate bunch of Bulgarians, who were complaining about being held unnecessarily – Rick Procter's pleas for his guests to be allowed to leave having fallen on the sergeant's deaf ears – the forensics team had arrived. They were closely followed by DCI Thistlethwaite and the two detectives from Harrogate, and the interviews had begun, Sergeant Clayton insisting that himself and Danny provide a local presence across both rooms.

With Gareth Towler and Ana Stoyanovic having already been questioned, and Rick Procter currently undergoing the same under Sergeant Clayton's watchful eye – with DCI Thistlethwaite in attendance – Danny had the pleasure of being on hand for Delilah's turn.

'Miss Delilah Metcalfe?' The detective from Harrogate looked at his notes and then across the table at the woman who'd just entered the room. 'Take a seat.'

Delilah sat, a small smile in Danny's direction. She

looked more like the Delilah he knew, having lost the wig and padding she'd been wearing when the Bruncliffe police arrived. Devoid of the heavy make-up, her face was pale, the strain of the day telling in the dark smudges under her eyes. Eyes which were back to her natural shade.

'So, Miss Metcalfe—'

'Call me Delilah, please.'

'Delilah, then,' continued the detective. 'You arrived on the scene shortly after the shooting?'

'Yes.'

'Can you tell me what happened, from your perspective?'

She shrugged. A bemused look on her face. 'I don't know what happened. All I know is I was heading out towards the courtyard when the shotgun went off. I started running, and then I heard Ana scream. When I got out there, I saw Bernard—'

She broke off. Blinked. And Danny had to fight the urge to console her. Offer her a cup of tea or something. But the detective didn't even pause.

'So Ana Stoyanovic was already in the courtyard when you got there?' he asked.

'Yes.'

'Can you tell me exactly where she was?'

'By the passenger door of the Land Rover.'

'Was the door open?'

'Yes.'

'And was there anyone else in the vicinity?'

Delilah nodded. 'Gareth Towler and Rick Procter were already out there.'

The detective wrote something down and Delilah shot

a glance at Danny. He smiled at her. Tried not to be too disconcerted by the bloodstains on her shirt.

'Right,' said the detective, looking back up. 'The victim, Mr . . .'

'Bernard Taylor,' said Danny, barely managing to conceal his frustration with the out-of-town detective. 'The town's mayor.'

The detective didn't even break stride at the implied criticism. 'Yes, Mr Taylor. What can you tell me about his mood today, Delilah? Did he seem any different to normal?'

Delilah didn't reply straight away, as though getting her thoughts straight. 'He seemed . . . preoccupied. Frightened almost.'

'In what way?'

'As though today had a lot riding on it. You know, in business terms.' She shrugged. 'He just didn't seem himself.'

'And how long have you known Mr Taylor?'

Delilah looked surprised at the question; Danny supressed a snort.

'All my life,' she said. 'He was my father-in-law for a while.'

'Oh. Right.' The detective scribbled away, making notes that Danny and Sergeant Clayton would have had no need for. 'So you know – sorry, knew – him well?'

'I suppose so.'

'Final question,' said the detective, leaning back in his chair to better focus on Delilah. 'Do you know of any reason why Mr Taylor might have wanted to take his own life?'

The last vestiges of colour drained from Delilah's face.

*

'She's been in there a long time,' said Will, looking at his watch.

With their presence still requested by the police, the remainder of the shooting party had congregated on the terrace outside the drawing room, the Bulgarians dragging out chairs to sit on, while Samson and the Metcalfe brothers sat on the steps that led down to the wide expanse of lawn, Tolpuddle lying at Samson's feet. At odds with the gorgeous sunshine and the glorious surroundings, a subdued air had settled on the two groups, the impact of the morning's fatal events sobering even the raucous Milan. What conversation there was, was muted.

'A man's died,' said Ash. 'They're going to want to take their time over this.'

'Going to want to know what the hell Delilah was doing in bloody disguise, too,' Will muttered, the dark mood that had been building in the oldest Metcalfe brother since he'd discovered his sister's subterfuge in danger of breaking.

'They certainly are going to want to know that.' The voice came from behind, Samson turning to see a casually dressed DCI Frank Thistlethwaite coming down the steps to where they were sitting. He leaned against the balustrade, his expression every bit as dark as Will's as he stared at Samson. 'Care to explain?'

'You're a bit off your patch, aren't you?' Samson couldn't help it, the churlish reply rising unbidden at this unexpected arrival. It was the second time in recent months that the Leeds detective had turned up in the middle of one of Samson's investigations. And Samson didn't believe in coincidences.

'I heard it on the radio and I was in the area so decided

to pop up and see what was happening. If that's okay with you?'

'In the area? Or did someone tip you off? I wouldn't like to think you're keeping tabs on me.'

Frank gave a dry laugh. 'Don't flatter yourself. I'm far more interested in Delilah. Which brings me back to my question. What the hell were you thinking, O'Brien?'

Samson dropped his gaze to the floor. He'd been asking himself the same question since the police arrived. When he'd come round that corner into the courtyard and seen Delilah there, looking like she'd been shot, his whole world had stopped. Then training had kicked in. The attempt to revive Bernard, Gareth helping him manoeuvre the mayor out of the car so they could get better pressure on the wound, Lucy and Elaine looking after a traumatised Ana while Delilah gathered the frantic Bounty out of her cage and tried to soothe her. Rick Procter had been the only one to remain frozen, rooted to the spot as he watched Samson's futile efforts, his Bulgarian guests keeping their distance, as though they wanted no part of this drama.

The turmoil had prevented Samson from dwelling on what was actually happening. But now, hanging around, waiting for the police to carry out their enquiries, all he'd been doing was thinking. About Bernard Taylor. About the investigation. And about how reckless it had been to involve Delilah.

He was such an idiot. For the last few weeks he'd been pushing her away because there was a chance his past might come calling and place her in danger. Yet here he was, for the second time in as many months, having thought his worst fears had been realised in an incident that had nothing whatsoever to do with the corruption case being filed against him, and everything to do with him having embroiled Delilah in one of his investigations.

While Frank Thistlethwaite's concern was something Samson couldn't stomach, Will Metcalfe had every right to be angry.

'It was a straightforward case. It wasn't supposed to be dangerous,' Samson murmured.

'Funny how things never turn out that way when you're involved!' snapped Will.

'Give it a rest, Will,' said Ash. 'No one could have predicted what would happen. I mean, Bernard Taylor, of all people . . . Was it suicide?' The question was aimed at Frank.

'Seems that way. Three witnesses all arrived on the scene at the same time, moments after the gunshot. They're all telling the same story. I'd say it's pretty clear-cut.'

'Jesus!' Will ran a hand over his face. 'I just hope for your sake, Samson – but mostly for Delilah's – that whatever you were up to has no connection to this.'

'It can't have,' said Samson. 'Bernard wasn't even aware we were here.'

He said it confidently. But whether he'd fooled his audience or not, he hadn't fooled himself, and he found himself hoping, as fervently as Will, that there was no link between the mayor's death and the Dales Detective Agency's investigation. Because he didn't think that would be something the town of Bruncliffe would forgive very lightly.

17

Sitting at the large table that spanned the length of the dining room, Sergeant Clayton didn't know what to think. On the one hand, things were turning out to be less of a nightmare than he'd first feared. Still a nightmare – the town's mayor was dead, for goodness sake. But with the angle the Harrogate detectives were taking, it would at least be a manageable nightmare.

Suicide was what they'd decided on, having heard the testimony from the key witnesses. It was the sergeant's opinion too. They had three people all stating that the doors on the Land Rover were closed when they got there, Bernard Taylor already shot inside it. At which point Ana Stoyanovic had raced to the passenger door, opened it, and the shotgun had fallen out. The preliminary findings of the forensics team backed up what the witnesses had said. It seemed clear beyond all doubt that Bruncliffe's mayor had taken his own life.

So, pending the more detailed results from the crime scene, it was looking like the investigation could be tied up in a neat parcel. No need to arrest anyone – although they were discussing the steps to take against the big Bulgarian lad who'd been found to have cocaine in his possession. The cocaine that seemed to have kicked the whole thing off. But other than that, it was looking like the incident, while tragic and devastating, wasn't criminal.

And yet, Sergeant Clayton was uneasy. He could tell from the drawn appearance of his constable as the lad joined him in the dining room, that he felt the same.

'What a mess,' Danny muttered, taking a seat next to his boss as the two Harrogate detectives came back in from the courtyard, where they'd been having one last look around the stables and the gunroom with Gareth Towler.

'Look on the bright side,' said the younger of the detectives, his smile jarring with the sergeant. 'Better than it being murder.'

Sergeant Clayton bit his tongue. What did they know? They came from a large town where something like this wouldn't reach into every corner of every home and shake the very foundations. Where there wouldn't be repercussions that would echo down the years amongst people blessed with long memories and a predisposition to condemn. A town that hadn't already been set reeling by murder and mayhem over the last six months. And when you considered who was going to get some of the blame for this latest tragedy – a black sheep cast out fourteen years ago and reluctantly welcomed back only recently. The same person who'd been at the centre of the dramatic events that had rocked the place of late. Forgiveness would definitely be in short supply.

But worse than that was the other person who was going to be implicated. Someone a lot less able to take on the role of town pariah. Someone the community would be horrified to learn was at the heart of what had happened here today. She was one of their own, after all.

'This Delilah Metcalfe,' continued the detective, 'do you think she's right? What she said about the trigger for the suicide?'

Sergeant Clayton nodded slowly. 'I'm afraid she is.'

Afraid, because he knew what would happen when the news broke in the town below. And it would break, because there was no way to stop something of this magnitude leaking out, no matter how much he and his constable tried.

A gentle knock on the door to the breakfast room prefaced a pale face appearing at the door.

'I don't know if this is a good time,' said Lucy Metcalfe, 'but I've got some hot beef sandwiches here if you can manage them.'

One of the detectives was already walking towards her, hands out. 'You're an angel,' he declared, taking the plate of sandwiches from her.

She nodded in the direction of the two local policemen before closing the door behind her.

'Here,' said the detective, offering the plate around, 'help yourself.'

But the sergeant didn't partake. For the first time in his life, Gavin Clayton simply didn't have an appetite.

'Who is she? This Delilah Metcalfe?'

The enquiry from Niko was delivered quietly, calmly, but shot a bolt of panic through Rick Procter just the same. A Rick Procter already teetering on the edge.

He'd just about held it together for the police interview, faltering only on the last question. Had he known anything about the investigation the Dales Detective Agency had been carrying out into his business partner and did he think that could have been a cause for the deceased to take his own life?

The deceased. It had such a permanent ring to it. It had thrown Rick as much as the question, seeing again the figure of Delilah Metcalfe, wig off, glasses abandoned as she held Bernard Taylor in her arms. And then Samson O'Brien hurtling around the corner moments after Rick had arrived on the scene, the private detective clearly having been hiding out somewhere on the premises.

A full-blown undercover operation from the Dales Detective Agency, mounted at a shoot organised by Procter Properties when the Karamanski brothers just happened to be in town. Was it a coincidence? Rick didn't think so. He was damn sure the man next to him wouldn't view it that way either, if Rick were to give a truthful answer to his question.

'Delilah Metcalfe?' echoed Rick, as he took a seat next to Niko out on the terrace, feeling like he couldn't breathe despite the copious amounts of fresh air. 'She's no one.'

'No one?' Niko's tone became frosty. 'She does not seem like no one. Wearing a disguise. Lying about who she is. Do you have any idea why she was doing this?'

Rick shook his head, beads of sweat beginning to form along his hairline. 'Not a clue.'

It was the truth. He didn't know. He only suspected. And he wasn't foolish enough to share that suspicion with Niko Karamanski.

Silence met his reply. A long silence, against the backdrop of the murmuring chatter coming from the rest of the

Bulgarians on the terrace. Rick couldn't understand a word of it. But he didn't need to. There was only one topic of conversation.

'Interesting,' Niko said finally. 'And this man with the grey dog?' He turned his laser-like regard onto the figure sitting on the steps with the Metcalfe brothers, talking to a man Rick didn't recognise. 'Who is he?'

'That's Samson O'Brien. He's . . .' Rick stumbled. How to describe O'Brien and not cause alarm? 'He's a corrupt copper. Kicking his heels in town while he waits for his court case.'

'Samson, eh?' Niko laughed softly. 'He has the look of a rogue policeman. I wonder what brought him here today.' He turned back to Rick. 'Most interesting. I will have to do a bit of research. Find out who these people are, this English "Samson and Delilah". And why they were here. As for the rest of this,' – he cast a hand in the direction of the police cars and the forensic vans – 'it is most inconvenient.'

It was said with typical understatement. A weekend of low-key activity for the Karamanski brothers and their entourage had resulted in a fatal shooting and a police presence. It wasn't something they were going to forget in a hurry. Or forgive.

'I trust I can rely on you to sort it all?'

'Yes.' It was all Rick could manage, a single word, his heart drumming in his chest.

'Good. And as for poor Mr Taylor . . .' Niko shrugged, eyes narrowed as he held Rick in his sights. 'While his . . . unexpected . . . death is of course tragic, it has to be said it is somewhat beneficial for our joint business interests. I hope you understand?'

Rick feared he did indeed understand. All too well.

While Niko was assessing Samson, Frank Thistlethwaite was doing some assessing of his own, his gaze coming to rest on the group gathered on the terrace. 'What's their story?'

'That's the shooting party,' said Samson. 'Guests of Rick Procter.'

'Not local, I'm guessing.' Eyes narrowing, Frank was all policeman now.

'From Bulgaria. They're supposed to be property investors.'

Ash gave a soft snort. 'Mafia more like, according to Ana Stoyanovic. Elaine said Ana "recognised their type".'

Samson's look said it all.

'You didn't know?' asked Ash.

'Not a clue. Did Delilah know?'

Ash nodded and Will's glower got darker. Frank too was staring at him, as though this was yet another fault to lay at Samson's door. Which Samson couldn't disagree with. He'd had his suspicions that the Bulgarians weren't your typical businessmen, but if he'd heard Ana's theories, he'd have insisted Delilah drop her disguise there and then. Delilah, of course, knowing this, hadn't said a word . . .

He felt sick to the stomach at just how much danger he'd put her in.

'Interesting.' Frank had turned his attention back to the camouflaged men. 'Bulgarian mafia, you say?'

'That's piqued your curiosity,' muttered Samson,

observing the DCI in turn. 'Wouldn't have anything to do with the body you found in the Leeds and Liverpool canal? You know, the one that was conveniently wearing my jacket around its neck?'

Samson could tell he'd hit a nerve. Frank stared at him and then gave a reluctant nod.

'You're good, O'Brien. I'll give you that.'

Samson shrugged. 'I find that being falsely accused of murder makes you develop an interest in a case. Going to tell me what you're thinking?'

A dry laugh came in response. 'You might be good, O'Brien. But you're a copper currently on suspension, so forgive me if I don't share details of an ongoing investigation with you. Now if you'll excuse me, I'll go have another chat with those who *are* here in an official capacity.'

The policeman turned to leave just as Will got to his feet, a hand raised in the direction of the main entrance.

'Delilah!' he said.

The figure that had appeared underneath the portico turned towards them. She looked so small. Without the padding and the wig and with that look of shock. She started to move towards them, her face blank. And then Samson realised she was crying. Tears tracking down her cheeks. Her appearance was enough to still all conversation, every man turning to watch her.

'It's my fault,' she said, as she reached the terrace, Frank by her side now, Samson unable to move, knowing that if he moved at all, he wouldn't be able to stop himself taking her in his arms. 'It's all my fault.'

'It's no one's fault,' Frank was saying, an arm going around Delilah's shoulders. 'You can't blame yourself.'

But she wasn't even aware of him or her brothers or the Bulgarians and Rick Procter, who were all listening. She didn't even seem to see Tolpuddle, who had trotted over to her with a low whimper and was leaning into her legs. The only person Delilah was focused on was Samson, staring at him, her eyes wide with panic, cheeks wet with her tears.

'He saw me,' she whispered. 'Bernard saw me just before he killed himself. He knew I'd been in disguise. That's what made him—' She broke off, a hand going to her mouth.

'Christ!' Will turned to Samson, furious. 'What the hell have you done?'

18

At first it was a trickle, coming down from the hills in a stuttering dribble of information. A phone call to Peaks Patisserie to alert family, the details – sketchy as they were – passed on to the group of pensioners still sitting at one of the tables. There it would have rested, held back by a dam of propriety that resisted the urge to gossip. But that phone call wasn't the only source of particulars relating to what had occurred up at the shoot. For in a town like Bruncliffe it's impossible to stem the flow of news and, before long, other rivulets were springing up: a comment in Whitaker's newsagents about the number of emergency vehicles seen heading up the hill; a sighting of the air ambulance flying away, bright yellow against the blue sky; a report of Nancy Taylor dropping her shopping basket in the Spar and running out, mobile to her ear, face blank with shock; and the clincher, a conversation between Mrs Pettiford and her niece, who happened to be dating a paramedic, in which it was mentioned that there'd been a call out to a shooting at the big house above Bruncliffe. The victim had been dead on arrival.

These trickles merged rapidly, running together to form a beck and then a stream, continuing to grow, swelled by rumour and speculation, until the town was awash with the news.

Bernard Taylor had been shot up at Bruncliffe Manor and had died.

The town went into a frenzy. Their mayor. Killed. Nothing like this had ever happened before in the collection of houses and businesses nestled beneath the limestone crag. The sense of shock had people gathering in groups, lingering in the marketplace to talk in low voices, casting sympathetic glances towards the double-fronted Georgian house overlooking the square that was the Taylor residence. There was no sign of movement from within. And no one was brave enough to go knocking.

By the time the two people working in Taylor's Estate Agents got wind of what was happening, it was early afternoon. Stuart Lister, caught up in his own worries about the irregular letting practices he'd uncovered, had spent most of the morning viewing potential rental properties and then a fretful couple of hours back at the office trying to concentrate, but flinching every time the front door opened. He was staring blankly at his computer monitor when the receptionist, Julie, burst in from the street and nearly killed him with fright.

'Oh my God!' she exclaimed, unaware that her colleague had gone an ashen shade of grey and clasped a hand to his chest at her dramatic entrance. 'Mr Taylor!'

Stuart felt a bolt of panic follow on from the fright. 'What . . . what about him?' he stuttered.

'He's been shot!'

Julie was in front of him now, expecting some sort of reaction, a sense of alarm to mirror the distress on her own face. But his brain was still dealing with it all. Putting it together with the unorthodox files he'd unearthed in the filing cabinet in Mr Taylor's office, and making no sense of any of it.

'Did you hear me? Mr Taylor's been shot at that shoot Rick Procter organised and they're saying he's *dead*!'

'Oh,' Stuart managed at last. 'Right. Bloody hell.'

While the lettings manager was trying to get his head around these startling new developments, across the square in Peaks Patisserie, Peggy Metcalfe was trying to clear what had become very muddy waters. But it was a slow process when the flood was already in full spate and the likes of her current customer were doing nothing to help the situation.

'It was suicide!' Mrs Pettiford declared, standing sideways on to the counter so she could assess the impact of her announcement on the entire cafe – the group from Fellside Court listening intently. 'Another one!' she added, with a regretful shake of her head, as if, after two such deaths in close proximity, Bruncliffe was somehow at risk of an epidemic.

'Suicide?' queried Peggy. 'Are you sure?'

Mrs Pettiford nodded. And then leaned forward to finally release the information she'd been hoarding for several days. 'And I'll tell you why – Nancy was leaving him!'

Peggy took a step back, as though to remove herself from the contamination of the other woman's gossip. 'I'm sorry, but I don't hold truck with such talk. The man is only just dead. It's no time to be speculating, either about the nature of Mr Taylor's death or the cause—'

'I'm not speculating! I got this information straight from the horse's mouth—'

A gruff laugh cut across Mrs Pettiford, Arty Robinson showing no shame at his rude interruption. 'I reckon you don't know one end of a horse from another,' he barked, sending Eric Bradley into a laughter-induced coughing fit, 'because you're talking sh—'

'Enough, Arty!' Edith Hird silenced him with a sharp rebuke, her eyes twinkling all the same. 'I think you're trying to say that perhaps Mrs Pettiford has the wrong end of the stick.'

'Aye, just not in such posh terms,' growled Arty in Mrs Pettiford's direction. 'Happen as Peggy's right. This is no time for your gossiping. If you've nowt constructive to say, bugger off!'

Mrs Pettiford was staring at the former bookie, jaw slack with incredulity at his language and his message, while young Nathan had walked around the counter and was now holding the door open, a huge grin on his face. With a humph of displeasure, Mrs Pettiford stalked out of the cafe.

'That woman!' exhaled Peggy, shaking her head before giving Arty a grateful smile. 'Thanks.'

'Any time,' he said.

'Could she be right, though?' asked Nathan. 'Could it have been suicide?'

'We'll find out soon enough,' said his grandmother. 'I'm just grateful Delilah and the girls are okay. Honestly, I don't know how she does it. Even when she's only wait-ressing she manages to get mixed up in a drama.'

A strained silence fell on the table by the window.

'What?' asked Peggy, noticing the looks darting between the group of pensioners. 'What's going on?'

Arty glanced at Edith, who nodded. The town was going to find out soon enough. And better the truth be told than to have the place drowned under a deluge of hearsay. They beckoned Peggy and Nathan over, out of earshot of the other customers.

'Delilah wasn't just waitressing,' Arty said in the grave tone of a newsreader with unpleasant facts to impart. 'She was up there in disguise, working on a case.'

Peggy stared at him and then slowly lowered herself onto the nearest chair. 'She was on a case?'

Arty nodded, casting a hand around the table. 'Same as us. That's why we're here. The Dales Detective Agency was investigating Taylor's.'

'I knew it! I knew you were on a stake-out!' exclaimed Nathan, grinning.

But the lad was young. He didn't yet see the implications of Arty's confession. For Peggy Metcalfe, however, there was no need to spell it out.

'You don't think . . . Could there be a connection?' she asked, looking horrified.

None of the pensioners replied. They just stared at each other, the same grim worry replicated on every face around the table.

If the town was in tumult, it was as nothing compared to the maelstrom currently besetting the passenger in the red Micra as it wound its way down the fellside in the afternoon sunshine. Delilah Metcalfe could barely lift her head to look out of the window, such was the burden of guilt she was carrying.

She'd been responsible for the death of someone. She

knew it, no matter how much Samson or Lucy or any of the others had tried to tell her otherwise. She'd seen the look on Bernard Taylor's face in that moment when he'd realised who she was. When the significance of who'd been following him around the fellside that morning hit home. And he'd gone straight out to the Land Rover and shot himself.

Nothing anyone said could change that. Or make Delilah feel better about it.

'Are you sure you don't want me to drop you and Tolpuddle off at home?' Samson glanced at her as they turned onto Back Street, the dog leaning forward from the back seat to nuzzle her on hearing his name.

Delilah nodded, stroking the grey head now on her lap. The last thing she wanted was to go back to her cottage. She'd grab a shower and change at the office and try to bury herself in work. Anything but be left alone with her thoughts.

Thoughts that kept going back to that Land Rover . . .

The Harrogate detectives had greeted her confession about why she'd been at the shoot and how she suspected she'd been the trigger for the terrible event that followed with indifference, as though, now that criminal acts had been ruled out as the cause, the why was of no significance. If anything, they seemed to view the reasons for the Dales Detective Agency's investigation as a convenient bow to tie the whole thing up: a man, suspecting his infidelity had been uncovered, took his own life. Case closed. And while they'd asked for a copy of the video footage from her spy cam, she sensed watching it wasn't going to be top of their list.

Not so Sergeant Clayton and Danny Bradley. Delilah could tell they appreciated the magnitude of her revelations and the impact this would have on the town, and her place in it. The sergeant in particular had showed unexpected solicitude as he made sure that she wasn't heading home alone. Like he was worried there might be another suicide before the day was out.

Her brothers, too, were concerned for her welfare. Once he'd calmed down, Will had put pressure on her to go back with him to the farm, Ash agreeing that it might be for the best. While they hadn't stated it explicitly, she knew that they were both worried about the reception she'd get in Bruncliffe when news broke about her part in what had happened today.

But Delilah wasn't a coward. If the town was going to condemn her, she'd take it on the chin. Especially when she felt their condemnation was justified.

As the car drove along the familiar stretch of Back Street, however, she felt herself shrinking at the prospect of facing the people who populated the shops and houses they were passing. Her misgivings were only exacerbated when they reached the Fleece, Samson pulling the Micra into the kerb opposite. He hadn't finished parking before there was movement across the road, the pub door opening, Troy Murgatroyd appearing in the doorway. He wasn't the only one. Barry from Plastic Fantastic had walked out onto the pavement at the sound of the car, face full of curiosity. And in Shear Good Looks, the hair salon on the other side of the office, Delilah could see several people peering out of the window.

'Thanks,' she said, turning to Samson as he switched off

the engine. 'For driving down but, even more so, for being there.'

It was something they hadn't yet addressed – Samson and Tolpuddle's timely arrival at the scene of the shooting. Clearly they'd already been in the vicinity, keeping tabs on her progress. But far from being annoyed, Delilah had just felt a surge of relief when she'd seen them in the courtyard.

'I didn't like the look of those men,' said Samson with an apologetic shrug. 'It wasn't that I thought you weren't capable or anything . . .'

'I'm glad you were there, whatever the reason.' She managed a smile. Then she sighed, a knot of tension in her chest at the thought of getting out of the car. 'Best get this over with and face the public.'

'Just ignore all of them.' Samson laid a hand over hers, squeezing her fingers gently. 'What they think doesn't matter. It's what you think that counts.'

Delilah shook her head, as much to free her eyes from the tears that were forming as to disagree. 'That's the problem,' she said, struggling to stay calm. 'I'm thinking exactly what they're thinking. And I hate myself as much as they do.'

Samson O'Brien didn't know what to do for the best. He'd been like a rudderless ship since Delilah had walked out onto the terrace of Bruncliffe Manor in a daze of distress. All he'd wanted to do was gather her to him and tell her everything was okay. But he'd just stood there, hating himself for having brought such trouble into her life.

Why the hell had he agreed to let her be part of the investigation? And in disguise, of all things! He hadn't needed Will Metcalfe to point out how irresponsible he was. He knew. It had been written all over Delilah's face as she stood there doing her best not to break down completely, the weight of her remorse an almost visible load on her bowed shoulders.

And now? Getting out of the car in Back Street under the scrutiny of the neighbours, he just wanted to shield her from it all. Because he knew what it felt like to be the centre of attention in this town. Yet still he did nothing. Simply walked ahead and opened the office door, like it was a normal day, some part of him telling him that this was the best course of action. Keep her occupied. Get her focused on something else. Because the despair he saw in her eyes terrified him.

'Have you got a minute?' he asked, as she entered the hallway behind him, Tolpuddle right next to her, grey head nudging her leg. The Weimaraner hadn't left her side since she'd joined them on the terrace, proving a far better source of solace than Samson. 'Perhaps when you've showered? There's something I'd like your help with.'

It had come to him on the drive down. The request from Edith Hird that he hadn't found time to deal with. Running a background check on a possible scam artist would take Delilah's mind off the day. And offer no risk.

She nodded, a perfunctory response, no flicker of interest. Until a deep cough came from behind the closed door of Samson's office, making her jump.

'There's someone—' Delilah's observation was stalled by Samson's hand across her mouth.

'Shhhh,' he murmured. 'Stay here.'

Creeping across the tiled floor, he leaned in towards the door panels, pressed an ear against the wood. Movement from inside. Someone pacing around. Judging by the heavy tread, someone of size. Friend or foe?

Despite having been wrong on occasion – thanks to the ridiculous Bruncliffe tradition of folk walking into places uninvited – Samson wasn't willing to take the risk. Not when he'd been warned that danger was coming. Slowly turning the handle, he eased the door open and then sprang into the room.

'Jesus!' Interrupted in mid-pace, the large man over by the window staggered backwards, tripped on a bit of torn lino and fell flat on his backside. From his undignified position, flat cap in hand, he stared up at Samson. 'Christ, lad! Tha fair startled me!'

'Makes two of us,' said Samson, taking in the checked shirt, the pressed trousers and the polished leather boots.

No foe. No friend either, the man's bushy black beard and weathered face not one he recognised. But definitely a farmer and in his auction-mart-best clothing.

'What are you doing here?' Samson asked, offering a hand to the man.

A firm grasp caught hold of his – the strength and roughness of it suggesting Samson's guess as to the profession of his unexpected visitor was spot on – and the man got to his feet, brushing off the seat of his trousers.

'Why, the same as thee, lad,' he said with a bashful grin, rubbing a hand through the thick thatch of his hair. 'Happen as I'm looking for a bit of love!'

A hiccup of laughter came from the doorway. Samson turned to see Delilah watching him, amusement briefly lighting up her face. And then behind her, the hollow-cheeked features of Ida Capstick appeared.

'Tha's found him, then,' she stated, making Delilah jump a second time at her unexpected arrival.

'Apparently so,' muttered Samson, still none the wiser.

'I was talking to Delilah, not you,' retorted Ida. She tipped her chin in the direction of the man, who looked as baffled as Samson did by the current proceedings. 'This is Mr Lee Iveson. From Muker.' The cleaner managed to make the village from a northern dale sound like an insult. 'He's a client.'

'A client? For me?' Delilah looked at the man and then back at Ida. 'I don't understand. I didn't have anyone booked in.'

'And that right there is the problem,' muttered Ida. 'Phone's been ringing non-stop since I got here this morning. Near drove me mad. So I answered it. In fact, I've been answering it the entire time since Samson left. Tha's got a stack of messages upstairs and then this fella, here.' She gestured at Mr Iveson again. 'Happen as he couldn't wait so I asked him to take a seat down here while I manned the phones.'

'Wait for what?' asked Samson.

'Why, love,' said Ida, the words sounding incongruous coming from her pursed lips.

'I read the article,' Mr Iveson finally spoke. 'That's why I'm here. I want thee to do the same for me.'

'What article?' Samson asked, wondering if he was the only one who felt like he'd fallen down the rabbit hole.

'Here.' The man reached into his back pocket and pulled out a rolled-up copy of a magazine. One Samson remembered from his youth, his father reading it religiously every Friday. 'That, right there.' Mr Iveson jabbed a sturdy forefinger at the glossy page. 'That's what I want.'

Delilah stared at the magazine and groaned. Plastered across a double-page spread of *Farmers Weekly* was Clive Knowles, farmer and Delilah's most recent client, looking freshly washed and dapper in a knitted jumper. The happy man depicted in the photograph was a far cry from the unkempt, lonely – and it has to be said, somewhat pungent – soul who'd first darkened her doors two and a half months ago, demanding she find him a wife. Beaming into the camera, this new-look Clive had his arm draped around a sour-faced woman whose attempt at a smile was far from comforting, Carol Kirby revealing she shared her cousin Ida Capstick's aversion to attention. According to the in-depth feature, the farmer had found love and a prospective partner, thanks to none other than the Dales Dating Agency.

From Delilah's office upstairs came the familiar jangle of the phone.

'Like I said,' muttered Ida, glowering in the direction of the noise, 'tha's got a stack of messages. And happen as that blasted phone won't stop ringing. If tha's going to be gadding around the countryside putting thyself in harm's way, than tha needs a receptionist.'

But Delilah was shaking her head, the spark of life of moments before extinguished. 'I'm sorry, Mr Iveson, but I really can't see you now. I'm going to have to reschedule—'

'Rubbish!' Ida interjected. 'Tha's said thyself tha's got nowt in the diary. Get thyself up and showered and out of them mucky clothes and I'll make Mr Iveson a cup of tea while he's waiting.'

Mr Iveson had been watching the exchange with a look of bemusement, his uncertain gaze now settling on the large blemish that had dried a rusty colour on Delilah's shirt.

'Is that blood?' he asked, nervously.

'Ketchup,' snapped Ida. 'Now come on,' she chided Delilah, motioning her towards the stairs. 'Get a move on.'

Delilah looked about to rebel, but then she simply sighed and beckoned her latest client to accompany her up to her office, Tolpuddle a grey shadow by her side.

'Thanks,' murmured Samson, as Ida made to follow them.

Ida turned to him, her expression softening. 'It's all over town,' she said, 'what happened up there. And folk are saying it's Delilah's fault.'

'It isn't—'

She cut him off with a snort. 'Tha doesn't need to tell me that. And don't go thinking it's tha fault either,' she added, a firm finger pointed in his direction. 'That lass makes her own decisions. But guilt has a way of taking over a mind left idle. Happen as those of us who hold her dear need to keep that from happening.'

Having delivered the longest speech Samson could ever remember her giving, with a final nod, Ida stomped off in the direction of the ringing phone, her footsteps heavy on the stairs. Samson was left alone in his office. He sank into the chair behind his desk and stared blankly through the window.

Looking for love. That's what Mr Iveson had presumed

when he'd seen Samson. And now Ida was talking about holding Delilah dear . . . Was it that obvious? The torment his heart was currently being put through?

Christ! Head pounding, he covered his face with his hands and let out a groan.

'Am I interrupting?' The voice came from the hallway and made Samson shoot up in his chair. 'Sorry. Didn't mean to startle you, but the front door was open . . .'

If his head had been hurting before, seeing the mass of blonde hair and the serious face of DC Jess Green, his suspension support officer, didn't help any.

'We really need to talk,' she said, closing the door behind her as she entered the office to take the seat opposite him.

Samson could tell from her expression that his day wasn't about to get any better.

19

Forty-three prospective new clients. It was like Christmas come early.

Showered, changed, and a cup of Ida's well-brewed tea to hand, it hadn't taken Delilah long to get ready to deal with Lee Iveson. Sitting in the armchair in the corner of her office, the farmer on the sofa opposite, she'd taken down his details and given him a run-through of how the Dales Dating Agency app worked, all the while Ida manning the phone at the desk in the background. Then, with her new customer fully signed up and on his way, Delilah had turned her attention to the messages her impromptu assistant had been taking.

All recorded in a neat no-nonsense script, devoid of curls and flourishes, each of Ida's notes included a name, a number and a handful of details.

Farmer. Reeth. Divorced.

Farmer. Clitheroe. Bachelor.

Farmer. Scarborough. Desperate . . .

As sparsely worded and to the point as their scribe, the messages detailed interest from around the country, not just the Dales, some of the callers from places as far away as Cornwall and Inverness. All of them were looking for the same thing. The very thing Lee Iveson had mentioned when Delilah had asked what had brought him to her door.

'Why, tha understands farming, lass,' he'd said. 'Tha knows what it takes to live this life. It's no good me finding some fancy lady from a city who loves me back but can't stand the smell of cows. Or is afraid to muck-in at shearing time. What I need is a woman who loves both me and what I do. And that's a big ask. I figure as tha's best placed to help, seeing what tha did for this fella.'

With that, Mr Iveson had gestured at the radiant features of Clive Knowles, still smiling out from the pages of *Farmers Weekly*. Staring at the pile of messages now in her hand, Delilah didn't know whether she should curse or kiss her former client for his glowing review of what she'd achieved for him. Not that she'd achieved much, if truth be told, her suggestion that he employ Carol Kirby as a housekeeper having been a practical necessity in the attempt to find him a partner, given the appalling state of Mire End Farm; a practical necessity which had somehow blossomed into romance.

But whatever the reality, the free publicity would either be the making or the breaking of her dating agency. Because there was no way Delilah could field the phone calls, enter client data in the system, set up the online profiles and monitor the dating app if the current stream of enquiries continued. She'd be snowed under within days. The only way she was going to be able to capitalise on the boost Clive Knowles's article had given her business was to expand. To take someone on. And take on all the risk that entailed, too.

'Tha's going to need help.' The sharp comment from Ida echoed Delilah's thoughts.

'Yes,' said Delilah, getting up from the armchair and

crossing to the desk where Ida was writing up yet another message. 'I think I am.'

'Has tha got someone in mind?'

'Not a soul. I wasn't expecting this. I guess I'll stick a note up in Whitaker's and put the word out on social media, see who turns up.'

Ida gave a grunt of disapproval. 'Tha'll need someone hard working.'

Delilah nodded.

'Someone tight-lipped too, given the personal nature of this. Don't want a Mrs Pettiford type who'll be blathering on to all and sundry about tha private affairs.'

'Yes.'

'Happen they should be punctual, too. And tidy. Not like there's a lot of office space.'

'Yes.'

'And able to make a good brew.'

'Ye—' Delilah paused. Stared at Ida. The cleaner glared back at her, at her most ferocious, which was always a sign that she was feeling vulnerable. And the penny dropped. 'You aren't thinking . . .'

'If tha's offering, I'm accepting.' Ida nodded, firmly. 'Happen I do three mornings a week to start off with. See how we rub along together.'

'Oh. Right. I mean . . .'

Ida waved a hand in Delilah's stunned direction. 'No need to talk pay right now. Tha's had a rum day and I've got to get on. Got cleaning to get done over at the bank. Let's sort it next week.'

And with that, Ida tidied the desk, gathered her coat from the back of her chair and headed for the door.

'Monday, then,' she said. And with what could have been described as a smile, she headed off down the stairs.

Delilah stared after her and wondered how it had transpired that Ida Capstick had just interviewed herself for a job as Delilah's assistant. And given herself the job to boot.

The heavy clomp of Ida Capstick coming down the stairs and exiting the building could be heard through the closed door of the ground-floor office. But Samson barely registered the fact. He was too busy trying to digest the latest bombshell that had hit his life.

'You don't have a lot of time to prepare,' DC Green was saying, a frown of concern on her young face as she leaned across the desk towards him, blonde hair escaping from the clasp pinned to the back of her head, a file spread open in front of her. 'You do understand that?'

It was the understatement of the year. The investigating officer overseeing the corruption charges – charges of the gravest manner which alleged Samson had been stealing drugs from the evidence locker and selling them on through criminal networks – had put the case forward to the Crown Prosecution Service. And in a lightning-fast move, the case was coming to court in twelve days' time.

Samson was struggling to take it in. Only three weeks ago he'd contacted DC Green, wanting to move things along, to get it all resolved and the threat against him removed so he could let Delilah fully back into his life. But this . . . it was a shock. The week after next he'd be going down to London to face criminal charges in a courtroom. Not an internal police enquiry, which would have been bad enough, but a real-life court case, with him in the dock.

'I'm sorry. But it didn't help that you missed your misconduct hearing . . .'

The exasperation in Jess Green's voice was audible. She sat back, staring at him, an eyebrow raised in expectation, waiting for an explanation as to why he'd not made it to the appointment with the investigating officer back in March, his absence another black mark against him and the trigger that had led to the case being passed to the CPS. So far Samson had refused to offer any excuses.

That wasn't about to change.

Because he didn't trust her. He didn't trust anyone within the institution he'd been so proud to be a part of. Not since his old boss, DI Warren, had revealed that someone within the system was setting Samson up, the text three days ago reiterating that warning.

So Samson remained silent.

'Bloody hell!' Jess Green stood up. Glowering now. The look out of place on her sweet face. 'You were the one who wanted this sorted. You were the one begging me to help. But how can I help you if you won't talk to me?'

'Thanks, but I've changed my mind. I don't need your help after all,' muttered Samson.

'Right! In that case, I can't do any more.' She slapped the file closed, shoved it in her bag and pointed at the letter in front of him. 'You have the date for the start of the trial. Try not to miss it.'

She was already striding towards the door. He managed to get there just ahead of her and pull it open.

'Sorry if you had a wasted journey,' he said.

DC Green stared at him. Shook her head. 'You need to wake up, Samson. Because you are in so much trouble. And by the time you realise that *I'm* the one you can trust, it will be too late.'

A noise on the stairs made them both turn to see Delilah there, holding a solitary mug of tea in her hand, Tolpuddle on his lead beside her. While she'd showered and changed, her hair still damp on her collar, the impact of the day's events were there in the smudges beneath her eyes. Samson felt a tangle of love, desire and guilt.

'Sorry, I didn't know you were here,' she said, speaking to DC Green. 'I've just made Samson a brew before I go home. Happy to get you one—'

'I'm not staying, either.' Jess Green jerked a thumb over her shoulder in the direction of Samson, standing in the doorway to his office. 'Perhaps you can talk some sense into him before you go. God knows I can't!'

With one final glare back at the man in question, DC Jess Green strode to the front door and let herself out of the building.

'What was that all about?' Delilah was staring at him now.

Samson made a gesture of dismissal with his hand. 'Nothing much. Just an update.'

She kept her gaze on him. He held it. And smiled. There was no way he was going to add to the stressful day she'd already endured by telling her now. He'd break the news after the weekend, when she'd had a chance to come to terms with what had happened at Bruncliffe Manor.

'Thanks for this,' he said, taking the mug from her before adding with a grin, 'How was Ida's telephone manner? Did she scare off all your prospective clients?'

A ripple of laughter met his questions, the sound

making Samson's heart feel lighter than it had in hours. 'You're never going to believe it,' she said, 'but she seems to have appointed herself as my new receptionist.'

Samson laughed and gave a fake shudder. 'God forbid!'

She smiled at him. Then she gathered up Tolpuddle's lead and turned towards the back door, taking a deep breath as though about to face an ordeal, her expression sombre once more.

'You're off then?' he said lamely. Reluctant to let her go in this state.

She nodded. 'It's for the best. I'm not able to concentrate.'

He gestured towards his office, making one last attempt to detain her. 'Have you got time to go over something with me before you leave? It's a case I could do with a hand with.'

She was shaking her head before he'd even finished speaking. 'No more cases, Samson,' she said gently. 'I think I've caused enough damage pretending to be a detective.'

He started to protest but she just held up a hand to silence him.

'Don't,' she said. 'I know you're trying to make me feel better. But the truth is, we both know that I'm right. Bernard Taylor would still be alive if it wasn't for me.'

'You can't say that for sure!'

She didn't argue. She didn't even get mad. She just gave a resigned nod of her head, and began walking down the hall towards the back porch, Tolpuddle following her. She'd reached the kitchen when the doorbell chimed, a fist thumping the door at the same time, as though the bell wasn't sufficient for the urgency of the situation.

'What now?' muttered Samson, turning towards the commotion.

Their latest guests weren't waiting, however, the front door thrust open before Samson could reach it, revealing Arty Robinson and Edith Hird.

'Didn't want to hang around out there,' said Arty, hustling Edith into the hallway ahead of him and then closing the door. 'Didn't want folk seeing us. But we really need to talk to you.'

'I'm sorry,' Edith was saying over him, 'it's not a great time, I know, but I'm so worried—'

Delilah was standing in the kitchen doorway, watching. Already pulled in by the distress of the former headmistress. 'What on earth is the matter, Edith?' she asked.

'It's Clarissa,' said Edith. 'I think she's got herself in a bit of a pickle. I mentioned it to Samson a few days ago, but now . . .' She paused, Arty patting her arm as she struggled to keep her composure.

Delilah was walking back up the hallway, instinctively coming towards the older woman, unable to bear her anguish. Samson could have told her to go on home, not to worry about it. But he didn't. He let her be drawn back into Bruncliffe life. Into his life. He even threw out a hook of his own.

'Actually,' he said, 'this is more Delilah's area of expertise. I just haven't had a chance to talk to her about it yet.'

Edith leaped on his words, hope in her voice. 'Is that right, Delilah? Will you be able to help?'

She was no fool, this partner of his. With a wry glance at Samson, she bent down to untie Tolpuddle's lead. 'Perhaps,' she said, 'once I know what it's all about. So why

Julia Chapman

don't we sit down and you can bring me up to speed while Samson makes us a cup of tea?'

As Edith and Arty led the way into the office, Delilah turned to Samson, one eyebrow raised. 'Are you sure you want me helping on a case?'

'Never been more certain,' he said with a smile, before heading upstairs to put the kettle on.

20

'Tell me everything you know about him.' Delilah had her notepad on her lap, pen ready, as she sat across the desk from the pensioners.

She'd listened in silence as Edith had filled her in on her suspicions about one Robert Webster, the man Clarissa had suddenly welcomed into her life. Suspicions that Arty Robinson now seemed to share.

'We don't have much,' he said. 'And what we do have is possibly a pack of lies anyway. Apparently he's in his mid-seventies, he was a commercial pilot for one of the major airlines, and he lives in Leeds.'

'And he likes ballroom dancing, hiking, and, from what we learned today, going on cruises.' Edith's tone was dry.

Delilah was shaking her head. 'This is all so vague. I'm afraid there's not much here if we're going to prove he's a catfish.'

'Catfish?' Samson queried. Having fulfilled his duties as tea boy, he'd been letting Delilah run the show, glad to see her animated with something other than remorse. But at the unusual terminology he spoke up.

'Someone who adopts a fake profile online with the intention of scamming others,' said Arty, with a know-ledgeable grin.

Delilah smiled. 'Excellent definition. But like I said,

we're going to need more if we're going to determine whether this Mr Webster is actually just a sham.'

'Like what?' asked Edith.

'The name of the online dating agency Clarissa used would be a great start.'

'It's called Silver Hearts.' Edith's mouth twisted in distaste as she said it. 'Always thought it sounded a bit tacky.'

'Silver Bullets would be more appropriate, given the bloody vampire they've got on their books!' muttered Arty.

Delilah laughed, making a note. 'Great. I'll get hold of Robert Webster's profile picture and maybe get something from his personal statement. A way he has of phrasing, which, if he is a catfish, he might have used for other personas on the same site.'

'People do that?' asked Samson. 'Set up multiple accounts to trap folk?'

'Oh yes,' said Delilah with a grim look. 'There's money to be made from these type of scams and the more bait you have in the water, the more likely you are to hook a victim.'

Edith looked worried. 'So do you think the cruise could be the hook you're talking about? Is that how he's going to con Clarissa?'

'Possibly. It's a classic trick – a trip of some sort that requires a deposit. And then the balance paying in full . . .'

'And all the time he's putting that money into his own bank account,' growled Arty.

'Goodness,' said Edith, her thin features looking even more gaunt with concern. But Arty had taken hold of her hand.

'Don't worry,' he said. 'Delilah will get this sorted. She's an expert in this field.'

A brief smile flickered across Delilah's lips at the compliment. 'Let's hope your faith is justified,' she murmured, before a frown settled on her forehead.

'I take it Clarissa doesn't know you're here?' Samson asked, filling in the silence his partner had slipped into.

'She thinks we're reporting back on the stake-out,' said Arty.

'What stake-out?'

'You know, for the Taylor case . . .' Arty trailed off and there it was. Right in the room. The reference to everything that had happened.

As Delilah's head dropped lower over her notepad, Samson could have kicked himself. He'd completely forgotten he'd assigned the pensioners to watch the estate agent's, simply as a diversion to keep them amused. Yet more people he'd unnecessarily drawn into this investigation that had turned so sour.

'Sorry,' he said. 'I forgot to ask. Things have been a bit . . .'

Arty waved a hand in the air. 'No need for apologies. We didn't see much of note, anyroads. And by the way,' he said, addressing Delilah now, 'we've heard the rumours doing the rounds. And for what it's worth, they're a load of bol—'

'Rubbish, I think you mean!' interjected Edith, with a glare at Arty. She turned back to Delilah. 'He's right, though. Whatever you might be thinking, dear, you had nothing to do with Bernard Taylor taking his own life.'

Delilah grimaced. 'I beg to differ. As would a lot of folk

out there.' She cast a hand towards the window and the town beyond it.

'Yes, well, there's plenty out there willing to cast stones while living under a glass roof,' retorted Edith with a disapproving sniff. 'Doesn't mean they're right. If what's being said is true and Bernard was having an affair, then it was his own guilt that killed him. You shouldn't be shouldering any of that blame. So,' she concluded, leaning across to tap the notepad in front of Delilah, 'forget about what people are saying and give this your best effort please. I really need your help.'

Delilah nodded like a dutiful pupil and Samson could have hugged the sharp frame of the former headmistress.

It was early evening by the time Edith and Arty finally left. As Samson closed the front door behind them and went back into the office, Delilah looked up from the desk with a smile and he was aware of only one thing.

He didn't want her to go home. And that emotion wasn't purely motivated by concern for her well-being.

'Fancy going to Rice N Spice?' he suggested.

He might as well have lit a fire under her.

'No, sorry,' she said, the smile slipping from her lips as she stood up and reached for Tolpuddle's lead. 'Not tonight.'

'Come on,' he cajoled. 'It's Saturday evening.'

'I can't,' she muttered. 'I just can't face anyone right now.'

'How about a takeaway, then?'

But the damage was done, her mood descending back towards melancholy. 'Another time, maybe.'

He nodded, not wanting to push her any further, despite the ache at the thought of her going home alone. He watched her bend over the dog in his bed in the corner to gently wake him, Tolpuddle stretching and yawning, looking as eager to leave as Samson was to have the pair of them go.

'I'll see you Monday,' she said, leading the sleepy Weimaraner towards the back porch.

Samson walked with them, hoping for another interruption. But the doorbell remained silent and they reached the back door undisturbed.

'Right then,' she said, stepping out into the yard, the late sun glinting off the Crag that swelled up out of the fellside above them, the evening golden. 'Have a good Sunday.'

She'd taken a couple of steps towards the gate before he spoke, the words bursting out of him.

'Delilah. I'm sorry!'

When she turned, her expression was one of exasperation. 'It wasn't your fault,' she said. 'It was my idea to go undercover, so there's nothing to apologise for.'

'Not that. Not today. I'm sorry for how I've been treating you lately.'

Delilah blinked. Looked away and then back at him, eyes narrowed. But she didn't speak.

'It's just . . . I don't know . . . I was trying . . .' He spoke in a rush, in staccato half-formed sentences. And all the time he kept seeing her there, by the Land Rover, the blood on her shirt, those dreadful moments when he'd thought he'd lost her. 'I was trying to protect you.'

'Protect me?' Her eyebrows shot up, eyes huge now. 'From what?'

'My past.' He grimaced. 'DI Warren didn't just give me that emergency phone when we met up last month. He also gave me a warning. He said I should be careful with those I . . . care about. That what's coming for me could hit them too.'

She was really staring at him now, her chin tipping up, a flare of temper building in her tired eyes. 'You mean this last month when you've been giving me the cold shoulder, that was because you were trying to protect me?'

'Yes.'

'Really? Because last I looked, the definition of protect didn't include hurting someone.'

'I'm sorry. Honestly. I just didn't know how else to keep you safe—'

'Christ!' She spun away from him, fists clenched by her sides, and Samson wondered whether this had been a sensible time to try and clear the air. A Metcalfe was a dangerous beast at any time. When wounded and tired, they were particularly volatile.

'I didn't want you hurt,' he soldiered on. 'I don't want you caught up in what might be coming so I tried to keep you at a distance. It was the only option. Can't you see that? And then when I saw you today in the courtyard . . . I thought you were dead.' The last words almost choked him.

She whipped back to face him. 'Who the hell do you think you are? My brother?'

Samson shrugged, suddenly unsure that this was the wisest course of action and unable to say anything more. Because the next thing he said would wreck their friendship forever.

'Here,' she said, taking two steps towards him, reaching out and pulling his face down to hers. 'Protect this!'

And right there, in the back yard, underneath the looming Crag, Delilah Metcalfe kissed Samson O'Brien. On the lips.

He felt the world expand and contract, everything pulling back to this one moment, the taste of her, the passion that made his head spin, the joy that fired through his cautious heart—

'Bloody idiot!' Delilah abruptly broke off, still glowering, and stormed off towards the gate, leaving Samson staring after her, stunned.

What had just happened?

The gate shot open, and Delilah disappeared into the ginnel, Samson left alone in the courtyard with Tolpuddle, the dog watching him, one ear cocked in what looked like sympathy. Before he too ran off.

Samson stood there for a moment, the Crag turning a burnished gold above him. But he may as well have been blind. For in his mind's eye, he was seeing Delilah, reaching up on tiptoes to kiss him, her hand behind his head, pulling his lips down to hers.

With a rueful shake of his head, he turned his back on the golden limestone and went inside the office building.

As the sun shone its late light on the Crag, it left in shade the narrow ribbon of Back Street. And while the steep gables of the gothic townhall in the marketplace were golden tipped, the double-fronted Georgian house on the far side of the square had long been cast in shadow. Not that it mattered. The curtains were already drawn.

The sole occupant sitting at the kitchen table, sobbing.

Across the square, oblivious to the glorious shades of bronze on the rock above the town, Stuart Lister was leaving Taylor's Estate Agents, his mind in turmoil as he pulled the door closed behind him and turned the key. His responsibility now, locking up, since his boss had killed himself. It was something the young lettings manager was struggling to come to terms with. And somehow he couldn't help thinking that this latest shocking development was linked to the anomalies he'd uncovered in the agency's files.

Head down, deep in thought, he walked by the now-closed Peaks Patisserie, Peggy Metcalfe alone inside as she wiped down the last of the tables. His movement past the window caught her eye and she glanced up, and saw the Crag, spotlit in splendour. She stood there, marvelling at it, her anxiety about her only daughter quelled for a couple of minutes. Then her concerns for Delilah resurfaced and, with a shuddering sigh, Peggy Metcalfe resumed her work. And her worrying.

While the sun had left behind much of the town, restricting itself to the higher points as it dipped below the fells to the west, the large balcony of one of the apartments on the first floor of Fellside Court was still blessed with its warmth. There Edith and Clarissa were hosting the rest of the amateur sleuthing team after their long day on stake-out in the cafe. Despite the copious amounts already consumed, with mugs of tea to hand they were discussing the latest news. For there was much to discuss. So engrossed were they in their analysis of the events up at Bruncliffe Manor and the rumours that had flooded the town, they failed to spot the man leaving the police station at the bottom of Fell Lane.

After many hours in Sergeant Clayton's office, doing what he could to help the local force with what was a major incident, Frank Thistlethwaite was glad to be out in the fresh air. Pausing at the corner of Fell Lane and Church Street, he lifted his face towards the Crag and nodded in appreciation.

At least, that's what it would have looked like to any casual observer. In actual fact, he barely registered the brilliant effect of the reflected sun on the limestone. Instead he was accepting the possibility that the shooting incident that morning, with its Bulgarian clients there at the invitation of Rick Procter, could somehow be linked to the murder he was trying to solve: that of an unidentified Eastern European, found strangled with a jacket last seen at a house in Leeds being developed by Procter Properties. In that single nod, DCI Thistlethwaite was also accepting the inevitable. That Samson O'Brien was somehow the key to all of this. With much food for thought, the detective made his way towards his car.

He wasn't the only one dwelling on the Dales Detective Agency's owner. On the other side of town, alone in his east-facing kitchen, which had lost the sun hours ago, Rick Procter had a whisky in his hands as he reflected on how close things had come to falling apart, all thanks to bloody Samson O'Brien.

O'Brien and the meddlesome Nancy Taylor – it was all over town that she'd set the detective sniffing around, unaware of the fates she was tempting. Or the dire consequences it would have for her own husband. To think everything Rick had built up had almost been scuppered by a jealous wife!

In truth, he should have been feeling relieved. A quiet conversation with Sergeant Clayton after Delilah Metcalfe's dramatic appearance on the terrace – Rick taking on the role of a concerned businessman, afraid of being tainted by a corrupt partner – had seen the copper assuring him that the investigation O'Brien had been carrying out had been into the mayor's private life. Add to this the fact that Taylor's unexpected demise was, as Niko had said, beneficial – no more loose talk about Pete Ferris or pressure to sever links with the Karamanski brothers – and Rick really should have been celebrating. While the shoot may have ended in disaster, he'd dodged several bullets.

Yet he couldn't shake the feeling of disquiet that had been with him from the moment Samson O'Brien came running into the courtyard, shouting Delilah's name. In those seconds, when Rick had realised the true identity of the woman called Denise, he'd felt sick. And while he hadn't been the focus of O'Brien's spying mission, he wasn't out of the woods when it came to the fallout from the disastrous day.

Rick drained the glass of whisky, placed it on the granite worktop and stared at his mobile. An hour ago Niko had called from Mearbeck Hall Hotel, quietly furious. The police had politely asked the Bulgarians to stay in the area for a few days, pending further investigation. Therefore, in light of the unwelcome attention currently on the brothers and their entourage, the scheduled inspection of their joint business ventures would have to be cancelled.

In the calm and measured way he had, Niko also informed Rick that he was to get his house in order or the Kara-manski brothers would send in a cleaning team. One capable of a deep clean.

The meaning was clear. Make sure there were no loose ends. No evidence left lying around that could tie Bernard Taylor to the operation being run by the Bulgarians. Rick had immediately thought of the filing cabinet in his part-ner's office, where the foolish estate agent had insisted on keeping the records for the phoney rentals he'd established. Rentals which were vital for laundering the proceeds of the drugs business being carried out in isolated properties across the Dales and beyond.

No amount of warning had changed Taylor's mind, the man convinced that the filing cabinet was the safest place to keep the files, claiming that his staff were too scared of him to access it, and too incompetent to under-stand what the files contained if they did stumble on them. Now it was Rick's job to go and retrieve them. A call to Nancy would do the trick – apologise for intrud-ing on her grief and persuade her that there were documents relating to the sale of some of Procter Prop-erties' developments in Bernard's office that Rick urgently needed, and gain access to the premises as a result. For now that would suffice. But long term, there would have to be changes. Radical changes. Because the other thing Rick couldn't stop thinking about was the manner of his partner's death.

Since returning from the shoot, he'd done everything he could to make sure there was no reason for Bruncliffe to question the notion of their mayor committing suicide.

Delilah Metcalfe stepping forward to take a share of the blame had played nicely into his hands, offering a distraction, giving folk a focus for their gossip. He'd happily added fuel to those fires where he could, taking the time to talk to people in the Spar, in the pub . . . Throw in some casual comments in the right ears about Nancy Taylor having hired O'Brien, and the image of Taylor as a cheating spouse taking a drastic way out became more than credible.

Because it had to be credible, if Rick was to survive.

Knowing he'd never been in more danger, Rick Procter picked up the whisky glass and flung it across the room.

At a distance too far to hear the resulting crash and with nothing stronger than a cup of tea in front of her, DC Jess Green was sitting in the sunshine on the terrace outside her hotel. It was a spa hotel, one that wouldn't normally be within budget. But with staying in Bruncliffe not an option, given that she wanted to be under the radar, she'd had no choice but to book into the larger premises on the outskirts of the town.

With hers the only table still capturing the sinking sun, she could have been forgiven for wanting to bask in the last of the day's warmth. But that hadn't been her consideration when choosing where to sit. She'd simply gone for privacy, choosing the spot furthest from the hotel's patio doors and from the two men at the only other occupied table, who were having a serious conversation in what had sounded like an Eastern European language to her untrained ear.

Mobile in hand, she was speaking quietly, providing an update on her meeting with Samson O'Brien.

'He was shocked. Like you'd expect,' she said.

'He doesn't suspect anything?' asked the voice, the same one she'd been reporting back to for months now.

'Not a thing.'

'And the woman? Do we need to worry about her?'

'Delilah Metcalfe?' DC Green cast her mind back to the strained features of the figure on the stairs. To the look Samson O'Brien had given her. The man might be one of the best undercover operatives the NCA had ever had, but in that moment, he'd been unmasked. 'She won't be a problem. If anything, she's his Achilles heel.'

'What about the shooting?'

'What shooting?'

A noise of impatience interrupted the usual calm tone. 'There was a fatal incident at Bruncliffe Manor. O'Brien was on the scene. He didn't mention it?'

'No.' DC Green couldn't keep the surprise out of her voice. She should have been used to her co-conspirator's omniscience, the insider knowledge that had proven the bedrock of their operation. Yet it had thrown her. Like bloody O'Brien had thrown her. 'He didn't mention it.'

There was a long pause. The information being digested. Then a sharp statement. 'He still doesn't trust you.'

There was no way to deny it. Three weeks ago, DC Green had been confident she'd won him over, that late night phone call from him, pleading with her to sort out the case. But today the stone wall had been back up. Bottom line was, Samson O'Brien had no faith in her.

'I'm working on it,' she protested. 'But it takes time—'

'We don't have time. If he doesn't trust you, that's a problem. A problem with only one solution. Understand?'

'I understand,' she said.

A murmur of satisfaction down the phone. 'So we're good to go, then?'

'Totally.' DC Green watched the sun finally dip below the hills, casting her table into shadow. 'O'Brien is never going to make it to court.'

21

She'd kissed him.

He'd been desperately trying not to think about it, the way she'd made him feel in that brief moment of pure joy. Before she'd walked away and left him standing there in the fading daylight of the back yard, feeling like she'd taken the sunshine with her.

What the hell had that been about? Did it mean anything? Or was he getting ahead of himself?

Sunday morning, at an hour even church-goers would have considered early, Samson was astride his Royal Enfield, riding out the Horton Road, relishing the sound of the engine, the sharp blue of the sky, and the brooding mass of Pen-y-ghent rising up from the fells on his right.

Anything but dwell on the thoughts that had been plaguing him all night.

Thanks to a combination of Bernard Taylor's suicide the day before, the news about his court case, and that bloody kiss from Delilah, he hadn't slept much. And when he had drifted off, he'd had tortured dreams which had concluded with him in a prison cell watching Delilah walk away with Frank Thistlethwaite. Waking up to the first trill of birdsong, alone in his bed in the top room of the office building, Samson had known that there was no point trying to go back to sleep. A ride out on the Enfield had seemed like a good alternative.

The bike swept around the last curve of the Horton Road and the long span of Ribblehead Viaduct came into sight, arching across the dale below. Samson rode to the T-junction and stopped. Not a car in sight. No coffee van either. With the bike idling, he sat there, staring at the immense structure that blended in so well with the landscape.

But he wasn't seeing it. He was seeing Delilah. The curve of her lips when she laughed. The tilt of her chin. That way she had of looking at you—

'Jesus!' Samson shook his head in disgust. He was like a lovesick teen.

Feeling a curdle in his stomach and not sure whether it was yet another symptom of his emotional affliction or simply hunger, he turned the bike around. He needed help. There was only one place he could think to get it.

He heard the bike coming up the steep kick of Fell Lane, that familiar throb of the engine; an engine he'd spent hours tinkering with back when they were a family, living out in Thorpdale. Before Kathleen had been diagnosed with cancer. Before he'd started drinking to block out his grief, never realising that he was blocking out his young son at the same time.

Feeling the years slipping through his mind, Joseph O'Brien watched the scarlet-and-chrome Enfield pull around to the back of the building. He glanced at the clock on the bookshelf. Not yet eight. Whatever had pushed Samson into calling round this early, he was going to need sustenance.

By the time the doorbell went, Joseph already had the frying pan on the stove.

'Bacon!' Samson stepped in to his father's small apartment, nose twitching, a grin lifting his weary features.

'Of course.' Joseph patted his son on the arm, gesturing towards the small table tucked into a corner of the open-plan space, two mugs of tea already on it. 'Sit yourself down, son.'

Samson did as he was told, struck by the normality of it. Him sitting at his father's table waiting to be fed. It had been far from normal, however. Probably no more than six months after his mother died before things began to tip and sway, the relationship between father and child getting skewed through the medium of alcohol. After that, it was more likely to be Samson at the stove, trying to persuade his father to eat while he sat slumped in his chair, cradling whatever bottle he was hell-bent on emptying.

'Two eggs?'

Samson nodded. Watched his father crack the eggs into the pan, flip the bacon and turn to spread butter on bread. Proper butter and a liberal amount of it too.

'I heard about yesterday,' Joseph said, back to his son as he cooked. 'Dreadful business.'

'Sure was.'

'And Delilah at the heart of it, too.'

'I didn't mean for her—'

Joseph cut across his son's protestations with a shake of the head. 'No reproach on my part, Samson. Delilah knows her own mind. I doubt she'd be one for taking no for an answer.'

'Understatement of the year,' muttered Samson.

From the kitchenette came the hiss of the bacon and then a sound he hadn't heard in decades. The slow tuneful hum of his father, a beautiful lilting melody, one that brought back memories of happier times. Before his father had turned into an alcoholic and long before that fateful day when Joseph O'Brien had chased his own son off the doorstep with a shotgun.

'You're happy, Dad.' If the statement contained an element of incredulity, it was because Samson couldn't really remember the last time he could have said that about his father.

Joseph turned, smiled, nodded. 'Yes, son.'

'Living here? You know, instead of up at the old place?' This time Samson didn't hide his bafflement, his eyes taking in the cramped apartment and comparing it – unfavourably – with the rambling old farmhouse and the spectacular scenery that surrounded the isolated Twistleton Farm.

His question was met with a philosophical shrug. 'Sure, I know that Rick Procter pulled a fast one when he bought the farm. But the truth of it is, Samson, if it wasn't for this place and the people who live here, I'd still be drinking myself to oblivion every day. If I was still here at all.'

Joseph ended the pronouncement by placing a plate in front of his son, piled high with sausages, bacon, eggs, black pudding and—

'White pudding!' exclaimed Samson at the sight of the treat he hadn't tasted in over twenty-five years. It had been a staple of Sunday morning in Thorpdale before his mother died, Joseph adhering to his Irish roots when it came to fried breakfasts. 'Where did you get this?'

His father laughed, tapped his nose and took a seat opposite his son, a much smaller plate of food before him. 'I have my sources.'

They ate in companionable silence, the clink of cutlery on china, the odd murmur of appreciation the only sounds. When they'd finished, Samson wiping the last piece of bread around his plate, savouring every last bit, Joseph smiled.

'So,' he said, reaching for his mug and then leaning back in his chair to look at his son. 'What brings you here?'

Samson sighed. Part contentment. Part agitation. 'I'm in a mess, Dad,' he said. 'And I couldn't think of anyone better to turn to.'

It didn't take any detective skills to spot the surprise on his father's face, eyebrows lifting, and then a pained expression in his eyes which he tried to mask with a slow smile. A surprise triggered by the simple fact that Samson had never sought his father's advice on anything. Not since the drinking started.

'Right,' said Joseph, a wariness about him now. As if he were afraid he wouldn't be up to the task. 'Something important?'

'You could say that.'

'A case perhaps? I hear Arty and Edith came to see you about Clarissa's fella.'

For a moment Samson was tempted to pretend that's what it was. Talking about online scam artists suddenly seemed infinitely more suited to a conversation between

two men who hadn't really interacted in over fourteen years than the personal matter he was about to raise.

'No, not a case.'

'Whatever it is, son, fire away. You know I'll do my best to help.'

And with those words, Samson was back at the kitchen table in Twistleton Farm, struggling to comprehend fractions, his father sitting opposite, using the segments of an orange to make clear what Samson's young mind was grappling with. They'd solved the maths problem and then eaten the orange, both laughing at the idea that homework could be so tasty.

'It's about women,' Samson said, staring at his mug, feeling his cheeks burning.

'Oh.' Joseph coughed. 'Anyone in particular?'

Samson looked up and saw the grin on his father's face. 'Maybe,' he said, grinning back. 'But my question is this: does it mean anything when they kiss you?'

'Ahhh!' Joseph shook his head, reached out and picked up his mobile off the table. 'To answer that, I am going to need reinforcements.'

While Joseph was about to tackle Samson's burning question, Stuart Lister was breaking into Taylor's Estate Agents.

At least, that was how it felt as he turned the key and slipped inside, unseen by anyone, the marketplace deserted at what was still an early hour for a Sunday. He stood for a moment, wondering if this was all a mistake, before picking up the courage he'd spent so long gathering in his flat. Resolute, he moved towards the rear of the reception area. Towards the closed door of Bernard Taylor's office.

Date with Deceit

The Kingston Holdings files were what he was after. He'd spent a long sleepless night, turning over the events of the past week in his restless mind. The bogus rentals. The repeated mentions of Kingston Holdings in the fabricated paperwork. His visit to Matty Thistlethwaite. And now the shocking suicide of his boss. While Stuart had never been described as having a fertile imagination – his English teacher at school having accused him of the exact opposite on many occasions – during the hours when he should have been sleeping, the lettings manager had been dwelling on the possible links between the things that were keeping him awake. So by the time dawn had crept through the window of his cramped bedroom, bringing with it the first birdsong, Stuart had been determined.

He would continue to be proactive, despite his promises to himself after his last attempt nearly backfired. After all, with Mr Taylor deceased and the business without a boss, there was less risk than ever, offering the ideal opportunity to get to the bottom of whatever was going on. He would go and get the files and bring them back to his flat. There he would have time to go through them at leisure and take photographs of the ones he hadn't already got, before deciding what to do with them.

It was a decision which had seen him rise from his bed, pull on his clothes, slip down the stairs past the closed Chinese takeaway and out into the fresh air of a brilliant May morning. He hadn't seen a soul, which should have calmed his nerves, but the unusual silence of the market-place only served to make him more jittery.

With his hand now on the door of his boss's office, he

had one last attack of cold feet. Turn around, and he could justify everything should he be seen exiting the premises on a Sunday. Get caught in Mr Taylor's private quarters and there would be no explaining it.

Persuading himself the chances of being interrupted were virtually nil, Mr Taylor in the mortuary and Julie visiting friends in Leeds, Stuart Lister turned the handle and entered, swiftly closing the door behind him. Then he made a beeline for the filing cabinet.

'I'm sorry it's so early.' At the top end of the marketplace, Rick Procter was standing on the doorstep of the Taylor residence. 'And I'm sorry to be bothering you at a time like this. But like I said on the phone last night, I really need that paperwork and I know Bernard was working on it. It's probably on his desk . . .'

'Not at all.' Nancy was dressed, make-up immaculate. It had taken an immense effort but she was determined not to show the grief that was tearing her apart. She gestured for him to come inside, closing the door behind him.

'How are you holding up?' he asked gently.

She grimaced. 'As good as could be expected.'

He nodded, his handsome features drawn down in shared sorrow. 'I just feel so responsible,' he said. 'Bernard's been under so much pressure. I feel like I should have seen it coming.'

'Ha!' She didn't mean the laugh to sound quite so cynical but in the silence of the empty hallway, it did. 'You and me both. I lived with him and I didn't spot a thing.'

Although that wasn't quite true. She'd spotted something, a pattern of behaviour that had her suspecting the worst. Yet instead of confronting Bernard, she'd set Samson O'Brien onto him, a move that had culminated in suicide.

That was the bit she was having trouble coping with. Suicide. The finality of that action hurt her more than the infidelity – because there was no doubting now that her husband had been cheating, the message he'd left on her voicemail as good as a confession. But Nancy could have lived with that. Worked it out with him. Instead, she'd never get the chance, the police claiming that Bernard was pushed over the edge by spotting Delilah Metcalfe at the shoot, driven to take his own life because his wife had set detectives on his trail.

Nancy may as well have pulled the trigger herself. And it was that which was destroying her. That and the declaration of love before the dreadful sound of the shotgun . . .

'Don't be so hard on yourself,' Rick was saying, touching her arm, concern in his eyes. 'None of us could have predicted this. That he would be capable of . . .' He made a helpless gesture.

'You think he did kill himself, then?' She asked the question in desperation.

'You don't?' There was genuine shock in the reply. 'I mean, all the evidence points that way—'

Nancy shook her head. 'I'm just finding it hard to believe. That Bernard would . . . I think there must have been some mistake.'

'But . . . the evidence . . . it's clearly suicide . . .'

She folded her arms without even noticing, defiant. 'He wouldn't have done that to me.'

'Listen, Nancy, I was there.' Rick had his hands on her shoulders now, his tone sympathetic but firm. 'Bernard took his own life. I know it's a shock but you'll only make things harder for yourself if you refuse to accept it.'

She felt her confidence waver, the convictions she'd had at dawn that her husband wouldn't have taken this route – *couldn't* have taken this route, given the weight of responsibility that would cast onto her – faltering in the face of Rick's certainty. 'But what about the cash?' she asked quietly. 'The police were asking me about it. Why would they be bothered with that if it was a simple suicide?'

'What cash?'

'I found a holdall with a hundred and twenty-five grand stuffed into it in Bernard's wardrobe last week. Maybe it's something connected to that?'

Rick was shaking his head. 'No way. Bernard was an honest businessman. There'll be a perfectly good explanation for that money.'

She bit her lip, feeling the tears rising. 'So you don't think it could have been murder?'

An emotion Nancy couldn't identify flickered over Rick's face. 'No! Not at all!' He squeezed her shoulders then let his hands drop. 'I'm sorry, Nancy. I can't imagine what you're going through, but letting yourself get caught up in wild theories like this is just going to make it worse.'

She nodded. Wiped the back of her hand over her eyes. 'Sorry. I'm all over the place. Here.' She opened the drawer of the console table next to her and passed him a bunch of keys. 'For the office,' she said. 'And thanks.'

'For what?'

'For being such a good friend to Bernard.'

Rick shrugged. 'He was a good man. And if there's anything I can do to help, you only have to ask.'

Minutes later, Rick Procter was walking down the marketplace, the keys to Taylor's in his hand.

Samson wasn't sure about the quality of the research panel Joseph had assembled. Sitting on the couch in his father's apartment were Arty Robinson and Eric Bradley, neither in the first flush of youth, his father in his armchair and Samson still at the table.

'What's this in aid of?' Arty asked, nose sniffing at the air. 'And did you have a fry-up without inviting us?'

'Yes, we did, and he needs your help,' said Joseph, grinning over at his son, who was squirming in his chair.

'Again? Who do you need tracking this time? And I hope it's a damn sight more interesting than the last job, because that was a dud—'

'It's nothing to do with detective work,' said Joseph, interrupting his friend's rambling.

'Oh.' Arty looked surprised. 'What, then?'

Joseph made a gesture with his hand, inviting his son to take the stage, his eyes twinkling. The old rogue was enjoying his son's discomfort.

'It's a personal matter,' muttered Samson.

'Viagra,' wheezed Eric. 'I hear it works wonders.'

Joseph and Arty burst out laughing while Samson shook his head in despair.

'Sorry,' said Eric, grinning. 'You were saying?'

'That it's a personal matter. And for some reason my dad thought you two would be able to assist.'

'Go on, lad, we're listening,' said Arty, sobering up at

the clear anguish on the young man's face. 'Whatever it is, we're here to help.'

Not convinced of the efficacy of that promise, Samson was desperate enough to take the gamble. 'It's about women,' he began. 'When a woman kisses you, does it mean anything?'

'That,' said Arty, folding his arms across his chest like a sage about to dispense wisdom, 'entirely depends on the woman.'

There were more files than he remembered. Lying in his bed, Stuart had come up with the idea that he would sneak them out under his jumper, and had subsequently dressed for just that, currently sporting a cable-knit pullover which wasn't helping keep him cool. Nor, he realised as he stared at the bottom drawer of the filing cabinet, would it help him transport the documents out of the office unseen. Not unless he wanted to cross the marketplace looking like someone in the latter end of their third trimester of pregnancy. With triplets.

He needed some other way to get the folders out of there.

Stacking them in a bundle on the floor, he scanned the office, looking for something suitable. Nothing. But there was a box in the kitchen area, one that had contained paper towels and which hadn't yet made it to the recycling. It would be perfect.

Stuart picked up the stack of files and crossed the office to the closed door. Pulled it open. And felt his already thumping heart rate rocket.

Coming across the marketplace straight towards Taylor's was Rick Procter, keys in his hand.

22

As he unlocked the front door of the estate agent's, Rick was cursing the man he'd been so recently eulogising to his widow.

That bloody holdall full of cash. He'd nearly choked when Nancy had mentioned it. Taylor's half of what should have been Pete Ferris's blackmail payoff had just been stuck in a bag in his wardrobe for his wife to trip over. The idiot! And now the police had wind of it. It was yet another item Rick was going to have to add to his long list of things that needed cleaning up.

Feeling stressed, he stepped inside the empty property, the space holding that stillness of all workplaces out of hours. More so, knowing that the owner wouldn't be making a return, thought Rick morbidly, as he closed the front door behind him.

The soft tick of the clock on the wall caught his attention. It was later than he'd thought, thanks to the amount of time he'd had to waste trying to nip Nancy Taylor's conspiracy theories in the bud, the woman's guilt pushing her thoughts along dangerous lines. So he'd have to be quick. The church crowd would be heading for the first service soon and, while he was on the premises legitimately, he'd rather not be seen walking out carrying a stack of files.

He moved swiftly through the reception area towards Taylor's office at the back, and was just level with the lettings manager's desk when there was a thump from behind the closed office door.

Someone was in there! At this hour on a Sunday, that was more than unusual. Rick didn't hesitate. He crossed the remaining floorspace in rapid strides and flung open the door.

A silent workspace met his gaze. No one in it. The only thing out of place was an upturned plant pot and saucer on the ground next to the filing cabinet, soil and plant spilling all over the laminate flooring, suggesting that had been the source of the noise.

Odd though, that it had fallen off of it's own accord.

He stepped out of the office and glanced around the corner into the kitchenette tucked in the back of the building. No one round there either.

A careless cleaner then, doing a quick dust and leaving the plant too close to the edge.

Aware of the clock ticking, Rick went back to the office, stepping over the mess on the floor to turn the key in the filing cabinet and pull open the bottom drawer.

Nothing! The bottom drawer was empty, save for a folder of genuine rentals – the ones used to house their illicit business – and a couple of lone paperclips. He pulled open the remaining drawers in ascending order, rifling quickly through the rows of folders. Just business documents. No sign of what he was after.

Taylor must have moved them. After all Rick's warnings, he had finally taken heed, but in doing so, had placed them beyond Rick's grasp. And now the man himself was also beyond reach, leaving the Kingston Holdings files out there somewhere. If they fell into the wrong hands, like those of a curious spouse or someone trying to help run the business in Taylor's absence, it would turn what was a difficult situation into an irredeemable disaster.

Furious that his partner's incompetence was outliving him, Rick slammed the top drawer closed. He'd been confident this little matter could be cleared up relatively easily. Now he was going to have to gain access to Taylor's home office somehow. See if the files were there. And soon, before someone stepped in to take charge of this leaderless business —

The idea, when it came, was so simple. After all, if he was worried about someone stumbling across things they weren't meant to see now Taylor was out of the picture, there was an obvious solution. Two birds and one stone. Stepping over the scattered soil and the uprooted plant, with no thought given to cleaning it up – that's what people like Ida Capstick were for – Rick left the office and strode towards the front door. Minutes later he was walking back up the hill towards the Taylor residence.

If Rick Procter had been more conscientious when it came to literal housekeeping, he'd have discovered two things. One was that there was a spare key to the filing cabinet lying under the plant, which would have given him pause for thought. The other was that he wasn't alone on the premises.

As the front door closed and the building settled back into silence, Stuart Lister let out his breath. It felt like the same breath he'd been holding since Rick Procter had walked in. Huddled in the dark of Ida Capstick's cleaning cupboard, files clutched to his chest, the lettings manager had spent the time in what he was sure was the beginnings of a heart attack, pulse thundering, every sinew strained tight to hold him still.

When he'd spotted the unwelcome visitor across the square, he'd been caught in the doorway of his boss's office with no time to replace the files, and had made the snap decision to hide. He'd been heading for the cupboard when he felt the cold metal of a key in his sweating palm.

The blasted key to the filing cabinet. Yet again he'd forgotten to put it back.

Whipping round, he'd lunged at the cabinet, lifted the plant, deposited the key, dropped the plant back on the saucer and hurled himself from the room. He'd made it into the cupboard as Mr Procter arrived at the front door. But as he squeezed past the vacuum cleaner, trying to burrow his way to the furthest recess, Stuart hadn't noticed that he'd left the door to his hiding place ajar.

When he'd turned and seen the light creeping in, he'd almost died.

How long had he been in there? It had felt like hours – a high-stakes version of hide-and-seek, waiting to be discovered, those damn files still under his arm, sweat beading on his forehead. Watching through that crack as Mr Procter opened the door to Mr Taylor's office and discovered the plant on the floor. And when the property developer stepped back out to look around the kitchenette, Stuart had thought that was it. Game up.

But Mr Procter had returned to the office and . . . Well,

that had been the strange thing. Whatever he'd been look-ing for, he'd gone straight to the bottom drawer of the filing cabinet. As though he knew what was in there.

Or *had* been in there.

His face on seeing the emptiness had been furious. All of which hadn't helped Stuart's heart rate any. If he was caught now . . .

But he hadn't been. Somehow he'd survived. Even the disaster that would have been Mr Procter coming for the vacuum cleaner – the same appliance that was currently digging into Stuart's hip – had been averted.

Feeling weak with relief, the lettings manager remained in the dark. Gave it five minutes after the clunk of the door being locked from outside – five long minutes which he counted off in his head in slow seconds – before he so much as moved. Which was just as well, as his first step was to trip over the cleaning bucket and almost go flying.

Emerging from the cupboard warily, he considered his options. Placing the files back in the cabinet was the rational choice. Step away from whatever this shady busi-ness was that Mr Taylor had been involved in – probably Mr Procter too, given how he'd just behaved. So put everything back as it was and forget having stumbled on the forged rental contracts and the mysterious Kingston Holdings.

Stuart moved towards Mr Taylor's office, thoroughly intending to take the sensible option. But he paused. A pang of conscience besetting him.

That was the coward's way out. And besides, if he replaced the files now, how would that be explained?

Mr Procter had already seen they weren't there. Their miraculous reappearance would only raise suspicion.

So take them home, then. But not in a carboard box from the kitchen as had been the original plan. Because if he bumped into anyone on the way home, they'd know he'd been in the office, the name and address printed on the side of the box. He needed something else . . .

He turned back to the cleaning cupboard. Pulled out the bucket he'd tripped over, tipped the cleaning paraphernalia onto the floor, and placed the files inside.

They fitted perfectly. Over the top, he spread out a yellow duster.

If anyone asked, he'd been shopping in Plastic Fantastic and had purchased some housekeeping items.

Carrying his stolen bucket, Stuart Lister let himself out of Taylor's Estate Agents onto the still-deserted cobbled square. Doing his best to walk at a natural pace, despite the urge to run, he got all the way past Peaks Patisserie and partway down Church Street before he saw a soul. And even then, it was only the two sisters from Fellside Court, Miss Hird and Mrs Ralph, walking down to get their Sunday newspapers. They nodded in greeting, seeing nothing untoward in a young man heading home with a bucket. It was the season for spring cleaning after all.

Except these were no ordinary sisters. These were sisters who had recently been assigned a sleuthing role and took it seriously – despite the case being in limbo thanks to the recent demise of the main focus of the investigation. As Stuart Lister walked past, Clarissa broke off from telling Edith about a dress she'd seen in Betty's Boutique on Back Street that would be perfect for her upcoming cruise to glance over her shoulder after him. Then she pulled a note-book out of her handbag and wrote something down, her sister nodding in approval.

While Stuart was making good his escape, Delilah Metcalfe was forcing herself to brave a walk into town. Tolpuddle by her side, she was heading down the steep slope of Crag Hill, feeling more nervous than she could ever remember.

It was ridiculous, she'd told herself earlier that morning as she looked out of her kitchen window at the grey roofs below. Staying cocooned at home because she was afraid of what people would say to her, how they would judge her for what had happened the day before. Besides, she'd been the subject of the town's gossip before. Her divorce from Neil Taylor had given some folk a field day and, more recently, her association with the local black sheep, Samson O'Brien, had caused tongues to wag. Still did in some quarters.

So, having chided herself for being so feeble, she'd slipped Tolpuddle's lead on him and set off, a shopping list in her hand. But as she made her way down the hill, she couldn't shake the feeling that curtains were twitching as she went by. That people were staring out at her. Heart thumping, she kept going, reaching the Spar and tying up Tolpuddle outside.

'Be a good boy,' she whispered, wishing she could take him in with her, his solid grey body better than a shield.

Picking up a basket at the door, she entered the shop. And that's where it all went wrong. Two women in the veg aisle stopped talking the moment she walked in. Both of them watching her go past. The same in the dairy aisle, a farmer from out past Hellifield giving her nothing more than a curt nod in greeting. Basket trembling in her grasp, she forged on, gathering the bits and pieces she needed. But when she turned a corner and saw Mrs Pettiford, Delilah's courage failed.

'Well!' exclaimed the bank clerk, lips pursed in disapproval. 'I'm surprised you have the nerve to show your face. Considering the hurt you've caused.'

Delilah went to speak. To offer up a curt rejoinder, like she'd done before when she was on the sharp end of Mrs Pettiford's tittle-tattle. But this time wasn't the same. This time she knew she was in the wrong and there were no words to defend her actions. Playing around in disguise and driving a man to suicide.

Overwhelmed with self-loathing, Delilah set down her basket, and meekly walked away. By the time she got to Tolpuddle, she could barely see to untie his lead, her eyes awash with tears. With her head hung low, she hurried back up the hill to her cottage.

'So the paperwork wasn't there?' Standing in her kitchen, Nancy Taylor was looking puzzled as she poured coffee into two mugs from a cafetière.

'No,' said Rick. He'd been reluctant to accept her invitation to stay for a drink, but with what he was about to propose, it wouldn't hurt to go through the motions of being civil. And so he'd followed Nancy into the kitchen and was currently sitting at the table, his back to the window, trying not to let his frustration show. 'He must have brought it home to work on.'

But Nancy shook her head. 'I doubt it,' she said, carrying the two mugs over and taking a seat opposite him. 'Bernard never brought work back to the house. He always said the two should be kept separate—' Her voice broke slightly and she held a hand to her mouth, as though containing the despair.

Rick had to muster all of his self-control to maintain the facade he'd spent so long building for the gullible folk of Bruncliffe. 'Sorry,' he said, reaching over to gently squeeze her arm. 'I know how upsetting this must be for you.'

She nodded. Head down as a tear escaped. 'It's awful. It's not just the grief. I feel so out of my depth with everything. Thank goodness the boys are coming home later today.'

The mention of Taylor's two sons, grown men with the potential to be thorns in Rick's side if they started dabbling in their father's affairs, was the trigger he needed.

'Have you given any thought to the business?' he asked. 'I mean, have you got someone to help you out?'

'Not really. I haven't had a chance. The boys are up to their eyes with their own careers and I feel so helpless. Bernard never wanted me working, so I know little about it . . .'

'Well, perhaps I can assist you with that.'

'How do you mean?'

'Step in for a bit, put a hand on the rudder until we know what's happening. It'd be a shame to lose everything Bernard worked so hard for.'

The offer presented just the right amount of peril to make accepting it seem the only option, and Nancy gave him a grateful look.

'Really?' she asked. 'You'd do that? I mean, you're so busy . . .'

'It's the least I can do.' He could sense the hesitation, the uncertainty on her face as she stared at the set of keys he'd left on the table. 'Come on, Nancy,' he said, gentle humour in his voice, beguiling her. 'I'm not just anyone. Bernard trusted me.'

She blushed. Nodded. And handed him back the keys. 'Thank you,' she said.

As he stepped out onto the marketplace ten minutes later, Rick Procter was congratulating himself on a deal well struck. With the access he'd have to Taylor's business, he would be able to locate the missing files and deal with any other evidence his imbecilic partner might have left lying around – like that damn holdall – all part of the housekeeping Niko Karamanski had demanded. And all while seeming to be helping out a widow left stranded.

It was a win-win situation. Which, considering how things had looked a mere twenty-four hours earlier, was a vast improvement.

With his spirits considerably lifted, Rick was in a good enough humour to cast a cheery hello to Miss Hird and Mrs Ralph as they walked past. And when he looked over his shoulder and caught a glimpse of Delilah Metcalfe hurrying up the hill away from town, her shoulders bowed, her head down, Mrs Pettiford watching her retreat from the Spar doorway, his mood got even better.

While two-fifths of the Fellside Court amateur detective group were in the marketplace, the remaining three were still sitting in Joseph O'Brien's apartment, all staring at Samson and expecting an answer.

'It's a hypothetical question,' muttered Samson.

Arty laughed. 'Sure, lad. You're asking for a friend.' His arms remained folded. 'But if we don't know which woman in particular we're dealing with, we can't offer frank advice.'

Samson looked at his father, who just shrugged. There would be no help from that quarter. He sighed. Wondered how it had come to this, that his Sunday morning – far from his undercover past where it would have been spent hanging out in seedy bars pretending to be hungover or holed up in some squalid conditions on a stake-out – could be passed in the company of three pensioners discussing his love life.

'If you must know,' he said, 'it's Delilah. She kissed me and I was wondering—'

'Bugger!' Arty exclaimed, Eric bursting into a cackle that morphed into a cough.

Joseph just smiled. And held out his hand. At which Arty pulled out his wallet and slapped a tenner in the outstretched palm.

It took Samson a second. Then he exploded.

'*Betting?* You were *betting* on me and Delilah?'

Arty looked indignant. 'Don't make it sound so sordid. Bookmaking is a noble profession, as old as the hills. Hence, we were merely indulging in an ancient pastime.'

'And using my life to get your sport?' Samson watched his father fold the ten-pound note and place it in his pocket. 'What was the bet, anyway?'

Eric, coughing fit subsided, supplied the answer on a gasp of breath. 'Which of you would be brave enough to make the first move.'

Another second passed and Samson turned to his father. 'You bet on Delilah?'

Joseph nodded. Unabashed at his lack of familial loyalty.

'On what grounds?' asked Samson, more than a hint of indignation to the words.

'You take after me, son. If it hadn't been for your mother taking action, I'd still be mooning over her but too afraid to do anything about it. Besides, the odds were too good to turn down.' Again that smile, the twinkle in the eyes, both melting any genuine affront Samson might have felt.

'Bloody insider trading,' muttered Arty, glowering at Joseph and then at Samson. 'What the hell was up with you, lad, that you didn't kiss her sooner? A woman like that . . .' The former bookie shook his head in disbelief.

'Well,' said Samson, 'now that we've established that I'm a disappointment in the romance stakes, can we get back to my initial question? Delilah kissed me. Should I take it as an indication of anything more serious?'

The three men looked at each other. And then nodded in unison.

'This is Delilah Metcalfe we're talking about,' said Arty. 'She's one in a million. If she kissed you, you don't want to let that pass.'

'I agree,' said Eric. 'That lass is something special. I'd walk through fire for her. I mean, after what she did for your father—'

At first Samson thought the abrupt silence was simply caused by a lack of oxygen but Eric wasn't coughing. He was staring at Joseph, aghast.

'Sorry . . . I didn't mean . . .' Eric was spluttering now, but nothing to do with his illness.

Joseph reached across and patted him on the hand.

'Don't worry about it. Samson would have found out sooner or later.'

'Found out what?' Samson looked at the three faces in turn, his gaze coming to rest on his father, who was smiling. But nervously.

'Delilah helped me out,' he said. 'Back in January. I had a bit of a problem and, well, she helped sort it.'

And just like that, Samson felt the twinges of doubt. Gone was the rapport of moments ago, the belief that he could have a father like everyone else, one that could be relied upon. In its place was the all too-familiar suspicion that had coloured their relationship from the day Joseph had picked up a bottle and started trying to drink himself to death.

'Are you drinking again?' Samson asked, a bite to the words.

'No, son, not now.'

'But you were?'

'It's not as straightforward as that—'

'Either you were drinking or you weren't. Surely it's fairly clear cut?' Samson had got to his feet unawares, fists beginning to clench.

'It wasn't his fault—' Arty's attempt to intervene was cut off by a flicked hand from Joseph.

'It's okay, Arty. Samson needs to hear this from me.' Joseph cleared his throat. 'It was at Christmas, you know, the stake-out.'

Samson didn't need reminding. A series of suspicious incidents at Fellside Court had culminated in him and Delilah carrying out surveillance in an operation that had almost cost the life of his father. 'What about it?'

'I accidently imbibed some alcohol—'

'What Joseph means is he was force-fed some whisky by that fiend that tried to kill him,' interrupted Arty.

Samson stared at his father and then slumped back into his chair. Stunned. 'You didn't tell me.'

'No,' said Joseph. 'I thought I could cope at first. But even that small amount was enough to fuel the thirst and I found myself in a real battle. Playing Russian roulette with a bottle every night.'

'So what did you do?'

'I called Delilah.' Joseph dropped his gaze to the carpet. 'She came round and got Arty and Edith on board and between them . . . I came through it.'

Samson was hit with conflicting emotions. A surge of love for the woman who'd helped his father through his torment – and hadn't breathed a word about it. And a deluge of guilt that Delilah had been the one his father turned to.

'But . . . but . . . why didn't you call me?' he asked.

His father gave a soft sigh. 'Because I didn't want you to know that I'd failed again. It's all I ever seem to do in our relationship.'

The words cut Samson to the heart. He sat there, hurting, feeling his own pain and his father's. Then he got to his feet, crossed the small lounge, and put his arm around the man he hadn't embraced in so long.

'Sorry, Dad,' he muttered, holding his father close. 'I should have been there for you.'

'Don't,' said Joseph, a break in his voice, as he hugged his son back. 'There's nothing to apologise for.'

'Bloody hell!' said Arty gruffly, blinking furiously

while Eric wiped a hand across his eyes. 'Spare us the bromance and let's get back to the real issue. What should lover boy here do next?'

Father and son both started laughing, releasing each other, Joseph pulling out a handkerchief and dabbing at his cheeks as Samson cleared his throat and stepped away to lean against the table.

'I'm all ears,' he said.

'Well, listen up, lad,' continued Arty, 'because like we said, Delilah is a keeper. But she's also got that Metcalfe temper. So we need to think this through carefully.'

'Roses,' said Eric. 'They'd work.'

Joseph shook his head. 'Not with Delilah.'

'Chocolates, then. Or a nice meal out at Rice N Spice.'

'New running shoes more like,' laughed Arty.

Still Joseph was shaking his head.

'What is it, Dad? What are you thinking?' asked Samson.

'I'm thinking all that would be trying too hard. She wouldn't go for it.'

'So what do you suggest, then?'

Joseph shrugged. 'Delilah Metcalfe is one of the most honest people I know. She's direct to a fault. But she has the most generous of hearts. So just tell her how you feel.'

'But what if she doesn't feel the same?' Samson couldn't help the edge of panic in his voice.

'It's a risk worth taking. If she doesn't feel the same, she won't mess you around. If she does feel the same . . . well, son, you'd be one of the luckiest men alive.'

Samson swallowed, hearing the advice he'd known was

right all along but least wanted to follow. Laying his heart out in front of Delilah terrified him more than any of the threats he'd faced in his life down in London.

'He's right, lad,' said Arty softly, not an ounce of levity in his words. 'You're going to have to bare your soul.'

23

It was a subdued Delilah Metcalfe who walked down the steep steps which led from Crag Lane to the ginnel at the back of the office building early on Monday morning, the sky overhead an unbroken blue. Having been up at dawn for a run with Tolpuddle in Hawber Woods, the bluebells at their stunning best, she'd returned to the cottage for breakfast and a shower and was still going to be at the office ahead of her normal time.

That's what being unable to sleep did for you.

Unsurprisingly, the two nights since the shooting hadn't yielded much rest, the hours when Delilah should have been sleeping having been spent dwelling on the dreadful events at Bruncliffe Manor. And as for the daylight hours . . .

The trip to the Spar the day before had really shaken her. Unable to bear the thought of facing anyone else, she'd arrived home and immediately called her mother to say she wouldn't be joining the family for Sunday lunch at Ellershaw Farm as usual. Instead she'd spent the remainder of the day sequestered in her cottage, fielding messages and texts from concerned family and friends. To ignore them would only have resulted in people turning up at the door to see how she was. She'd let Frank Thistlethwaite's calls go to voicemail, however. All four of them.

By the end of the day it had been hard to say who was the most restless at this self-imposed confinement, herself or Tolpuddle. So she'd taken him up onto the fells at twilight for a long run, hoping that might help her sleep.

It hadn't.

She'd woken from troubled dreams to lie there in the dark, wishing the dawn would arrive. Only for her thoughts to turn to the other matter that was weighing her down.

That bloody kiss. A full on, lip-to-lip, no-holds-barred smacker with Samson O'Brien. All instigated by Delilah herself. Even the thought of it now, as she reached the ginnel, made the heat well up her cheeks and, not for the first time, she was ruing her impetuous nature.

What the hell had possessed her?

Shock? Fatigue? Guilt? Or . . .

It was the 'or' that bothered her most. That and the fact that part of her didn't regret her actions at all.

Still, the upside of not being able to sleep and being a social pariah was that she'd spent most of Sunday working, trying to find Clarissa Ralph's suspected catfish. And she'd got news for Samson. Shocking news. Although how she was going to be able to face him after her ridiculous behaviour on Saturday evening . . .

She'd had a solitary message from him over the last twenty-four hours, simply enquiring if she was okay. Unsure whether he was asking about her mental state following the shooting or whether she'd recovered from whatever lunacy had afflicted her at the time of their parting two days ago, she'd replied with an ambiguous thumbs-up emoji. Even though the real answers were 'not good' and 'not yet'.

It was little wonder, then, that her stomach was churning as she followed Tolpuddle along the ginnel to the back gate and into the yard. The Royal Enfield was parked to the left, covers off, gleaming in the sunshine. Delilah was just musing over whether that meant Samson had been out on it over the weekend – and trying to stifle the sudden yearning to be up on the pillion behind him, riding through the dales in this glorious weather – when the back door was flung open.

'Morning!' she said, bracing herself to see him.

Instead, Ida Capstick was standing there, looking cross.

'Someone's stolen my bucket!' she exclaimed.

Delilah had no idea how to respond.

The bucket was still over by the sink, where he'd left it. The Kingston Holdings files back in it, covered with the duster. And sitting on the sagging couch in his flat, Stuart Lister was plucking up the courage to take action.

There wasn't much he could do about the properties represented in the files he'd stolen. Establishing what role they played in the scheme Mr Taylor and Mr Procter had concocted required legal expertise, something Stuart didn't have. But what he did have was a working knowledge of property and rental contracts. And a hunch that the high-end rentals Mr Taylor had been so cagy about might be a good place to start.

He'd settled on the house on Henside Road. He couldn't say why he'd plumped for this one when he'd come up with his next step in his proactive plan. Perhaps it was the history of the place. Not the history of its owners, a long line of farmers only recently broken, but his own history with it.

It was where he'd been nearly killed the autumn before, lured out to a fictitious late-night viewing and then set upon. But for the timely intervention of a group of Bruncliffe Harriers, he would have been dead for sure. Stuart shuddered at the memory. He hadn't been out there since, the remote former farmhouse having been rented to a Mr Dugdale and the paperwork all sorted while Stuart was still in hospital, recovering from the injuries he'd sustained that night. The house was now one of the high-end rentals that Mr Taylor had overseen, never passing across Stuart's desk. One of those with paperwork irregularities . . .

He would pop over there this morning. He didn't have the keys but he'd bluff his way in. Explain away the lack of a formal appointment, blame the computer system being down or something. If everything was above board, he could complete the much-needed inspection and start getting the file in some sort of order. If everything wasn't above board . . .

Stuart was trying not to think about that. Not just through fear, although that was a large part of his reluctance to dwell on things. But also because he literally couldn't think of anything that could be behind the oddities he'd uncovered.

At least this way he'd find out.

Feeling far from brave, Stuart Lister picked up his briefcase and left his flat before his courage failed altogether. He headed down the stairs, returning the greeting of Mrs Lee, who was mopping the entrance hall, and stepped out into a bright May morning, the clear sky a promise of a great day to come.

*

'I've cracked it!'

Samson hadn't even had time to get his breakfast. The moment he'd come down the stairs from his bedroom, hair wet from the shower, mind still not fully awake, Delilah had accosted him outside the kitchen.

'Sorry?' he said, taking in her folded arms, the tilt of her chin.

Whatever she was talking about, Miss Metcalfe was on the defensive, a shield erected around her – whether because of the rumours going around town or their last interaction, he couldn't tell. What he could tell was that she was putting on a brave front, the dark shadows below her eyes suggesting she'd had a troubled weekend. It took every inch of his self-restraint not to lean over and kiss those defiant lips.

But then he was only half-asleep, not completely stupid. Delilah in this mood was as liable to right hook him as she was to kiss him back.

'What are you talking about?' he asked, moving into the kitchen and reaching for the kettle.

'There's a pot already made,' called out a voice from Delilah's office. 'And tell him about my bucket!'

Samson raised an eyebrow in Delilah's direction.

'Ida,' she murmured. 'She's at my desk, going through the answering machine messages. Apparently her cleaning bucket has gone missing from Taylor's.'

'It was stolen!' came a shout from the other room, confirming that there was nothing wrong with Ida's hearing.

'Stolen? How?'

Delilah shrugged. 'Maybe "why" would be a better question?'

'Bright red. Brand new. Plus a duster.' Ida had appeared in the doorway, her thin face pulled into sharp displeasure. 'And it wasn't someone wanting it for cleaning – they left all the products on the floor.'

'Have you mentioned it at Taylor's?' asked Samson.

'Mention it to who? The young lettings lad wasn't there when I left and young Julie called to say she's got a migraine and won't be in. Anyroad up, I'm mentioning it now. Thought tha could keep an eye out for me.'

'Right.' Samson felt a burning need for sustenance, his faculties not clear enough for dealing with both Ida and Delilah at this hour. He reached for a mug.

'Best pour it,' said Ida, nodding towards the teapot on the table, a colourful cosy over it. 'Been brewed a while and tha won't want it stewed.'

'Right,' Samson said again, heart sinking. He lifted off the cosy, picked up the teapot and poured. Treacle-brown liquid issued from the spout. The week wasn't starting on a good note.

'So tha'll keep an eye out? Perhaps have a word with Danny Bradley for me?' Ida was still there, glowering, the loss of her bucket clearly painful.

Samson nodded, noticing the corners of Delilah's lips twitching. Ida let out a grunt and turned to go before adding, 'And tha needs to call Mrs Hargreaves, too. She wants an update on that search for whatever mongrel keeps fouling her front step.'

With that, she headed back into the office at the end of the landing to resume her receptionist duties.

'Are you seriously going to ask Danny about the bucket?' Delilah murmured once Ida was out of earshot, her words edged with laughter as she watched Samson add milk to his tea. 'I mean, it's not like Bruncliffe's police have anything on their hands at the moment.'

'What choice do I have? First time she sees Danny, Ida will ask if I mentioned it.' Samson shook his head, smiling ruefully. That was the thing with being a private detective in a place like Bruncliffe. One day you were dealing with suspected marital infidelity, next minute you were on the lookout for a missing red bucket.

Taking his mug in both hands, he took a sip of the beverage Ida passed off as tea and grimaced, running his tongue over his teeth to check he still had enamel left on them.

'Anyway,' he said, placing the mug back on the table, 'you were saying? Before Ida came in?'

'You need to call Edith Hird. Tell her and Arty to come in, if they can. I think I've cracked the catfish case.'

Samson stared at her. 'Already?'

'Yes.' Delilah's arms folded even tighter across her chest, if that was possible, her chin tilting to a higher angle. 'I worked on it all day yesterday.'

His partner's diligence triggered a flash of guilt – Samson's own thoughts in the last twenty-four hours not having strayed much further than the woman he was currently talking to. After he'd left his father's, he'd spent the rest of the day riding aimlessly round the Dales on the Enfield, fighting the urge to go and see her, figuring that after the weekend she'd had, she didn't need him declaring his love. Plus he hadn't trusted himself to be alone with her. Yet while he'd been mooning around in a lovelorn daze, she'd been working hard on a case.

'Right,' he said yet again, his vocabulary still not fully awake. 'And?'

'He's a catfish all right.' There was something in the way she said it, like she was holding something back.

'You've found his real identity?'

She nodded. 'It was ridiculously easy. I mean, he didn't even try to cover his tracks. Once I had his personal statement and profile picture from Silver Hearts, I was able to track down an Instagram account and from there I traced his user name to an old forum post that had his email address on, and after that it was simple.'

'I'll take your word for it,' said Samson, her efforts beyond him even at a more decent hour of the day and with some food in his belly. 'So, who is he?'

She held out her mobile and showed him the screen.

'Christ!' Samson stared at the photograph and then at Delilah. 'This is going to have to be handled really carefully.'

'I know. We don't want anyone getting hurt.'

He looked at the mobile once more and then nodded. 'I'll give Edith a call.'

Delilah was already moving away down the landing.

'By the way,' he said, making her pause to look back at him. 'That's bloody amazing detective work, Delilah.'

His reward was a beaming smile that made his heart soar. Then she turned and headed back to her office, Ida grumbling something at her as she entered. Samson was left in the kitchen, his morning cuppa undrinkable, his stomach rumbling and his mind pondering over whether it was wrong that he'd felt slightly dismayed on hearing that Delilah's entire Sunday had been spent preoccupied with the catfish case, and that what had happened in the courtyard the evening before hadn't even merited her contemplation.

Deciding it was best not to dwell on it, Samson reached for the bread and began making himself some toast.

Stuart Lister was regretting his rapid departure from his flat, wishing he'd taken the time to make himself some toast. Instead, he'd dropped by the office to pick up the keys for the company car, fully intending to leave a vague note for Julie telling her he had an appointment and would be late. But when he got there, he'd seen a message from Ida to say Julie had called in sick.

Relieved at not having to lie, even in written form, Stuart had made the most of the empty office and grabbed the Henside Road file, thinking it might make him seem more legitimate when he turned up on the doorstep to carry out an unscheduled inspection. He'd been about to leave when he decided he might as well go the whole hog – seeing as Julie wasn't going to be in before his return – and so had taken the keys for the property as well. Ten minutes after leaving town, the orange Mini with the company name emblazoned down the side was out in the middle of nowhere and Stuart's stomach was rumbling with hunger.

At least, he told himself it was hunger. Better for him to believe that, as he approached the turn off for Henside Road, than to think it was nerves.

Indicating right, he turned onto the narrow lane, stone walls lining each side, the tarmac dropping immediately down the fellside. This was where it had happened. Somehow it was worse in broad daylight, the steepness of the road more dramatic, the isolation more apparent, nothing but fields stretching out on either side. Hands gripping the steering wheel, Stuart guided the Mini slowly down the hill, staring straight ahead, unwilling to look at the mound of stones where his car had been slammed into a wall. He didn't even glance at his briefcase when it slid off the passenger seat and tumbled onto the floor as the descent got steeper.

Instead he concentrated on approaching the cattle grid in the dip with care, the Mini rattling over the metal bars before starting the even sharper climb on the other side. Engine groaning, the car inched up the incline, Stuart marvelling that anyone had ever decided this deserted spot would make a good place to live. He crested the hill and to his left saw the property in the distance. A large farmhouse, completely alone on the slopes of the fells.

He turned off the road and onto the track that led to the house. Stomach cramping, he told himself he really could have done with that slice of toast.

'Well, is he too good to be true?' Edith Hird was sitting bolt upright across the desk from Samson and Delilah, Arty Robinson in the chair next to her, looking no less tense. They'd come straight to the Dales Detective Agency after Samson's call, declining the customary offer of tea in their impatience to hear what had been discovered.

'I'm afraid so,' said Delilah.

'Oh no!' Edith sagged, as though her strings had been severed. 'I was so hoping I was wrong.'

With a stricken look, Arty reached across to take her hand. 'Sorry, lass. I should have believed you straight off.'

Edith looked at him, face twisted with worry. 'Poor Clarissa. How are we going to tell her?'

'Poor Robert Bloody Webster when I get my hands on him,' growled Arty, turning to Samson. 'What kind of bloke would take advantage of a woman like that?'

Samson didn't say anything. He'd seen plenty of men in his lifetime whose behaviour was beyond comprehension. But there was something particularly reprehensible about someone deliberately setting out to target a pensioner.

'So how did you do it?' asked Edith. 'How do you know he's a catfish?'

'I did a reverse search using his profile picture,' said Delilah. 'Straight away it popped up online in adverts for men's hair dye.'

'Are you saying he's a model?' Arty asked in surprise.

'No, I'm saying the photo he used is of a model. From there I did a search of his name and discovered that Robert Webster is actually a pilot. Or he was. Until he died . . .' Delilah flicked open her notepad to consult her notes, 'three years ago.'

'This bloke has no shame!' muttered Arty. 'Robbing a dead person's identity like that.'

'But what about the man behind all this? Have you found out who he is?' asked Edith.

'Aye, because I know a few folk who'd like to give him a talking to,' Arty rumbled.

Delilah glanced at Samson, who leaned across the desk.

'We're not a hundred per cent certain just yet,' he said. 'Give us forty-eight hours and we should be able to name him. And then it'll be a matter of letting the police—'

'Sod that!' growled Arty. 'When you have a name, you let me know. I fancy a chat with this bloke.'

Samson was shaking his head. 'Not going to happen, Arty. This one is being played by the book.'

Arty started to object but Delilah reached across to place a hand on his arm.

'Please, Arty. For my sake?' she said. 'I don't want anyone getting hurt. I've caused enough pain in the last few days and I couldn't bear to be responsible for any more.'

'Delilah's right,' said Edith, gently. 'Let the authorities deal with it. No need for you to put yourself in harm's way, Arty.' She smiled at him and he sighed.

'Okay,' he muttered. 'But keep us posted.'

Samson nodded. 'Of course we will.'

'And Clarissa?' asked Edith. 'How on earth do I break this to her?'

'Hold fire for a couple of days,' said Samson. 'Let's make sure we're right about all this before we go upsetting her.'

'But in the meantime,' Delilah added, 'make sure she doesn't make any payments towards the cruise you mentioned. Keep her distracted if you can.'

Edith nodded, the concern on her face no less than it had been when she'd walked in the door. 'I'll do my best,' she said, getting to her feet and leaning on her stick, the others all standing too. 'And thank you, Delilah. You've just saved my sister from making a terrible mistake. One that would have devastated her.'

Delilah blushed at the praise from her former teacher while Samson stepped around the desk to offer Edith his arm, leading her into the hall. Arty grinned at Delilah, sweeping a low bow in her direction.

'He's not the only one who can do chivalry,' he said, nodding towards the office doorway. 'Ladies first.'

Delilah laughed and followed the others, her foot only just hitting the tiles of the hallway when the front door burst open.

'Samson! Delilah!' Lucy Metcalfe was standing there, face smeared in flour, Peaks Patisserie apron still on. 'You've got to help!'

'Lucy! What's happened?' Delilah was by her sister-in-law's side in an instant.

'It's Ana! The police have just arrested her. They're saying she murdered Bernard Taylor!'

Three mouths dropped open, Lucy's audience all too stunned to notice that Arty was still in the office. On Samson's side of the desk.

24

The Taylor's-branded Mini bumped and jolted along the unsurfaced track towards the farmhouse before Stuart crossed another cattle grid and onto gravel. He pulled up some distance from the front door, noting the lawn was badly in need of cutting. The ivy which climbed over the stones of the porch could do with being trimmed back as well.

When he'd last been out here it had been pitch black, not a street light in sight, so it was hard to tell how much the property had been neglected by the current tenants. But Stuart had learned that, as a rule of thumb, if the outside of the rental had been let slip, there wasn't much to be expected of the inside either.

Preparing himself for a difficult inspection, he retrieved his briefcase from the floor – hoping it would give him the air of authority that his youthful features never did – and fastened the front clasp, which had popped open in the fall. Then he got out of the car and looked at the house.

Curtains still closed, even though it was gone nine o'clock. Actually, they were blinds, not curtains, the type his mum had in her bedroom for when she worked nights at the hospital, the type that blacked out the daylight. They were pulled down over every window.

Strange.

Crunching over the gravel in shoes that could have done

with a polish, he approached the front porch of the substantial property. With six bedrooms, the original farmhouse having been extended into the adjacent barn, it was definitely worthy of being called high-end, the current owners having spent a fortune on it. En suite bathrooms, a top of the range bespoke kitchen complete with Aga, three reception rooms and a utility larger than Stuart's living room and kitchenette combined. The inspection would take a while.

Clearing his throat, Stuart reached out and pressed the bell. Listened and heard nothing, only the call of a black and white bird which was wheeling about above the fells, sounding like a squeaky toy he'd had as a child. He smiled, thinking how Julie would have known what it was and teased him in his ignorance for being a townie from Skipton.

He pressed the bell again. Put his ear to the door and heard only the thud of his pulse coming back at him. So he knocked. Hard. And waited.

When still no one was forthcoming, Stuart took a few steps back from the unopened door and looked up at the front of the house. No sign of any of the blinds being rolled up. Given the lack of vehicles on the forecourt, it didn't bode well. Thinking he should have made an appointment, he decided to try his luck around the back.

Following the gravel to the right, he arrived in a yard, a long outbuilding stretching away, its roof offset, lower on one side than the other. No cars in sight here, either. He looked up at the rear wall of the farmhouse, the windows not as uniform as on the front, some small, some large, one running the height of the building. All of them stared blankly back at him, the glass covered in blinds.

Not holding out much hope, Stuart knocked on the

kitchen door. When there was no answer, he didn't bother a second time. Instead, he wandered over to the outbuildings, noting the shininess of the padlocks on the three sets of doors. He also noticed the yellow box on the wall nearest the house. An alarm, on the outbuilding. That wasn't listed in the specs, and besides, it looked new.

Intrigued, he went up to the gable wall, to a small window just about reachable on tiptoes, and pressed his face against the dirty glass. Some kind of workshop, an old bench inside. Nothing that looked valuable. He looked back at the farmhouse. No alarm on it. Although there was a small security camera above the back door, again looking newly installed.

All very curious.

Feeling frustrated at his wasted journey, Stuart was very aware that in his hand were the keys for the property. He knew he shouldn't. That it was against the law for him to enter without permission. But there was something fishy going on. The paperwork for a start. And now this . . . he couldn't put his finger on it. The strangeness of it – the blinds, the padlocks, the alarm, the camera.

Without giving himself the chance to chicken out, Stuart Lister slipped the key marked 'Rear' in the back door. From within the house came the sudden sound of a dog barking.

'Slow down, Arty!' Edith finally had to say as they came out of Back Street onto the marketplace in what would have been record time for Edith in her heyday. Now in her advanced years and with a dodgy hip, it was leaving her breathless, her stick tapping dementedly as she tried to keep up with her companion. 'What on earth has got into you?'

He'd been like a cat on hot bricks since they'd left the Dales Detective Agency, shooing her out of the door while Lucy Metcalfe was still talking to Samson and Delilah, not even waiting to hear what was going on. He'd made the excuse that Lucy needed privacy, but Edith wasn't buying it.

Arty glanced over his shoulder before easing to a more natural pace. 'Sorry, but I wanted to make sure we put some distance between us in case they noticed.'

'In case who noticed what?' She pulled on his arm, making him stop outside Whitaker's, allowing her to catch her breath.

He grinned at her and took his mobile out of his pocket. 'In case Samson and Delilah noticed that I'd taken a photo of their records.'

On the screen was a picture of Delilah's notepad, the page covered in writing. And at the bottom, handily circled, was a name and address. Edith looked up at Arty.

'Is that . . . ?'

He nodded. 'I'd bet my life on it. I could tell there was something shifty going on when you asked if they knew who Robert Webster really was. Delilah went all coy.' He gestured at the phone. 'And here we have it. The identity of the catfish.'

'I hope you're not planning on doing anything stupid, Arty Robinson,' Edith said in her strictest voice.

Arty shook his head, all innocence. 'Nothing stupid. Just planning a spot of fishing with the lads.'

*

It turned out Stuart Lister was a coward after all.

Key in the lock, a half-twist already completed, he froze at the sound of barking coming from the other side of the rental property's rear door. Not the high-pitched yap of a lapdog but the deep, resounding barks of something a lot larger. A Dobermann, perhaps. Or a Rottweiler. A guard dog to go along with the security camera and the shiny padlocks.

Not the kind of dog you could calm with a few soft words and the promise of a belly rub.

It was enough to give the lettings manager pause for thought. And then his mobile sounded, alerting him to an incoming text, yet another excuse to hesitate. Stepping away from the door, he consulted his phone.

A brief message from Nancy Taylor to inform him that Rick Procter was temporarily taking over the business, as of today.

Like now. Possibly already in the office and wondering which keys should be hanging on the empty hook in the key safe in Mr Taylor's office. Or perhaps even checking the bottom drawer of the filing cabinet and noticing that, as well as the Kingston Holdings files, there was now one of the high-end rentals files missing, too.

How long before he joined the dots?

Stuart felt sick at the thought. So he turned away from the property, walked back around to the front of the farmhouse and got in the Mini, a large part of him relieved at not having to brave the inspection. But as he drove down the rutted track, despising his lack of backbone, he came to a decision.

Yes, he might not be made of the stuff that could see him illegally enter a house, confront a barking dog, and put himself in possible danger in order to find out what was going on with the irregular lettings. But he had enough moral fibre to know he couldn't continue to work for Taylor's either. Especially not now Mr Procter was taking charge, the man clearly involved in whatever the skulduggery was that Stuart had uncovered.

So that was it then. Decision made. He'd head back to the office, hand in his notice and start again. A new job. A new life. The possibilities were endless. And as for everything he'd uncovered, he still had the Kingston Holdings files. Perhaps he could make sure they landed on Matty Thistlethwaite's desk? The solicitor would know what to do with them. By which time, Stuart would be far away from any possible repercussions.

In a better frame of mind, Stuart Lister drove towards what he hoped was a brighter horizon. A horizon that, right at this moment, was filled with an approaching Range Rover.

After two weeks of dieting, Sergeant Clayton wasn't in the best of moods. Throw in a shooting incident on his patch that had turned from suicide to murder, the victim none other than the town mayor, and Bruncliffe's senior policeman was feeling stressed, grumpy and hungry. His mood had been in no way aided by seeing Samson O'Brien and Delilah Metcalfe walk in the door of the police station, accompanied by Delilah's dog. And now they were sitting opposite him in the small office, demanding to know more about the latest developments.

'Stop!' he said, holding up his hand to halt O'Brien, who was trying to outline why Ana Stoyanovic couldn't

possibly have been responsible for shooting Bernard
Taylor. 'I don't have time for this.'

'But—'

'No buts!' Sergeant Clayton shook his head, the sharpness of his words brooking no opposition. 'This is a grave
matter and believe it or not, we have it firmly in hand. Your
interference in this instance is not welcome, and I'm not at
liberty to discuss the case with you.'

Samson O'Brien sat back, surprised by the outburst.
Not so Delilah Metcalfe. She lifted up a paper bag and
placed it on the desk with an impish smile.

'Are you at liberty to have a coffee break?' she asked.

It was a Peaks Patisserie bag. Sergeant Clayton knew it
was also a blatant bribe. Sitting at his desk and pretending
to work, young Danny was stifling a smile.

'What's in here, then?' asked the sergeant, pulling the
bag towards him, vowing that he'd just see what she'd
brought and take it no further.

He peered inside and groaned. Plum-and-almond slices.
One of the top ten in the Lucy-Metcalfe-baking chart, and
it was a chart that took some beating. The sergeant was
vaguely aware that Danny had stood up and put the kettle
on and was taking down four mugs . . .

'Damn it!' he muttered. 'What do you want to know?'

'The grounds for Ana's arrest would be a good start,'
said O'Brien. 'It seems like a dramatic change to go from a
verdict of suicide to one of murder.'

'Aye,' said Sergeant Clayton. 'I was a bit surprised
myself when they called over from Harrogate to fill me in.
But the test results don't lie.'

'What do they say?'

'That Bernard Taylor couldn't possibly have killed himself, because there are none of his prints on the shotgun.'

O'Brien stared at the policeman. Delilah looked stunned, too.

'Pretty conclusive, wouldn't you say?' added the sergeant.

'And Ana's prints . . .' murmured O'Brien.

'Are all over it.'

'But that's because she carried it through the building and put it in the Land Rover,' protested Delilah. 'It doesn't mean she fired it.'

'There was sufficient gunshot residue on her hands to suggest that she did,' countered the sergeant.

O'Brien was shaking his head. 'Still not enough proof. She's already testified that she opened the passenger door when she reached the Land Rover and the gun fell out. She caught it as it fell. That would explain the traces on her hands.'

'Very convenient, don't you think?' Sergeant Clayton leaned back as Danny deposited four mugs of coffee on the desk, his eyes tracking the constable's movements as he drew the plum-and-almond slices out of the bag and put them on a plate. Five of them. One each and one spare . . . Delilah Metcalfe was a smart woman. Tearing his attention away from the cakes, the sergeant continued. 'I mean, if Ana Stoyanovic wanted to give herself an alibi in terms of gunshot residue, that's quick thinking.'

'You can't seriously believe this?' exclaimed Delilah, exasperated. 'Isn't it possible Bernard fired the gun using . . . I don't know . . . a stick or something?'

'Not unless he was ambidextrous. He was holding his mobile in his right hand.'

'He was on the phone when he was shot?' O'Brien's voice was full of curiosity.

'He was indeed. He left a voicemail for Nancy. But before you ask,' the sergeant said, anticipating the next question, 'no, you can't have a copy of the recording. And furthermore,' he continued, turning his attention back to Delilah, 'nothing was found at the scene that could have aided Bernard in a suicide attempt. But anyway, that's all moot. Because the clincher from the forensics team is that, according to the blood spatter analysis, the passenger door must have been open when he was shot.' Sergeant Clayton reached for his coffee and picked up one of the slices, letting his last revelation sink in.

'Open?' O'Brien was already working it out. 'Yet all three of the first witnesses to arrive on the scene have said it was closed when they got out there.'

'Aye,' mumbled the sergeant through a mouthful of cake. 'Pretty neat trick for a dead man to close a car door, wouldn't you say?'

It silenced them. Briefly.

'But even if it was definitely murder, what about motive?' persisted Delilah. 'Apart from the fact that she's not capable of killing someone, what reason would Ana have had for shooting Bernard Taylor?'

Sergeant Clayton shifted in his chair. Because this was the bit he was least comfortable with. 'I have to admit, we were struggling with that. But there are two strands of thought. One is that, as Ana herself said, she was trying to keep a low profile at the shoot to avoid a confrontation with her former boss, Rick Procter. But we know, thanks to you Delilah, that Bernard had seen her.'

Delilah nodded, her testimony having included the last words she'd heard Bernard speak: that puzzling reference to Ana. 'How is that relevant?'

'Well, we think that Ana knew she'd been rumbled and went out to the courtyard to beg Bernard not to say anything to Rick. And things turned heated . . .'

'Rubbish!' said O'Brien. 'Ana wouldn't have killed him just because he could have identified her.'

'You know her that well? Don't forget she'd already spent time here on a false passport.'

'That's a long cry from murdering someone.'

'That's as maybe. But there's another scenario. Thing is, we came across a bit of an anomaly during the digging we did over the weekend – a substantial amount of cash Nancy Taylor admitting to finding in Bernard's wardrobe.' The sergeant could tell from the glance that passed between his two guests that this wasn't news. 'Aye, she mentioned that to you, did she? Because she told us that's what made her hire you both. That she thought Bernard was hiding his assets in the run-up to divorcing her. But what if she had the wrong end of the stick?'

'In what way?' O'Brien was frowning now, trying to see where this was going.

'Blackmail.' Sergeant Clayton leaned back in his chair. 'Bernard Taylor was being blackmailed by Ana Stoyanovic because she knew he was having an affair.'

'So basically, it was a disaster,' muttered Delilah, concluding her account of their visit to the police station as she stirred her coffee with more vigour than it warranted.

In the post-lunchtime lull, Samson was sitting across

from her at a table by the window in Peaks Patisserie with Lucy Metcalfe next to him, while Tolpuddle lay on the pavement outside, basking in the afternoon sunshine. Of the four, the Weimaraner was by far the most contented.

'We went in there to help Ana's cause,' Delilah continued, her spoon clattering onto her saucer, 'and instead my testimony has ended up being part of the case against her.'

'It's like a bad case of déjà vu,' said Lucy, shaking her head. She'd finally found time to be brought up to speed by the detective duo, having been left short-staffed following the very public arrest of Ana Stoyanovic at the cafe that morning. Agreeing to cover for Elaine, who'd been offered extra lecturing hours at short notice, Ana hadn't even started her first shift before she'd been taken away in a police car, apron still around her waist. 'Poor Ana. That business at Fellside Court at Christmas was bad enough and now this – Bruncliffe seems to be determined to label her a criminal. And I wouldn't mind but she was doing me a favour. She shouldn't even have been here.'

'Makes no difference.' Samson pushed away his plate of apple pie, appetite gone after the frustrating morning. 'They'd have arrested her somewhere else. At least here she had you to raise the alarm.'

'Not that it's done much good,' said Delilah with a grimace.

'But surely they can't make this stick?' insisted Lucy. 'As if Ana would know who Bernard was having an affair with! And even if somehow she did, why would she kill a potential golden goose? It just doesn't make sense. And as for killing him to hide her presence at the shoot . . . pah! These motives are so flimsy.'

Samson gave a fatalistic shrug. 'Unfortunately, you don't need a cast-iron motive to prove a case. Quite often the balance of forensic evidence will do the trick. And Ana has her fingerprints all over that gun and residue on her hands to boot.'

'And Sergeant Clayton? Is he going along with this nonsense? Or are the Harrogate detectives driving it?'

'He seems to be on board,' said Delilah. 'He even suggested as we were leaving that I ought to be too. You know, because I don't need to feel guilty any more if Bernard didn't kill himself.'

'You should never have been feeling guilty in the first place,' retorted Lucy.

'I'd rather keep carrying that burden than have an innocent person convicted.' Delilah shook her head. 'All the evidence seems so inconclusive.'

'Apart from the fact that Bernard Taylor didn't kill himself,' countered Samson. 'That's fairly conclusive from the test results. Which means someone at the shoot is guilty of murder.'

It was a sobering thought. That what they had witnessed two days ago up at Bruncliffe Manor hadn't been the desperate action of a man under pressure, but rather the deliberate taking of another person's life.

'It just doesn't seem possible, though,' said Delilah. 'How did someone manage to shoot Bernard and get away before Ana, Gareth and Rick all arrived on the scene.'

'You were there moments later. You didn't see anything that could shed any light on it?' asked Samson.

'Nothing. I went out of the kitchen, through the breakfast room and out of the dining room doors. I didn't pass a soul. But it'll all be on the camera footage, so we can double check.'

'What about you, Lucy? What did you see from the kitchen?'

'Not much. With where Gareth's Land Rover was parked, I could only see the boot from the window. But I wasn't even looking out when the gun went off. I was at the stove.'

'So the gun going off was the first you knew about it, like the rest of us?'

Lucy tipped her head in contemplation. 'I guess so, although just before it went off I saw something reflected in the splashback above the range. A movement of some sort. It pulled my attention to the window and I was still in the act of turning round when I heard the blast. And then I just ran.'

'What kind of movement?' Samson was watching her with interest.

'I don't know . . . a flash of something brown . . . I really can't say any more than that.'

'And how long after that did you hear the gun?'

'Oh, no more than it takes to turn around. A couple of seconds?'

'I presume you told the police about this?'

'For what it's worth.' She shrugged. 'It was one of the Harrogate detectives and he didn't seem bothered. Why? Do you think it could be important?'

'If we're going to prove Ana didn't kill Bernard Taylor, then yes, everything's important. Especially when you're describing something that happened in the moments before the gun went off.'

'So is this it, then?' asked Delilah, trying not to show her delight at his casual use of 'we'. 'We're taking the case?'

Samson nodded. 'We have to. Because I'm damn sure Ana Stoyanovic didn't kill Bernard Taylor. All we have to do is prove it—' He broke off at the ring of his mobile, frowning at the unknown number. 'Hello?' he said.

A gabble of words tumbled out of the receiver, Delilah watching as Samson's forehead pulled into an even tighter frown.

'Right,' he finally said. 'Leave it with me for now and I'll call you back.' He placed the mobile back on the table and shook his head. 'You're not going to believe this,' he said, looking at Delilah and Lucy in turn. 'That was Gareth Towler. The police have just had him in for questioning.'

Delilah's eyebrows shot up. 'In connection with the shooting?'

Samson nodded. 'From the tone of the questions, he thinks they suspect him of murdering Bernard Taylor.'

'This is getting crazier by the minute!' exclaimed Lucy.

'Tell me about it,' muttered Samson. 'He called to ask if we could take his case. He wants us to prove he's innocent.'

25

A stunned silence had settled over the table at the window of Peaks Patisserie. Two people, both suspected of murdering the same man, both wanting help from the Dales Detective Agency.

'You have to say yes,' Lucy finally said. 'You have to agree to investigate on Gareth's behalf. The man doesn't have a bad bone in his body. There's no way he could have done this.'

'That's what you said about Ana,' said Samson, with a wry smile.

'But wouldn't it be unethical?' asked Delilah. 'To represent Ana *and* Gareth?'

Samson shook his head. 'We're not lawyers. We don't have to worry about conflict of interest in that respect. It's more a matter of whether we'd be setting ourselves an impossible task.'

'You mean, by proving one innocent, we'd have to implicate the other?' said Delilah.

'Exactly. Especially given that Ana and Gareth were first on the scene, which sets them up to be considered as suspects.'

'Are we to include Rick Procter in that, too, then? Seeing as he got to the courtyard the same time as them?'

'Definitely.'

'Blimey! Three possible suspects, two of whom want us to work for them and all of them known to us,' muttered Delilah, rubbing her forehead. 'This case is already giving me a headache.'

'What's with the long faces?' A smiling Herriot hailed them as he walked in the door and over to the table. 'Stuck on an investigation?'

'Something like that,' said Samson, shaking the vet's hand.

'Morning, Herriot,' Lucy said, getting to her feet. 'Usual?'

The vet's smile widened. 'Please.' He watched her walk to the counter before turning back to Samson, more sombre now. 'Terrible news about Gareth.'

'You've heard?'

'He called earlier. He's afraid he might get taken into custody at any minute so he's asked me to look after Bounty for a couple more days, seeing as he doesn't know what the hell is going on.'

'Bounty's with you?' asked Delilah, feeling bad that she hadn't thought about the springer spaniel since she'd handed her over to the gamekeeper after the paramedics arrived.

Herriot nodded. 'Gareth brought her in to me on Saturday after the shooting. He was worried about her.'

'And how is she?'

'Not so good. She's sound physically but she's really shook up by what happened. Any loud noise at all and she's terrified, just curls up in her cage. I'd say her days as a gun dog are over.'

'Poor thing. What'll happen to her if . . .'

'If Gareth gets detained?' The vet shrugged. 'I guess—'

'Herriot will just take Bounty home and lavish love on her like he does with all the strays,' said Lucy, placing a takeout coffee and a wrapped-up sausage roll on the table before putting an arm around the vet. 'Because he's a really good person.' She kissed him on the cheek and he blushed.

'Thanks,' he murmured. 'For the food, I mean. Right. Got to go.' Herriot grabbed his coffee and headed for the door, Lucy walking with him.

'Christ,' muttered Samson. 'What a mess. For everyone involved.'

'For what's it worth,' said Delilah, lowering her voice to a murmur, 'if you had to choose from the three candidates we have so far, who would you pick for the guilty party?'

Samson gave a dry laugh. 'What a question! While my heart would want it to be Rick, I have to say that I honestly don't know. I can't help feeling that there might be an element of truth to Sergeant Clayton's hypothesis.'

'Blackmail?'

'Yeah. It makes sense. Having a large amount of cash lying in your wardrobe is highly irregular.'

'But we saw no evidence that Bernard was having an affair.'

'No, but there are other reasons to extort money from someone. He was the town mayor and an estate agent. Maybe he got caught with his fingers in the wrong pie?'

'Which could rule out Rick as a potential suspect, seeing as he was Bernard's business partner. God, we're just going round in circles—'

'You're not the only ones!' This time the interruption was from PC Danny Bradley, standing at their table and looking as furtive as the lad was capable of, given that he had one of the most honest faces Samson had ever seen. He held out his hand to Delilah and let something fall into her open palm.

'What's that?' asked Samson.

'It's a recording of the phone call Bernard Taylor made to Nancy before he was shot—' The constable paused, grimaced and corrected himself. 'Actually, *while* he was shot. It's not pleasant listening.'

Delilah looked at the memory stick in her hand and up at the policeman. 'I take it Sergeant Clayton isn't aware that you're giving us this?'

'You're right,' said Danny. 'He'd kill me if he knew. But Sarge is on a diet and not thinking straight and the rest of the investigation team don't seem to think it's worth analysing. Whereas I can't help feeling we're missing something and the answer might be there, on that.'

'You don't think Ana Stoyanovic shot Bernard, then?' asked Samson. He knew enough of the lad to know his opinions were always worth respecting.

'I wouldn't go that far. But I'd like a motive. And before you repeat Sarge's blackmail scenario, I'm not buying that. Not for a minute.'

'What about the latest suspect in the frame? Gareth Towler?'

The question triggered a flash of surprise on the constable's face. 'You've heard already?'

Samson nodded. 'From the man himself.'

There was a moment of silence, then Danny sighed. 'That's why I'm really here. They're saying Gareth might have killed Bernard because he threatened to have Gareth sacked. I've known Gareth Towler all my life and he just isn't capable of killing someone.'

'You and Lucy both,' murmured Samson.

'Yeah, well, Sarge and the detectives from Harrogate won't listen to me,' continued the constable, 'so I'm begging you to keep investigating this. Find out who really shot Bernard Taylor.' The young policeman turned to go, paused as if considering something, and then turned back to Samson with a pained expression. 'And by the way, that DCI Thistlethwaite. I'm not sure you should trust him.'

The way he said it brought a moment of clarity to Samson. 'He's asked you and Sergeant Clayton to keep tabs on me?'

Danny nodded, looking even more miserable. 'He didn't say why. But Sarge made me call him when we got to Bruncliffe Manor on Saturday. Sorry.'

'Not your fault. But thanks for letting me know.'

Danny regarded him for a moment, then gave a small smile and walked off towards the door, Delilah already getting to her feet. If she was thrown by the revelation about Frank Thistlethwaite, she wasn't showing it.

'Come on,' she said, gesturing at Samson's untouched apple pie. 'Eat up. We've got work to do.'

Feeling his appetite returning, triggered by the buzz of adrenalin that came from knowing they had a lead to work on, Samson pulled his plate towards him and, in four rapid mouthfuls, finished off the pie, Tolpuddle watching on mournfully from the other side of the window.

If the third member of the Dales Detective Agency team was perturbed at having missed out on a slice of apple pie, it was impossible to tell as he trotted contentedly along between Samson and Delilah on the walk back to work. But that contentment disappeared the minute they turned the corner onto Back Street, Tolpuddle starting to growl. It was a low rumble at first, but grew steadily into something more threatening. Samson reached down to slip a hand under the Weimaraner's collar.

'Easy boy,' he murmured. Then he saw the reason for the dog's reaction.

On the doorstep of the office building was Rick Procter. Tolpuddle was outright barking now, straining towards the property developer, every muscle and sinew pulled taut as he fought to get free from Samson's grip.

'I'll take him,' said Delilah, possibly sensing that Samson was more than tempted to let go of the Weimaraner altogether. Taking hold of Tolpuddle's collar, she turned him around, talking to him all the time as she eased him back up the street, his barking gradually subsiding to a low growl.

'Quite a welcome,' said Rick Procter, backed up against the front door where he'd retreated, handsome face drained of colour.

'Believe me, it's a lot warmer than mine.' Samson stared at the man. 'What do you want?'

'I didn't expect open arms, O'Brien. I'm here on business. Is there somewhere we can talk?'

Samson knew what Bruncliffe hospitality would dictate – that he show Rick into his office and offer tea. But Samson had never felt more out of sync with the conventions of his birthplace than at that moment. All he wanted to do was punch the man, a raw burst of anger burning in his gut, blocking out every rational thought—

A light touch on his arm cut through the red mist. Delilah was standing next to him, a quieter Tolpuddle by her side, his growl reduced to a low continuous rumble.

'That's him all calmed down now,' she was saying, a smile on her face, the subject of her statement ambiguous. 'Come on inside, Rick. We can talk in there.'

Samson opened the front door and stood aside. With a wary glance at the dog, Rick entered the building and went straight into the downstairs office.

'You okay?' Delilah murmured, catching Samson before he could follow the property developer.

He nodded. 'Yes. But don't offer him any tea.'

Delilah blinked at the odd request, nodded anyway and entered the room behind Samson, leading Tolpuddle to his bed, where she persuaded him to lie down.

'You're not going to let go of him, are you?' Rick was already moving back towards the door at the sight of the Weimaraner, the dog regarding him with equal distaste.

'Sit down, Rick, you'll be fine,' said Delilah with a bright smile, taking a seat next to Samson. 'Honestly. And if Tolpuddle does make a move, we'll do our best to catch him before he can reach you.'

There was a moment of silence, Rick trying to work out if she was joking or not, then he gave a forced laugh and took the chair across the desk from them, shifting it slightly so the dog bed was in his line of sight.

'So, what do you want?' Samson asked.

'I need your help.' Rick smiled, hands held open in supplication as if he'd never made threats against the man he was talking to, nor robbed his family blind in an unscrupulous property deal. 'I'm in a bit of a predicament.'

'The police suspect you of murdering Bernard Taylor.'

The smile slipped and Samson caught a glimpse of what he could only describe as panic on the property developer's face before the man nodded, lips curving once more. 'Yes. Ludicrous as it sounds, I think they do. I had the two Harrogate detectives at the office this morning, asking questions, and I didn't care for their tone.'

'So how do I come into this?' asked Samson, no intention of making it easy.

'I want to hire you. If anyone can get to the truth of what happened on Saturday, it's you, O'Brien.'

'Why Samson?' Delilah's blunt question made both men turn in surprise. She shrugged, a smile as sunny as Rick's on her face. 'Sorry, but I'm just curious. You haven't exactly been the most welcoming of people since he came home.'

Again Rick's hands spread out, seeking understanding. 'I admit we've not always seen eye to eye. But the Dales Detective Agency comes highly recommended. And I've a feeling I need the best there is.'

'Did the police give any hint as to why they suspect you?'

'Not overtly. But from the slant of their questions, I'd say they heard reports of a tiff Bernard and I had at the shoot. Perhaps you noticed in your guise as Denise? When we broke off for refreshments up on the fell?'

'What was it about?' asked Samson, rescuing his partner, who looked uncomfortable at the mention of her undercover operation.

Rick shrugged. 'Oh, you know, a business disagreement. Nothing we wouldn't have worked out over a couple of drinks that evening. Certainly not something worth killing someone over.' Again, the high-wattage smile, which Samson suspected was masking genuine alarm. 'So, will you take my case? Prove I didn't do it? You'll have the full weight of Procter Properties behind you – funds, resources, anything you want that I can provide you with, all you'll have to do is ask.'

But Samson was deaf to the offer of such assistance, the thought of representing the man making his blood curdle. 'Sorry. No can do. I'm already working for someone else connected to the case.'

'Who?' asked Rick.

'I'm afraid I can't discuss that with you. Client confidentiality.'

Rick nodded. Then he tried one last time. 'Not even if I pay triple the going rate?'

Before Samson could reject the offer in more brutal terms, Delilah spoke up.

'It's a deal,' she announced, leaning across the desk to get her notebook, a sharp kick landing on Samson's ankle in the process, stifling the objection he'd been about to verbalise. He glared at her but she ignored him, focus on their new client. Whose face was showing a visible sense of relief.

'Thank you, thank you so much,' Rick said.

'Save the thanks for when we've saved your backside,' said Delilah. 'Now, let's start at the beginning. Tell us what happened in the lead up to the shooting from your perspective.'

Samson sat back in his chair, arms folded, furious. But also curious to hear Rick's side of events.

'There's not much to tell,' said Rick. 'I went round to the courtyard—'

'Why?' asked Delilah, her tone one of interrogation. 'The rest of the shooting party were at the front of the manor. What took you out the back?'

'I was worried about Bernard. He didn't take the decision to end the shoot very well, so when I noticed that he'd disappeared from the drawing room, I was afraid he'd gone to try and confront Gareth again. So I went looking for him.'

'And that brought you to the courtyard?'

'Yes. I walked round the house from the terrace, down the south side—'

'Not out past the cars and down the track?'

'No.' Rick grimaced. 'My guests were gathering out front and . . . well, truth is they'd been complaining about the shoot being cancelled and I didn't want to have to deal with them. Plus, it was quicker to just go straight out of the drawing room.'

Delilah nodded. 'Fair enough. So walk me through what happened next.'

'I was almost at the back of the house when I heard the gunshot. I started running and came around the corner into the courtyard as Ana Stoyanovic and Gareth Towler got there.'

'Which direction did they come from?'

Rick took a moment to think. 'Ana must have come from the opposite side to me and Gareth emerged from round the back of the stables.'

'And who was nearest the Land Rover.'

'Ana Stoyanovic. But there wasn't much in it. She ran

to the passenger door, opened it and then bent out of sight and started screaming. I couldn't see what she was doing as the vehicle was between us but I gather she caught the shotgun as it fell out. And that's when you came out of the French windows from the dining room.'

'So, why do the police suspect you could be involved? Have they said what evidence they have?'

Rick nodded. 'My fingerprints are all over the gun.'

Samson had watched the exchange in silence, but now he sat forward, compelled by the response to intervene. 'How come? Wasn't it Milan's gun?'

'It was. But after Milan threw it down in annoyance after the first drive, I picked it up.' Rick gestured towards Delilah. 'You must have seen that?'

'I did,' confirmed Delilah, cheeks going pink.

'Right,' said Rick, with a dry tone. 'Never thought I'd be grateful for having you spy on us.' He glanced at his watch. 'I'm sorry but I'm going to have to leave it there for now as I've got a stack of work on. I'm running the estate agency for Nancy as an interim measure and I'm flat out.'

'That's incredibly generous of you,' said Delilah. 'I'm sure Nancy is grateful.'

'She is. Just as I'm grateful to you two for taking on my case.' With one last smile, Rick stood, a cautious glance shooting to Tolpuddle in the corner as the dog lifted up his head, growling slightly. Then he turned to go.

Samson let him reach the door before slowly rising from his seat. 'Actually, there are a couple of things you might be able to help us with.'

The property developer paused in the office doorway, nodding. 'Anything. What is it?'

'Can you describe your outfit the day of the shoot?'

Rick looked puzzled. 'You were there. Surely you saw it? A brown tweed jacket and plus fours. Bloody ridiculous clothing but, you know. . .when in Rome and all that.'

'And Gareth?'

'Very similar.'

'Brown?'

'Yes, why? What's this got to do with anything?'

Samson shook his head. 'Just ruling things out, that's all.'

Rick stared at him, as though he was going to press for more. But then he simply said, 'And the other thing?'

'The other thing,' said Samson, 'is that in the course of our enquiries, it's come to light that Bernard had a substantial amount of cash hidden in his house. The police are speculating that he was being blackmailed. Can you think of anything Bernard might have been trying to hide?'

Rick's laugh was loud. 'Blackmail? Seriously? Is that the best motive they have?'

'It's the one they're going with. You don't think it has legs?'

'Not for one minute.'

'So how can the presence of that much cash be explained?' asked Delilah.

'Taylor's is a successful real estate business,' said Rick, an element of frustration in his voice. 'What the tinpot police in Bruncliffe consider a substantial amount of money is probably peanuts to the likes of Bernard and myself.'

'A hundred and twenty-five thousand pounds?'

'Like I said, peanuts. I'm sure a look at Taylor's accounts

will explain it.' He turned to Samson, smile back in place. 'Anything else?'

'Nope.' Samson made no move to show the property developer out, leaving Delilah to maintain Bruncliffe's high standards of hospitality as she walked around the desk and followed Rick into the hall. Samson waited for them to say their farewells and the front door to close before he let out a sigh and sank back into his seat. In his bed, Tolpuddle did likewise, a long exhalation followed by the flopping of his head onto his paws.

'So,' said Delilah, returning to lean against the door-jamb. 'A full set. Ana, Gareth and now Rick, too.'

'Thanks to you!' Samson grumbled. 'I can't believe you said yes to that man.'

Delilah just grinned. 'You know I was right. This way we get to grill Rick about his movements that morning and he pays us for the privilege. In triplicate.'

Samson couldn't argue. In fact, as the interview had progressed, he'd seen the genius in Delilah's decision to accept Rick Procter's request. And as for her questions . . . She'd handled herself like a real detective.

'What do you think, then? Of the three, who takes your fancy now?' she asked.

'Hard to say. Ana seems to have been on the scene earlier, which could suggest she was already there and merely pretending to be arriving. But Rick and Gareth—'

'Were both wearing brown.' Delilah nodded. 'I guessed that's why you were quizzing Rick about his attire. You think one of them could be the flash of brown Lucy saw?'

'It's a thought. A chance reflection in the splashback as the killer moved away from the Land Rover?'

'Or simply a bird flying past!' retorted Delilah.

Samson nodded. 'It's all so tenuous. Let's hope the recording Danny gave us can shed some light on this impossible case.'

'*Three* impossible cases,' said Delilah, still leaning in the doorway, a smile on her lips.

And suddenly Samson caught himself staring at those lips, knowing what they were capable of, wishing they were—

From the corner of the room came a loud Weimaraner sigh and Delilah laughed.

'I don't know which of you two had to work harder at self-restraint while Rick was here!' she said, grinning at man and dog. 'You both deserve a biscuit before we get back to work.'

Her footsteps retreated up the stairs, closely followed by the sound of the kettle being filled. Samson was left with a now snoozing Tolpuddle to ruminate on Rick Procter's unexpected visit. And to acknowledge that his self-restraint when it came to the property developer was as nothing compared to the efforts he was going to in order to maintain his behaviour around Delilah.

Rick Procter was along Back Street, out onto the marketplace and down the cobbles to the estate agent's before he stopped sweating, a condition that had nothing to do with the brilliant sunshine that was flooding the town with light.

Bloody Taylor! When it came to the funds intended to pay off Pete Ferris, the idiot mayor had left a luminous trail behind him. A trail so easy to follow that even the moronic minds of Sergeant Clayton and the Bradley kid were putting two and two together.

That wasn't the worst of it, however. The worst of it was O'Brien. That way he had of pinning you down with a stare. The sharpness of his questions. He was formidable enough on his own but teamed up with Delilah Metcalfe, they made for a couple of problems that were long overdue being solved.

But first things first. And first of all, he needed their help.

Some would call it madness, to allow O'Brien so close to him at a time when things were so tense. The man had a sixth sense for trouble and Rick was pretty sure that he must be reeking of it right now, the way things were going. But he had his reasons for putting himself in the lion's den, not least because he needed to be out of the spotlight, the intense police scrutiny that would come with a full murder investigation not being something his business partners would appreciate. He was banking on O'Brien and Delilah proving him innocent and deflecting that attention. He also needed to glean as much about the progress of the investigation into the shooting as he could, for his own peace of mind. And while O'Brien hadn't been particularly forthcoming on that front so far, he'd at least alerted Rick to the fact the police were considering blackmail as a motive for Taylor's actions. An unsettling disclosure, but an invaluable one, which Rick would have to try and deal with. Because blackmail was a topic he couldn't have the police digging into.

Using the keys entrusted to him by Nancy, Rick let himself into Taylor's, the place as quiet as it had been the

Date with Deceit

day before, thanks to staff absences. Which suited him perfectly. With the coast clear, he could make the most of his legitimate right to be in the office, and access Taylor's computer. A few tweaks here and there, covering tracks, and before long there'd be no digital records left to worry about. All he'd have to do then was locate the missing Kingston Holdings files. Feeling somewhat calmer, Rick set to work.

26

Listening to Danny's recording brought a shiver to Delilah's spine, the brilliant late-afternoon sunshine beyond Samson's office window dulled momentarily as she was transported back to the terror of Saturday morning. Opening with a stressed Bernard Taylor leaving a garbled message for his wife, the audio quickly descended into a cacophony of panic – Bounty barking frenziedly as Bernard tried to apologise to Nancy. And then that fatal blast from the shotgun, followed by an abrupt silence as the phone went dead.

'Are you okay?' Samson was sitting opposite her, looking at her as the voicemail ended.

She cleared her throat. 'Yes. Fine. Just . . . you know . . . it's just so raw. He sounds so desperate and I can't help thinking it's all because he saw me . . . Sorry.'

'No need to apologise.' He reached across the desk to put a hand on her arm and it took all of Delilah's control not to pull him across the desk towards her.

Instead, she sat back, tactfully withdrawing herself from his touch and forcing her attention onto the harrowing soundtrack of the mayor's final seconds. 'It's not much help, is it?' she said, gesturing at the memory stick that held the audio. 'Apart from revealing that Bernard *was* having an affair. I mean, he pretty much admits it. Poor Nancy –

imagine that being the last communication with your husband.'

'It must be dreadful for her,' said Samson. 'But like you, I'm struggling to see how this is going to produce the miracle Danny was hoping for in terms of the case. Could you bear another listen?' He was leaning forward, concerned.

More concerned that he was going to touch her again than about the impact the recording would have second time around, Delilah stood up. 'Go for it,' she said, walking over to Tolpuddle, who was lying in his basket, head on paws, dozing. She reached down and fondled the dog's ears, and wondered whether she ought to take Ida Capstick on full-time. Because if she couldn't trust herself to behave in Samson's presence, having Ida around would at least mean she could be chaperoned by her new receptionist.

Samson clicked on his laptop, the audio no less shocking on a second listening. Nor was it any more helpful. Until Samson stopped it just short of the shotgun being fired.

'There,' he said. 'Listen to this bit again.'

Bernard's final words, just about discernible against the barking dog, echoed around the room once more: '*I never meant to hurt you.*'

The mayor fell silent, Bounty's demented barking filling the void and then, just before the explosion of gunshot, another sound.

'That silence,' said Samson, frowning. 'What the hell is that all about?'

Delilah was as puzzled as he was. 'I know what you mean. If this was still a case of suicide, then that could be

Bernard, reaching over to fire the gun. But if it's murder, then what made him pause like that? Do you think he saw his killer?'

'Possibly. But what about the other noise at the very end? Did you catch what it was?'

Delilah shook her head. But there had definitely been something else audible in the milliseconds before the shotgun was fired.

'Let me see if I can isolate it,' she said. 'Maybe slow it down a bit, too, make it a bit clearer.' She made to approach the desk, pausing when Samson simply pulled a chair around to his side, gesturing for her to sit next to him.

It was worse than being a teenager again.

Acting like her heart wasn't rattling her ribcage, Delilah took the proffered seat and forced herself to concentrate. Focusing on the last five seconds of the voicemail, she began editing, cutting it into shorter sections and then playing around with the speed settings.

'How's that,' she finally said, clicking on the modified recording and sitting back.

The reduced speed made the mayor sound slurred, his final declaration more like a drunken lament, Bounty's barks seemingly amplified in contrast. And then that pause, lengthier now, the dog getting louder and then the mysterious sound, rendered terrifyingly audible:

'*No!*'

It was the last word of a dead man.

'It's Bernard,' whispered Delilah, ashen-faced.

Samson nodded grimly. 'All we have to do now is work out who he was talking to.'

*

With the evening just around the corner, the detective duo decided to call it a day, the revelation from the voicemail audio doing no more than adding yet another unanswered question to a case that was already proving vexing. Feeling exhausted, especially after an early start on the back of little sleep, Delilah was relieved when Samson didn't suggest they go for a meal. All she wanted, she thought, as she came down the stairs from having turned off her computer, was a hot bath and her bed. Although if Samson were to offer that . . .

'What are you smiling at?' Samson was standing in the hall, watching her, Tolpuddle next to him, lead already on.

'Nothing . . . just, er, thinking about tomorrow,' she stuttered, face on fire. 'You know . . . Clarissa's catfish . . .'

Rather than proceed with the Taylor case the following morning, they'd agreed that they needed to draw Clarissa's case to a conclusion, the danger that she'd hand over funds for the cruise ever present until the scam was exposed. Which meant a trip to Leeds to deal with the man behind Robert Webster, a situation Delilah wasn't looking forward to, given the potential for it to all go badly wrong.

Samson nodded. 'Don't worry, we'll get it done first thing. Best to get it out of the way, now we have three other cases to solve.' He was grinning at her.

'Right. So I'll see you at eight.' She took Tolpuddle's lead from him, careful not to let his hand touch hers.

'I'll walk you out,' he said.

'No need!' It came out sharper than she'd intended, induced by panic. The last thing she wanted was another farewell in the courtyard. 'We'll see ourselves out. Catch you tomorrow.'

Giving what she hoped was a cheery smile, she set off

through the back kitchen and out of the porch with Tolpuddle. It wasn't until they got into the ginnel, the gate shut behind them, that Delilah's heart rate settled back to something more normal. But as she climbed the steps up towards the Crag, it started racing again. Nothing to do with the pace of her ascent – Tolpuddle pulling her onwards in his rush to get home – but more that her thoughts had returned to the same topic they'd been distracted by when she'd been coming down those very steps that morning.

That bloody kiss!

He watched them go from the downstairs kitchen window, knowing Arty Robinson wouldn't have been impressed. Yet again, Samson had failed to take the initiative and tell Delilah how he felt.

It wasn't a good time, he told himself. She'd had a stressful couple of days. Perhaps when things calmed down a bit.

He laughed out loud at the thought. If the six and a bit months since he'd arrived back in Bruncliffe were anything to go by, he'd be waiting a long time to make his declaration, calm seemingly in short supply in this town.

He turned away from the window and promised himself that he would do it before the week was out. He would tell Delilah Metcalfe that he loved her. He'd done it once before, after all, when they were facing death in the freezer. But this time he would make sure that she was conscious.

'Do you think this is sensible?' On the other side of town to the Dales Detective Agency, Joseph O'Brien was sitting in Arty's lounge in Fellside Court, trying to be the rational voice amongst his fellow conspirators. But it was proving hard not to get caught up in their enthusiasm.

'Not at all,' laughed Arty. 'Sensible would be staying here and joining in with the pottery class. Personally, I'd rather be helping out a friend.'

Arty had waited until after tea to invite Joseph and Eric back to his, supposedly for a game of poker. But once there, the plan he'd outlined had far higher stakes.

They were going to pay Clarissa's catfish a visit. In person.

'You don't think we should leave it to Samson and Delilah to sort out?' asked Joseph.

Arty shook his head. 'Not with everything they have on their plate. They were talking about needing forty-eight hours to resolve this. We can't wait that long. And besides, last I heard, they had both Gareth Towler and Ana Stoyanovic asking for their help in the Taylor case. I wouldn't want either of them wrongly convicted of murder because Samson and Delilah were too busy dealing with something we're capable of sorting.'

It was a good point, one sure to appeal to his audience. While they didn't know the gamekeeper that well, they all remembered the former manager of the retirement complex with particular affection and would do anything to help clear her name.

'And you think we'll be able to cope if this Robert bloke turns nasty?' wheezed Eric.

Arty gave a confident nod. 'I still know a few moves from my odd shifts as a bouncer and I reckon Joseph could be handy with his fists. If all else fails, we could clock the fraudster with your oxygen tank.'

'But what are you hoping to achieve?' insisted Joseph. 'Surely it's enough to simply tell Clarissa the man is a con artist and that's the end of it?'

'And leave the bugger to cheat some other poor soul out of her life savings?' Arty shook his head. 'I'm not having that on my conscience. Anyway, enough talking! Are you with me or not?' He glared defiantly at his two friends.

'I'm in,' said Eric.

'Me too,' said Joseph.

Arty clapped his hands. 'Excellent. Seven o'clock sharp tomorrow then, for the train to Leeds.'

'What about Clarissa? Won't she be suspicious when we're not here?' asked Eric.

'I doubt she'll even notice,' said Arty with a grin. 'It took a bit of persuading, but Edith's agreed to take her to Harrogate on the pretext of buying a dress for the cruise. Which leaves us boys free to go fishing.'

Joseph's laugh was tinged with nervous excitement. 'Let's just hope we don't catch more than we can handle.'

Hours later, with darkness settled on the town and the two-day-old moon offering little illumination against an inky sky, the gentle wind that had been blowing over the Dales shifted in direction. Coming from the east now, it morphed into a more forceful beast, gusting down the fell-sides and into the streets, tipping over bins in ginnels and blowing garden furniture aside.

In the bedroom of one of the two flats situated above the Happy House takeaway, Mrs Lee was woken by the rattling of the sash window, a single-glazed relic from the past that had been known to fall out of its casing when the wind really whipped up. Tonight it was merely shuddering against its frame. Not a problem in itself, but if it roused the baby in the cot on the other side of the room . . .

She lay there in the dark, listening for the first stirrings of a child about to wake.

Nothing, just the heavy breaths of her husband, almost snores but not quite, the man exhausted after his evening shift in the kitchen. Then, through the thin wall that divided one dwelling from another, footsteps.

Her neighbour, walking around. Knowing Stuart Lister wasn't a night owl, hearing him up and about was unusual enough to make her look at the alarm clock. It was gone two o'clock.

Perhaps he had company? She smiled at the thought, hoping it was a woman. Someone who'd cook for him, because he was too thin. The lovely young man deserved to be looked after.

Another gust on the window, this one enough to judder the sash loudly. And from the cot came a whimper. The baby was awake. He'd remember he was teething soon and then there would be no quieting him. Moving softly so as not to disturb her husband, Mrs Lee got out of bed and crossed the room in the dark. She gathered up the restless child, blankets and all, cuddling his warmth to her chest, and crept out into the lounge, the cold lino a shock under her bare feet.

A rice cake was what she needed. Give the baby something to chew on before he started really grizzling. Opening the cupboard above the cooker in the kitchenette, she reached for the packet, prising one lose and passing it into the plump fist that had appeared from within the bundle of blankets.

In that moment of quiet, Mrs Lee smiling down at her son and caught as always by wonder that she had helped create this gorgeous being, the sound of the door to the neighbouring flat closing echoed down the short landing outside her lounge. She lifted her head, listening. Footsteps, heading past her front door and starting down the stairs.

Mrs Lee wasn't what you'd call a busybody. But activity of this sort at this hour was enough to spark curiosity. Baby still on her hip, she eased open the front door and peered down the stairs. The dim light in the hall picked out the tall figure of Stuart, a hoodie covering his head and a large rucksack on his back as he stepped out into the night.

Now she was really curious.

Baby, rice cake and all, she hastened back into the bedroom, to the rattling sash window. Pulling the curtain to one side, she peered out – nothing moving, Bruncliffe fast asleep apart from what looked like a dog slinking across the cobbles of the marketplace in the distance, two smaller shapes in its wake. And then Stuart came into view below her, crossing Fell Lane, heading up into town. Heading into the easterly wind.

The easterly wind that blew down his hoodie, letting Mrs Lee see a glint of what she thought was blond hair under the streetlight opposite the police station, before the hoodie was yanked back into place.

But Mrs Lee didn't have time to muse on the oddness of this – Stuart Lister's hair being mousy at best – for at that moment the baby hiccupped, dropped the rice cake and began to grizzle. Catching the cake before it hit the floor, she crept from the bedroom. She was only just in time, the baby letting out his first wail as she closed the door behind her. In the morning, Mr Lee would find wife and child fast asleep on the sofa. And after a sleep-deprived night, the nocturnal goings on of her neighbour would be the least of Mrs Lee's worries.

27

By eight thirty on Tuesday morning, Arty, Joseph and Eric were standing outside Leeds station, having an argument.

'It's too early to head straight there,' Arty was insisting. 'He might not even be up!'

'Or he could be heading for work and if we linger here, we'll miss him,' said Eric, holding on tight to his portable oxygen cylinder as the morning commuters flowed round them.

'Well I say we wait, and that looks as good a place as any to kill a bit of time.' Arty tipped his head in the direction of a small cafe built into a railway arch, the aroma of frying sausages wafting out of the open door.

'And I say you're thinking with your stomach and not your head, as usual,' muttered Eric.

Arty laughed and turned to the so-far silent member of the group. 'Your call, Joseph. What's it to be? A coffee and a sandwich or hop straight on the bus for Roundhay?'

'Well,' said Joseph, 'much as I agree with Eric's assessment of your thought processes, I also think that we might all benefit from a bit of sustenance before we go tackling this fella.'

'Spot on, my friend,' said Arty, slapping him on the back. 'Never wise going into a brawl on an empty stomach. The cafe it is!'

Sincerely hoping they wouldn't have to put Arty's maxim to the test, Joseph and Eric followed their friend across the road.

Samson and Delilah were late leaving Bruncliffe. And this time it wasn't Delilah who was to blame. She'd got to the office with Tolpuddle just before eight as promised, only to be met by an irate Ida Capstick at the back door. Following the cleaner up the stairs, Delilah knew from the even heavier than normal footsteps that Ida was in a real state. And so when Samson came down from his room, expecting to be on the road in minutes, the kettle was on, three mugs stood ready and Delilah was sitting with Ida at the kitchen table while Ida poured her heart out.

It was all Rick Procter's fault. Having arrived at the estate agent's to do her cleaning as usual, Ida had come across the property developer working in Bernard Taylor's office. Although surprised at the early hour, she'd heard he'd taken on the temporary running of the business and so his presence wasn't unexpected. In fact, she'd decided to make the most of it and had broached the subject of her missing red bucket.

To her chagrin, Mr Procter had dismissed her out of hand, telling her not to bother him with 'trivial nonsense'. It was the word trivial that had really got the cleaner annoyed. The idea that what she did counted for nothing when, if it hadn't been for her, the very floor under his feet would be still covered in soil from the upended plant she'd walked in on the morning before.

In high dudgeon, she'd got on with her duties, making sure she ran the vacuum cleaner for longer than usual, it's high-pitched whine enough to disturb anyone. Then she'd left the premises, slamming the door behind her and stomping over to the Dales Dating Agency – as the building would forever be known in her mind.

Samson stood at the sink listening to the tale with a frown, mug in one hand, toast in the other, before disappearing down the stairs, the front door closing behind him. Five minutes later he reappeared.

'I'll speak to Danny about your missing bucket this afternoon,' he said. 'But in the meantime, I got Barry next door to open up early.' He was holding out a bright red bucket, a packet of yellow dusters contained within it. 'Nothing you do is trivial, Ida. This place wouldn't be the same without you.'

Ida was speechless. She looked at the bucket. She looked at Samson. And then she gave one of her humph noises, which were always hard to interpret, used for both admonishment and praise. But the shine in her eyes and the slight curve of her lips suggested she was inclined towards the latter.

'Thank you,' she simply said, before heading upstairs to start cleaning, surreptitiously dabbing her eyes with the sleeve of her cardigan as she went.

Aware they were running very late, Samson hustled Tolpuddle and Delilah down the stairs and out to the Micra. Minutes later, just after eight forty-five – about the time Arty and company were tucking into their sausage sandwiches in the cafe in Leeds – the little red car hit the A65 and Delilah put her foot down.

Which to Samson's relief, was a lot less hair-raising than he'd been expecting, having suffered Delilah's speeds around the narrow lanes of the Dales. For with two adults and a large dog on board, the Micra was only capable of sixty miles an hour. And on a major road, with no tight bends or stone walls to worry about, that really wasn't so bad. By the time they reached Otley fifty minutes later, for the first time ever, Samson was enjoying a car journey with Miss Metcalfe at the wheel. He just wasn't looking forward to what was at the end of it.

While Samson and Delilah were speeding towards Leeds, Julie, receptionist at Taylor's Estate Agents, was getting off the train at Bruncliffe Station. She was running a bit late, but after the migraine that had flattened her the day before, it was a wonder she was heading into work at all. She probably wouldn't have been, but for the awful events that had overshadowed the place in the last few days.

Mr Taylor, killed up at Bruncliffe Manor, in what at first had been considered a suicide, but now, according to the local news, was reported to have been murder.

Murder! Her boss, shot!

Julie couldn't get her head around it. And if she was struggling, poor old Stuart with his gentle approach to life would be completely swamped by it. Which was the real reason she'd forced herself to come into work today. Stuart Lister was a soft soul who would be left adrift by all this upheaval, trying to man the office on his own. She owed it to him to offer a bit of support. To Mrs Taylor, too, a lovely woman who always went out of her way to have a chat whenever she popped in. She also always remembered that Julie was looking after her mother, who'd got early-onset Alzheimer's, and never failed to ask after her.

It was the little things, thought Julie, as she walked down Station Road to Church Street and turned right up towards the marketplace, that made a workplace a happy space. She glanced up at the flat above the Happy House takeaway and smiled. Stuart was one of those things. He didn't know it but her work life had been a lot more enjoyable since he'd joined Taylor's back in the autumn. Just having that other person to talk to for one thing. Having someone else to bear the brunt of Mr Taylor's recent bad moods was another.

Not that they had to worry about that any more.

Chiding herself for being disrespectful, Julie approached the marketplace, Peaks Patisserie on her right. She was almost past it when she stopped. Turned. And went in.

'Two Americanos to go,' she said. 'Oh, and a couple of those pecan slices, too.'

The woman behind the counter was new. Blonde. Stunning. But a very serious expression on her face.

'Morning, Julie!' Lucy Metcalfe had appeared from the kitchen. 'Are you feeling better?'

'A bit. Thought I'd best come in and rescue Stuart,' she said with a laugh.

Lucy nodded, looking grave. 'It's got to be difficult over there without Bernard in charge. What's going to happen, do you know?'

'Apparently Mr Procter is stepping in for a while,' said Julie. She couldn't help but notice that the blonde woman flinched at the name. 'I've no idea what Mrs Taylor will do long term, though.'

The blonde woman placed the coffees and the pastries on the counter and took Julie's money, a small smile now gracing her pale features.

'Thanks,' said Julie, heading for the door.

'Thank you,' said the woman, Lucy waving from the kitchen.

It was only as she crossed the marketplace that it came to Julie just who the mystery woman was. That accented English. The stunning good looks. She was Ana Stoyanovic. The woman who'd been arrested for the murder of Mr Taylor.

Seeing a shadow inside the office building, Julie hurried across the cobbles, anticipating bringing Stuart up to date on this latest bit of news.

The joviality that had accompanied Arty, Eric and Joseph on their train journey from Bruncliffe and continued during their unscheduled refreshments, faded once they were on the bus. As the three friends travelled north through the city, they became more sombre, aware that what they were about to do could get dangerous.

'What's his name again? This catfish?' asked Eric, leaning forward to speak to Arty and Joseph in the seat in front.

'Robert Webster.'

'No, his real name.'

Arty consulted his phone. 'Bob Rushworth. At least, that's the name Delilah had written down.'

'Bob Rushworth,' mused Eric. 'He sounds okay. The kind of bloke you'd go down the pub with.'

'Don't be going soft on me, Eric,' warned Arty, twisting round to speak to him. 'He's the kind of bloke willing to fleece old ladies out of their pensions.'

'Doesn't sound like a fighter though,' said Joseph, with a hint of hope in his voice.

Arty grunted. 'Aye, well, let's hope not. I wouldn't want him getting hurt.'

'Roundhay Park,' the driver shouted from the front, looking at them in the rear-view mirror.

'That's us!' Arty said, jumping up. With a thumbs up to the driver in thanks, he ushered the others off the bus.

They stood there in the green of the park, looking around. From the rows of tennis courts behind them came the soft whack of balls being hit, the courts busy for a weekday morning. And from across the road came the gleeful shouts of children playing.

'We could just get an ice cream and call it a day,' said Eric, pointing towards a van parked up further along the road, its windows covered in stickers of lollies and 99s, a bench handily situated opposite it.

Even Arty was tempted. The sky was blue, the sun warm, and they were on a day out after all. But then he remembered his duty. 'Come on,' he said, leading the way across the park, 'there'll be time enough for ice creams when we're done.'

'It's the next right.' Samson glanced up from the map app on his mobile and watched the junction they wanted go past, the car showing no signs of turning. 'That right back there,' he said dryly, pointing over his shoulder now, 'which, once you've done a U-turn, will be a left.'

Delilah glared at him, already slowing up and indicating, pulling the car into a sideroad. 'Some navigator you are! Have you got the map the right way up?'

He just grinned as the car swung round in a tight arc, Tolpuddle swaying on the back seat.

They were on the edges of Roundhay Park – would have been in the park proper, if Delilah had kept going – an area of Leeds Samson knew well. Not just from his time as a constable on the beat before he moved to London, but from a more recent visit with Delilah on a case. By a sheer coincidence, the residence of Clarissa's catfish was a stone's throw from the property they'd come to see on that occasion.

'How do you want to play this?' Delilah asked, as she took the now-left turn onto Old Park Road, the nerves that had caused her recent flare up visible in the worried look she gave him.

'As peacefully as possible,' said Samson. 'We can't afford to make him angry. Here,' he pointed at the next side road, 'park down there. We'll walk back to the house.'

While Delilah pulled up at the kerb, Samson looked at the photograph she'd shown him the day before, part of an article in the *Yorkshire Post* and the reason she'd uncovered the man's real identity so easily.

'Ready?' asked Delilah.

'Ready,' he murmured.

The three of them got out of the car.

With two coffees and the bag of pastries in her hands, Julie backed into the estate agent's, using her hip to open the door.

'You'll never guess who just served me at Peaks, Stuart,' she said, talking before she was even fully in the door. Before she'd turned round. 'That Ana Stoyanovic. She doesn't look like a killer to me—' She halted. Stared. Blushed.

'So what exactly *does* a killer look like?' Mr Procter was sitting at Stuart's desk, smiling at her.

'Oh, I'm sorry, I didn't know you were . . .' She faltered to a stop. Acutely aware that Mr Procter himself – who looked more like a movie star than a murderer – had also been the subject of rumours when it came to the fatal events up at Bruncliffe Manor on Saturday. 'I thought you were Stuart,' she concluded.

'He's not here.' Mr Procter's smile flipped to a frown and he pointed towards her desk. 'Read for yourself.'

Julie placed the coffees down, shrugged off her denim jacket and threw it over the back of her chair, and reached for the piece of paper lying on top of her desk. She read the first line and felt her legs go empty. Sitting down, she read the rest.

As resignations go, it was brief. Stuart had quit his job at Taylor's owing to the pressures arising from the unexpected death of Mr Taylor, and had gone travelling.

That was it. He was gone. No note for her. No popping in to say goodbye. Not even a text.

Her vision grew blurred and she was fumbling in her trouser pocket for a tissue, feeling like life had just kicked her in the guts.

'I'm going to have to look for a replacement,' Mr Procter was saying. 'I don't suppose you know of someone suitable?'

Julie thought of Stuart and those ridiculous knitted sweaters he wore in the winter that just swamped his gangly frame. The way he always had a cuppa waiting for her when she got in. The way he loitered around her desk when things were quiet.

He'd had a crush on her, she'd known that. Perhaps even more than just a crush. But she'd never pushed him to make a move, thinking he'd always be there. That he was reliable. A compass pointing north in her world that was all over the place since her mum's diagnosis.

'Sorry,' she murmured. 'I don't know of anyone who could take his place.'

Mr Procter nodded. Got up from Stuart's desk and turned towards the back office. 'Hold all calls,' he said. 'I've got some important business to catch up on.'

The door closed behind him and Julie let out the sigh she'd been holding, her bottom lip trembling. Then she spotted the two coffees and the Peaks bag and the tears began in earnest.

'Is this it?' Joseph was looking through open iron gates at a driveway which led to one of the biggest houses he'd ever seen. 'Seems a bit posh for a scam artist.'

'Maybe that's what he spends the money on,' said Eric.

'Park View,' confirmed Arty, checking Delilah's notes. 'That's the one. You two ready?'

Eric looked at Joseph and Joseph looked at Eric, and neither seemed prepared for battle. If anything, Eric was wanting a lie down and Joseph, well, he was regretting the coffee, which had just gone right through his system. The adrenalin wasn't helping any, either.

'Maybe we should just leave a note, or something,' wheezed Eric, the walk through the park having been at a faster pace than he was used to, Arty being on something of a mission.

Arty scowled at the pair of them. 'Look, I'm going in there whether you two are coming or not. Now, are you with me?'

'We're with you,' said Joseph, sounding more resolute. 'But what's the plan?'

'We'll just walk up to the front door and ask for Bob Rushworth,' announced Arty.

And that's what they did. Up the length of the long drive to the massive house, the huge front door already open, they stepped inside, into a tiled hallway. In the middle, a magnificent staircase rose up, twisting to the right, and beyond the stairs, through a set of double glass doors and across what seemed to be a dining room, they could see out onto a large expanse of lawn.

'Can I help you?'

They turned to see a young man standing to the side. He was smiling.

'We're here to see Bob Rushworth,' said Arty, Eric and Joseph struck dumb.

'Of course. He's in the garden. If you'd like to follow me?' The man walked ahead of them, towards the double doors, the trio falling in behind.

'He's got a bloody butler,' muttered Arty.

'This catfish business clearly pays,' said Eric, his oxygen trolley rumbling across the tiled floor.

Through the double doors they went, across the wooden floor of the dining room, a long table at the far end already set for lunch, and then they were stepping through the patio doors and onto a small terrace, bordered with tall shrubs.

'This is it, lads,' whispered Arty. 'Be ready for anything!'

'I'll give him a shout for you,' the young man was saying, a bit ahead of them and reaching the end of the terrace, looking around the shrubs to someone still out of sight to the others. 'Bob!' he called. 'Bob! Some friends to see you.'

'Friends!' muttered Arty, fists curling by his sides.

It was the point at which Joseph wanted to turn back. Before anyone got hurt. But he followed the others until the three of them came around the edge of the terrace and could finally see the full extent of the garden.

They all stopped in their tracks. And stared.

'There has to be some mistake . . .' Arty was saying.

'The only mistake,' came a voice from behind, 'is you three being here in the first place.'

Arty, Eric and Joseph turned around to see two people and a Weimaraner. Only the Weimaraner looked pleased to see them.

28

There was no time for explanations. Or for arguments. The young man was already looking at the group from Bruncliffe curiously.

'Bob Rushworth,' said Samson. 'We're all here to see him.'

'Over there,' said the young man. 'With the book on his knees.'

They looked to where he was pointing, past all the other people sitting in chairs and on benches, to see a man in a wheelchair, waving.

'This is an old folks' home?' Arty asked, incredulous.

The young man smiled. 'We prefer the term "care home".' He gave a small nod and then turned and went back inside.

'But . . . I don't understand,' said Eric, looking round in bemusement. 'This Bob bloke . . .'

'Come on,' said Samson. 'Let's go and chat to him. But I'm warning you, no threats or anything. The man is ninety-two and has a heart condition.'

He set off across the grass with Delilah and Tolpuddle, the dog already getting lots of admiring comments from the other residents. The three friends followed, still stunned.

'Bob Rushworth?' Samson double-checked as he

approached the figure in the wheelchair, a large stamp album open on his lap.

'That's me. Who's asking?' Bright eyes looked out from a wrinkled face.

'Perhaps we could sit down?'

Bob nodded, gesturing a hand at the empty chairs scattered about the lawn. 'Be my guest.'

They gathered around him, Arty rendered unusually silent by the strange turn of events, leaving Samson to do the talking.

'We've come to chat to you about Robert Webster,' he said.

Bob cackled. 'Oh Robert! He's a right one.'

'He's also not real,' said Samson. 'And we think that maybe one of our friends is about to be hurt by that.'

'Hurt?' Bob shook his head. 'No one ever gets hurt. Just a bit of romance and a bit of dreaming, that's all it's about.'

'So you admit that Robert Webster is fake?'

'Oh, he's fake all right.' Bob slapped the sides of his wheelchair. 'He lets me do all the things this bugger doesn't.'

'But you're not afraid that you might mislead someone too much?' Delilah asked.

'Or ask them for money?' said Joseph.

'Money never comes into it!' declared Bob, indignantly. 'What would I do with money? Apart from buy more stamps, maybe.' He gave a wistful smile. 'Thing is, it's not until you reach my age that you realise half the fun in life is planning for living. But when you reach my age, no one expects you to be planning for anything except death.' He shrugged. 'Robert Webster allows me to plan. Afternoon tea. A walk in a rose garden. A hike up Pen-y-ghent. All the things I can't do, I can plan for. With someone else who wants to do them.'

No one spoke. From beyond the high hedge came the sound of people playing tennis in the park and the distant chime of an ice cream van, children's laughter floating over it.

'So you see,' said Bob, breaking the silence, 'no one gets hurt. My ladies know the score because I tell them up front.'

'Ladies?' Samson's eyebrows shot up. 'You have more than one lady on the go at once?'

Bob reached down the side of his wheelchair and pulled out a tablet, tapping the screen to activate it. 'Here they are,' he said proudly. 'Now, who is your friend that you're worried about and I'll sort this all out.'

'Clarissa Ralph,' said Arty, finally finding his voice.

But Bob Rushworth shook his head. 'Don't know any Clarissa,' he said. 'You must have made a mistake.'

'Can we have a look?' asked Delilah, gesturing at the tablet.

'Of course.'

She scrolled through the website, photos of elderly women rolling past. And then she paused. Turned the tablet so the others could all see.

'Josephine Shaw!' exclaimed Arty.

'Ah! Josie,' said Bob, eyes sparkling once more. 'She's something special. Wants to go camel trekking to the Pyramids! By God, she makes me feel young.'

Samson started laughing, Delilah and Joseph smiling while Eric was shaking his head, a huge grin on his face.

Not so Arty Robinson. He was staring at the photo of Josie Shaw – the grey hair, the petite features. Clarissa Ralph was smiling back at him.

'Seems like Bob's not the only catfish out there,' said Joseph, patting Arty's arm.

Arty was still too stunned to speak.

It was some time before they were able to leave the company of Bob Rushworth and his fellow residents, Tolpuddle in particular proving to be a hit. When the Bruncliffe contingent finally walked away from Park View care home, the dog had been petted by every pensioner in there. With promises to bring the Weimaraner back for another visit soon, Delilah followed the men out onto the road.

Which is where her heart went out to the three friends, who were facing a long journey back home on public transport. Overriding Samson's objections – him being of the belief that they should see it as penance for their miscreant behaviour – she offered them a lift. And an hour and a quarter later, with Samson at the wheel, Eric alongside him with his oxygen cylinder between his knees, Arty, Delilah, and Joseph in the rear and a cramped Tolpuddle in the boot, the little Micra pulled up at Fellside Court.

'Go easy on Clarissa,' said Delilah as the men got out of the car, knees popping and backs creaking. 'It wasn't her fault you all went off looking to do battle.'

Arty grinned back at her, Delilah now in the passenger seat and Tolpuddle already stretched out in the rear. 'Aye, but what a day, eh? Wouldn't have missed it for the world!'

'Yes,' said Eric, tapping his portable oxygen cylinder. 'It's made me appreciate what I still have, that's for sure.'

'Just one thing,' said Joseph. 'How did you find him so easily?'

'"PennyBlackBob",' said Delilah. 'Bob used that as his username in the guise of Robert Webster. It just so happens he also uses it in real life on philately forums. And then I found an article in the *Yorkshire Post* about a pensioner who'd been responsible for finding a Penny Black in his youth when he'd been helping with a house clearance. It had a photograph of a certain Bob Rushworth. Once I saw that, I realised that our catfish might not be as dangerous as we'd thought.'

'I should have listened to you when you told me not to get involved,' said Arty, apologetically.

Samson grinned. 'Now where would be the fun in that?'

Arty started laughing, then he slapped his forehead. 'Almost forgot,' he said, reaching into his jacket pocket and pulling out a small notebook. 'Edith asked me to give you this. It's the notes we took at the stake-out of Taylor's.' He shrugged. 'Don't see as you'll have any use for them now, but Edith insisted.'

'Right. Thanks.' Samson took the notebook and slipped it into the side pocket of the car door.

'And don't forget, if you ever need more help – detective stuff or advice, maybe – you know where we are,' added Arty with a devilish grin, Joseph and Eric laughing behind him.

Samson glared at them, put the car in gear and drove off, the three men waving as the Micra pulled away.

'What was that about? The advice bit?' asked Delilah, as they turned down Fell Lane.

'Nothing,' muttered Samson.

She looked at him and then just shrugged. 'So, what's next?'

'Next,' said Samson, cutting across the marketplace to pull up on the square, 'we've got an interview scheduled at Peaks Patisserie.'

'With one of our clients?'

'Not one,' said Samson, 'but two of them. At the same time. Ana contacted me while we were in Leeds – the police released her last night and she wants to talk. I figured it made sense to get Gareth in, too.'

'You think that's wise? Interviewing them together?' Delilah queried as they got out of the car, Tolpuddle yawning at the fresh air.

'To be honest, I'm not sure what's wise and what's not any more when it comes to this blasted Taylor case. We just seem to be chasing our tails. At least this way, we're guaranteed hearing the truth, because with both of them in the frame for murder, they won't hesitate to correct any inaccuracies in each other's accounts of what happened. And let's face it,' Samson added with a grim look as they reached the cafe door, 'Ana and Gareth are looking like the most viable suspects. So this could be the interview that cracks this case wide open.'

Feeling sick at the thought of unmasking either of her friends as a murderer, Delilah tied Tolpuddle up outside and followed Samson into the cafe.

'I went into the courtyard to find Gareth,' said a very pale Ana Stoyanovic, gesturing towards the gamekeeper, who was in the chair next to her, the immense proportions of him dwarfing her. They were sitting at a table in the far corner of the cafe, Samson and Delilah opposite them. 'I saw him go past the kitchen window and I remembered the shotgun. I ran out to tell him about it.'

Samson nodded, her timing tallying with what he'd seen of the gamekeeper walking past him while he was hidden behind the hedge. 'Did you find him?'

'No. When I got out there, I couldn't see him.' The glance she gave Gareth was apologetic, knowing her words could be incriminating. 'I went over to the gunroom and then doubled back across the yard and went up the track along the north side of the house, but he was nowhere to be seen.'

'I was round the back of the stables,' said Gareth, cheeks flushed above his russet beard. 'I was having a cigarette.'

'I didn't know you smoked!' exclaimed Delilah.

'I don't, as such. I just keep a packet out in the gunroom for emergencies. And Saturday counted as an emergency.' He shook his head. 'I was stressed out by those bloody Bulgarians so I nipped into the gunroom, grabbed a cigarette, and then went round the back of the stables to smoke it on the sly.'

'I presume you told the cops this?' Samson asked.

'They know. They also have the cigarette butt, for what it's worth. I keep a tin round there to put them in.'

'So you were there when you heard the gun go off?'

'Aye. But that wasn't what got me moving. It was Bounty. I'd glanced over when I walked past and saw she was fast asleep but suddenly, when I was having a smoke, she set up barking. Proper cross barking. I stubbed out the cigarette, intending to hurry back, and then the gun went off. By the time I rounded the corner of the stables into the courtyard, Ana was already there, off to my right, coming round the far side of the house. And Rick Procter was running in from my left.'

'You didn't see anyone else?'

The gamekeeper shook his head.

'What about you?' Samson turned to Ana. 'You said you started up the track at the side of the house. How far did you get before you turned round?'

'Not far. Like Gareth, it was the dog barking that made me go back. I knew I'd left the gun on the seat—' She broke off, a trembling hand to her mouth. 'Sorry,' she murmured. 'But I can't help thinking that if I hadn't left it there, none of this would have happened.'

Gareth put an arm around her. 'Don't,' he said. 'Whoever pulled the bloody trigger is to blame for killing Bernard Taylor. Not you. And not me.'

Ana nodded, giving him a grateful glance, and Samson found himself thinking that this was one of the most unusual interviews he'd ever been part of. Instead of trying to trip each other up, the two suspects were supporting each other, a genuine concern apparent in their interactions. And while it was heart-warming to see, it didn't bode well in terms of providing a breakthrough in the case.

'You said you turned back when you heard Bounty . . .' Delilah gently prompted Ana to continue.

'Yes. I was worried someone was at the Land Rover. So I started to rush back but, like Gareth, I was still out of sight of it when the gun went off. When I came round the corner, I went running to the passenger's side – it was nearest me and that's where the gun was. I pulled the door open and the gun fell out. It was instinctive, to catch it, but as I did, I saw Mr Taylor . . .' She bit her bottom lip at the memory. 'I dropped the gun and I screamed.'

'And that's when you came running out of the dining room,' said Gareth, looking at Delilah.

Samson supressed a groan. There was nothing in the testimony of either Ana or Gareth to provide the answer as to how Bernard Taylor's killer had managed to execute the deed and then disappear within seconds of the gun going off. Which meant they now had three separate people – four if you counted Delilah – approaching the courtyard from every conceivable angle. Yet none of them had seen anyone running away. And all three principal witnesses-cum-suspects had affirmed that the Land Rover door was closed when they arrived on the scene. It was that detail which puzzled Samson the most.

Why close the door if you were fleeing from a murder? Had the intention been to make it look like suicide?

Still lost in his thoughts, Samson was aware of Delilah leaning across the table. 'Just a few more questions, Ana,' she was saying. 'Did you know that Bernard had seen you at some point during the morning on Saturday?'

'Not at all. The first I heard of it was when the police asked me. They said Bernard told you . . .'

Delilah nodded. 'In a roundabout way. He mentioned you when he saw me out of disguise. As though seeing the two of us was the final straw, somehow. Do you have any idea why you being at the shoot would have thrown him?'

'Blackmail.' She gave a lopsided smile. 'That's what the police think. I was blackmailing him and he thought I was there to expose him.' She sighed. 'I know nothing about the man, apart from him being Mr Procter's associate. He never spoke to me in all the time I worked at Fellside Court. It's just a crazy accusation.' Ana glanced at her watch, the cafe filling up steadily around them, lunchtime in full swing. 'I'm going to have to go,' she said. 'Lucy needs me.'

'One last thing,' Delilah persisted. 'Did you know the shotgun was loaded?'

Ana shook her head. 'That was the first time I'd ever handled a gun. I wouldn't have known how to check if it was loaded or not. And I wouldn't have dared, anyway.'

Her admission elicited a moan of self-reproach from the gamekeeper. 'I should have just put the damn thing away when Elaine told me about it,' he said ruefully.

'Hindsight is always perfect,' murmured Ana, placing a hand on Gareth's arm. 'Like I said, I wasn't sure about leaving the gun in the Land Rover but, under the pressure of the day, I did.'

'But if you didn't know it was loaded,' asked Delilah, 'why were you so nervous about leaving it there?'

There was a pause, Ana finally shrugging. 'Because it was a gun. They have a dangerous habit of killing things.'

While Ana made her excuses and hurried off towards the kitchen, tying her apron back on as she went, Gareth, in contrast, was showing no rush to be gone.

'Which of us is in the most trouble then?' he asked with a grim smile.

'You both are.' Samson's blunt reply was met with an appreciative nod, the gamekeeper not being one for flannel. 'Ana because she was first on the scene and then there's the whole thing about her knowing the gun was there. And you, because you have the better motive.'

Gareth laughed. 'Motive? Jesus! The man threatens me twice with losing my job and suddenly I'm a killer. It's ridiculous.'

'There's also the blackmail angle,' said Delilah, softly. 'The money Nancy found in Bernard's wardrobe. We haven't really addressed that from your perspective.'

'Like I said to the police when they raised this, why would I be blackmailing him? And what about?'

'An affair—'

'What do you take me for?' Gareth cut her off. 'Bruncliffe's answer to Hercule Poirot? You know as well as me, Delilah, that if Bernard Taylor was having an affair, there'd be plenty more folk out there would know about it before I got wind of anything. I live halfway up a mountain, I spend my time with my dog and a load of pheasants for company and I don't dabble in gossip. How the hell would I know if our mayor was having a bit on the side?'

It was a strong argument. But Samson wasn't deterred.

'Perhaps the blackmail wasn't over an affair. Perhaps it was over some sort of business deal. Like the lodges your boss wants to install across the road from the manor?'

This time the gamekeeper's reaction was a snort of derision. 'Again, why would I try to extort money over that? Those lodges are what will secure my position on the estate. Without them, the place becomes less viable every passing year. So I'd have to be stupid to scupper the best chance I have of staying on here. Besides . . .' He paused, glanced down at the table and then shrugged, as though he had nothing left to lose, before giving Samson a defiant look. 'Happen as there's another explanation for that cash,' he said, voice no more than a murmur.

'Like what?' asked Samson.

'Everyone investigating this mess is assuming Bernard was the one paying out. That the bag full of money was destined for someone else. What if it wasn't?'

It was like a light bulb going on. A completely different perspective on the case. Samson nodded. 'A bung?'

'Why not?' said the gamekeeper. 'I know for a fact the Luptons were desperate for the lodges to go ahead. And that's just one of the projects the mayor was dealing with. Why couldn't someone have given him that cash as a sweetener?'

Delilah groaned, sensing that rather than narrowing down possibilities, the interview with Gareth had just thrown even more avenues wide open for consideration. 'Oh God. This case is driving me mad,' she muttered.

'Try being in my shoes,' said Gareth, despair thickening his voice. 'At least you're not going to end up in jail over it.'

When they emerged from Peaks Patisserie, the despondent mood of the Dales Detective Agency team seemed at odds with the bright sunshine bathing the marketplace and the blue sky arching over the limestone crag above the town.

'What a morning!' declared Delilah as she untied Tolpuddle, the dog at least in a better frame of mind, greeting them with a wagging tail.

'Been a long one all right,' said Samson. 'So long it's already well into the afternoon and we haven't even had lunch. And the worst thing is, nothing seems any clearer when it comes to the Taylor case. We've got three people relying on us to exonerate them and we don't seem to be getting anywhere.'

'Maybe we need to widen the net in terms of suspects?'

'What, add more conjecture to an investigation already riddled with it?' Samson's tone was dry.

'I'm serious,' insisted Delilah. 'If Ana, Gareth and Rick are telling the truth about their actions, then maybe one of the others from the shoot is responsible.'

'One of the Bulgarians?'

Delilah shrugged. 'Why not?'

Samson scratched his chin. 'Feasible in some respects. Apart from the fact they were all in front of me when the gun . . .' He stopped, halfway across the marketplace to the car, remembering the scene – the group of men standing around on the gravel in front of the manor, Ash and Will on the doorstep. 'Milan,' he said. 'Milan wasn't there. He wasn't by the 4x4s with the others when Bernard was shot.'

'Where was he?'

'Don't know. But I do know his prints would have been all over the gun.'

'And,' said Delilah, excitement in her voice, 'he was wearing a brown T-shirt.'

Samson stared at her, nodding. 'Lucy's brown flash . . . okay, but before we go haring down another dead end, how feasible is it that he ran out to the courtyard, killed Bernard, ran back inside and still had time to appear round the corner with the rest of the Bulgarians at the end?'

'Let's go and find out,' said Delilah with a grin, leaning down to pat Tolpuddle, who was bouncing along between them like a spring waiting to uncoil. 'What do you say, boy? Fancy a bit of sprint training?'

The Weimaraner barked in approval.

Despite the fact they were trying to catch a murderer, by mid-afternoon Samson O'Brien was having the most fun he'd had in a long time. He was watching Delilah, along with some dubious assistance from Tolpuddle, trying to recreate the actions of each of the principal suspects in the lead-up to the killing.

'Any faster?' she gasped, hands on her hips, sweat on her brow, Tolpuddle panting beside her.

'A bit. But still not fast enough.'

Delilah groaned, grabbed a quick drink of water from the supplies they'd bought at Peaks Patisserie, and turned to have another go.

They were up at Bruncliffe Manor, in the courtyard, Samson representing the Land Rover, standing on the spot where a rusty stain informed them Bernard Taylor had died. Meanwhile, Delilah was running sprints away from the crime scene, following the trajectories each suspect had arrived from, before doing a U-turn and coming straight back.

The theory was that whoever had shot Bernard Taylor needed to have had time between the shot being fired and their arrival back in the courtyard, supposedly as a concerned witness, to disappear out of sight. But it was a tight margin, because if they took the shotgun firing as the beginning of the sprint and the arrival of the first witness – Ana – as the end, the killer had only a handful of seconds to make good their escape, before reappearing again.

'Go!' said Samson, hitting the stopwatch on his mobile.

Delilah and Tolpuddle took off for the south side of the building in the direction Rick Procter had appeared from. They raced round the corner, the Weimaraner almost taking Delilah out, so tight was his turn, and then they raced straight back, Samson stopping the stopwatch the minute they reappeared. He looked at the time and shook his head. 'I think this counts Rick out,' he said, with a twinge of regret. 'There's no way he could have covered the distance from here to there in the time needed. Want to have another go at Gareth now you're warmed up?'

'Okay.'

It was more of a wheeze than a word, making Samson smile. It wasn't often he got to see the far superior runner that was Delilah Metcalfe – champion fell runner, in fact – suffering for her sport. Usually it was him who was left puffing like a steam train on their runs together.

'Right, let's go. The sooner we're done, the sooner we can finally have something to eat.' Samson reset the stopwatch. 'On your marks, go!'

They raced past him, a blur of legs, Tolpuddle pulling away this time, disappearing around the stables ahead of Delilah, only for her to reappear first, the hound chasing her seconds later.

Samson checked the time. 'Nope. Not fast enough.'

'Bloody hell,' muttered Delilah, collapsing onto the ground in a heap, Tolpuddle helpfully licking her ear. 'That leaves just Ana and Milan.'

They hadn't tried the Bulgarian's route yet, knowing it was a long shot.

'He came down the track with the others, hot on my

heels,' said Samson, pointing to the corner where he himself had appeared, the copse climbing the fellside behind it.
'There's no exit from the house along that side, so he must
have come out the front door. Which means he had to have
run like the blazes to go from here, through the dining
room, out the front and then round the side to catch the
others as they got here. Do you think it's worth a shot?'

Delilah looked up for the challenge. 'Let's try it. He was
one of the last to appear, which means he had longer to play
with.'

Having secured a key to the building from Gareth, they
opened up the French windows to the dining room,
unlocked the huge front doors and then Delilah and
Tolpuddle took their places.

'Go!' shouted Samson.

They ran inside, Tolpuddle immediately hitting trouble
on the polished floor, claws skittering over the surface, a
couple of chairs crashing over as he smacked into them.
Delilah was around the corner and out of sight while the
dog was still untangling himself, leaving Samson doubled
over laughing. It wasn't long before the sound of gravel
crunching heralded their arrival, woman and Weimaraner
neck and neck as they came into sight at the far side of the
building.

'Way out,' announced Samson, shaking his head.
'Nearly a minute. Even if he's an Olympic athlete in disguise, there's no way Milan's our man.'

'Damn,' muttered Delilah. 'I really hoped we could put
him in the frame.'

'So that just leaves Ana. Are you up for one more sprint?'

Delilah nodded. Gave her legs a shake and resumed her

position by the rusty stain, Tolpuddle immediately standing next to her.

'And for the last time . . . Go!'

This was the fastest of them all. Straight out towards the
copse, round the corner onto the track and back, but as
Delilah and Tolpuddle came haring into view again, Samson
shook his head in disbelief.

'Too slow,' he said, Delilah in a heap on the ground once
more, breathing laboured. 'Not one of these people could
have fired the gun, got out of sight and come back again.
This case is ridiculous!'

'And I'm ridiculously shattered,' groaned Delilah.
'How about that food you promised?'

Samson helped her to her feet and they walked round to
the south of the building, sitting on the vast lawn below the
terrace to have their late lunch. The peaceful atmosphere
was a stark contrast to the last time they'd been there, lull-
ing Delilah into lying back on the grass when she'd finished
eating, her eyes closed, cheeks still pink from the sprinting.
Sprawled out next to her with his belly full of ham,
Tolpuddle was already dozing. Samson watched them both,
thinking that this was the most perfect moment he had ever
known. The fells rising up on all sides, a lapwing wheeling
above the neighbouring field, the warm sun shining down,
and the woman he loved—

This was it. The ideal setting. If he didn't tell her now,
he'd never get a better chance.

Butterflies besetting his stomach, he leaned over
towards her. 'Delilah,' he said softly.

She opened her eyes and smiled at him, the languid
curve of her lips making his pulse skyrocket.

'There's something I need to—'

'Just a sec,' she said, sitting up and pulling out her mobile, which was ringing. 'Hello? Danny?'

Samson knew by the way her hand went to her mouth, her eyes widening, that it was bad news.

'Thanks for letting us know,' she said. 'We'll get straight on it.' She hung up and turned to him, panic on her features where there had been peace only moments before. 'Danny said they're talking about charging Ana tomorrow. With murder. If we're going to prove she didn't do it, we need to think of something soon.'

29

'So, what have we got?' Showered, changed and sitting in Samson's office, notepad on lap, Delilah was all business.

'Not a lot,' said Samson. 'We have three primary witnesses – one of whom is about to be charged as a suspect – and they all agree on two things: that they all reached the courtyard about the same time, and the Land Rover doors were all closed.'

'Which rules out suicide, thanks to the lack of blood on the passenger door.'

'That and the absence of the victim's fingerprints on the weapon. Which is another thing we've got. While Bernard's prints aren't on the shotgun, the other three had all handled it.'

'As had Milan,' added Delilah.

Samson nodded. 'All of them also tested positive for gunshot residue, which, in the case of the men, is hardly surprising considering they were at a shoot.'

'So, on the surface,' Delilah said, tapping her pen against the list of names she'd written down, 'it looks like one of these three – possibly four, if we include Milan – must be the killer. And with Ana closest to the Land Rover at the time of the murder, combined with a less credible explanation for the residue on her hands, she remains the main suspect. However, if we accept

Lucy's sighting of something brown moving out in the yard . . .'

'Ana's eliminated because she was dressed in a white shirt, while all of the men were wearing something brown.'

'Right.' Delilah flipped the page over on her pad. 'Moving on to motive—'

'Weak to non-existent,' muttered Samson. 'A dubious accusation of blackmail for Ana or, even more tentative, a result of having had her presence at the shoot uncovered. Likewise a weak blackmail claim laid against Gareth or, more believably, the desperate act of a man about to lose his job.'

'While for Rick Procter, we have an argument caught on video with his business partner, but given their business interests are so intertwined, he probably stands to lose a great deal because of Bernard's death. That weakens that motive a bit.'

'And Milan?'

Delilah pulled a face. 'He'd been harassing Bernard all day. And then he lost face when the shoot was called off. Is that enough to make him go and kill someone?'

'Maybe, if he was hopped-up on cocaine.'

'But . . .'

Samson sighed. 'Yes, but. After your amazing efforts this afternoon, I don't see how any one of these suspects can have committed the murder and not have been seen. It's just not possible.'

'It has to be,' said Delilah. 'Because between the missing fingerprints on the gun and the lack of blood on the passenger door, the test results have shown that Bernard Taylor didn't kill himself. Which means somebody there had to have pulled the trigger, closed the passenger door and then run off.'

'Reappearing seconds later in a time even you couldn't produce?' Samson let his head drop into his hands and groaned. 'Ana's relying on us and we're letting her down.'

'We're missing something,' said Delilah, putting a hand on his arm. 'That's all it is. Just a little something which, if we go back over it all, we'll see. How about I go upstairs and watch the spy cam footage again?'

Samson raised his head and nodded. 'Okay. I'll work on the audio clips and go through the statements. Let's hope we can find something that will finally break this case.'

With a last pat on his arm, Delilah left the room, and, out of an obligation to Ana Stoyanovic more than a belief in his own abilities as a detective, a despairing Samson pulled his laptop towards him.

Over in Fellside Court, Arty Robinson was far from despair.

Things were back as they should be amongst his friends. In fact, in some ways, they were even better. While indignant on first hearing that they'd been interfering in her love life, Clarissa had soon backed down when the lads confronted her with Josephine Shaw, Edith both shocked and fascinated to discover her sister had an online alter ego. Once all the deceptions were out on the table, they'd spent a companionable afternoon, discussing what they'd all been up to, the tale of Arty, Eric and Joseph being the most adventurous.

'I can't believe you were ready to fight someone over me,' laughed Clarissa. 'And all the time I was perfectly safe.

Even if Bob hadn't told me his real identity, I would have found it anyway. I know better than to get involved with anyone online without googling them first!'

'How were we to know you were such a whizz on the internet?' grumbled Arty good-naturedly. 'But this Bob character! What a card. You should go over and meet him one day.'

'We all should,' said Edith. 'Do us good to get out a bit.'

'Agreed,' said Arty.

'And as for you, little sister,' said Edith, looking at Clarissa, 'what on earth possessed you to get involved in all that imaginary nonsense in the first place?'

Clarissa shrugged, her smile dimming slightly. 'I wanted a bit of sparkle in my life.'

'You mean romance?' asked Arty.

She nodded. 'Yes. Why not? Just because we're older doesn't mean we have to stay on the shelf.'

'I agree,' Eric piped up. They all stared at him and he rattled his oxygen tank crossly. 'What? You think this ties me down? Look at that poor bugger today. I can do a lot more than he can and it's time I did!'

Joseph let out a burst of laughter, Arty joining in, and that was it, they were all laughing, quietening down only when Eric's laughter turned to coughing.

'So, what do we do about it?' asked Joseph.

'Talk to Delilah,' said Edith. 'Get her to set up a dating group just for folk like us.'

'We could call it "Grey but Game"!' said Arty.

'Sounds like a pheasant that's been hung too long!' quipped Eric, setting them all off again.

'I've got it,' said Joseph. 'How about "Silver Solos"?'

'Ooh, that's good!' said Clarissa, to nods of agreement all round.

'Except Arty would be excluded,' said Eric, with a grin. 'Seeing as he's bald rather than silver.'

Edith leaned over and kissed Arty on the cheek. 'We'd make an exception for Arty,' she said, smiling.

Arty Robinson felt like his heart would burst.

By late evening, the search for a breakthrough in the Taylor case was proving even more hopeless than Samson had feared.

'Damn it!' He flung himself back in his chair, his office empty, Delilah and Tolpuddle both upstairs, trying to conjure something from the video footage.

He hoped to hell they were better magicians than he was, because so far all he'd conjured up from repeated listenings to the audio was a headache. Nothing that could be used to clear Ana Stoyanovic of the charges she was facing.

'Damn it!' he muttered again, staring at the computer screen.

In desperation, he picked up the phone and called Danny, the constable answering immediately.

'Well,' asked the lad, 'have you found anything?'

'Apart from having spent the afternoon basically ruling out all of the suspects, not much,' muttered Samson. He quickly brought the policeman up to speed on the sprint tests, a soft whistle coming from Danny in response.

'So you're saying none of the primary witnesses could have killed Bernard Taylor, if they're all telling the truth about who they saw where at the moment they arrived in the courtyard?' Danny swore. 'This case is insane.'

'Which is why I want you to run the forensic results past me again – specifically the ones that ruled out suicide. Maybe we've all been too hasty to dismiss it.'

'You've timed it well. I've just got a copy of the full set of tests – Sergeant Clayton has asked me to go over them during any downtime on my shift tonight.'

'Is he having second thoughts about Ana being in the frame?'

'I think he's more concerned that the Harrogate lads are rushing things through just to get a tick in a box. Either way, I've got carte blanche to go through everything to do with the case. So, let's see . . .' There was the sound of pages being shuffled around a desk before the constable spoke again. 'Right, the test results with regards to suicide being eliminated as a line of enquiry – the absence of Bernard's fingerprints on the gun and the absence of blood spatter on the inside of the passenger doors are the main ones. Apart from that, the amount of gunshot residue on the passenger seat suggested that the gun was close to or on it when fired, and at that range, Bernard would have needed Inspector Gadget arms to pull the trigger.'

'Damn,' muttered Samson. 'There's no arguing with that. Okay, thanks.' He was about to disconnect when he thought of one more thing. 'Oh, Danny, before you go, what happened to Bernard's mobile?'

'How do you mean?'

'Where was it found in the vehicle?'

'Let me check . . .' More rustling of paper and then Danny spoke again. 'Here we go, according to the report, the victim's mobile was found in the front footwell on the driver's side. Why do you ask?'

'Just making sure I've covered all the bases,' said Samson.

He bade the constable farewell a second time and as he sat back in his chair, he stared at his own mobile. There was something in what Danny Bradley had just told him, but he couldn't think what it was. Something on the edge of his consciousness—

The front door closed, Delilah coming into the hall, Samson not having even been aware that she'd gone out.

'So, are you getting anywhere?' she asked, standing in the doorway, a paper bag in her hand that was giving out the most divine smells. 'Got time for a curry?'

They didn't linger long over the food, bringing each other up to date on their respective progress – or lack of – as they ate. Delilah had gone through the full footage from the spy cam and isolated a few key areas that were worth Samson's consideration, a copy of the highlights now in his inbox. While the only good news Samson was able to pass on was that Danny was adding his weight to their search for a solution to this baffling case.

'I just can't help feeling we're missing something obvious,' muttered Samson, as they finished eating and began clearing up the takeaway containers.

Delilah sighed. 'I know what you mean. It's like we're looking for the elusive "third man".' She gave a wry laugh. 'Although in this instance, it's more like a fourth man.'

'Fifth if we include Milan as a suspect.'

'God,' she groaned. 'What I'd give for an open-and-shut

case!' With a weary look, she headed back up the stairs to continue her efforts on behalf of their friend, leaving Samson to return to his desk.

He clicked on the first of her edited video clips and, chin on hand, began watching.

As the rest of Back Street turned in for the night – the Fleece long since closed, Plastic Fantastic shuttered up, the hairdryers in Shear Good Looks silent and the mannequins in Betty's Boutique staring out into the dark – a sole light still burned in the downstairs office of the Dales Detective Agency. Past midnight, on into the new day, still the light stayed on as Samson went over and over every possible aspect of the case.

'It's got to be here,' he murmured, rubbing his eyes and reaching for the mug of tea next to him. He took a swig and nearly choked. Cold. How long had it been there?

The clock in the corner of the computer screen told him it was twenty past two. Delilah had brought him the tea at midnight. Where the hell had the time gone? And what had he got to show for it?

Nothing.

He stretched his arms up above him, easing his aching back. One more look at the spy cam videos and then he was going to have to call it quits.

Delilah had sent him seven excerpts in total, mostly concentrating on the three main suspects but with a couple of oddities thrown in. Settling himself back in front of the screen, Samson started with Rick's argument with Bernard, the two men some distance from where Delilah had been standing. It was impossible to hear what they were saying, but it was clear Bernard wasn't happy. Samson watched the dispute unfold for the umpteenth time, nothing standing out as noteworthy.

Next he skimmed through the two clips showing Bernard threatening Gareth Towler, one in the gunroom, the other just as Gareth cancelled the shoot, again without any new insight that would help the case.

In terms of Ana, there was only one bit of footage and that was from the minutes following the shooting as Delilah burst out into the courtyard, the camera capturing a distraught Ana on the other side of the Land Rover. Samson could feel the weariness seeping into his bones as he tried to concentrate. The clip finished and he clicked on the next one.

Milan was up next, Delilah having included two short pieces of footage that showed him at his worst. Samson fast-forwarded through them, feeling his eyelids beginning to droop.

Last one. It was from inside the kitchen, Lucy sitting on a stool, clearly discouraged by the cancellation of the shoot. Delilah was opposite her, the camera showing the window and the boot of the Land Rover in the courtyard. In her email accompanying the clips, Delilah had explained that she'd included this bit of video to show what Lucy could see when she turned round to the window after the gun was fired. Samson let it play, but his focus wasn't really on the screen. He was tired. His vision blurring.

Maybe that's what it was. By not looking intently, he finally saw something of interest.

Suddenly he was sitting bolt upright, wide awake. Thinking. About Delilah. Only not in the way he'd been doing recently. He was thinking about the curry they'd just shared and the conversation that had come with it . . .

'"Third man"!' he exclaimed, slapping himself on the forehead. '"Open-and-shut case"!'

He went back to one of the other clips. Let it roll, looking at it differently now, in the light of what he'd just seen. And there it was. The answer.

He nodded, grinned, nodded again, and reviewed the spy cam footage once more. Then he reached for his mobile. Bruncliffe's on-duty constable answered on the first ring despite the hour.

'Danny? I think I've had a breakthrough, but I need your help,' said Samson, wasting no time on small talk. 'It'll involve a ride on the Enfield.'

There was no need to dangle that particular bait. On the other end of the phone, Danny Bradley was already saying yes.

When the light finally went out in the downstairs office, it was an excited, but shattered, Samson O'Brien who climbed the stairs to the first floor. The door to Delilah's office was still open, her desk lamp still on, but if Samson had been hoping to share his news with his partner, he was to be disappointed.

Not that he could ever be disappointed by her, he thought, looking down at the sleeping features of Delilah Metcalfe where she lay on her couch, curled up, her laptop on the floor. A soft whine came from the basket in the corner, Tolpuddle watching him from sleepy eyes.

It passed through Samson's mind that he could carry her upstairs, let her have the benefit of his bed while he did the chivalrous thing and took the couch. It was a thought swiftly dismissed. This was Delilah. There was every possibility she'd wake up while they were halfway up the stairs and lash out in surprise, sending them both down to the landing below in a heap. Instead, he took the fleece blanket lying across the back of the sofa and spread it across her. Let her sleep. His news would wait.

With a stroke for Tolpuddle, Samson turned off the desk lamp and crept up to bed. He'd be able to grab a couple of hours kip before he had to be going.

30

It would be Thursday morning before Bruncliffe heard anything more about the Taylor case. As for Wednesday, it turned out to be a slow day all round. Apart from the start. For Delilah Metcalfe, the day began as she woke to the gentlest of kisses, Samson's lips on her cheek, his breath in her ear, his nose—

'Tolpuddle!' Finally identifying the correct instigator behind what she'd thought was a romantic awakening, Delilah pushed her affectionate hound away and sat up. Only to discover she was lying on the couch in her office, covered in a blanket. And Ida Capstick was standing in the doorway, arms folded and both eyebrows raised.

'Tha didn't even make it home last night?'

There was more than a hint of suggestion in the tone, an implication of impropriety.

'We were working,' stammered Delilah, still mentally adjusting to the dog kisses and the couch and her office and now Ida. 'That's all it was.'

'Aye. Well when tha decides to get up at last, there's a brew on.' She'd walked off down the landing before throwing over her shoulder: 'And there's a note on the dog.'

'What?' Delilah rubbed her eyes, not yet fully awake, and pulled Tolpuddle towards her. 'Thanks for waking me,' she murmured, rubbing his flank. And sure enough, there under his collar was a note.

Morning Sleeping Beauty!
Out and about all day – be in touch soon.
Samson

No kiss. No information about the case either.
'This tea is stewing!' came a call from Ida.
Wondering if she'd ever had a stranger start to her day, Delilah shuffled off to the kitchen.

While the morning may have started with a bang, the remainder of the daylight hours proved to be one of waiting and frustration. With Ida having gone after she'd done her cleaning – Wednesday apparently not being a day she had earmarked to be a receptionist – Delilah was left on her own. Realising how unused she'd become to being alone on the premises, she made herself a cup of tea and got down to business, one ear permanently cocked for the back door opening. For the rest of the working hours, she barely left her chair, apart from to check that Samson hadn't appeared downstairs, which she did about every half an hour. Or to go to the window to see if the Enfield had somehow silently returned without her knowing. So in fact, she left her chair quite a bit. But on the whole, her day was focused on work.

By late afternoon, she'd caught up with the flood of applications for the Dales Dating Agency, registering new accounts and setting up online profiles on the website. Thanks to the magazine feature on Clive Knowles and to

Ida's sterling work manning the phone, the dating agency had never been in better health. At this rate, Uncle Woolly was going to be in raptures when they next met at the bank to discuss the financial health of Delilah's businesses.

With hours still left to be filled, Delilah even managed to do a bit more on Taylor's IT system overhaul, although there didn't seem to be much point in rushing that particular job right now, everything up in the air with Bernard Taylor dead and his killer still at large. Presumably. Not having heard from Samson, Delilah could only assume that was the case.

Her final task of the day was one that had been outstanding for a while – catching up with the footage from the CCTV camera the Dales Detective Agency had installed outside Hargreaves' butcher's back in March, in an attempt to catch the elusive dog which had been fouling the shop's doorstep. Aware that Mrs Hargreaves' request for an update on Monday had gone unheeded, Delilah had been informed by Ida over their breakfast cuppa that the butcher's wife had called twice yesterday while Delilah and Samson were 'gadding about', as Ida so succinctly put it. According to the cleaner, Mrs Hargreaves had awoken that morning to yet another mess besmirching her front step and she wanted action. Feeling guilty at neglecting a client for so long, Delilah cued up the video and was about to start watching it when her mobile beeped.

A brief message from Samson, asking her to do some very precise editing on the recording of Bernard's call to Nancy. It took her an hour. Burning with curiosity, she sent the adapted audio file to him, asking what he wanted it for. But she heard nothing back.

Too impatient to sit in front of a screen any longer, Delilah logged out of the computer and tidied up the paperwork littering her desk. She liked to consider herself as naturally tidy, but desk-sharing with Ida Capstick raised the bar somewhat. The cleaner had pointedly moved all of Delilah's work to one side when she'd taken up residence the other morning, lining up the pencils and pens neatly and aligning the edges of the folders with the edge of the desk.

It wasn't a situation that could continue. If Ida was to become a permanent feature in her role as receptionist, she was going to need her own space. A desk in the corner, perhaps. Or even in another room . . .

Hardly believing she was in the position to be considering employing another person after struggling so long to simply keep the business afloat, neither could Delilah believe that the person in question was Ida Capstick. She wasn't exactly welcoming on the phone, and yet, people didn't seem to be put off. Maybe her blunt approach was what people looking for love needed.

Perhaps it was the approach Delilah ought to take with the issue she'd yet to tackle with Samson. That bloody kiss . . .

Refusing to let her thoughts go in that direction, she roused Tolpuddle from his slumber and headed home for a run on the fells. After a day on tenterhooks, waiting for Samson to appear, she needed to clear her head. But of course, she spent the run thinking about him. Wondering where he'd got to and what he was up to. And what was happening with the Taylor case. When she finally got a text from him late that evening, it did nothing to answer her earlier questions. Instead the message merely directed her to meet him at Bruncliffe Manor at ten thirty the following morning, without Tolpuddle but with her tablet. And not to be late.

Needless to say, that night Delilah didn't sleep a wink.

On Thursday morning, a thin trail of white cloud icing the edges of a blue sky, it was a somewhat apprehensive Delilah Metcalfe who was driving up Hillside Lane once more. No disguise this time. Or companions. Instead she was alone in her Micra, a knot of tension in her stomach. It was perturbing returning to the scene of the shooting, flashbacks of Saturday's terrible events playing in her mind as she turned onto the tree-lined drive, in a way they hadn't when she'd come up with Samson and Tolpuddle to do the sprint tests the other day. When she came around the last bend, she was relieved to see the Enfield already parked up in front of the manor, Samson standing next to it. Before Delilah had even turned off the engine, he was walking over to the Micra.

'You okay?' he asked as she got out of the car, her pale face telling him everything.

'I'm fine,' she lied.

'What about Tolpuddle? Is he with Dad?'

She shook her head. 'Ida's at the office all morning so she offered to look after him. Though I don't understand why he couldn't come along—' She broke off at the sound of another vehicle approaching along the drive. 'You expecting more company?'

Samson grinned. 'Oh yes.'

Delilah refused to rise to the bait, despite being desperate to know what was going on. Seconds later, two police cars drove into sight, pulling up next to the Micra. Sergeant Clayton and Frank Thistlethwaite got out of one, the two Harrogate detectives out of the other.

'This had better be good, O'Brien,' muttered a tense Sergeant Clayton. 'I've had to stick my neck out to authorise this.'

'We'd best get on with it then,' said Samson, gesturing for them all to follow him.

He led them down the track that ran along the side of the house, and into the sunlit rear yard where two more vehicles were already parked. One was a Land Rover, in the middle of the courtyard, exactly where Gareth's had been parked on the day of Bernard's death, the other a small van tucked away in the corner. Standing by the Land Rover were Herriot and an out-of-uniform Danny Bradley. The latter had a shotgun in his hands.

'What the hell?' muttered Sergeant Clayton, clearly surprised to see his constable being part of whatever was about to unfold.

'If everyone could stand over there, please,' said Samson, pointing at the French windows leading out of the dining room. He waited for them to all shuffle into place before he continued. 'For the purposes of this demonstration, Danny is Ana Stoyanovic, the prime suspect in this investigation, and I'm Bernard Taylor, the only two people who matter so far as this case is concerned.'

Sergeant Clayton grunted, intrigued despite himself, the two Harrogate detectives looking sceptical, while Frank Thistlethwaite was watching on with interest.

'Ready, Danny?'

'Yes.' The constable moved round to the passenger side

of the Land Rover and placed the gun on the seat, gently closing the door. Then he walked back the way the others had come to stand at the north corner of the building, where Ana Stoyanovic had been seen to arrive from.

'From all the witness testimonies and the footage we have from the spy cam,' said Samson, his focus on the detectives and Sergeant Clayton, 'when Delilah arrived on the scene, Bernard was slumped at the wheel, already shot, while Ana was standing on the other side of the car with the passenger door open. Agreed?'

Mutters of consent came from the group of spectators, Delilah nodding, the memory triggering a twist of anxiety in her guts.

'But it's the run-up to the shooting that we need to concentrate on,' continued Samson. 'We know from the voicemail recording that Bernard was already on the phone when he sat in the car. We also know that Ana, according to her statement, was around that corner.' He nodded at Danny and the constable moved round the side of the building out of sight. 'Danny has gone to stand on the exact spot Ana was in when she turned round to run back here. As for the other witnesses, Gareth Towler was behind the stables having a cigarette on the quiet, and Rick Procter was coming along the terrace on the south side. So,' he concluded, 'what we're going to do now is show you what I think happened in the last moments before the gun was fired. Okay?'

Delilah could feel a sense of anticipation building amongst the policemen around her. She found herself getting tense.

'If you're ready, Herriot?' Samson turned to the vet.

Herriot nodded, a concerned look on his face. 'Don't forget, you only get one shot at this.'

'Best make it count then,' said Samson. 'Here goes.'

Moving up to the Land Rover, he pulled his mobile out of his pocket and tapped the screen and suddenly they were there, back at the scene of the shooting, Bernard's panicked voice clear as the audio clip Delilah had prepared the day before started playing. With the mayor's frantic monologue cutting through the expectant hush that had settled on the watchers, Samson opened the driver's door and sat down. And then came the sound of barking.

Loud barking. Frantic barking. A dog in deep distress. Then suddenly, in a blur of brown body, something leapt from the rear of the Land Rover, across the back seat and onto the passenger seat. At which point the deafening explosion of a shotgun echoed off the stones of the manor and Samson slumped over the steering wheel.

'Samson!' screamed Delilah, lunging forwards, Frank Thistlethwaite holding her back, while Sergeant Clayton let out several expletives, a hand on his chest, and Danny came tearing around the far corner.

'It's okay!' Samson had sat back up and was looking straight at Delilah. 'It was just a recording. No one got shot. Not this time.'

'Are we done?' demanded Herriot.

'We're done,' said Samson, getting out of the car and nodding at the vet. 'And I think we have our culprit.'

'We do?' asked Sergeant Clayton, still stunned.

The Harrogate detectives were looking towards Danny, who, in his role as Ana, had only just reached the scene of the crime. But Samson pointed instead at the rear of the

Land Rover, where Herriot was opening the doors. Inside, confined in a cage, Bounty the spaniel was curled up in a corner, whimpering.

'The dog?' The oldest of the detectives stared at the spaniel, now being lifted out by Herriot and carried to his van, the vet soothing her the entire time. 'You seriously think it was the dog that shot Bernard Taylor?'

'I'm damn sure it was. You've just seen for yourself.'

'Lucy's flash of brown,' murmured Delilah. 'That's what she saw reflected in the splashback!'

Samson was nodding, but the detective wasn't having it.

'It's all such conjecture,' he said. 'It's just as likely that the Stoyanovic woman leaned in, picked up the gun and fired the shot.'

'Not quite,' said Danny Bradley, walking over to join them. 'For a start, you've just seen me re-enact Ana's movements, culminating in the exact position she was in when the other witnesses arrived on the scene. Thanks to Samson and Delilah, we can prove that it would have been impossible for her to fire the gun, run from the Land Rover and yet still be at that spot by the time Gareth and Rick got here. What's more, I had another look at the forensic report. There was a significant amount of gunshot residue found on the passenger seat, consistent with the gun having been lying on it when it was fired, not held in someone's hands.'

'But I don't understand,' said Delilah. 'How can Bounty have jumped over the seat and back? Her cage was closed when I lifted her out of it on Saturday after the shooting, so she can't possibly have got out.'

Samson grinned. 'All thanks to a faulty catch. Look.'

He took Delilah's tablet, holding it so they could all see, and played a video clip. It was from Delilah's spy cam, the images inside the kitchen before the shooting, Lucy sitting on a stool bemoaning the cancellation of the event. Outside the window was the back of the Land Rover.

'There,' said Samson, freezing the image and enlarging it. 'See?'

In the boot, it was possible to see Bounty, asleep in her cage. The cage was open.

'But . . . it was closed when I got there,' murmured Delilah.

'Which is exactly what happened just now. Herriot left it open when he put her in and yet you saw for yourselves it was closed when he took her back out. Want to show them, Danny?'

They gathered around the rear of the Land Rover, Danny raising the door of the cage, an up-and-over type that rested on the top when open.

'Now watch this,' said the constable. He leaned in and bounced the floor of the cage with his hand. The cage door snapped down, Danny just getting his arm out of the way before it slammed shut. 'The pressure of Bounty landing back inside would have been more than enough to make that happen.'

'So let me get this right,' said Sergeant Clayton, scratching his head. 'You're saying the dog left her cage, presumably thinking someone was breaking into the car or something, jumped over the seat to get at Taylor and landed on the gun, setting it off. And the resultant noise was enough to send her scampering back to her cage, the door falling closed behind her.'

Samson nodded. 'That's exactly what I'm saying. We spoke to Gareth and he said it's a habit of Bounty's, leaping over the seat.'

The Harrogate detectives didn't look convinced. Neither did Frank Thistlethwaite.

'I don't think a bit of gunshot residue on a seat and a defective cage door is enough to make a case, O'Brien,' he said.

'Luckily, that's not all we have,' said Samson. 'Danny went back through the full forensics report and discovered some surprises that didn't make it into the report sent through from Harrogate.'

'Like what?' The older detective bristled.

'Gunshot residue, found here, on the bottom of the cage.'

Sergeant Clayton stared at Samson. And then at the cage. 'How much?'

'A significant amount. Consistent with what you'd expect to find after a dog with residue on its paws had stood there. Not only that, but there were also traces of blood.'

'Taylor's?'

Samson nodded.

'We thought it was transference,' muttered the detective. 'All the witnesses said the dog was locked in the cage when everyone got to the scene, so we presumed the evidence had transferred from people handling the dog after the shooting.'

'A fair assumption.' Herriot had joined them again. 'Apart from the fact Bounty never went back in her cage from the moment Delilah lifted her out of it. Delilah passed her to Gareth, who passed her into Lucy Metcalfe in the kitchen until Gareth was free to bring her down to me.'

'And the cage was closed when I arrived at the Land Rover,' said Delilah, growing excitement in her voice. 'So there's no way anyone could have tampered with it between the shooting and my arrival. Which means the gunshot residue and the blood can only have come off Bounty!'

'Which means Bounty was next to Taylor when he was shot,' said Samson.

'But surely the dog would have been covered in blood if she'd been that close?' protested the younger detective.

'She was,' confirmed Herriot. 'But it didn't show in her coat, thanks to her colouring. It was only when I gave her a bath when we got back to the surgery that I noticed. And then I made the same mistake as you – I just presumed it had come off Delilah or Gareth's shirt. They'd both been holding her after they'd tried to tend to Bernard Taylor.'

Sergeant Clayton was nodding as the pieces clicked into place. 'And the lack of blood spatter on the passenger door,' he said. 'That's what sent us looking for a murderer, thinking the door must have been open during the shooting, when in fact it was closed all the time and the dog was standing in front of it, keeping it clean.'

'Add to all that the fact that the tests also found traces of gunshot residue on the back seat,' said Samson, 'and poor Bounty becomes a credible suspect.'

'Bloody hell,' muttered the sergeant. 'We nearly charged an innocent woman.'

The two Harrogate detectives looked grey.

'Just tell me one thing, O'Brien,' said Frank Thistle-thwaite, making no attempt to hide the fact that he was impressed. 'How the hell did you come up with this as an explanation for what happened?'

'Someone mentioned that we were looking for a "third man",' Samson replied with a grin aimed at Delilah. 'It made me think about what I was missing. Having ruled out all the obvious candidates, who would the third man be? Which is when I started thinking about Bounty. The audio had already been throwing me, the fact that the dog's barks got louder on Bernard's call to Nancy, which would suggest that the phone must have moved closer to Bounty, because she was confined in a cage and couldn't move. Yet the mobile was found in the driver's footwell, no closer to the rear of the Land Rover than when Bernard started the call. So if the mobile didn't move back towards the dog, that meant the dog had to have moved towards the mobile, even if that seemed impossible . . . I was going back over the video when I spotted the anomaly with the cage.'

'And then persuaded young Danny to get you access to the Land Rover yesterday so you could test it all out?' said the sergeant with a knowing look.

Samson grinned. 'How well you know me, Sergeant! We inspected the cage, discovered the faulty lock, and then spent a couple of hours testing the trigger on the gun Milan used that day, seeing whether a dog of Bounty's weight could realistically set it off. When I was satisfied it was worth testing it out for real, I called Herriot. He refused at first, Bounty still being traumatised, but finally agreed with the proviso that we only have one attempt, so as to limit her exposure to further stress. And as you saw, it paid off. An open-and-shut cage, you might say.'

Sergeant Clayton grunted. Stroked his chin and then ran a hand across his belly, which let out an alarming gurgle. 'Bloody hell, O'Brien. You could have waited until I was off this blasted diet before throwing a spanner in the works.'

31

With the demonstration successfully concluded, Samson, Sergeant Clayton, Danny Bradley and the detectives gathered around the Land Rover, to discuss some of the finer points of Samson's theory. Herriot had already left, going to meet Gareth Towler to hand over Bounty, the spaniel no longer needing to be in the vet's care. So, making the most of the sunshine, Delilah wandered round to the south-facing terrace of the impressive manor and sat on the steps. She was only there a matter of minutes before someone sat down next to her.

'You've been avoiding my calls.' The smile Frank Thistlethwaite gave her was lopsided. As though he knew it was a lost cause.

'Sorry,' murmured Delilah, feeling awkward. 'I've had a lot on.'

'I've noticed.' Frank grinned. 'Bruncliffe seems to be a right hotbed of activity.'

She laughed. 'These days it is.'

'Since O'Brien came home?' It was said casually, but there was a sudden intensity to the detective.

Delilah could feel the burn on her cheeks, knowing they were scarlet. 'He's livened things up, for sure,' she said.

Frank nodded, his smile turning into one of resignation.

'I know when I'm beaten,' he said softly. 'He's a lucky man. Don't let him break your heart.'

Then he moved, as if to go, before turning back to her.

'I know this is probably falling on deaf ears, but just be careful around him, okay? And if you ever need help, call me.'

'Delilah? You ready to go?' Samson had appeared with the rest of the men, looking over towards her, face impassive.

She stood, Frank catching her hand as she did. 'I mean it,' he said. 'You can trust me.'

Delilah nodded mutely, and walked away. All the time Danny's warning in the back of her mind. Perhaps this charming detective from Leeds wasn't what he seemed – even if he was a Thistlethwaite with relatives in the town below, a pedigree she'd normally stake her life on.

Aware of Samson's curious gaze on her, she followed everyone to the cars.

The drive back down Hillside Lane to town was a burst of colour. Up ahead of the Micra, the Royal Enfield was a dazzle of gleaming scarlet and chrome in the sunshine, the fells an abundant green flecked with the white of cavorting lambs, and Delilah found herself wishing she could be on the back of the bike, arms wrapped around Samson on a ride through the Dales. When she pulled up on Back Street, she was thoroughly miserable.

Which was mad. They'd just solved an impossible case. Her dating agency was doing amazingly well. And the sun was shining, which, living in the Yorkshire Dales, was not to be taken for granted.

But yet she felt deflated. It would have been easy to blame the disconcerting conversation with Frank Thistle-thwaite, the man's warnings getting under her skin as always. But Delilah knew that wasn't what had unsettled her. No, the root of her malaise was far more trivial.

That bloody kiss.

'For god's sake,' she muttered, getting out of the car. 'Just deal with it.'

Or deal with him, more like.

Resolved to talk to Samson before the day was out, Delilah entered the office building, the back door slamming shut as she stepped into the hall.

'Tha's both back, then?' called out Ida from the first-floor landing, Tolpuddle almost knocking her over as he raced down the stairs in welcome, tail wagging furiously.

'Afternoon, Ida,' said Samson, joining Delilah in the hall and patting the excited Weimaraner. With a wink at Delilah, he glanced back up at the cleaner. 'Any sign of your missing bucket?'

Ida glared down at him. 'Not a sausage.'

'I mentioned it to Danny Bradley yesterday. He said he'd keep an eye out.'

The fierce expression on Ida's face softened slightly. 'Tha's a good lad.'

'Did you use your new bucket in Taylor's when you were over there?' asked Delilah, aware of Samson's lips twitching and feeling a strong urge to start laughing. Or kissing him.

'Happen I didn't,' replied Ida. 'Bit of a commotion over there this morning so I just gave the place a lick and a promise and left them to it.'

'What kind of commotion?'

'That lad's gone and Mr Procter and Mrs Taylor were having a bit of a set to as to how to go about replacing him.'

Confused by the reply, Delilah looked at Samson, who shrugged. 'What lad?' he asked.

'The lanky one. Him as got almost run over last autumn by the tractor.'

'Stuart Lister? The guy that does the lettings?'

'Aye, him. Seems he's up and gone. Left a note for young Julie on Tuesday morning, saying he was off travelling. Leaving Mrs Taylor in the lurch like that. Husband murdered and now this lad does a runner.' Ida gave a sharp tut of disapproval. 'He picked a right time to get itchy feet.'

'Poor Nancy,' Delilah murmured. 'She'll be in a right state.'

'I'll give her a call,' said Samson. 'I need to talk to her about this morning anyway. I doubt the Harrogate detectives will give her the full story and I'd rather she heard it from me.'

'And *tha* needs to call Mrs Hargreaves,' Ida said, addressing Delilah sternly. 'She rang again earlier, after I told thee yesterday to call her.'

'Right,' Delilah sighed, not keen on wading through more hours of CCTV footage. 'I'll be straight up.'

Ida turned towards the kitchen and the sound of the kettle being filled broke the awkward silence that had fallen between Samson and Delilah.

'Tea,' said Delilah.

'Great!' said Samson with a grimace, making her laugh. 'Thanks for your help this morning,' he continued. 'Sorry

I didn't fill you in on what was happening but I thought it would have more of an impact on Sergeant Clayton and the others if you were seeing it for the first time too.'

'That's okay. Pretty good sleuthing on your part.'

Samson shook his head. '*Our* part. If it hadn't been for you, I'd never have taken all three cases. And it was your comment that made me consider Bounty as a possibility. We're a team, don't forget. Us two and this gorgeous fella.' He bent over Tolpuddle, making a fuss of him until the Weimaraner flopped on the tiles in ecstasy.

Delilah felt her heart swell with love. She swallowed, took a big breath, and was about to speak when Samson turned to her.

'There's something we need to talk about,' he said, looking at her in a way that made her limbs wilt. 'Not now. But later. When I've told our three clients the good news and you've dealt with Mrs Hargreaves, and Ida's gone.'

She nodded. Mouth full of words about to spill out. 'Right.' She nodded again and turned to walk up the stairs. Suddenly, combing through a CCTV video was about all she thought she could manage.

Some time later, sitting at Bernard Taylor's desk, Rick Procter was marvelling at how fortune had favoured him.

He'd just had a call from Samson O'Brien – a call that totally justified the risk he'd taken in going to Bruncliffe's private detective. By some miracle, O'Brien had managed to prove that Taylor had been shot by the gamekeeper's dog! No charges were to be brought against any of the three witnesses, including Rick himself.

Rick felt like ordering in champagne. He was off the

hook, the threat of a police investigation removed. Not only that, but the fears that had been plaguing him since he'd come round the corner and seen Taylor dead had all been unsubstantiated. Fears that he'd held even when the police were saying it was suicide. Fears he hadn't wanted anyone else sharing, so he'd pushed the idea that Bruncliffe's mayor had taken his own life; had actively encouraged folk to believe that the only guilty party was Delilah Metcalfe and her ridiculous disguise. When the verdict became one of murder, those same fears had threatened to engulf him. But finally they had been allayed.

Bernard Taylor hadn't been eliminated in a callous act by the Karamanski brothers, after all. He'd been killed by a bloody dog!

In his elation, Rick sent a brief text to Niko to update him on the conclusion of the investigation, the brothers and their entourage having finally flown back to Bulgaria, and then sat back, savouring the sense of relief. It was worth the bill O'Brien would be sure to send through. Every last penny of it.

Sitting there in his deceased partner's chair, the property developer mused over the sudden twist of fate, the fact that Taylor's death had turned out to be caused by something as trivial as an over-excited mutt – such a meaningless end to a life. Then the thought came to him.

What if he were to take over the estate agency permanently?

It was the perfect solution. With Taylor gone, this was the ideal opportunity to charm Nancy into selling the company. Persuade her she was doing it for her health. That she didn't need the stresses and strains that came with a business like this. And who better to take Taylor's off her hands than her husband's best friend?

It would be an addition to the Procter Properties portfolio that made total sense, solving a lot of headaches and keeping the Karamanski brothers off his back. No need to move the cannabis farms. No need to worry about the funds being laundered through the bogus rentals. What's more, it would give Rick a chance to lay his hands on those missing files.

Grinning at the way his luck was changing, the partner who'd become a liability no longer a threat and his own business about to expand, Rick got to his feet, intending to celebrate. To take the pretty receptionist out for a meal at his brasserie in Low Mill.

He'd reached the office door when his mobile went. A text from Niko that made Rick slump back against the filing cabinet.

No more mistakes. Bruncliffe can't afford to lose another leading figure.

He stared at the screen. Felt his throat constrict. Was it a simple warning, deadly enough in itself? Or was there a suggestion of something else? An insinuation that Taylor's death might not have been—?

A knock at the door and the receptionist was standing there. 'I'm off, Mr Procter. Is there anything you need before I go?'

Rick shook his head, aware of the sweat on his brow.

'Is everything okay? You don't look so well.'

'I'm fine,' he snapped, closing the door and collapsing into a dead man's chair.

A dead man who'd allegedly been killed by a dog . . .

Rick's fears came flooding back. Despite all his plans for the future, he was still standing on quicksand.

It was early evening, Ida long gone and the working day drawing to a close, when Samson heard the clatter of feet coming down the stairs. He could tell from the haste that Delilah had news. Grinning in anticipation of his partner's appearance, he turned towards the doorway.

'Guess what!' she exclaimed before she was even on the bottom step, a huge smile on her face.

'Ida's signed up so many clients for the dating agency that you're treating us both to dinner this evening?'

Delilah laughed. 'Not quite. It's to do with Mrs Hargreaves' doorstep . . .'

'You've found the dog?' Samson jumped up and Delilah nodded, holding out her laptop to show him, her face alight with pleasure.

'It wasn't easy to spot,' she said, pressing play as Samson leaned in next to her. 'But it's the culprit alright.'

And there on the screen, slinking around the edge of Bruncliffe marketplace shrouded in night, was what looked like a dog. On the grainy CCTV footage, it stopped by Rice N Spice before trotting across the cobbles to the butcher's and then—

'It's a fox!' exclaimed Samson, as the creature answered the call of nature in full view of the camera. 'All this time and it was a fox!'

'Yep. Don't think that was what Mrs Hargreaves was expecting, but at least we've solved it. But that's not all. Look.'

Samson watched as two smaller shapes appeared on the camera. 'Cubs!' he murmured. 'A vixen and her cubs.'

He didn't think. He grinned. Turned to Delilah, placed a hand either side of the face and kissed her. On the forehead.

He felt her jolt backwards. Like he'd just put a couple of extra volts through her.

'Sorry . . . just it's brilliant news . . .' he stammered. 'Good to have it tidied up. Mrs Hargreaves will be pleased . . .'

'I've already called her,' Delilah said, hurriedly taking a seat, putting the safety of the desk between them. 'She said she'd deal with it.'

Composure regained, Samson raised an eyebrow. 'That sounds ominous.'

'To be honest, foxes are protected under law so there's not much she can do. What about you?' Delilah smiled. 'Did you tell all three of our clients the good news?'

'I did indeed. They're over the moon. I also spoke to Nancy Taylor. She seemed relieved to hear that it was all just a terrible accident.'

'The poor woman,' said Delilah. 'Losing your husband in any circumstances must be tough, but she's really been put through the mill.'

'And yet still remains a class act. She even offered to pay for our truncated investigation into Bernard, which I refused. I suggested she make a donation to the mountain rescue team instead.'

His words were met with a nod of approval. 'That's a lovely idea.'

'Nancy also asked if we could continue to look into the origins of that holdall of cash,' added Samson. 'Seems she's not comfortable not knowing where it came from. And finally, talking of cash,' he grinned, 'seeing as Rick has paid – in triplicate, as agreed – I've waived the charges for Ana and Gareth.'

Delilah's face creased with laughter. 'Brilliant thinking! So that's two Dales Detective Agency cases successfully solved in one day. Think it's you that should be buying dinner.'

Samson nodded, feeling suddenly nervous. 'Before that, I've got something I want to say.'

'Me too,' said Delilah, a shy smile curving her lips. 'You first.'

'Okay. I want to apologise.' He reached into his desk drawer and pulled out a letter. 'I got this on Saturday. DC Green brought it up with her.'

Delilah twisted the paper round so she could read it, then looked at him, worried. 'You're going to court? Next week?'

'So it seems.' He tried to keep his tone light. 'I'm sorry I didn't mention it until now. What with us just getting back from the shoot and everything that's happened since . . . I didn't think it was a good time.'

She glanced sideways at him, devilment in her eyes. 'You weren't trying to protect me, were you?'

He grinned. 'I wouldn't dream of it.'

And she laughed. The sound hit his heart, spreading warmth through him, making him just want to go round the desk and —

'Is there anything I can do to help?' she was asking, gesturing at the letter.

'Not really.'

'Are you worried?' She was looking at him now, really looking at him. And he made the decision. No more lying. No more deceit. Not when it came to Delilah.

'Yes,' he said. 'I'm afraid I won't get a fair trial. Not when someone in the force is behind all the fabricated accusations being levelled against me.'

'But there must be a way to fight this?' The fire in her eyes made him love her even more.

'I think there's too much stacked against me. I'll just have to take my chances in court.'

'And if you're found guilty? Will you go to prison?'

He nodded.

'Jesus!' She stared at the letter and back up at him. Fists clenched. Like she was about to go into battle. 'But Samson . . . !'

Samson smiled. He'd just laid bare his worst fears and yet, he'd never been happier. Because he was pretty sure this woman loved him. This amazing Delilah Metcalfe, with her passion and her ferocity and her heart that was capable of so much generosity.

'I think we should have dinner,' he said, getting to his feet. 'And then you can tell me whatever it was you wanted to say.'

But she was getting to her feet too. Crossing the room. Pulling his face down to hers and kissing him. Not on the forehead. But on the lips. Every ounce of her passionate nature contained in her embrace.

When she pulled away, Samson felt the world crash back around him.

'Wow!' he said.

'Wow, indeed.' She grinned. 'I'm going to get dinner.

Reckon it's my treat. And then we'll talk about how we keep you out of prison.'

He nodded. Still not able to form words of any meaning.

'Don't go anywhere,' she said, a smile on her face that he knew was just for him.

He heard the back door close and he sank into his chair. It was a while before he was capable of coherent thought.

'We've run out of time. We need to go with Plan B. Are you ready?' The question was blunt and to the point, the speaker on the other end of the phone not one to mess around.

DC Jess Green didn't hesitate. 'More than ready.'

'Good. My colleague is on his way to meet you. And remember, no more kid gloves. O'Brien can't make it to court. It would ruin everything.'

'I understand.'

'Let me know when it's done.' The call ended as abruptly as always, Jess Green left holding a mobile with no one on the other end.

Heart racing, she got up and packed her bag. She wouldn't be coming back to Mearbeck Hall Hotel that night. It was too risky. After what she was about to do, she'd be lying low for a while.

Bloody O'Brien. If only he'd trusted her, it would have all been a lot easier. Fewer people would have had to get hurt. But now . . .

Plan B. It wasn't an option she favoured, but with the news coming out of London, their backs were against the wall. It was either this or the last two years of DC Green's life would come crashing around her ears. And she wasn't willing to pay that price. Not after everything she'd put into this.

She finished her packing, left the room and checked out of the hotel, the receptionist too polite to enquire what had prompted her departure at an hour when most guests would be heading out for an evening meal. When she got out into the car park, there was a man standing by her car. A large man. The kind you didn't mess with. More than sufficient for what was needing to be done.

A few minutes later, DC Green drove towards Bruncliffe, her passenger sitting silently next to her. Plan B was in operation.

32

The trill of his mobile pulled Samson back from his day-dreams, Delilah's kiss having fried his senses like the strongest narcotic.

'Samson?' It was Danny. Samson managed a grunt in reply and the constable continued. 'Thought you'd want to know that Ana Stoyanovic is officially no longer a person of interest in the investigation. They've gone with your theory. And Sarge is going round like a dog with two tails for getting one over on the Harrogate lot – you'd swear the whole Bounty thing had been his idea!'

Samson laughed, finally focusing on the here and now. 'Seeing as it was him who managed to delay charges being brought against Ana until we'd carried out the demonstration, I'm happy to let him have the credit.'

'Gets Rick Procter off the hook, too,' said Danny. 'Although Gareth is still facing investigation for possible gross negligence.'

'What's your gut feeling on that?'

There was a pause, the young constable giving the question serious consideration. 'I'm not sure the prosecution service will go ahead with it,' he finally said. 'But either way, Gareth will be lucky to come out of it with his shotgun licence intact.'

Danny knew he didn't need to spell it out for Samson:

a gamekeeper without a shotgun licence was unheard of.

'Still,' continued the policeman, 'if it hadn't been for you and Delilah, an innocent person could have been convicted of murder. I owe you one.'

'I think we're more than even, Danny.'

Samson hung up, thinking about the case and the twist it had taken. Thinking about how it had all started with the bag of money Nancy Taylor found and – given the Dales Detective Agency's latest assignment – was ending with it too. That much cash, hidden in a wardrobe. From his experience, Samson doubted it had an innocent reason for being there. Which begged the question, what had Bernard Taylor been planning on doing with over a hundred grand in cash if he wasn't being blackmailed?

Some other illicit payment, maybe, like Gareth Towler had suggested? Or a dodgy property deal? Or maybe Nancy had actually been onto something and the mayor had been squirreling away money in preparation for divorcing her? It wasn't like Samson and Delilah had had long to investigate the man before he'd been killed. A couple of days in the ginnel across from Taylor's was hardly enough to gather the evidence required if he had indeed been planning on betraying his wife.

As he was thinking this, Samson's gaze happened to rest on Delilah's laptop, the screen still showing the CCTV image of the furtive fox. And something clicked. A memory of himself in the ginnel watching Taylor's combined with an earlier memory of going through other CCTV footage, in a case for Rice N Spice. Then he was tapping keys on his own laptop, searching for a file, opening it.

There. Pete Ferris, caught on a hidden camera Delilah

had installed in an attempt to catch a thief at the Indian restaurant. The camera pointed towards the till and out through the window and had captured the poacher skulking across the marketplace not long before he committed suicide. But what Samson found interesting was that Pete Ferris had emerged from the exact same ginnel he himself had been using to spy on Bernard Taylor.

Samson checked the date on the image. More searching on the laptop and he opened another file, this one footage from the CCTV camera above Mrs Hargreaves' shop, the same side of the square as the ginnel. Same date. Same time. But a completely different view. The camera angle wasn't wide, but it was enough to show Taylor's Estate Agents. To show Bernard Taylor coming out onto the square and hurrying away up the cobbles in the direction of the town hall. And then Pete Ferris, from behind, leaving the ginnel and going after the mayor, like a lurcher on a scent.

A bag of money. Blackmail. Was it possible? Pete Ferris, who'd turned down Lucy's offer of a reward for finding Nathan. The man who'd left a message on Samson's mobile that he wanted to report a crime and then committed suicide not long after. It had been a long eight days since they'd buried him, when Herriot's comments about the drugging of the lurchers had sparked Samson's interest in the pub. Now he found himself wondering, could Pete Ferris have been—?

Samson cut himself off with a laugh. He was hungry and a nervous wreck, on tenterhooks for Delilah's return. It was making him see conspiracies in every shadow – not the best time to start dealing with the investigation into the dodgy holdall. Closing down his laptop, he was about to do the same with Delilah's when he heard a noise out in the hallway.

It had him on his feet in seconds. Across the lino to the door, his heart thumping. Back against the wall, he peered around the doorframe.

'Bloody hell, Tolpuddle!' Samson exhaled as the dog looked back at him, head on one side. 'You frightened the life out of me!'

Tolpuddle crossed the tiles towards him, yawning, unconcerned by the alarm he'd caused. He leaned into Samson's legs and gazed up at him pleadingly.

Perhaps, thought Samson, rubbing the dog's flank, it was no bad thing the court case was coming soon. At least it would get it all over with. Remove the ever present threat that had been hanging over him since he'd fled London with bruises on his face and body from a message delivered in blows. Life would be a lot safer once it was done with.

Although how safe it would be if he ended up spending a long time in prison wasn't something he wanted to think about.

The Happy House had been empty, Delilah waiting no more than fifteen minutes to get her order – which was just as well, because for the first time in weeks she was starving. She'd had just enough time to nip to the Spar and grab a bottle of red. Talk about pushing the boat out.

Chinese takeaway in one hand, bottle of wine in the other, she headed back across the marketplace towards the office, grinning to herself.

That kiss. She'd never made the first move in her life, and now she'd done it twice in one week. And both times it had felt amazing. But the kiss today, that was something different. She hadn't been in a temper for a start. So she couldn't claim to have been acting irrationally. And there was no denying the tension leading up to it. That's what was different. This time Delilah was pretty sure Samson felt the same way.

Well, she was about to find out. Because she wasn't going home this evening until they'd been honest with each other. No more lying. No more deceit. She'd tell him exactly how she felt and if he didn't feel the same, at least she'd know.

Her grin widened. She knew already. That kiss . . .

In a delicious daydream, Delilah Metcalfe walked on past Back Street to reach the narrow opening that led to the rear ginnel. Turning into the gloom of the alleyway with her head full of love, she didn't see the person at the far end, walking slowly towards her. And when she did see them, she didn't think anything of it.

'Hello!' she said, going past the back gate as she carried on down to meet them. 'What are you doing back here? Is Samson not answering the door?'

DC Jess Green smiled. 'It's not Samson I'm here for,' she said.

Delilah didn't get a chance to reply. Two strong arms grabbed her from behind, a hand over her mouth, a hand around her waist, the Chinese meal and the bottle of wine falling from her grasp. She just had time to kick out, heels connecting with shins and eliciting a grunt of pain, before she was lifted off her feet and bundled into a car. With a roar of the engine, the car sped away.

*

Delilah was taking her time.

Samson checked his watch. She'd been gone forty-five minutes. Maybe there was a queue. He was about to text her when his mobile beeped. Delilah. *Running late*, was all it said.

In the corner of the office, Tolpuddle let out a long sigh. He was hungry.

'You're not the only one,' said Samson, stomach grumbling. 'How about a biscuit to tide you over?'

The dog's ears shot up and he was at the door before Samson had even stood up.

'I guess that's a yes!' Samson laughed, letting Tolpuddle lead him upstairs to the kitchen.

Not sure if Delilah would feel flush enough to get wine, Samson put the kettle on as backup and then reached for the biscuit boxes, one marked *Hound*, the other marked *Human*. One for each of them. Lunch felt a long time ago and there'd been a lot of energy expended since then. Maybe even more to come . . .

Samson caught his own reflection in the window, a grin wide across his face. And he marvelled at how he could feel so good when his life was at such a critical point.

Delilah. That was how.

The kettle finished boiling, Tolpuddle finished a second biscuit and Samson was just putting two plates out on the worktop in readiness when he heard a noise downstairs.

'She's back!' he whispered at the dog, feeling as excited as a kid on Christmas morning.

Trying to be cool and collected, he went down the stairs, Tolpuddle behind him.

First thing he noticed was that the door to his office was

almost closed. That wasn't how he'd left it. Moving more quietly now, he crossed the tiled hall and approached the door.

He'd done this so often in the last six months. Burst into a room thinking danger was behind it. Frightened numerous innocent people in the process. Maybe, for once, he should just behave normally. Maybe the door had closed as he'd left the room.

So he didn't burst in. He simply pushed it open. Which is how he saw her, standing at his desk, the emergency mobile DI Warren had given him in her hand.

'Everything okay?' he asked.

Delilah dropped the phone on the desk. 'Totally,' she said.

He looked at her, face pale, eyes wary. And no sign of food. 'What's going on?'

'I've got a headache. I just want to go home. So if you don't mind . . .' She was calling Tolpuddle over to her, face hidden as she bent down to clip on his lead.

Samson didn't know what to say.

'Sorry,' she murmured, as she walked past him.

He watched her walk down the hallway with Tolpuddle, the dog at least looking back, whimpering slightly. Then the back door closed and Samson was left alone in his office, wondering what the hell had just happened. And whether he'd ever truly be able to understand Delilah Metcalfe.

The sun had slipped below the horizon by the time Samson finally moved from his office chair. And then it was only because he knew he needed to eat. Heartsore and confused, he dragged himself up the stairs and into the kitchen and began making a meal for one. A meal he knew he wouldn't be able to enjoy. Not when his mouth was full of the bitter taste of heartache.

By contrast, over in Skipton, in a one-bedroomed flat just off the high street, a relieved and happy Ana Stoyanovic was on a video call to her son back in Serbia, telling him that soon he'd be coming to live with her. She'd been waiting until she could afford a bigger place but after the last week, she'd decided not to wait any longer. A sofa bed in the lounge would be fine if it meant they could be together. The smile on his face at the news made her heart feel like bursting.

Also relieved, but a relief that was tinged with guilt and fear for the future, Gareth Towler was having a glass of whisky in the lounge of the small cottage up on the fells that came with his position. Curled up on the couch next to him was Bounty. The gamekeeper had heard from the Luptons that afternoon that planning permission for the lodges had been granted. That the paperwork had been rubberstamped the day before the shoot, the mayor's threats having been nothing more than bluster from a man at the end of his tether.

It was good news for the estate. Although it was unlikely to be Gareth overseeing this next chapter of life at Bruncliffe Manor. With the possibility of gross negligence charges being filed against him, he knew he wasn't out of the woods and that, at the very least, losing his beloved job might be the price he had to pay. Which was nothing compared to the cost Bernard Taylor had paid. With a heart full of regret, the gamekeeper raised a glass to the dead man.

Down the fellside in Bruncliffe, Nancy Taylor was also

raising a glass to her dead husband. And she was making a vow. She would make sure that the business Bernard had spent so much of his life building up would continue. With her at the helm. It was the least she owed him. For despite the day's news, she still carried a burden of guilt that she doubted she would ever shake. She took a swig of wine and then took out her mobile, and began making a list of all the things she would need to do if she was going to start running Taylor's Estate Agents, glad to have something to occupy her overwrought mind.

Nancy wasn't the only one thinking about Taylor's. Julie, the receptionist, was in the Coach and Horses on High Street on a rare night out, celebrating a friend's birthday. But she wasn't really in the mood. All she could think about was Stuart Lister and that note. It wasn't just the abruptness of it. It was the fact it was completely out of character – him going travelling. He was the last person she'd imagined setting off round the world with a backpack.

But there was something else, too. The note itself. It was in Stuart's hand. It had Stuart's tone to it. Except for one thing.

He'd addressed Mr Taylor as 'Bernard'. Something she'd never heard him do. Not even when they were talking about their boss informally.

It was an oddity that had Julie preoccupied. One that saved her from thinking about how hurt she was by his actions.

Round the corner from the pub, in the marketplace, in one of the windows on the top floor above the butcher's, a figure stood at the edge of the closed bedroom curtains, peering out. With darkness having settled on the town, Barbara Hargreaves was on the lookout for the fox that had been fouling her doorstep. She'd been knocked for six when Delilah Metcalfe told her. Didn't really believe it until she saw the footage Delilah had emailed through. A fox, slinking around the town, making a mess.

She'd told Delilah she'd deal with it. Which she had done.

'Well?' Ken Hargreaves had joined his wife at the window. 'See anything?'

Just as he said it, a shape emerged from the dark, creeping along past Peaks Patisserie and heading across the cobbles, two smaller shapes tight on its heels. Husband and wife watched in silence as the trio made their way towards the butcher's, disappearing out of sight directly below them.

'Did you do it?' asked Ken.

Barbara nodded. And tapped the mobile in her hand, the CCTV footage live on her screen. The fox was at the step, sniffing it, no doubt getting a good dose of bleach from the clean Barbara had given it that morning. Then it spotted the lump at the side. It sniffed it suspiciously, and started eating.

'You big softie,' said Ken, wrapping his arms around his wife's broad frame.

For the way she'd dealt with the fox was to feed it, a few small offcuts of beef left on the step. After all, this was a vixen and cubs. Happen as Barbara Hargreaves remembered what it was to be the mother of young. She also knew what it was to lose a child. So while there were plenty of folk around who'd have slipped something in the meat and no one would have been any the wiser, there was no way she could harm this animal.

Together, the Hargreaves watched the fox devour her unexpected treat before trotting off into the night with her cubs, the step left as clean as a whistle.

And up at the back of Bruncliffe, in the cottage that overlooked the town? There Delilah Metcalfe sat, staring into the dark beyond her kitchen window.

She was fighting tears. Fighting panic. That mobile, the one his boss gave him, his only lifeline – she'd seen the texts on it. Warning of a danger that was already here. A danger that had her in its grasp.

Could she do it? What was being demanded of her?

She had no choice.

It was either comply with their ultimatum or Samson O'Brien, the man she loved, would be killed in the coming days. And she wasn't able to tell him a single word.

With a heart full of deceit, Delilah Metcalfe had never felt more alone.

Acknowledgements

This, the sixth book in the Dales Detective Series, was written during a strange time. A time of pandemic; a time of lockdown; a time of global uncertainty. So an even greater debt of gratitude than normal is owed to the following, for keeping me focused when my attention was running wild. And for keeping me balanced when real life threatened to swamp my imaginary one. While a bag of plum-and-almond slices from Peaks Patisserie won't repay the full cost, here's hoping it holds the same sweet attraction as for Sergeant Clayton!

First up for a round of applause, three friends who helped in their own ways . . . Catherine Speakman for not only being my go-to veterinary expert but also for wielding a camera and taking some cracking publicity photos that even incorporated my bike! Harry Carpenter, who never fails to answer my off the cuff questions about modern day policing in a rural environment – and who is patient with my bending of those truths. And to Jo Robinson, who twice rescued me from the depths of writing despair with homemade cakes left on the doorstep.

When it came to researching gamekeepers and shoots in general, I'm grateful to my friend Isabel, who gave me the benefit of her ninety-plus years of knowledge. I also had some timely input from my dad with his brilliant tales of working on shoots in Ireland. As for the lovely teller in a certain bank who took it all in her stride when her customer suddenly started asking questions about life behind the counter – thanks for not having me thrown out!

As always, family plays a part in keeping me on track, even when I wasn't allowed to visit them because of lockdown restrictions. A particular mention for Claire for dropping everything to read the draft version, and to my mum, for sending me photos of flowers every day for four weeks while I wrestled with a rewrite!

In terms of the publishing world, the team that gets this series to the shelves just keeps getting better and better. In the UK, a huge thanks goes to Gillian and Vicki for expert editing; to Matt for fielding my odd enquiries during lockdown; to Ellis for handling PR in what had to have been the strangest publicity period ever!; to the amazing editing crew of Charlotte, Fraser and Natalie, who pushed me to be even better; and to the rest of the Pan Mac stars who continue to show passion and support for the Dales Detective series.

In France, it's *merci et au revoir* to the wonderful Camille – a Frenchwoman with her heart in the Dales – and *bonjour* to Nathalie who has joined Glen and the fabulous *équipe* at La Bête Noire. A special mention also to Dominique and Stéphanie, a formidable translation team who worked under tough conditions to get this book ready on time. You are amazing! And finally, to the festival organisers who had invited me before coronavirus took hold of the world and cancelled everything, and to all the French readers who were hoping to see me at those events, here's to the future and meeting up in better times: *à la prochaine*!

A name that always appears in these final notes is that of my agent, but this time the thanks are needed more than ever